# LOST

# LOST

*a novel by*

## GARY DEVON

ALFRED A. KNOPF    *New York*    1986

THIS IS A BORZOI BOOK
PUBLISHED BY ALFRED A. KNOPF, INC.

Library of Congress Cataloging-in-Publication Data

Devon, Gary. Lost: a novel.

I. Title.
PS3554.E92824L6   1986      813'.54      86–45265
ISBN 0–394–53836–6

Manufactured in the United States of America

FIRST EDITION

*This book is dedicated to my family:*
*to Mom and Dad and my three sisters,*
*but especially to the memory of*
*my brother Rudy, 1945–1953.*

*I want to express my gratitude to*
*Dr. Virginia Lowell Grabill,*
*without whose early encouragement and assistance*
*this work might never have been done.*
*And to my wife, Deborah,*
*who saw it through.*

*Because there is wrath, beware*
*lest he take thee away with his stroke:*
*then a great ransom cannot deliver thee.*
*Desire not the night, when people are*
*cut off in their place.*

*—Job 36:18, 20.*

# LOST

# PART ONE

# 1

The bullet entered his head slightly above and behind his left ear, and the air pocketed with the report. The shot jarred him off balance and his tense face hurtled sideways, blurred like a swiftly unwinding bobbin of thread. His name was Sherman Abbott; he was twelve years old.

Thrown out loose by the recoil, his upturned hand wavered daintily in the evening air, his fingers bent back twitching under the weight of the dangling revolver. Suddenly he slumped as if to curtsy, then bolted erect. He staggered forward a step or two, weaving from side to side; the revolver jiggled from the end of his thumb, and he fell headlong in the high grass.

His sister Mamie, who was almost seven and the youngest of the Abbott children, watched him go down. She was standing less than ten feet from him when it happened, close enough for the resounding shock of the noise to hurt her ears. Clutching the tin pail with the nine berries in it, which she had picked and counted, she hurried to reach him. Small for her age, she squatted beside him, peering at him. "Sherman," she said, leaning down through her spread knees. But if he saw her or heard her or knew who she was, he didn't let on.

He burrowed among the yellow stalks of grass, lurching and rocking up and down, as if he were trying to lift himself and crawl. Spasms flew through his body like tiny flickering fish. Then he stopped moving. Slowly his head settled on the crook of his unbuttoned shirt sleeve. The hurt side of his face was bone white and it was blood-pocked and embedded with grit, like a knee scraped on gravel. His still eyes were half shut and very blue. In the thin bristle of his new haircut, in the cheesy-white skin above his ear, the ruptured carbuncle of the wound was crusted with black dust. A rising puddle of bright blood filled his ear and broke down across his cheek.

Again Mamie spoke to him, a nudging worry in her voice. "Sherman," she said, "you better get up." But she didn't comprehend the terror of what he'd done or the gravity of the pain it would cause—she couldn't believe it was real until she touched him.

Irresistibly, even as the dread knotted tight inside her, she lowered her fingertips to the side of his face. Ever so lightly and gently. And the skin there was cool-hot and clammy like a fever. "Sherman," she whispered, "what'd you do?" She was about to pull away when something happened: she lost her footing or her hand shook of itself, and her fingers smeared across the sticky blood drying on his cheek. At first she couldn't breathe; when at last she caught her breath, a shriek rode out of her body so high-pitched it snapped in and out of frequency. It was like a corrugated sound she couldn't stop. She jerked back, kicked back, flinging out her hand. She came to her feet and turned, and turned, stumbling in an aimless zigzag, her cry continuing as shrill and piercing as a chalk squeak.

She ambled in loops, unable to get her bearings. Again and again, she found herself coming upon him. She wanted to pick him up, impossible as it was. She kept thinking, I should pick him up and take him home. But she knew she couldn't lift him —he was nearly twice her size. Each time she saw her blood-dirtied fingers, she screamed. With the air almost gone from her lungs, she finally gasped, "Sherman . . . Sherman . . . Oh,

Sherman," so frightened she couldn't call for help. She kept her bloodied fingers extended before her. She didn't know what to do—she couldn't dirty her dress, put *blood* on it. Suddenly she dropped to her knees, wiping her hands viciously on the grass, pulling out clumps of grass and scrubbing it across the palm of the bloody hand. Again, inadvertently, she touched him, his arm this time.

She sat back on her haunches. Breathing hard and moaning, she wiped her face on her hunched-up shoulders. She couldn't bear to look at him, but she did look and the blood was trickling out now in a pink foam—from his nose and mouth. Quickly she squeezed her eyes shut; she put her hands on top of her head, one on top of the other, and just sat there, still and numb. "Oh, Sherman," she babbled in her desperation, "I wish you wouldn't do things like this to me." After she said it, she thought it sounded like something her mother might say. She sat there beside him on her haunches, unable to help him, afraid to touch him. And she covered her eyes with her hands but she couldn't stop the tears running through them. At last, shivering uncontrollably, she pushed to her feet and whirled away, running for home.

Some of the men in the neighborhood brought Sherman home that night and put him on the wicker lounger in the living room —the lounger their wives had pulled in from the porch and hastily prepared with starched white linen.

Mamie sat halfway up the stairs, clutching the varnished spindles, peering down on the commotion. Above her, on the dark landing of the stairs, Toddy Abbott, who'd just turned eight, stood motionless in his pajamas as if by being quiet he could hide. He'd stayed in bed that afternoon and evening with a croupy summer cold. They listened as their mother frantically tried to decide what to do, changed her mind and changed it again, but none of the neighbors questioned her judgment. Finally, sobbing as she spoke, she blurted out what she wanted most. "If he has to die," she said, "it should be here at home. Don't you think so?" The longer she talked, the more she pleaded. "I want it to be here—in his home—among his own things when it happens. Not in some cold hospital room. I want him to be home, at least. Don't you think that's right?"

Outside, police cars pulled up, one, then two of them, their red lights beating irregularly against the front windows. Car doors slammed and voices shouted outside beyond the doorway, but it was the doctor, followed by a nurse dressed in white, who wove through the tangle of neighbors in the foyer. Without a word, they went directly into the bright living room, where the doctor paused and drew the tall sliding doors shut behind him. Almost immediately from that closed-in place, Mamie heard her mother's heartbreaking wail—a sound as thin and relentless as wind on wire. The cry tore through Mamie like a dagger; startled, she clung to the spindles, unable to stop her tears.

Her mother's voice rose and fell like a loud heartbeat: "Don't . . . hurt him . . . please . . . don't hurt him . . . any more." Just when Mamie thought she couldn't bear it any longer, the sliding doors rumbled apart. Escorted on either side by neighbor women, her mother wandered out, coming down the shaft of light and into the foyer where the dim wall lights lit the stairs. She hugged a small oblong box to her breast. Her face was white as plaster.

The doors slid shut. The hot August night dragged on.

By the time their father arrived in his work clothes, the police cars were gone. He had been running; sweat soaked his shirt. He stumbled through the crowd, saw their mother, and turned toward her, unsteady on his feet. And their expressions were so tender and full of longing they were painful to watch. Their mother's fingers picked at the oblong box, and she kept saying, "Oh, Ray, I'm so sorry," over and over again. They stood less than two feet apart, unable somehow to touch each other, their eyes full of tears. She said to him, "All my life I've been afraid of something like this."

When he could speak, their father said, "Where is he?" his voice raspy and tired. One of the women nodded toward the double doors; she said, "The doctor's in with him now." He glanced at the sharp light outlining the doors, stepped back, and turned. Their mother said, "Don't, Ray. Let them do what they can," but he paid her no heed. Moving out of her reach, he went to the closed-up room, grasping the handles to draw the doors open, but suddenly he slumped there. Another man from deep in the house—the dining room or the kitchen—called to him, "Ray, is that you?" and hastened to meet him and lead him away. Their mother, comforted by strange hands, let herself be drawn down on the edge of the foyer settee.

As Toddy came down the stairs to sit by Mamie, the nurse slipped from the bright living room. Dodging questions, she hurried outside. Mamie could feel the heat radiating from Toddy's body; when he bumped against her, she cringed from him. Clasping his arms around his shins, he said, "Can I stay down here with you?" He was trembling all over like a rabbit.

She couldn't begin to tell him how awful she felt; her skin seemed to draw tighter and tighter, and the ache of dread and regret sank deeper within her. Without looking around, she said, "Toddy, he was dead, I think. He's really dead. I saw him. I reached down . . ." She began to sob.

As her voice shriveled, he let out a shuddering sigh. "He can't die, Mamie. He just can't, y'know. He can't die and you can't die and I can't die, because we're all brand-new people. Him and us."

The weird logic of what he was saying escaped her.

The crowd withdrew and dispersed. A few of them ventured forward to mutter their awkward goodbyes. With his shadowy friend in tow, their father had circled the house and was now on the porch with the last of the departing neighbors, smoking a cigarette. The nurse walked by him when she returned, carrying some metal apparatus and a large canvas bag. The two remaining neighbor women speculated that it was an oxygen tent.

Still perched on the settee, their mother tapped her foot. Then, she stood and paced and sat down again, muttering something to one or the other of the ladies. Suddenly she seemed to realize that she was still holding the oblong box. She lowered it before her and opened the lid with her thumb. It was Sherman's schoolbox, tattered and crudely marked.

"We had such a hard time with him in school," she said quietly, as if only to pass the time. "I worked with him till I was blue in the face, but nothing helped. He started a year late, you know, because of the stupid birthday law and it just got continually worse. He failed the fifth grade. Always so haphazard and happy-go-lucky. Just couldn't've cared less." She went on talking calmly about his ups and downs for quite a while. "Then he got in that trouble and it shook him—really upset him—and he seemed to snap out of it. This summer we sent him to remedial class, and for the first time he really started to try. And now this ... *this!*" Struggling for breath, she cried again, more easily than before, but when she tried to cover her face, the schoolbox spilled, the gnawed pencils with the erasers bitten off scattering on the floor. The ladies closed around her.

In that way, with unpredictable outbursts and moments of ordinary conversation, they waited. Eventually, Toddy said, "I'm afraid to watch. It makes me too nervous. I'm goin' back upstairs." And a few moments later, without saying anything more, he was gone from Mamie, who still clung to the railing. It was well after midnight before the doors rumbled apart and the doctor stepped out in the harsh span of light, mopping his face with a handkerchief. Then, with his arms spread, he caught the handles and pulled the doors shut, allowing just a fleeting glimpse of the wicker lounger, the makeshift apparatus beside it, and the shrouded shape under the gauzy tent. He scanned the foyer as he turned.

Their mother came to her feet, dazedly. Her thin face lolled like a mask on a scarecrow. "Where's Ray?" she said.

"He went with them to look for the gun," the nearest woman told her.

"Tonight?" she said, visibly trembling. "In the dark?" She tried to smooth her hair as she gravitated toward the doctor, hardly able to keep her balance.

Mamie stood when her mother turned, then rushed down the stairs as her mother went forward. But the two neighbor ladies were ahead of her, taking up their positions behind her mother, so that Mamie had to squeeze past their hips, clasping her mother's thigh through her skirt, to hear what the doctor was saying.

He was speaking low. He said the bleeding had stopped and that Sherman was in a coma. So softly she could hardly be heard, her mother said, "Then maybe we should move him to a hospital, after all." The doctor studied what she had said at length, his dire thoughts apparent in his long hesitation. Presently he said, "No, I don't think so. At least not right now. His condition is very . . . extremely delicate just now, very critical. It's too dangerous. The risk . . . If he hemorrhages again, Mrs. Abbott, death would be instantaneous." He was an elderly gentleman with baggy eyes and he had a small trimmed mustache that looked painted on.

The woman nearest Mamie stooped down and drew her aside. "Mamie, you should go to bed," she said. "It's way past your bedtime. We'll take care of your mama. Really, it's okay now. Go on and go to sleep." But Mamie shrugged away from her and went around to her mother's other side.

". . . centrifugal force," the doctor was saying as he massaged the base of his skull behind his right ear. "It's lodged roughly here," he said, holding his fingers stiff to that place. "It's possible the bullet was deflected somehow and moved inside his head for several seconds like—like—"

"Like a bee, in a bonnet," her mother said distractedly.

"Yes, I suppose," he said, and nodded. "Something on that order. But try to remember, Mrs. Abbott, even if he should live through this—even if he does, the extent of the damage won't be known for a very long time. He could be an invalid . . . or seriously impaired." He cleared his throat. "Even with the most sophisticated equipment, we couldn't know this soon."

"But he will live, then—won't he?" her mother asked. She leaned toward him, anxious for his confirmation.

The doctor's face did not change. For a moment, he stared at her intently. His eyes drifted aside, then refocused on her. He opened his mouth but said nothing.

She began to fold where she stood, and the women swept toward her. She staggered, caught herself, motioning them off. "Then I have to see him. Please, I have to go in to him."

Attentive, but without any further talk, the doctor accompanied her to the doors and slid them apart for her to enter. Too late, Mamie ran around the four legs blocking her path, but from inside the room her mother called out, "No, Mamie, not now. Not this time. Maybe tomorrow, okay? Tomorrow, maybe," and she instructed the women to put the children to bed. She was nearly transparent with light.


Mamie heard her father cross the hall; under the rug the floorboards snapped. He went to Toddy first. Drifting in and out of sleep, she heard the gruff rumble of his voice. A drawer squealed open, then shut.

Through the open window came the distant funnel-like shouts of children playing in the yards below. Despite the residue of her distress and the mood of strife that had descended on the house the night before, the cheerful noises beckoned her like slow, enticing music. Her eyelids wobbled; she dozed. Immediately it seemed, although it could have been longer, an angry uproar erupted in the gray distance—the neighbor's dog lashed out, growling and barking. Mamie thought, Those boys're tormenting him again. In her imagination, she could see them sneaking along the right-of-way behind their house to throw rocks into the dog pen. All hackles and teeth, the dog would lunge at them, his snapping chain flipping him cross-wise in the air. He was a crazy-mean dog with scary eyes, and the bet was to see if they could goad him into breaking his chain. Once in a while he did break it, his teeth slashing at the fence wire.

"Oh, Chinaman," she muttered. Mamie wanted to get up, poke her head out the window, and yell at them to stop it. She reached for the bedpost to pull herself up, but in the air her fingers bumped across a scratchy face. Her entire body flinched. She lurched crablike on the bed to escape it. The room was too full of sunshine to see clearly. With her pulse pounding, she rubbed her eyes and squinted. "Oh, Daddy," she gasped. "You scared the daylights out of me." He was seated on the small chair by her bed.

"Mamie," he said, so softly, and his face turned pale like a foggy image of himself. "I want you to tell me some things." Again she wiped her fists across her closed eyes, and when she looked once more, he struck three matches from a little paste-board box—the first two broke to pieces in his fingers. Smoke curled on his lip. He was unshaven, the drag of the comb still showing in his neat, wet hair.

She scooted up from the pillow, but stammered, said nothing.

Flattening his hands on his knees, with the cigarette glowing between his fingers, he asked where the gun had come from; did she know where Sherman got it?

He's dead, Mamie thought and, slipping out from the twisted quilts, remembered in detail the night before.

"He had no business with that gun," her father said. "Somebody's just as responsible for this as he is. I mean to find out who that is."

This time he's dead, Mamie thought, and they won't tell me. And the sickening ache that had stayed with her through the night spread vividly along her nerves.

"I'll find out," he said, "one way or the other. So you'd better tell me. Mamie, do you know where he got that gun?"

She shook her head. She wanted to tell him without lying that Sherman lied all the time, that he'd told her different made-up stories about how and where he got the gun, but she shook her head. "Let me hear you say it." And she muttered, "Dunno," and asked was he dead. Her father glanced toward the elm twig scratching the windowpane. "Maybe he will be," he said. For a moment, his eyes glazed. "Probably." He's lying to me, Mamie thought. Sherman's already dead. Her father cleared his throat. "Mamie, do you know anything about this?"

Matching the cadence of his words, she again shook her head, five, six times. He put the cigarette to his lips but his fingers trembled; a long stub of ash splashed down his shirt. He kept his dark head tilted toward the window. "Why'd he shoot himself, Mamie?" He frowned, studying his cigarette. He wiped his eyes. "Something's been wrong here a long time for this to happen. I just didn't see it. Why would he do such a thing? You were around him all the time. If anybody knows about this, you do. You're the one. You have to."

"I really liked him," Mamie said and nodded, without looking up.

His cigarette had gone out. He held it pointed up in a pinch of his thumb and fingernails. "We found the gun last night," he said. "I've never seen it before. . . . Well, I'll find out whose it was and how he got it if I have to go from door to door of every house in Graylie." As he talked, never once loud or hateful, he pulled from his pants pocket a small green plastic water gun. "Here," he said, and thrust it at her. "Show me, Mamie." His voice became firmer. "Show me what you saw . . . how he did it."

She cowered from it. "No, Daddy, don't make me. I don't want to. Please, please don't make me." But regardless of how much she begged, he insisted. Reluctantly she cupped her palm around the handle and placed her forefinger through the slot until it rested on the tension of the plastic trigger. She looked at him to see if he would tell her not to, but he said, "Go ahead." Drawing her arm up crooked, she held the water gun to her head.

He wiped his face and ran his hands through his hair. "All right," he said. "Give it here." She handed it back to him. "Mamie, if you know anything else about this—anything at all —you have to tell me now. And tell the truth, because I don't want to find out you're in on this. I'll be watching you, every move you make." Like God does, she thought.

"But I dunno," she said, crossing her feet off the edge of the bed, one on top of the other, then reversing them. "I already told you." His hand came down close to hers, but she got up and went to the dresser. When she glanced back, the door was ajar; smoke hung in the doorway.

All that day the double doors to the living room didn't open except to allow their neighbor Mrs. Jackson to enter and leave at suppertime with a tray covered by an embroidered cloth. Toddy stayed in bed, taking his medicine, and their father roamed the house, smoking his cigarettes. Some of the bouquets of flowers that had come were left on the table in the dark vestibule. Again the next day, except for brief necessities, the doors remained shut. Twice the nurse left and came back; the doctor arrived shortly after two o'clock and stayed in the room for most of an hour; otherwise the room was closed. Her father went in and out a few times, taking a glass of water or a wet washcloth, but Mamie did not once glimpse her mother. The room must be full of flowers by now, Mamie thought.

As she changed into her pajamas, she tried to question her father. Where would Mama sleep? She had to go to sleep some-time, because she had never stayed in the living room so long. But her father shrugged off her questions. "Your mama sleeps on the couch when she's tired," he said.

Mamie had made a place to play on the landing where the stairs turned, bringing down shoe boxes from the closets to build an imaginary room and dragging out all her paper dolls, but she played with them distractedly, watching the tall doors below through the bannister spindles. Late in the afternoon of the third day, their father helped Toddy pack his tin suitcase to go stay with the Connerlys down the block, where Jeff Connerly, a friend in his grade at school, lived. Watching from the bedroom doorway, Mamie saw her father do the things usually left to her mother. His large hands looked so strange folding and packing the small clothes while Toddy tracked behind him from the bu-reau to the side of the bed and back, asking how bad was Sher-man, how long would he be sick? "I don't know," her father said. "We don't know for sure." That evening, for Mamie, he made peanut-butter-and-jelly sandwiches for the fifth time in a row. She couldn't eat more than a few bites. "When's Toddy comin' home?" she asked him, but he didn't seem to hear.

She waited as long as she could, hoping for a time when she could be with her mother by herself. Night came into the house and the staircase grew steadily dimmer. The nurse left at six o'clock, telling Mamie's father she would return at eight. He followed her outside as far as the end of the walk, talking. Mamie dumped the clutter of paper dolls off her skirt and crept down the stairs. Standing at the window beside the front door, she saw that they were still talking. She hurried toward the sliding doors, faintly etched now with light. No sound came from the other side. Grasping one of the handles, she slid the door until she could slip inside. She noticed in a glance that the room was empty of flowers.

A single bedside lamp burned on an end table, its dark lampshade capturing much of the light. The oxygen tent was gone. The couch had been pushed up beside the wicker lounger, and on the couch a shape moved. Inching forward, she saw that it was her mother, nestled alongside Sherman. She was murmuring to him when she saw Mamie. They stared at each other. Quiet as a cat, Mamie stopped at the foot of the lounger, rigid. Finally, her mother broke the silence. "Sherman, look who's here," she said, her voice croaky but kind. "Mamie's come to say good night." Slowly she lifted her face from his. "Look how much better he is today. The color's come back to his cheeks. He's so much better—so much better off here at home where we can take care of him. What a fine boy he is. So strong. Mamie, don't be scared. Come on around here and say good night. Come on, now. He's fast asleep. He can't hurt you."

With her hand trailing on the wicker, Mamie moved slowly up along the side of the lounger toward the place her mother had indicated with a nod.

"Now see," her mother said even more quietly, "that wasn't so hard, was it? Go ahead. Tell him good night." The stench of antiseptic and perspiration was stifling.

Everything seemed terribly wrong; nothing was the same as it had been. She could not see that Sherman was breathing at all. The sheets did not move upon his body, and his head—his lolling head was enormous with bandages. As she stood trembling at the bedside, peering over at his swollen, almost unrecognizable face, she was dumbstruck with how thoroughly everything had changed. Even her mother had suddenly been transformed. In the three days she had stayed in the room, her hair had turned white in places and her eyes smoldered in her gaunt face.

Tears ran loose in Mamie's eyes. "Mama," she said, bracing herself. She stammered for breath; then she blurted it out: "Mama, is he still dead?"

Shooting across the narrow width of the lounger, her mother's hand sank into Mamie's hair, clasped the back of her head, and pulled her down across the white sheets until their faces were inches apart. "Don't you ever say that," she whispered sharply. "Don't you ever. He's not dead and he's not going to die. You know how I know? Because"—wincing under her grip, Mamie begged to be let go, but her mother only tightened her hold—"because the good Lord tells us he will not give us something we cannot bear and—and I can't . . . bear . . . it." All at once, she sounded absolutely exhausted. Her fingers relaxed their grip and Mamie pulled away with such force that she fell on the floor. She picked herself up and stared at her mother, but she didn't cry any more; she backed away, blinking the tears from her eyes.

Her mother had returned her attention to Sherman, crooning to him and straightening the bedclothes around him. Watching them while she rubbed her sore scalp, Mamie realized that she was completely on her own. She'd wanted to go to her mother, had waited these three days to sit on her lap and tell her everything—the truth about what she and Sherman had done together. But she couldn't now. She would do his bidding as he had asked, as he had taught her. She was afraid to tell her father, afraid of what he might do, and now that her mother had given herself to Sherman, there was no one left to tell it to—except, maybe, the Chinaman.

The next morning, in the hour before daybreak, Mamie awoke quite suddenly for no explainable reason. She sensed someone near, watching her, almost asking her to turn around. She peered through the half-light, this way and that, but there was no one. She rolled from her bed and padded down the hall.

The water drummed from the faucet as she filled the basin.

Standing on her short red stool, Mamie doused her face, put soap on it, and rinsed it off. Toddy's hair was dark with a natural wave, but her hair was almost the same color as Sherman's—what her mother called dishwater blond. Staring at her own face in the mirror, she stretched the skin white over her nose and lowered her eyelids just slightly, trying to make Sherman's face. But where her nose was thin and straight, his was thicker, with a gristly lump in the middle from when he broke it; where her gray-green eyes were long-lashed and open, his were blue and droopy and quick. And besides, she thought, she had freckles. But trying to conjure his face caused her mind to whirl with memories.

"Look," Sherman said.

"What is it?" she asked him.

"A button."

"Whose button?" She laughed through her hands.

"Dad's. I just got it while he's asleep. Now it's your turn."

"But what should I get?"

"Whatever you want. Anything you want. It's a game."

She squinted at him. "What kind of a game?"

He said, "You have to get something from them while you're very close. It's like you trick them and you have to do it so they don't know. See? A hair would be good or—or something hard, like an eyelash."

The house had seemed labyrinthine then, all hallways and hiding places where they could share their triumphs and laughs, and if discovered, they always knew where to meet later—in the attic below the circular window where the glass bulged out like an eyepiece. There, panting for breath, they would have a quick laugh before they revealed the surprises in their hands, buttons and ravelings and hairs. Afterward, standing on boxes, they gazed down through the distorting window on the pattern of the town, overlooking the streets and blocks all the way to Main Street, with the stream meandering beside it; gazed down like invincible rulers on their kingdom of Graylie in the land of Pennsylvania.

It was a game only she and Sherman had played; Toddy was always afraid he'd get in trouble. As Mamie remembered all this, stepping down from her stool and pushing it aside, it dawned on her where Sherman must've put their sack. Now she would do what he couldn't do. As she had promised.

She wasted no time. She changed all her clothes down to her underwear. She put on the simple smock-dress and buttoned the back, but got it crooked. She couldn't reach it; it pooched and gapped. Finally she left it that way. Very gently she shut the bedroom door behind her, slapped the damp hair from her forehead, and moved down the hall on sock feet, carrying her shoes.

She glanced into the room Toddy and Sherman had shared, and saw that the beds were neatly made. It seemed odd not to have Toddy there; she wished he'd just come back home. Ten feet farther and she entered her parents' bedroom, tiptoeing quickly to the bed. Her mother's side of the bed was empty, unrumpled. Her father's mouth hung partly open, his cheeks telling breath, and his eyes were crinkled skin. She backed away, easing the door shut so the knob barely clicked. The sun was coming up.

Retreating to the top of the stairs, Mamie opened a white door that looked like a closet door. As she turned the wooden latch, the trapped hot air engulfed her. She stepped into the swarming heat on the first step and pulled the door to, leaving it open a crack. Faint pencils of light cut the dark hemisphere of rafters above.

Feeling her way in the attic room, she lifted the curled shade on the back window to let in the early light; it was a pure, harsh light falling in a long trapezoid on the floor. "You can find it," Sherman had said. She opened the chifforobe where they had hidden things before and rummaged through the clutter of old magazines and years-old dresses, found nothing. She searched the other side of the partition. Gingham quilt pieces, embroidery patterns and floss, a ragged clump of discharge papers, a newspaper print of *The Last Supper*, and more, but in all of it she couldn't find the paper sack. When she closed the chifforobe door, the air fumed with dust. She sneezed into both her hands.

Slowly, Mamie turned until she saw the camelback trunk standing on end. She pushed it aside a few inches and squeezed past. Picking up an old shirt, she wiped the cobwebs and dust from the large ox-eye window and looked down on the summer landscape, the wide perspective of houses to the meandering creek, and, at the other extremity, the highway and the blackberry patch where they had gone to pick berries the evening he . . . shot himself. She stood back, turning her head. Then she saw it.

Reaching as high as she could, she took the grocery sack with the wadded top from the exposed timber above the window. The top of the sack had been rolled and unrolled so many times it was as soft and pliable as chamois. One piece at a time, she emptied the contents of the sack to separate her few things from his, arranging them on the rough-sawed cross-member below the round window.

A half-empty pack of Lucky Strike cigarettes, his latest acquisition, the red target beneath the cellophane beginning to fade.

A marbleized fountain pen with the name J. T. Ivers burned in gold along its side.

A tie clasp in the shape of an ocean liner taken from the home of Mr. and Mrs. Bledsoe the same night she took the brand-new tube of lipstick encrusted with rhinestones. This she set aside.

A tiny spyglass, on a beaded chain, with a hootchie-cootchie dancer in it.

Two cigars, one broken, but both with their bright chromoliths intact, which he liked.

A rubber, the use of which he would not tell her about; just what it was: a rubber.

A tissue with a red kiss on it taken from Marilyn Haupt's dresser at 3:00 a.m. one night. Mamie remembered that night in particular because the clock in that bedroom glowed in the dark and she wanted it, but Sherman said it would take up too much room and make too much noise in the sack. Marilyn Haupt didn't sleep with any of her clothes on.

A huge knobby class ring with mohair around it and the initials R.G.

A red-and-yellow box of bullets.

A five-dollar bill, four tens, twenty-seven ones, and two silver dollars.

A postcard from the Everglades; the scribbled handwriting on the back side neither of them could read, but they liked the picture of the alligator on the front. And, taken that same night, a love letter addressed to Miss Peggy Dunnhurst, 273 Stockton Ave., Graylie, Penn.

Matching hair barrettes with laughing clown faces whose eyes dangled on springs—her absolute favorite things, but Sherman had told her she could never wear them because they had belonged to Suzie Rawlings, who lived only two doors away. These she left among the array of Sherman's things to be returned to the sack.

A charm bracelet of state capitals, which she set aside not to wear but to keep and look at.

Three speckled bird feathers they had found in the street one clear morning.

A Gem razor, still in its green plastic case, and a green plastic dispenser of single-edged razor blades.

In a separate, smaller sack, a collection of old Army medals and ribbons.

Two chocolate bonbons in their white paper cups, which she promptly ate. They had melted so many times they tasted funny.

An empty bronze-colored locust shell split perfectly down the back. It was huge in her small hand, the largest one they had ever found. She fastened its claws into the front of her smock, wearing it like a pin.

In soft rolled wads, a pair of gray silk stockings.

Books of paper matches and wooden matches with chalky red tips.

Pieces from a Zippo lighter and a pocket watch Sherman had taken apart to see how they worked. And, at the bottom of everything, Mr. Atherton's small brown spiral-bound notebook half full of his cryptic notes and figures. The rubber band around it was notched and limp with age. It broke when she tried to remove it. Licking her thumb, she turned the small pages until she found what Sherman had written. On one page, his name had been repeatedly drawn in flamboyant curlicue letters. The next page contained his note.

I AM GOIN TO KILL THEM   I NO WHERE A GUN IS AND SHELLS   NOBODY WILL BE OK BUT US   NALE THE WINDAS AN DOORS SHUT THAN SET IT ON FIRE

Mamie could read only part of it, but she knew what it said. She had watched him write it, laboring over each word, talking it out. Their father had asked her why Sherman had done it; now she tried to recall the day he'd written the note and everything leading up to it, because maybe hidden in the note, like a riddle, was *why*. . . .

One evening last spring, walking home from the baseball diamond, Sherman saw a pretty blonde woman getting into her car. The grocery boy had put her bags of groceries in the back seat, and he held the door open for her while she arranged herself behind the steering wheel. She wore a sleeveless blouse with a sailor collar, and Bermuda shorts. Her name was Lila Stiles; she was recently married and Sherman had noticed her many times before. On impulse, as he passed down the side of her low-slung car, he stuck his head through the open window and kissed her. With his quick left hand inside her blouse, he tugged at her brassière. Moaning against the press of his mouth, she dug the heel of her hand into the chrome horn ring on the steering wheel and he fled under the blare of the noise. He arrived home out of breath, in a state of agitation. When he told Mamie about it, he said he thought his heart would stop when he did it—the feeling of power and excitement went way beyond anything they'd felt when they took things. It was like a jolt of lightning. He said he would try it again. Mamie asked to go along, but he said not with this. It was too dangerous.

Two days later, a woman stood at the corner of Main and Grand Avenue, freshening her lipstick. The usual flow of passersby moved easily about her. In one hand she held a compact before her face, in the other a tube of lipstick. Her purse was tucked under her left arm. Suddenly, in the small frame of her mirror, she saw a flurry of movement behind her. Her skirt flew high above her hips, exposing her completely from the waist down. Yelling, she whirled around and saw a young boy running away. Her purse lay spilled on the sidewalk.

A week passed. It was noon on Saturday. Sherman cut through the alley and stooped below the top ridge of the picket fence for the third day in a row. Through the crevices, he watched the woman in her bathing suit sunning herself. She was lying propped up on her lawn chair. She wore sunglasses, and the book she had been reading had tumbled to the ground. He thought she was asleep. He slipped through the gate and was inches from her, coming toward her from the side, when she sat up, the black ovals of her sequined sunglasses fixed upon him. "What do you want?" she asked him. She started to stand up. But he was there and she was there, and he kissed her as she tried to get to her feet. At least, he almost kissed her. They tumbled over, fell, the top of her bathing suit sliding down like a candy wrapper, her breasts bobbing against him. That was his story. Sherman never admitted, even to Mamie, that he pulled down her top. He said that when she cursed him and called him by name it made him nervous, and that's when he pinned her to the ground and said if she told anybody, he'd come back and shut her up good. She claimed he tore her swimsuit and struck her repeatedly.

The woman, named Sarah Coveleski, called their father and their father notified the police. "This is the last damned straw," he told Sherman in front of the other two children. "You're nothing but trouble. I've tried to be good to you but nothing gets through. And I won't put up with this any longer. It's just the last God-damned straw." And he slapped Sherman's face with the flat of his hand so hard that it made a loud pop and Sherman stumbled and fell. He drove Sherman to the police station and turned him over to the officer in charge. Sherman was identified by the two women, Stiles and Coveleski, and was detained for questioning for nine hours. It was nearly eleven-thirty at night before he was released into the custody of his father. More to preserve the reputation of the women than anything else, the matter was kept out of the Graylie newspaper. And yet the word got around. Sherman wouldn't talk about his detainment, but he was properly chastised and seething.

Later, his mother had tried to explain that they only meant to teach him a lesson, but Sherman had never trusted them again. He was convinced his father would betray him with any chance he had, and he hated his mother for letting his father get away with it. Sherman already had the gun when he wrote the note. . . .

It was not yet five-thirty that early August morning when Mamie left the house by the back-porch steps. In her dress pocket she carried two lumps of brown sugar; in her right arm she carried the sack of Sherman's loot. The severe change in light from the interior of the house to the brilliant glare of the yard blinded her. Hugging the paper bag, she shielded her eyes, stepping into the cooler house shadow.

She followed the walk parallel to the house until it ended, then hurried across the wet grass. At the hedge, she ducked into the tunnel made by the thick branches of the privet hedge and the adjoining iron fence. All but hidden from view, she crawled down the length of the iron fence, dragging the sack with her to the end of the yard, where she emerged in the thicket of ragweed and goldenrod and wild crape myrtle. She stood and dusted her knees.

She crossed the weedy right-of-way.

She could hear the Chinaman before she saw him—a low, throbbing, nerve-numbing growl. The pen was constructed with two high fences, one set inside the other, because when he was mad enough to break his chain, the Chinaman could chew through one layer of fence in nothing flat. The back of the pen faced the right-of-way; its front and the gate were flush with the Ambroses' back yard, which meant she would have to skirt the fence and enter their yard in order to reach the gate. Picking her way carefully, she started down the sloping embankment alongside the fence. The low throb of the dog's growling neither quickened nor faltered.

More than halfway down the side of the pen, the weeds gapped and she saw him: the ruff of his black hair framing his pug face, the slanting Chinese eyes with no irises, just black holes to see through, the muzzle of his black mouth drawn back on long slashing teeth, saliva hanging from his jowls. It was the face of absolute rage and, as always, for a moment she found herself mesmerized by it, unable to move. He must have sensed her fear—the low, guttural growl rose an octave. Slowly he came to his feet, the chain attached to his collar clinking as he stood. His matted tail curled up and back on his hindquarters. His dust-mottled coat fell at odds with itself along his shabby length, clotted with chunks of dirt. He was no longer growling; his black lips were stretched thin, his nose ridged. Then he sprang, hurtling through the air, his growl twice as loud as it had been, teeth snapping, cracking together on empty air, till the chain caught, whipping him backward. He hardly touched the ground before he flew at Mamie again, his massive black muzzle ripping through the air only two feet away.

Frightened, she fumbled in her pocket for the sugar. The first lump crumbled to powder in her hand, and she quickly pulled out the second one. She reached through the outer fence and tossed the lump into the pen, underhanded. As often as she'd come here with Sherman to bring the dog some sugar, these first minutes never became any less terrifying. "Chinaman," she said, but her voice sounded shaky. She tried again, forcing a firmer voice. "Chinaman, you stop." He stepped over his chain and backed away, eyeing her. "There's your sugar. There it *is.*" Mamie pointed to where it had disintegrated on the ground. His pug face came up tilted and quizzical. "There," she said, and pointed again. "You know me. You remember me, doncha? I'm going to come see you now. You be a good boy. Don't you bite me." His growls were mellowing to short, snorty grumps and groans. He barked at her once, ran sideways a few steps, dragging his chain, and barked again; then he ambled toward the sugar, sniffing the ground.

The Chinaman was nearly as tall as she was, and she was as tall as a regular doorknob. His enormous tufted paws were as big as fists. Their father had told them to stay away from him. He said the Chinaman was half chow, and for all he knew the other half was timber wolf. When Sherman asked how he knew, he said the face and the black tongue came from the chow and the size and the coat came from a big breed, a German shepherd or a wolf; but he wasn't muscular like a shepherd, more lanky and lean like a wolf. And he told them there was no meaner breed alive than a chow that had been mixed. Sherman said it was no wonder he was mean, because Mr. Ambrose beat him, and their father said that was his privilege, it was his dog. But Sherman pitied him enough to start taking him sugar. He said they understood each other.

When Mamie opened the gate to his pen, she stepped directly into the bare circumference of his chain length and allowed the Chinaman to sniff at her from top to bottom. After his inspection, he nuzzled her and licked her with his black tongue. First he licked her face, then he licked her sugar-dusted palm, and finally, while she held it open, he licked the inside of her sugary pocket. She petted him and hugged his face and told him Sherman was hurt. The rolled-back tail twitched. She talked to him. She told him he was a good boy. Along his back she could feel hard welts under his fur. Then, while he watched, she went into the doghouse.

Inside, the air smelled heavily of damp dog. She lifted the straw mat in the far corner and hid the paper bag under it. Outside, the gate squeaked open and closed. Mr. Ambrose's house slippers walked past the square doghouse doorway, and his hand and sleeve set down a tin basin of water. She huddled in the darkest corner, careful not to shift in the straw. "Scat," he said. He stamped his foot and the Chinaman backed from him. With the side of his slipper, he scraped something shiny along the ground. His hand came down and he picked it up. "Well, I'll be," he said. With her heart pounding, Mamie looked down her front and at her arms and hands, trying to determine what she might have dropped. Had she torn a hole in the sack and lost something? She wanted to dig the sack out of the straw and check it, but she was afraid to move. "Biggest damned shell I ever saw," he said. Her hand searched the front of her dress, and it was gone—the bronze-colored locust shell she had saved, gone. His slippers came toward the doghouse door. Her mind

raced. He's gonna find me, find the sack, know what we did, tell
. . . But the footsteps turned away. The gate clapped shut. The
Chinaman sat, then lay down, wary and alert, peering at Mamie
from the swelter of his domain. His eerie eyes squinted to slits
as he yawned.

She crawled out and peeked above the low roof in time to
see Mr. Ambrose go into his house. She patted the Chinaman's
ruff, slipped from the pen, and went home the way she had
come, down the tunnel of hedges to the walk and into the
kitchen, catching the screen door. Without hesitation, she
crossed through the dining room, where the table gleamed like
a mirror. The doors to the living room holding Sherman and her
mother were closed. She thought she heard her mother softly
weeping. Carefully, Mamie moved toward the doors, but the
sound, whatever it was, had stopped. When she heard nothing
more, she backed away on tiptoe and climbed the stairs to her
room. Then she changed into her pajamas and climbed back into
her bed.

# 2

After the night she pulled Mamie down across the wicker
lounger, her mother never again spoke of Sherman's injury. She
treated him like a revered guest. To her, it was no longer a
question of whether he would live or die, but when he would
get well, as if his condition were a disease they could conquer
together.

As the days turned to weeks, she established a regime by
which she read to him from the Bible every hour on the hour
as long as she was awake. This practice never varied.

For the next eight months, she rarely left his side. She bathed
him, gently turned him first on one side, then the other, to

prevent bedsores; she learned to administer his injections and the intravenous-feeding device. Talking to herself, she kept up a conversation about everyday matters—the weather, the little gossip she'd heard, events Toddy and Mamie reported from their play outside—because, she told anyone who'd listen, she believed that his subconscious mind heard everything she said and stored it, so that eventually he would remember what he had missed. And, besides reading the Bible, she prayed. On the hour.

With the passage of time, the neighbors came by less and less frequently. Only Mrs. Jackson continued to show up every so often with a covered dish. The two younger children had gone back to school—Toddy went to Mrs. Shaw's third grade and Mamie was in the first grade with Miss Durbin—and their father was back at work full time. After the first two months, the nurse limited her visits to once a week to help their mother change the bedclothes. Their father explained they couldn't afford her any more than that. In early October, the doctor talked about surgery to remove a blood clot and, perhaps, the bullet. He described Sherman's condition as stable but unchanged, and stressed that the present situation might continue indefinitely. Her mother took the report in stride, but about the operation she said, "Maybe in a few weeks, we'll see. If there's no immediate danger, I can't bear to think about having him cut right now." Before the doctor could go on, she returned to the sickroom, shutting the doors.

The desolation hung over them all; it went to school with the children and came home with them. They often walked home alone. The other kids shied away, whispered behind their backs. Just when the worst effects of the family crisis seemed to be lessening, trouble would unexpectedly crop up again. One bright, chilly morning, during recess, word reached Mamie that Toddy was in the principal's office, crying. She thought he'd been spanked. It seemed impossible—he always behaved himself. She ran down the corridor to the office. Sitting on the edge of a chair, Toddy was weeping convulsively. His teacher was there, trying to talk to him. "It'll be all right," Mrs. Shaw said. "We've called your father."

"What'd you do?" Mamie asked, bending to him very close. "What's the matter, Toddy?"

"He started to cry uncontrollably during class," Mrs. Shaw said to the school nurse, who had come in. "It's . . ." She motioned the nurse aside, speaking quietly.

It took Toddy a little while to sob himself back to silence, and then their father arrived and Mrs. Shaw and the nurse met him with explanations. Toddy looked at Mamie as if pleading. "Sherman never liked me," he whispered to her. "He never, never did. Ever since I wouldn't do what he wanted. You know"—his voice grew even softer and quieter—"go and take things. Sherman never liked me after that. He was mean to me. And now he's hurt, and he's never gonna get well. I just keep thinking about it. I can't stop. I don't think he ever will like me." He began to sob again.

"Oh, Toddy," Mamie whispered, "I like you."

Then their father lifted him up in his arms, and Mrs. Shaw said, "It's a shame. Toddy's really a good boy, Mr. Abbott. He works so hard. You should be proud of him. None of us knew he was so deeply troubled by—by—well, you understand, your other son's injury."

"Daddy," Mamie said, "can I come home, too?" She didn't want to be left there in school by herself. But he said no, she ought to stay so he could spend some time alone with Toddy.

Fall was ending; the trees were suddenly bare, drifts of leaves knee-deep in the yards and gutters. On those dreary afternoons, after the children came home from school, their mother permitted Mamie to spread a quilt on the living-room floor and bring in her shoe boxes and paper dolls so she could keep an eye on her. Sometimes, without leaving Sherman's bedside, their mother helped Toddy with his arithmetic problems. And although Toddy always kept his distance, Mamie learned in time to speak to Sherman as casually as her mother did. Once, when no one else was in the room, she whispered to him where she had stashed his things.

But while their mother was absorbed with Sherman and, for the most part, neglected everyone else, their father intensified his watchfulness over Mamie, just as he had said he would do. Through that early winter, he talked to the neighbors, one by one. Mamie knew what he was doing, and her nerves twitched with the fear of what he might have discovered every evening that he was late coming home from work. And again, on Saturdays, when he left the house at midafternoon without telling them where he was going. She knew. He never let her put it out of her mind. With his accusing glances, with questions and hints, with quick descriptions of what he'd found out from Mrs. Graves or Mr. Mallory, he let her know that his pursuit of the truth about the gun had not slackened. When she was outside playing, it was not uncommon for her to glance up and see him watching her through one or another of the windows, or to see the curtains suddenly shifting. Once, when her mother had sent her to the corner grocery for a loaf of bread, she saw him leaving the Iverses' house. She remembered the marbleized fountain pen and a chill ran through her. She stood behind a tree until he had turned the corner.

He kept a notebook with him. When she came upon him jotting in it, he immediately put it away. It preyed on her thoughts. Now and then, as she crossed by a window, she would gaze in the direction of the dog pen or, while her father was at work, she would take the Chinaman a lump of sugar and talk to him. If the dog was in a good mood that day, she would even reach her fingers through the two layers of fence and stroke his stubby nose. But she didn't go into the pen.

Usually it was during supper that her father baited her. "Mr. Briggenschmidt said he had a gun that was stolen some time back." They'd eat in silence, Toddy stealing glances at her and Mamie mechanically lifting her fork. "But I showed him the gun Sherman used and it wasn't it." Afterward, Mamie was so tense she couldn't sleep. "Why don't you just tell him?" Toddy asked her late one night. "Because," Mamie said, utterly exasperated, "Toddy, *I don't know!*" Finally, one night, she set down her fork and exploded at her father: "Daddy, I don't know where he got that gun! I don't know, I swear I don't. I wish you'd stop it. Please stop telling me—stop telling. I don't know!" The tears were streaming down her face. "I want you to stop it. I can't stand it. If I knowed where he got it, I'd tell, but I don't. . . . Okay? Okay?"

But he didn't stop, and her fear mounted and mounted.

On Tuesday evening, November eighteenth, Mamie took a bath by herself, sweetening the bathwater with splashes of perfume and a cake of L'Eau de Paree. Sitting before her mother's vanity with a powder puff in one hand and the atomizer in the other, she dampened and patted her face with still another coat of perfume. She cut her hair, using the fingernail scissors, until it looked worse than when she had started, but she liked it. She dressed herself in her very best Sunday clothes—her taffeta dress, her white shoes and socks—and she carried her blue plastic purse with thirty-one cents in it. She waited that evening on the stairs and on the settee and at the dusty dining-room table. Her mother went by and patted her head. When her father, who had been working overtime, came home at seven-thirty, he told her to go change out of her play clothes and come help him get ready for supper. She lay across her bed and cried. On that day she was seven years old.

Somehow Toddy realized what had happened. When they were getting ready for bed, he gave her a present. "It's for your birthday," he said, and he handed her the old cuff-link box, unwrapped. "Go ahead. Open it." Inside was his skull ring, like the Phantom's. A summer ago, he'd sold garden seeds and saved box tops and sent away for it; it had one red eye and one green eye. The ring was just like the Phantom's ring in the funny papers; it could dent your jaw and leave its mark forever. "But, Toddy," Mamie said, "I can't take *this!* This's *your* ring you sent off for."

"You have to," he said. "I don't have nothing else you'd want." The back of the ring was adjustable and he bent it to fit tighter on her finger. He told her it would probably turn her finger green, but in that moment it became her most favorite of all her favorite things. She wore it to bed.

At Christmastime, their parents had a disagreement that lasted several days. Their father wanted to have Christmas as always, with a tree and presents underneath; their mother said that since Sherman couldn't participate, she wanted to put it off until they could all be together again. The two younger children heard them arguing in the night after the lights had been turned out. In the end, their father decided it. He took Toddy and Mamie through the bright glittering stores, where they bought armloads of presents, but on Christmas Day the three large presents wrapped for their mother and the four wrapped for Sherman remained untouched under the tree all that day and the next.

In the evenings of those months, they listened to the radio: "Junior Miss" and "Lux Radio Theatre," "Edgar Bergen and Charlie McCarthy," "The Shadow," and then "Boston Blackie." For New Year's Eve, they stayed up to listen to Guy Lombardo and the Royal Canadians.

The condition of the house fell steadily into decline. Balls of dust rolled underfoot. Their mother went through the motions of keeping herself going; that was all. She moved through the house like a hollow-eyed ghost. For a long time, Mamie and her father kept the kitchen halfway clean, tidying up each night after supper while Toddy did his homework. None of it seemed to matter. Their upside-down lives drifted on without any reversal in sight. Sherman lay unconscious on the wicker lounger. He was now thirteen.

A few nights into February, as Toddy set the supper table and Mamie laid out plates, their mother came from the living room. She stood in the doorway with her back to them, to Mamie and Toddy and their father. When she turned, her face was contorted and alive. She tried to speak, but her mouth just worked, her eyes opened wide. Toddy said, "Mama, what's wrong?"

"He talked to me," she stammered. "Just now he talked to me. Our prayers are answered. Just now he said, 'I'm in the light.' That's what he said. Of course, he sounded weak, but I heard him. 'I'm in the light, the red light.' That's it—it exactly."

They filed into the room and stood around the lounger, but Sherman looked no different from the way he had yesterday, and no sound came from him except his ragged breathing. It was like a terrible joke. Her mother studied their sad faces. "You don't believe me. I didn't believe it myself at first." Tears stood in her eyes. "You think I made it up—it's all over your faces. But I didn't. . . . Just wait, you'll see." She had begun to tap her foot. "You'll see."

The following afternoon, she had the children stand with her beside the makeshift bed. "I want you to feel how much heavier his arm is. He's getting stronger. Really he is. So much stronger. I can see it." The arm placed first in the upturned hands of Toddy, then in Mamie's, seemed heavy, but they didn't know how to gauge it.

It was another three weeks, toward the end of February, before Sherman opened his eyes. According to their mother, this time he said, "Oh, Mama, I'm so tired." The doctor was called, and again the children were kept from the room overnight. To dampen their impatience, their father said that evening, "You can see him tomorrow. That's plenty soon enough. The doctor said we have to take it slow. And Mama wants to give him a bath first and cut his hair." He headed back downstairs, but they trailed after him in their pajamas.

"Will he know who we are?" Toddy asked.

"Sometimes he will," their father said with his hand on the bannister, and it seemed an odd and baffling reply.

It was noon the following day before they were called into the living room. The window shades had been lifted. The purity of the winter light magnified the room, making it appear vast and sparsely furnished. The couch had been pushed back against the wall; a plain spindle-back chair replaced it at the bedside. "Toddy, come on," their mother said. "And, Mamie, close the door as you come in, sweetie. It's too drafty. We don't want him to catch cold."

Mamie did as she was told. Charged with anticipation, but not knowing what to expect, she lagged behind Toddy. She kept her eyes fastened on the lounger as they went to join their father on its far side. She leaned forward as she walked, trying to peer around her mother's shoulder; after a few more steps she could see Sherman propped up on pillows, his head pitched slightly downward. She moistened her lips and bit them and swallowed hard.

All this time, her mother was speaking to Sherman in a soft voice. "He's doing just fine. Yes, he is. Just fine, but look how tired he is. He's slept so long he wore himself out. So tired . . ."

Vaguely nodding and swaying, his head lifted by slow degrees.

It was as if everything else disappeared. Only his incredibly blue eyes looked up from below his eyelashes, and the room began to slide around Mamie. The smart-alecky, devil-may-care glint that had been so much a part of him was gone; in its place was something hard, and cruel, and blunt. She wanted to scream, No! He's not all right. He's not just fine. His eyes're wrong. Can't you see? It's all wrong!

And for as long as that moment lasted, it was like a horrible dream that wouldn't go away.

Then, as if moving it through heavy air, Sherman lifted his hand toward her and her mother's voice broke through that first stricken impression. "Mamie, don't be bashful," she said. "Take hold of his hand and tell him who you are, because he remembers you, really he does, but he's kind of confused. Everything seems so brand new to him. You'll have to help me watch out for him. Will you do that? Help me take care of him?"

Deliberately, Mamie nodded. She wanted to take his hand and help him, and then she did take it and she knew she must never tell them that he wasn't just fine, because he was her brother who had watched over her and taken her out into the night. Only he knew how to undo the trouble they were in; only he could help her return the things they had taken and not get caught. So for now he couldn't be anything but fine, because now that he was coming back, he was really all she had.

They knew from that day that he would never be the same as before the shooting, and yet it was like an unspoken secret they kept to themselves. Their mother acknowledged nothing but the glory of his improvement, and the others, the children and their father, realized instinctively what had to be done. With subtle, innocent glances, they communicated what they couldn't say out loud, what they couldn't have put into words if they'd wanted to, except to admit that he was different; changed. The glint was gone. They missed his smirky smile, his cockiness, and the gleam of mischief in his eyes, but with their silence they wove a cocoon around the truth—around the pain and sorrow and disappointment.

Within the week, their mother was more like her old self than she had been in eight months. Humming, she tied an apron around her waist and put her hair up in a scarf triangle. She went to work downstairs, mopping and cleaning, and she cooked expansive suppers, complete with dessert. As soon as Sherman could sit up for any reasonable length of time, she tied pillows to the back and the seat of her granddaddy's rocker, and when their father came home from work, he carried Sherman to the dining room and placed him in the padded rocking chair. In that way, he was with them each evening.

With his blank blue eyes, Sherman appeared more confused than docile, and when he did not looked confused, Mamie saw the hardness in his glance that chilled her to the heart.

Seldom was he cross, even more seldom did he complain, but he had frightening spells where he blacked out. In the beginning, only the simplest acts made sense to him. Did the sandwich taste good? "It's good," he'd say, staring into the distance. When he slumped back on the pillows and their mother asked if he was tired, "I'm tired," he'd say, ". . . sleepy," as if the connection between the two words were abstract and difficult. And when it was nine o'clock and he wasn't sleepy, she gave him medicine to put him to sleep. In time, he did remember who they were and called them by name—their mother initially, then Toddy, then Mamie and their father. It took a long time; he seemed to have to dredge their likenesses from the depths of his memory. But every day he grew a little stronger and a little more aware.

And their mother's praise of him never faltered. Her cheerful patter embraced him completely. Even in the early morning, as their father shaved to go to work, they sometimes heard her. "There goes Jimmy Porterfield to deliver his newspapers. See him? There he goes. One day you'll ride a bicycle just like his." She spent most of her time coaxing him to walk another step, to take one more bite; she urged him to speak without slurring. "How strong you'll be," she would say. "As good as new. That's my good boy." As if she could leave the past behind. But Mamie thought, Not for long will he be good. Not for very much longer.

During those months, those slow, rainy months when winter telescoped into spring, Mamie gently shared her things with him, even when he had no patience and tore her paper dolls or sent the toy lead soldiers she'd chosen for his Christmas present flying under the swipe of his hand. When their mother was out of earshot, she told him about the Chinaman. "I took him one of your old socks," she said, "so he'll remember you." In the chair too high for her, she sat beside his bed, talking quietly as their mother hovered nearby, or when he was finally able to walk from the chair to the couch to the doorway, she stood with him. She wanted to talk to him, really talk to him, but the chance didn't come and he was very reticent about talking to her. In all those early months, he didn't think to ask what had happened to him. "I'm hurt," he would say. "Yes," their mother would say, "you hurt yourself. But we're going to fix it. You'll be good as new." And the room would start to slide behind his gaze and Mamie would want to cry out, No, no, he's not! He's changed! He's not good . . . not good.

At the supper table early that summer, their mother said, "He's getting too strong for me. It wears me out just to have him lean on me. He's almost as tall as I am, and solid as a rock."

"Five foot two and eyes of blue," Toddy said.

One day weeks later, when the doctor had been to examine him, the doctor said to their father, "Walk with me out to the car. I have one of the prescriptions in my other case." But they didn't reach the car; they stood on the sidewalk with their backs to the house and seemed to stay out there endlessly. A little over a year had passed since that awful night in the blackberry patch. It was the middle of August; school would start soon. The doctor carried his coat, blotted his face with a handkerchief. And Mamie watched them through the blur of the ticking window fan. Finally, the black sedan drove away and their father came in empty-handed. "What did the doctor say, Daddy?" Mamie asked. With his fingers, he smoothed the sweat from his eyebrow. "Oh," he said, preoccupied, "nothing's very clear-cut right now. We have to decide what to do about Sherman."

Then, for several weeks, every night, it seemed, after she and Toddy had gone to bed Mamie heard them talking downstairs, their faint voices rising sporadically through the joists and plaster and lath like buried hearts. On the nights she couldn't sleep, she went quietly down to the landing to listen. Their voices sometimes buzzed and hummed inside the walls; only pieces of what they said came to her undistorted. One night, her father said, "I'm going to do what the doctor said to do, Ellie. Or else, before we know it, it might be too late." And her mother replied, "Not yet, please, not yet. Haven't you seen how well he walks? He's doing so well. Just today I was thinking we should move him upstairs. He needs more time. Give him a little more time, Ray . . . another few weeks." A shadow came to the lighted doorway below, and Mamie slipped up the stairs.

Another night, she had to go all the way down the stairs to hear. Light glowed beneath the closed kitchen door; she inched toward it. "Doc Lasher said he needs tests and he needs specialists. Even then we can't be sure. Maybe he'll never be—"

Her mother was adamant. "I won't put him away. You might as well tear the heart right out of me. I can't . . . I won't."

A long silence followed. One of them stirred something; a spoon tinkled against china. Her father said, "He's been out of the house again. I checked his shoes this morning when I got up. And they were wet. You know all this and still you persist."

Without any detectable increase in the pitch of his voice, suddenly he was near; inches from Mamie's eyes, the brass doorknob turned clockwise. As if hypnotized by it, she stood locked in her tracks. She couldn't move, the fear pounding through her. The door cracked open a slit and a thin blade of light scored her in half. But before she could think what to do, the knob jiggled and the door closed. "What if he is depressed," her mother said. "He'll come out of it." Mamie was already on the stairs, her fingers swinging round the pillar post. "Depressive," her father said, and the walls muffled his voice.

On the landing, Mamie hastened up the remaining stairs and back to her room.

But she dozed and tossed and dozed again. The house settled into a deep plinking silence, like a well. She couldn't think what it would be like to be put away, except that it would be a room with bars in it. Every few minutes, she woke up slick with sweat. She had to tell him, warn him.

In the deepest ebb of the night, she made her way down the dark stairs, crossed in front of the window fan that ruffled her hair and made her suck in breath, and entered the living room through the double doors, now left open. Her mother slept sprawled on the couch. Mamie paused long enough to watch the slow, even fall of her breath. Then she hurried toward the white island of the lounger.

To hide, she knelt on the back, shadowed side of it, checked the dark peripheries, and nudged Sherman's shoulder. As smooth and controlled as ball bearings, his eyes flipped open and they were like the lightless eyes of an animal stirred suddenly from an alert sleep. Placing her finger straight against her lips, she whispered, "Sh-h-h." He started to raise himself on his elbow, but she motioned him down. "Sherman," she said, uttering his name so low it was hardly more than the shape of her lips. "We have to go away. Go far away like we used to want to. Okay? Go far, far away. I put all your things in the doghouse. The things we took." She couldn't tell if he was listening. Like cobalt disks, his eyes were fixed on her, unblinking and expressionless. "We have to go, Sherman, just as soon as we can. I'll let you know when. Maybe Saturday when they go upstairs to sleep. If we don't go, they'll put you away in a place with bars in it. They're going to. I heard 'em."

Though quiet, his voice was gruff like a man's. "They did this, didn't they?" he said.

"What?" she murmured. "Did what?"

"Hurt me. To make me stop."

"No, but they're going to if we don't leave. So we have to. Or they'll put electricity things on us and make us talk like they did on the radio. On 'Boston Blackie.' "

"I know what they did," he said, shifting his head on the pillow. "I'm tryin' to remember . . . all day." The words oozed from him, his eyes beginning to squint. "I looked in the mirror. I had to do somethin'. And I had to do it."

"But they're going—"

"I know what they're tryin' to do. I heard them." Then he said, "Look." He slipped his hand under his pillow and pulled out a crumbling white pill. "I fooled her." His mouth worked and a strange broken smile widened his face. He started to giggle. Amazing bright tears clung in his eyes. "I fooled her." And he laughed. For the spark of that moment, he was the old Sherman again, having a good time, and nothing else mattered. She couldn't help it; she was laughing, too. And as she laughed she whispered to him, "Don't be mad at Toddy any more. He's been so worried about you." Sherman put his hands over his mouth and she put her hands on top of his, because if he stopped laughing, maybe she would, too, but it was too late. Their mother stumbled toward them. "What d'you two think you're doing? It's the middle of the night."

They looked up at her, no longer laughing.

"Well, come on. Somebody tell me."

"We're just telling jokes," Mamie said.

"Oh, Mamie, you don't know any jokes. Now run back to bed."

That was on Monday.

. . .

On Thursday evening, as they sat around the dining-room table passing the serving dishes back and forth, a knock came at the back screen door. It had been a sultry day for September, and it seemed an odd time for someone to call. Their father pushed his chair away from the table and went to answer the door.

They heard him say, "Well, Russell . . . come in, come in." He always said it twice. The other man said he couldn't stay, apologized for interrupting their dinner, but he had seen their father come home from work and he had something he thought he might want to see. Would Ray step outside?

"Who's Russell?" Mamie asked Toddy, who shrugged and grimaced and dug his spoon into his peas.

"Why, I'm ashamed of you two," their mother said. "You know who Russell is. It's Mr. Ambrose. He lives right behind us."

Very carefully, Mamie sat back in her chair. She left her fork on the edge of her plate, slowly withdrawing her hand to her lap. She licked her lips. "What does he want, do you reckon?"

"How should I know?" their mother said. "Toddy, don't play with your potatoes. It's something to do with your daddy."

"I want to see," Mamie said. She rolled from the chair and dropped to her feet even as her mother told her she couldn't. She went to the window, but the projection of the porch blocked her view. She pivoted and ran through the kitchen to the screen door.

On the palm of his left hand, her father held the brown paper sack. It was open at the top. He was taking the things out of it one at a time, glancing at them and dropping them back in, while Mr. Ambrose talked. For a moment Mamie felt dizzy; the air began to waver. She turned and stepped into her mother. "I told you no, Mamie. Now come have your supper before it gets cold." Steering her by the shoulders, she marched Mamie back to the table.

Keeping her eyes downcast, Mamie turned her peas with her

spoon. Fine prickly goose bumps nibbled her legs as the worry gathered in her mind. Still she didn't move, sneaking sidelong glances at the empty plate, then at the empty blue eyes peering at her across the table. The minutes stretched indefinitely. Knowing the screen door would bang shut when her father came in, waiting for it and steeling herself, did not lessen its startling surprise. It was like waiting for the cuckoo to spring from a striking clock—when the screen door slammed, she jumped so hard she upset her plate. And he still didn't come for her. He stayed in the kitchen.

He made himself scarce. At eight-thirty, Mamie was helping her mother put the supper dishes away when she heard him in the living room. "Toddy, you better go on up to bed."

Toddy said he wasn't through with his geography questions.

"Then you can finish them upstairs. And stay up there. What I have to do won't concern you. You better go on up right now."

Mamie took a deep breath. Under her skin, her muscles tightened as if straining for a place to hide. She heard Toddy climb the stairs. Her father called her into the dining room and closed the door behind them. By then, she was far too tense to cry. She stood in front of the closed door, tucking her lower lip in over her bottom teeth with three of her fingers, breathing very fast. "Sit down," he said, and she did, at her place at the table. "Mamie, when things were really bad, I asked you to tell me the truth and you wouldn't." He was fuming, his words sawing across her nerves. In the shine of the tabletop, the ceiling light reflected an inverted ghostly pool. She fixed her gaze there.

"Is there something you want to tell me now?"

She did not flinch; her eyes began to smart.

"Mamie, you were in on this from the very beginning. You're just as guilty as he is. Maybe more. All along you've lied to me. Now tell me you don't know about this." He dumped the contents of the sack on the table, the harder things—the fountain pen, the silver dollars, and the tiny telescope—bouncing and skittering on the tabletop, the noise deafening, then clattering to a standstill. "Now, what am I going to tell all these people—all our neighbors?" A web of bleary light skimmed across her eyes. She couldn't gulp her tears any longer. She twisted from the chair, but he caught her in midair and thrust her down on the seat. "Oh, no, you don't," he said. "I'm putting an end to this right now. Tonight. I want to know what you did. Everything you did. If there's more than this, you'd damned well better tell me."

Her mother opened the door to the kitchen and stood there, wiping her hands on a dishcloth. He didn't glance at her or pause. "There's more to this than meets the eye. You didn't do this by yourself. You couldn't have. So let's find out who helped you. And stop that bawling. Don't you dare cry." She choked and swallowed and wiped her face.

She would never know what caused him to notice her ring at precisely that moment. But he did. "I suppose that's part of it, too," he said, and for a second she didn't know what he was talking about. "All this time you've been parading it right in front of me, and like a damned fool I didn't even look. What d'you want with this trash?" Suddenly he pulled her fist up from her lap, forcibly undid her fingers, and yanked off the skull ring —all while she was begging, "No, Daddy! Oh, no, Daddy! *That's my ring!* Toddy gave it to me! Daddy, it's *my* ring! Please, Daddy! Please! Oh, please! *Oh, please, Daddy, that's my birthday ring!* We didn't take *that!*" But he had gone to the window and shoved it up and, with a snap of his wrist, the Phantom's skull ring sailed into the night. Shocked, she stood completely still, her voice like a rock stuck in her throat, astonished at the irreversible suddenness of it. Her ring was gone.

Her father crossed the dining room, threw open the living-room doors, and strode toward the lounger. Her mother followed after him. "Ray, don't, for God's sake. Let it pass."

"Don't start on me, Ellie," he answered. "I won't live in a nest of trashy thieves."

From under Mamie's hair the sweat trickled down her back. She shuddered.

Her father brought Sherman into the dining room, with Sherman in front. In dungarees, a plaid shirt, and his Pirates baseball cap, the boy looked like any other strapping thirteen-year-old, except for his cold, blank eyes. Immediately he saw the jumble of trinkets on the table and sauntered to a stop.

"Sherman," their father said, "have you ever seen any of this junk before?"

Mamie saw the realization flicker on his boyish face. Almost imperceptibly his expression drew tight—his jaw muscles clinched, his brow peaked slightly as he squinted, the rekindled hate flowed in his eyes. "I been tryin' to remember," he said under his breath.

"Oh, you remember, all right. There's nothing wrong with your *memory.*"

Recalling that other time, Mamie rushed between them. "Daddy, don't hurt him," she cried. "Don't hit him! He don't know any better." The bile rising in her throat was so sour it burned. She tried to cover her mouth but couldn't in time, vomiting into her hands and down the front of her dress. Every-thing blurred. Doubled over, she retched and vomited and blindly stroked the air. She didn't know when her mother came or where she came from, but she was there, holding her at the waist and forehead. "That's it. Get it out. Let it all out." The room and the side of her mother's face swam out of Mamie's focus. She couldn't find Sherman. Her father had picked up the telephone.

"Ray, put that down and help me," her mother said. "What's the doctor or the police or anybody else going to do anyhow . . . after all this time?"

Mamie couldn't remember being taken to bed that night or

how the two heart-shaped pillows from the sofa came to be under her head. She awoke in her petticoat as Sherman lifted her in his arms. Nestling upright against his chest, she put her tired arms around his throat and shoulder in a loose hug. "Are you okay, Sherman?" she murmured.

She could feel him nod against her hair.

"What time is it?" she asked, her voice as droopy as her eyes.

"Almost daylight," he said.

"Where are you taking me?" she asked. Slowly the room wheeled; she nodded against him lightly as he walked. Still blinking with sleep, she glanced down the back slope of his shirt, seeing the cuffs of his pants and the slide of the carpet beneath them.

"Far away," he said. Blades of cut grass were stuck to the backs of his shoes.

Mamie batted her eyes hard. "My purse," she moaned, still woozy. They went back for it; he turned and stooped and she caught the strap in her fingers; they turned again.

The door to her room rasped as it opened and they went through it, with Mamie jogging gently against him. They crossed to the top of the stairs. "Are we going right now?" she said.

"I'm taking you to a safe place," he said.

The pictures in the stairwell loomed up and passed beside her as they went down the stairs. "One last thing I gotta do," he said, "then I'll come after you." He turned on the halfway landing and went on down, and she bounced with him, the top of the stairs receding and curving away with every downward step. "Something smells funny," she said, "like gas." Her voice snagged and bumped on his shoulder. "I think I smell smoke."

"I've got it ready to blow," he said. "Everything's fixed. It's already started."

"Why?" she said, still yawning, fighting sleep. "Is Toddy comin' with us?"

"He's all right. He's asleep."

As they cut through the foyer, he dropped almost to his knees and they moved down and up like climbing a ladder. "Put this around you," he said, and covered her with a quilt.

"It's wet," she said.

"That won't matter," he said.

She squirmed under it, shrinking from its icy chill, and she felt it run wet on her cheek. She wiped at it with the hand she kept around his shoulder and saw a dark stain. It took a moment for her to realize that it was blood. "Oh, Sherman, did you hurt yourself again?"

They went through the kitchen. "It's not so bad," he said, "just a nick."

She tried to twist forward and sit on the perch of his forearm, but he held her pressed tight with his hand between her shoulder blades. "But it's getting on me. All over my petticoat."

"Then we'll have to take it off."

Later, she would remember him telling her to cover her mouth with the wet quilt as they went through the basement door and he turned sideways in the doorway to swing the door shut with his elbow. The air was mottled dark and hazy in the basement—one lonely cricket chirped along with the methodic grind of his shoes. She peered above her wet mask.

Great swarming coils of smoke hung between the black studs.


In the last few minutes of night, as the warm rising dew eddied and idled on the ground and the Chinaman lumbered from his opened pen, an explosion emptied the air like a massive spontaneous eruption—it rocked the foundation and shattered the first-story windows of the Abbott house. Old Mrs. Weatherholt, who lived across the street and reported the fire, said she felt the force of the concussion run up the corner posts of her bed and reverberate through her bedsprings so hard they strummed and tinkled for five minutes. "I thought it was an earthquake. I swear I did." In the beginning, she saw only smoke billowing from crevices in the foundation, then small shooting flames. She said she thought the house looked out of kilter, off plumb, tipped a little like a top hat.

Before she could get back to the window from calling the fire department, the fire had spread to the first-floor windows and a festoon of curling black smoke encircled the broad front of the house. When she came to the second part of her eyewitness account, she broke down; she couldn't tell the authorities what it was like to watch poor Mrs. Abbott tear at the smoky upstairs window that wouldn't open—her soundless, wild face smeared against the glass as her white fists went on pounding against it more and more feebly until she was engulfed in smoke. And all this time, Mrs. Weatherholt yelling, "Throw something! Throw something through it!" But it didn't help, nothing helped. Mrs. Abbott was beside herself with fear, then gone so quick, so unbelievably quick, already gone. When the firemen knocked the front door in, flames shot out of the house in a blast that scorched the geraniums at the end of the walk.

In their nightclothes, bathrobes, and wraps—some wearing slippers, some shoes, others in their stocking feet, their faces still puffy with sleep—the neighbors gathered and were cordoned off behind barricades on the other side of the street. They gathered to pray and wonder and bear witness, finding it unbearable to watch, but even more impossible to look away.

When all had been given up for lost, the fire spitting from the asphalt shingles on the roof and flapping in all the windows, when none of the neighbors staring into the gassy waves of heat could understand how the house went on standing, little Mamie Abbott wandered down the path beside the house through smoke and soot and sparks, clutching a wet and smoldering quilt around her shoulders with one hand and swinging a blue plastic purse by its broken strap in the other. Except for her awful retching coughs, she appeared abstracted, almost unconcerned, out for a morning stroll. Her hair, eyelashes, and brow were singed from one side of her head. Under the quilt, she wore only her panties. One of the firemen caught the child up in his arms and carried her to an ambulance. The siren sounded its shrill warning as the ambulance sped away. Some of the onlookers began yelling, "There's someone else in there! In the front room! I see Ray in there!" And everyone crowded to the barricade for a closer look. But it was impossible to tell whether the shape was that of a man or a smoke trick, and it made no difference. The house collapsed into itself in a grating, slow-folding crash. Tossed out in the sudden convulsion of the wreckage, chunks of burning debris were strewn as far as fifty feet away.

The firemen continued to drench the facing sides and roofs of adjacent houses, but the fire had been contained. Later that same morning, as the men collected their implements, they found in the right-of-way behind the Abbott house a bicycle and a pile of newspapers belonging to Jimmy Porterfield, who had been reported missing earlier that morning. A few of the newspapers were freckled with blood. The police were called to the scene.

At approximately five-fifteen that afternoon, it was concluded that four charred and unrecognizable bodies, two adults and two children, had been recovered. Mamie Abbott was admitted to the Nathan County Memorial Hospital in stable but guarded condition, with second- and third-degree burns on thirty percent of her body.

Like a particularly devastating dream, the first night in the hospital would remain in Mamie Abbott's memory for the rest of her life.

She awoke in the night, trying to talk. "Oh, please," she mumbled. "Oh, please, don't . . . oh, please . . ." Her lips shaped the same combinations of words again and again. When she eventually stirred and opened her eyes, she stopped murmuring, because she was in a black place, a steep black hole without shadows or limits. Where is this? she thought, and deep shudders shook her.

Blinking slowly, she glanced first to one side, then the other, until she could hold her eyes open. But she couldn't see anything, and she hurt all over. She rolled her tongue on her lips; they were swollen and cracked. The dark was impenetrable.

She tried to get up, but things were stuck in her arms and they pulled and tore when she moved. She felt lifeless and yet her heart was hammering so hard it beat in her ears. Her hands seemed fat as mittens—when she touched herself, they had no feeling. She couldn't tell what the things were in her arms or why they were there.

Where's everybody at? she thought, and bits of what had happened began to trickle through her senses. *Where's Toddy? Is he comin' with us?* She remembered that someone had picked her up and she had glimpsed the burning house. They're all gone, she thought. Oh, Mama! Mama! Mama! She felt raw inside, cauterized with the fearful knowledge that she was entirely alone . . . forever. They're all dead! I'm sorry, she thought, and said, "Sorry," as the tears welled and ran from the corners of her eyes.

She was gasping for air when she remembered Sherman's promise, and two thoughts crossed in her mind. They're all dead . . . except Sherman. He must've got out. Her eyes searched the dark, but only tiny disappearing pinpoints of light met her gaze. Careful of the things girding her arms, she shrugged up, wiping her face against her shoulders. Quietly, she said, "Sherman, are you there?" But with her thick lips and tongue, her voice was so unfamiliar she thought that even if he heard her, he wouldn't know who she was.

She wanted to cry again, but instead she forced her eyes to search the darkness once more. As well as she could, she called to him, "Sherman . . . ," and the fear and anger and longing grew so intense that her teeth chattered. "Why didn't you take me with you?" She lurched up through the dark, betrayed and forsaken. "Why didn't you take me?" Her chattering teeth chopped her words in two. She wanted to get up; she found an edge to the place where she lay. Something metallic crashed to the floor and the scream rising out of her was like that of a trapped animal, a forlorn and vicious bawling.

A door flew open and, streaming in through the light, white shapes flocked toward her like the hosts of God. "Don't take me!" she shrieked. She flailed out against them, still screaming and trying to talk, but they gently pinned her down and gave her a shot with a needle. As the shroud of her loneliness overtook her, she heard one of them say, "It's the medicine making you say crazy things. You shouldn't try to talk, Mamie . . . You're not making sense. You don't want people to think you're crazy . . . now do you?"

After that night, it would be a very long time before Mamie Abbott again tried to speak of her hope and her terror, her love and her wrath.

# 3

She had seen it before in the picture show when the projectionist got the reels mixed up and backward—the fragments swooping up, the sloshed coffee flying back into the cup pieces, the teetering cup of coffee restored to perfection on the arm of the sofa —but she had never expected to have it happen to her. If life could have reversed itself—if the shattered fragments of a cup lying in a brown spill on the floor could actually reassemble themselves complete and uncracked and full of steaming coffee —then perhaps Leona Hillenbrandt could have explained the sensation of fullness and completion she experienced as she stooped by a hospital bed one evening and little Mamie Abbott, still dangerously in shock and wrapped in bandages, reached out and grasped her thumb. The memory of that evening had haunted and held her ever since.

At the age of thirty-four, Leona believed that everything always turned out for the best, and that the least significant everyday events were guided by some unknowable, mystical force. Even in the worst of circumstances, her belief seemed to hold true, from this moment back to that time sixteen years ago, when, soon after her eighteenth birthday, she had had to leave home.

Rather than submit to her mother's arrangements and hide herself away at her Aunt Suid's until the baby came, she had taken the bus as far from home as she could go for two dollars. The day's journey took her to Livingstone, Kentucky, a river town of four or five hundred inhabitants. There, heartsick and alone and losing blood, she stumbled into the office of an elderly doctor named Merchassen. About to pass out, she told the doctor that she couldn't pay him with money; she had taken nothing with her from home except the clothes she wore and a five-dollar gold piece, half of which she'd already spent. She had planned to work and save until her time came.

With unreserved kindness, the doctor and his wife took her in and cared for her when she lost the child. She had stayed with them afterward, in gratitude, but more because of an affection they came to enjoy and, later, because she had promised Dr. Merchassen she would stay with his wife until the end. She often thought how remarkable it was that she had been saved from her destructive self. It was almost as if she had been guided to their door so that she could emerge years later, changed and with a new and better life.

And yet, as much as she believed in the unseen trigonometry of things, she also believed in coincidence, the two almost whimsical forces meshing together like ever-changing, parallel gears. Hardly a week passed that some coincidence was not played out in her life. An advertisement for tires would arrive in the mail and the next day she would have a flat, or she would mention an old friend and that evening the friend would call. Over the years, many of these haphazard events had manifested themselves. There was no way to predict them, no way to use them to her advantage. They happened and she noticed and remembered.

Coincidence had brought her to Graylie, Pennsylvania, to live with her married sister, Emma. A call from Cornelia Dunham, her oldest and best friend, whose tone of voice seemed to imply more than it said, conspired with Leona's imagination to suggest that Emma's health was failing (even if she wouldn't admit it), and Leona thought she should make one last visit while she still could.

The day after she arrived in Graylie, after all the hubbub and excitement of seeing each other for the first time in nearly four years, and while Emma was still hovering about, Leona said, "I don't want you to feel that you have to entertain me." Emma replied offhandedly, "I couldn't entertain you here in Graylie if my life depended on it. I'm afraid *you* may have to entertain *me,*" and they laughed.

But for all the good it did, Leona might have been talking to a box. Emma was determined to include her in her daily routines, and as long as Leona lived there, she never got used to Emma's fluttery invitations to go to church, to play canasta, to visit the neighbors. She understood Emma's hospitality, but she resisted being drawn into a frivolous social life with people she didn't know. She had come to Graylie to spend time with her ailing sister; she could only rejoice that the illness she imagined did not exist, but her purpose had never been to make

Emma's friends her friends, or to be jealous of the time Emma spent with them. It was a delicate, difficult balance: to go along with Emma on her excursions often enough to keep from hurting her feelings, and to not go often enough to remain uninvolved.

By the end of summer, she had turned Emma down so many times she was beginning to feel self-conscious and guilty. To make amends, she reluctantly agreed to accompany her sister to the hospital to visit a neighbor Leona hardly knew, Rosie Caldwell, who was recovering from surgery.

They asked for Mrs. Caldwell's room number at the nurses' station and had started down the hall past the intensive-care unit when Mamie Abbott wandered out of a room, her bandages coming loose, getting dirty, and Leona veered from Emma's side to go to her. She took the child's unbandaged hand and said, "I believe you're going the wrong way," and guided her back into the room as nurses darted toward them. Listening to the nurses' chatter, she realized this was the little girl who had survived that awful fire. A few minutes later, with Mamie safely tucked in bed and the intravenous tube re-attached to her bandaged arm, Leona leaned down to say good night and the little girl grasped her thumb. Leona motioned for Emma to go on without her.

She kept promising herself she wouldn't go back to the hospital, but in the middle of the morning or late in the afternoon she would go out for bread or a bottle of milk, or with some other excuse, and drive up the hill to the hospital, looking at the windows, wondering which one was Mamie's. Late in the night, lying awake, she listened for the spongy whir of the paperboy's bicycle tires and the wallop of the newspaper on the front porch to mark the time she could leave her hot, disheveled bed without disturbing anyone. She felt reborn.

More than once in the preceding months when she thought her welcome might be wearing thin, Leona had attempted to leave, but since she really had nowhere specific to go, each time she allowed herself to be talked out of it. The last time—some weeks back—Emma's appeal had been "Why don't you stay and help me put up my garden? I always have more than I can do." Now she waited for the town gossip to inform her of Mamie's release from intensive care. When word finally came, five days later, she told Emma she wanted to see if there was anything she could do to help, and she went to the hospital.

In the narrow private room, Mamie lay huddled in bandages beside the covers she had kicked away, her shadowed eyes fixed on some point in the air. An odor rose from the bed—a mixture of disinfectant, scorched ironing, and urine. Leona, sitting in the wing-backed bedside chair, lost her cheerful composure.

She found a lipstick-smudged teacup on a cleanup tray in the hall. In the bathroom adjoining Mamie's room, she washed the cup with hand soap and filled it with cold water. The only washcloth in the room had been used and left to dry in rigid folds on a wall hook. With a twinge of regret, she took her lace-edged handkerchief from her purse, dunked it into the cup of water, and wrung it out over the cup. Then she wiped the child's forehead and cheeks and gently washed the dried milk from her upper lip. "You needn't worry any more," she said, her voice sounding as strange and swallowed as a ventriloquist's. "I'll stay with you."

She dunked the handkerchief again, wrung it out, and folded it twice into a pad, which she held against the small forehead until the cloth felt as feverish as the skin beneath it. Then she did it again. And again. And the blank, staring eyes gradually fell shut. "That's right," Leona murmured. "That's better, isn't it? Go to sleep."

When visiting hours ended, at eight o'clock, two different nurses told her she would have to leave, but she ignored them as long as she could. On their third or fourth try, she interrupted them by holding up her hand and standing. "Could we discuss this in the hall?" she asked softly. "The child is asleep." With grim faces, they followed her out and she closed the door.

"I've been trying to decide what to do about this," Leona said as she turned. "And I've decided to stay."

"But that's not possible," said the nurse who had been doing most of the talking.

"Of course it's possible. What do you mean it's not possible? Mothers and fathers sit up—someone sits up with someone all across this country every night. I've seen it many times."

"Yes, but Mamie's parents are— Are you related?"

"No, but that's all the more reason why she needs someone."

The dispute went back and forth until Leona ended it. "You do what you have to do with your rules," she said. "And I will do what I think is right. If you want to know the truth, I don't think she's getting very good care here. But I'd rather not make a case out of it," and she turned and went back into the room. Ten minutes later, a third nurse brought in Mamie's medication and woke her up to give it to her, but nothing else was said. Leona drew fresh water in the cup and rinsed the handkerchief and, bending down at intervals through the night, she dabbed what little comfort she could onto the beautiful, vacant face.

Mamie was fast asleep and dawn had filled the room before Leona really paid much attention to the stack of dolls on the floor behind the door—gifts sent by sympathetic neighbors and family friends. Many of the dolls were still in their original cartons, and the others, without packaging, were heaped on top, legs and arms protruding every which way. Leona found the mere fact that they were there immeasurably sad, and couldn't bear to look at them for long. Shivering in the cool morning air, she stretched, wiped her face, and moved toward the window. On the windowsill stood seven red roses in seven thin glass vases, the red buds regressing from fresh to faded. They struck her as excessive and even unwholesome; it seemed inappropriate for someone to be sending roses frequently to a little girl. She thought of roses as a woman's flower and the frequency implied a lover's gesture, yet . . . It all seemed so ridiculous. She glanced about for a card and found nothing but the florist's tag. Then she heard the hasty steps of nurses in the hall. She put the tag in her purse, collected her sweater, and whispered, "So long, see you later" to Mamie.

Going home that morning, as she walked through the dew-laden air still silky and fresh from the night, she was reminded of playing, years ago, among wet clothes hung out to dry, and how refreshing the wet flapping had been against her face. But this morning she was bone tired and the air did little to invigorate her. A cup of hot coffee gave off its bittersweet aroma at her place at the table. "Look what the cat dragged in," Emma said, and Leona told her only what she thought could bear repeating.

A few days later, in the afternoon, she drove across town to the Forget-Me-Not Florist and wandered among the claustrophobic profusion of flowers on display. When no one came to wait on her, Leona found a woman seated behind the cash register braiding a wreath from greenery. Leona explained who she was, giving the barest facts, and asked the woman if she could remember who sent the roses to Mamie Abbott. The woman knew immediately what she was talking about, smiled, and shrugged. "Your guess is as good as mine," she said. "The order came in the mail. I've got the note here somewhere." She flipped through a file and held up a small sheet of paper torn from a spiral notebook. Written in a gawky, childish hand, the note said: PLEASE SEND 1 ROSE EVERY DAY TO MAMIE ABBOTT TIL MONEY GONE. IL NO IF YOU DONT. That was all. No signature or date or other markings. "Don't that take the cake?" the woman said, her hands again shaping the wreath. "So we did what it said. Oh, I remember now—it didn't come in the mail. Somebody stuck it under the door along with a ten-dollar bill."

"Is that so?" Leona said, just to keep her talking.

"We think it must've been some kid, one of her friends at

school, or maybe—you know, by the handwriting. The envelope was all beat up." The woman went on and on, even to the point of recalling the multiple Abbott funeral. Leona was obliged to listen to her politely until another customer came in some fifteen minutes later. The woman's notions seemed logical enough, and without an alternative theory of her own, Leona laid the small mystery to rest in the back of her mind.

Now suppers at Emma's seemed even more subdued than usual, a soft tinkling of dinnerware and china, followed by the news on the Emerson television set Emma's husband, Frank, had just acquired. When Emma had settled into her pink chair, busy with her crochet hook, Leona slipped quietly out the kitchen door and walked (or, if it was getting dark, drove) the twelve blocks and up the hill through the humidity of the evening to the hospital.

Tuesday was rain, and Wednesday was ten quarts of Rutgers tomatoes, and then it was Friday and Emma was hurrying to meet Frank after work to go to the V.F.W. for a blue-plate special and a few rounds of bingo. Knowing what the answer would be, Emma no longer asked Leona to join them. Leona spent the afternoon shopping and arrived at the hospital early.

Church-still, they sat side by side next to the bed, a man in a blue gabardine suit so new it still held the hanger creases, and a woman in a faded print dress, their weathered faces rotated toward her as she entered the room. She could have stumbled in her surprise. One look at their gaunt, sunburned faces and she knew who they were and why they were here. She went to stand across from them on the other side of the bed, and she said, "You must be Mamie's relatives?"

They nodded that they were. She asked where they were from. "Redland, Texas," the woman said. She asked how their trip had been. "Long and tedious," the woman replied. The man's gnarled hands rested like carvings on his knees and the woman's thin bony fingers clutched the black purse in her lap. Mamie had not moved on the bed, her expression slack and remote. "Does she recognize you?" Leona asked, and they shook their heads. To make conversation, Leona said, "I was wondering—how old is she?" The woman frowned. "Seems like the first or second grade, wasn't it, Charles?" Taking his time, the man nodded.

The withered roses had been thrown out, but ten tube vases still occupied the windowsill. "Mamie had such pretty roses," Leona said. "Did you send them?"

"No," the woman said. "We meant to, but with the funerals, we just couldn't."

After a while, Leona asked them if they were related to Mr. or Mrs. Abbott and the woman said, "Ray was my sister's boy." That would make them Mamie's great-aunt and great-uncle on her father's side. For what it was worth.

Unmistakably they were as slow as they appeared—slow, slow-speaking dirt farmers from Redland, Texas, come to take Mamie away. The evening light eroded into red and purple streaks and the long silences loomed between them. Finally, although Leona had made up her mind not to tell them who she was unless they asked, she blurted out that she lived nearby and came to see Mamie because she seemed so terribly alone after the fire. She felt better having said it. The woman said, "We appreciate it," and stood, brushing the back of her dress, and the man stood with her and they turned for the door.

"Will you be taking Mamie with you?" Leona asked in a rush.

"When she's well enough," the woman said. "The doctor said we could probably take her home after her check-up this coming Wednesday." And the man said, "We bide by our own." They stepped out into the white corridor, leaving Leona behind in the darkened room with the handles of her shopping bag cutting marks in the palm of her hand. The murmur of Mamie's sleep drew her down like a seductive lure. "Good Lord, Mamie, what will become of you?"

The nurses came and went, the noises dwindled to silence, and when Leona thought to look at her watch, it was nearly two o'clock in the morning. All night she sat in that bedside chair, deeply troubled, her mind a whirl of thoughts and memories. She remembered a time when she was four years old and Emma was—what? Eleven? And her mother had come down with diphtheria. As soon as the illness was diagnosed, the two girls had been sent to stay with their Aunt Cora, who lived on a farm several miles away. Leona still remembered that dark stifling house, the curtains that were never opened, the photograph portraits of Aunt Cora's brothers and relatives who had died in World War I. She and Emma had stayed there for two and a half months and she had never been so frightened for such a long time before or since. She never felt loved, never understood her stern, neurotic aunt. Her mother had nearly died. But Leona had prayed to be sick like her mother so she could go back home. It was one of her earliest memories. If Mom had died, Leona thought, what would have become of us? Even today the idea of it still made her feel sick to her stomach. I can't let this happen, she thought. If Mamie's experience with relatives was as unhappy as hers had been, it would be unendurable. This coming Wednesday, the slow woman had said. I have four days, Leona thought. Only four days. There was so little time. And so much to do.

How could she ever have imagined that the next evening the hospital would use her chance meeting with Mamie's relatives as an excuse to keep her out of Mamie's room and, to all intents and purposes, put an end to her nightly visits? On the pretext that she was too emotionally involved, they called her into an office and explained that the relatives had complained, which she didn't believe, and how necessary it was to maintain a certain detachment, a certain emotional equilibrium—and on and on, until her mind swam.

Overnight, Indian summer ended and the weather turned

dreary; a cold snap laid waste to Emma's garden; the vines and stems and hardy leaves were suddenly black and limp. Emma, of course, went to work clearing the patch first thing the next morning, bundled up in sweaters and pants, and before long, Leona joined her. "I'm glad you came out," Emma said, leaning on the rake handle. Her windburned cheeks were red, her eyes watery. "I was about to come get you. Come here. I want you to look at this."

Leona followed her sister across the tangle of cucumber vines to the iron birdbath in the center of the garden. On the back side of the ornament was a trampled place where the ground was packed hard. Around it, odd bits of stuff had been scattered: matchsticks and bits of cloth, a knot of crinkled thread and two Lucky Strike cigarette butts. It looked like the remnants of a destroyed nest. "What do you make of it?" Emma asked. "Frank smokes Lucky Strikes, but I know he doesn't come out here. Somebody's been standing on this very spot." She stooped and poked among the debris with her gloved finger.

As worried and preoccupied as she was about Mamie, Leona had to grin. She had seen Frank checking the garden on his way into the house, but to egg Emma on, she said, "Looks to me like we have a peeping Tom."

"Oh, come on, Leona. Be serious," Emma said. "I swear to God, some of the things you come up with. Who'd want to watch us anyway?"

They looked at each other, trading glances and winks, and burst out laughing. How different they were. Emma, always the realist, prematurely gray now, stockier, the good German matron. And Leona, younger by seven years, impulsive, taller and darker, and considerably more attractive. Only in their eyes did they resemble each other; they both had been blessed with their mother's warm brown eyes. When Emma stood, she went wading off across the frostbitten garden, bundled up in work clothes as heavy as a bear, switching her hips and waving her arms in a hula-dance mockery. Then Leona followed, swaying from side to side, and they laughed and laughed, finally draping their arms around each other to keep from falling.

At noon on Monday, during her appointment with a lawyer in Scranton, Leona fared no better than she had in the encounter at the hospital. Tapping her foot, she sat in the waiting room for more than an hour before the bearded, middle-aged man would see her. "There's no doubt," he told her, "that you could provide for the child. But—and there's no gentle way to say this—considering that you're alone, that you've never been married, I'm afraid adoption is out of the question. With living relatives willing to take her, no court would take your petition seriously."

"I see," she said.

Numb with the news, she rode the elevator down, turned the wrong way in the marble foyer, and went out a delivery door. The door locked automatically behind her and she found herself stranded in a grimy alley. A burst of freezing wind snatched her ivory-colored hat from her head and sent it spiraling up along the inner walls of the sooty brick airway. She spent the rest of the afternoon in a Scranton bank arranging for the withdrawal and transfer of all her money from the bank in Livingstone, Kentucky.

Returning to Graylie, it suddenly dawned on her that what had happened was like something both preordained and coincidental, a peculiar coalescence of events falling into place like loaded dice. Clearly, she had no other choice: she would do what she had to do.

# 4

At the foot of her bed, Leona stacked the last of the things they would take with them, new things she had bought for Mamie still in their wrappers and boxes: shoes, none of them bigger than her opened hand, a pair of white sandals with an eyelet design cut in the toes, small red moccasins, black patents for Sundays, lavender cowboy boots with yellow stitching, brown hightops just like some she had had as a girl, and a pair of fuzzy pink slippers; socks, mostly white, but one blue pair had a repeating design of pink giraffes; underwear and petticoats in every pastel color imaginable, dove gray and salmon and soft lime green; jeans and bib overalls, dirndls, a red sailor suit, striped and patterned T-shirts and blouses, with watermelons and kittens and happy smiling bears; jumpers and sweaters; and, finally, a special white Sunday dress, all ruffles and lace. This last dress she held up and out at arm's length. "Look at this. Isn't this something?" she said quietly in the still room, and she gathered it up to her for a moment before folding it and putting it down on the stack of dresses and skirts. Just one suitcase to go. She didn't have time for her flights of fancy; she had planned to be gone by now.

Then she heard it, a noise she should recognize but couldn't, a sound both muffled and metallic, like an iron skillet drawn across a grate far away. For several empty seconds, she remained in a posture of arrested motion, listening with her breath held, waiting for the noise to come again. Nothing. She crept to the door, looked down the hall to the landing, and listened. Nothing. Wouldn't it be a panic, she thought, if a burglar stumbled upon her packing to leave when she had taken all those precautions to keep Emma from finding out?

She had been waiting three days now for this evening, the

minutes ticking through her like waterdrops in a Chinese torture chamber. Emma's Women's Auxiliary luncheon had been
changed to a dinner meeting at the church so more members
could attend in preparation for the Thanksgiving bake sale, and
Emma's husband, Frank, exercised his only vice (according to
Emma) of the week: he played pinochle with his cronies on
Tuesday nights come hell or high water.

Leona had planned everything painstakingly, from this afternoon's excuses and declining Emma's offer to be a good sport
and come along and be friendly, to their five-o'clock so-long-
see-you-later at the front door, to looking down from the upstairs window in time to see Emma stop halfway across the street
as if she had forgotten something, then tilt the umbrella away
from her head and glance back toward the house as she closed
the spokes of the silky black cloth, hooked the bamboo tongue
over her arm, and went on around the corner. Now it was
almost seven o'clock and she was nearly finished, her own suitcases already packed and stowed in the trunk of her car.

As Leona opened the last suitcase, the bottom of the bedroom door scrubbed over the carpet and she closed the suitcase
empty, letting her fingertips linger on its top as if that light
touch would help her keep her balance. Emma was standing by
the half-opened bedroom door, clasping her purse in both hands
in front of her, glancing first at the empty closet, then at the
suitcase and stacks of clothes on the bed.

"Whew!" Leona said. "You scared the wits right out of me
just now," but she was caught red-handed and she knew it, her
voice trailing off without breath to carry it. She couldn't find a
comfortable place to put her hands. "You're home early."

Emma let out a long breath, her face scarlet. As she came into
the room, she was biting the inside of her cheek, and she let her
purse swing in her left hand. Her voice quivered as she spoke.
"I'm not even going to ask you what this is all about," she said.
With a defiant wave of her arm, she caught an edge of the white

ruffled dress and sent the dress sailing in the air. "Surely you're not serious, Leona. You can't be doing this."

With delayed reaction, Leona noticed that, over her apron, Emma was wearing her cardigan with the sleeves pushed up. So that was what the noise had been: Emma putting away her umbrella, hanging up her coat, the wire hangers scraping. Neither of them spoke, standing as they were, staring down at the stack of clothes and the suitcase. When she could stand it no longer, Leona turned and cleared a place on the bed to sit.

"I've been wanting to talk to you about this," Emma said. "It was no good from the very beginning."

Sitting on the edge of the bed, Leona closed her eyes.

As Emma sat on the bed, too, she said, "This has gone too far." She paused as if she expected a reply. "Leona, don't do this. Please don't do this."

Leona opened her eyes and studied her sister's kind, faintly quilted face, her sad brown eyes, and said nothing.

"You don't know what you're doing, running back and forth to the hospital every night. Look what it's done to you. You're exhausted and you're not thinking straight." Emma was leaning forward, holding her arms straight down between her knees, her fingers fumbling at the pennies in her shoes. It struck Leona like a long-overlooked discovery, and for that moment she loved Emma more than she had ever loved anyone or anything in the world—a woman forty-one years old, her older sister, with the innocence and terrible taste not only to be still wearing penny loafers, but actually to put pennies in them. It was heartbreaking and it was wonderful and Leona wanted to hold her, to make her happy, to give in. The back of her throat was so dry it hurt.

"It's time to put this aside," Emma said, staring at her shoes. "You can—"

Leona interrupted her. "No, Emma, I can't. I just can't."

"It's more than you bargained for."

For a moment, Leona couldn't sort her thoughts; then she said, "No, actually, it *is* what I bargained for. Though I didn't know it at the time. I want it all . . . for her. And I don't want her to suffer as I did once."

"It's already too late, then. I'm wasting my time."

"Emma, I know how you are, but I don't want you to worry about this. I know what I'm doing."

"That's just it. I don't believe you do know. I can't help my worrying." She rose and went to the door. With her hand on the glass doorknob, she turned and they looked at each other.

"I thought you had changed," Emma said, "and I felt better about things. But you haven't, not in the slightest. You're just as headstrong as ever. I look at you and I see that whizbang, hot as a firecracker—remember, when you were about sixteen you used to say that? 'Boy,' you'd say, 'I'm hot as a firecracker,' and our daddy'd smile like he'd died and gone to Heaven, God rest his soul. Well, I look at you and I still see that hot-as-a-firecracker sixteen-year-old who would ruin our family—still hell-bent for destruction."

Leona felt cut and numb. She turned away.

"What are you going to do when they catch up with you?"

"I don't know," Leona said without looking up. "I guess I don't intend to be caught."

"Ha! Listen to yourself. They'll send you to the pen and I'll have to live with *that.*"

Leona glanced up in time to see her sister's eyes, magnified with tears, before the door closed. "Damn," she said, falling back crosswise on the bed. She heard a door slam downstairs, then the squeak and whap of the screen door. Only the back door had a screen.

By the time Leona caught up with Emma, she was near the clothesline that ran alongside the house. She was weaving as she walked, her sloped shoulders heaving. When she stopped, Leona stopped, too, a few steps behind. Emma freed one hand to wipe her face. It made Leona ache. "Emma, if you don't stop bawling, you're going to get me started, too."

When Emma spoke, her voice sounded blubbery and hollow, as if she were holding her nose. "Oh, no, you won't. You're too tough."

Leona waited, shivering, the air as crisp and sour as the taste of cold green apples. She stared at the gray wooden clothespins left on the line. She started to go to Emma, but Emma was coming back, the wet patches under her eyes glistening, her face swollen and streaked. Emma took up a corner of her apron and wiped her face, then twisted the printed cloth until it was wrung tight.

"I don't understand it," she said, and choked. "I don't understand any of this. It's beyond me. Should I worry about you and what you're doing to yourself and the trouble you're going to cause? Or should I worry about that poor little girl being carried off into the wild blue yonder by the likes of you? And besides, what do you really know about her? Her older brother tried to kill himself some time back. Shot himself. That should tell you something. There had to be something wrong in that house." When she could twist the apron corner no farther, she picked it apart, smoothed it flat on the palm of her hand, and started twisting it again. "Why a woman alone would want the responsibility of a child like that, who probably"—she raised her eyebrows and leaned forward—"probably is not quite right"—she poked at her own head—"if you know what I mean, I'll never know. *That* is beyond me. You could've done anything you wanted. . . ." She shook her head. "With all that Merchassen money."

Emma lurched off again in another direction, wandering toward the two desolate concrete urns standing sentinel to her rose trellis, dragging Leona along in her wake.

If anyone's watching, Leona thought, we must look ridiculous. She tried to imagine how they might appear from a neighbor's window. A head taller than her sister and full-figured, Leona knew she had an angular kind of attractiveness. This afternoon, she'd taken particular pains with her appearance, choosing a tailored skirt and silk blouse that flattered her dark eyes. She had pinned up her auburn hair in a loose chignon, though the wind was now taking it apart in frazzles. Years ago, their father had said, "Leona, when God passed out His parcels, you got the looks and Emma got the leftovers and the common sense." At the time, it had been true and it had stayed with Leona as a kind of admonition. Ever since, she had tended to overcompensate in her dealings with Emma, as if she were somehow responsible for her sister's plainness. Just as she was doing now.

"Stop it, Emma, come on. Please. I don't have time for this." But her efforts to persuade her sister to stop went unheeded. The day had started with such promise, such a sense of expectancy, only to have it end like this. She wanted to grab her and shake her. "Emma, stop crying, or as far as I'm concerned, this conversation is over and I'll be out of here in five minutes."

Emma's face contorted, baring her teeth as if she were going to bite. "I know you will! That's the kind of mind I have to contend with."

"Emma, I *have* to do this."

Emma's eyes welled up again, and she spit the words out: "I should've said something sooner, but I didn't want to meddle in your affairs. I thought if I kept my mouth shut you'd stay longer and behave yourself. All along something kept telling me, 'This isn't right. This is wrong.' Every time you left to go to the hospital, a feeling of dread came over me. I didn't know what it was exactly. It just felt bad."

A cold wind rattled the brown hydrangeas caught in the fence and whipped the clothesline, and Leona turned her back to it. "Emma, I'd rather not talk about this out here. Couldn't we go inside?"

Emma didn't move. Stubbornly holding the apron corner, she crossed her arms.

"Okay, then," Leona said. "You only see the obvious. That little girl *needs* somebody. She needs somebody to be there when she wakes up from a bad dream or when she wants a drink of water. She *needs* somebody when she goes to sleep, so she'll know she's not alone. She needs to know somebody cares. And, Emma, *nobody cares.* They *don't.* Until I took it upon myself to start going to see her, she wasn't getting any better. You should've seen her. Skin and bones. She wasn't getting well." Either from the cold or her own desperation, Leona's voice was beginning to quaver.

When she stopped for breath, Emma butted in: "Yes, but you've gone way overboard with it. Way overboard!"

Holding her arms across her body, Leona hugged herself to break the chill. Talking about Mamie was like a spell; it put her back in that room all those nights. "She wouldn't help herself. Emma, she wouldn't eat, wouldn't talk, or, as far as I know, wouldn't cry either; wouldn't go to the toilet, wet the bed, and day in and day out, hour after hour after hour, she just stared off at—at I don't know what, a place in the air. And you know what they fed her? Pablum, just like a baby."

Emma slowly shook her head. "I know," she said. "That's what they say."

"Okay, so the last time they let me see her, she'd stopped wetting the bed and started going to the bathroom by herself. Most of her bandages had been taken off. But they call me in and say I'm doing more harm than good, I'm not detached enough, but they can't help her because they're *too* detached."

"But, Leona, you have to admit this is wrong. It's just *crazy.*"

"No," she said. "I don't. I don't have to admit anything. I've tried to think this through. Her relatives don't have anything; they're barely scraping by. You could see it in their faces. They don't want her; she's just another problem. But they'll take her because, as they put it, 'We bide by our own,' and for the insurance money. And there's no time left. They're taking her tomorrow. *They're taking her, Emma.* I can't stop it any other way. But what if they don't? She'll be put up for adoption. And I can't do a blessed thing, can't lift a finger to stop it. I can't adopt her, the lawyer told me, because I'm not married. What does that mean? That I'd care for her any less? Anybody else'll want to adopt a perfect baby. Well, she's not a baby, and she's not perfect."

"That's what worries me most," Emma said. "That's why I wouldn't want to take her myself. What if she's not quite right?" And she poked at her own head again.

"Will you stop doing that?"

"I have to say what I think."

Leona shuddered from the cold and tensed her arm muscles tight. Her nose was beginning to run and she had to sniff every few seconds. "Anyway, Emma, what's left? One of those *homes?* There's no bright spot in this. It never gets any better. It's all too iffy and time has run out. Put yourself in my place and tell me what I'm supposed to do. Lay it all aside, the way you said to? I can't, Emma, I just can't. I've got to get her out of this."

Emma cocked her head to the side and a smile stretched in her wind-chilled face. "Leona, you know what this reminds me of—the way you look right now? It's like it was when we were kids and one of us would have a crush on somebody and we'd have those endless talks about do you think he likes me? Do you think he really likes me? How could I have missed it? My God, Leona, it's all over you. You've fallen in love."

"Oh, Emma . . ." She wanted to laugh and tried to, but her teeth chattered too much. "Don't be ridiculous."

"And you look so good. Nobody'd ever guess there was anything wrong with you."

"Well, think what you will, Emma. I can't take any more of

this, and besides I've got to get in there and pack." She put her arm around her sister. "Aren't you cold?"

They went toward the house with Emma refusing to be still. "I'm the one people'll talk about. I'm the one who'll have to put up with it. You stayed at my house, so I'm responsible. . . . And besides, I wanted you to stay with us through Thanksgiving. The boys'll be home then. Bad weather will be here any day, and, Leona, you can't drive worth a hoot."

"I know you wanted us to spend Thanksgiving together, but you should spend that time with your family without me tagging along."

"You're part of my family," Emma said. For a split second, her voice sounded blubbery again.

"Oh, for Christ's sake. I am not. How old are your boys now? Eighteen? Twenty? Out on their own. They're practically strangers to me."

"That shouldn't be either."

"No, it probably shouldn't, but it's true. Sad, but true. Emma, why don't you stop this and help me?"

"That's just like you! If you think I'm going to be a party to this, you've got another think coming!"

But as they neared the back door, Emma ducked and pulled out of Leona's arm. "I want to say one thing, though, Leona. These past few months before this trouble came up, that's the way we should've been all these years. And I don't want you to go, because now that I finally feel like we know how to get along. . . . I feel like I'll never see you again."

"Why, Emma May Mattingly, I do believe you're jealous. Shame on you. *Shame on you.* Bite your tongue."


Still it was another half hour, quarter past eight and pitch dark outside, before the upstairs bedroom she had used for almost five months was put back in order, the last suitcase stowed with the other six in the trunk of the blue Buick, and she was ready to go. Grumbling and complaining, Emma had been up and down the stairs more times than Leona cared to count, bringing a box Leona didn't need, asking questions, and all the time arguing with herself: "I could stop this, you know. I could call the hospital and warn them what you're going to do. But then I suppose they'd suspect I was in on it."

"You could always be anonymous," Leona told her, and grinned.

"Well, it wouldn't take a mental giant to figure out who it was, now, would it? But don't you tempt me."

Leona went up to the bedroom one last time. "For a final check," she said. "I always feel as if I'm forgetting something."

Actually, what she went back for was the black lizardskin briefcase she had left under the far side of the bed. It had come to her as part of the Merchassen estate. To Leona, it somehow represented all the years she had been with the Merchassens, first as housekeeper, then as secretary (and nurse in a crisis), and finally as companion to Helen Merchassen until she had died at the age of eighty-two the summer before last.

The black briefcase was what the doctor had affectionately called "a smuggler's wonder," and he had bought it simply because it was clever. It opened in half and she laid it flat on the bed. On one side there was a series of pockets and dividers with zippers that seemed to fill the space quite well. But underneath was another compartment at least two inches deep; here is where Leona kept the small vials of medicine wrapped in cotton batting and the compounds and few instruments she had taken from the office before the auction. The doctor had been a fastidious man, so there weren't many other things she thought she should take, except for the personal documents he and his wife had left behind—drivers' licenses, birth certificates, appointment books, a diary. She decided it would be disrespectful to allow these small personal items to be passed on to strangers, and the relatives had no use for them. So she kept them—and she kept them in the pockets and dividers that held the medicines it was probably illegal for her to have.

The other side had an actual false bottom. She cleared this half of everything she had originally put in it. There was a slot in the spine of the briefcase, and by fiddling with the small blade of a penknife, she triggered the release of a panel in the bottom, revealing an inch-deep space the full length and width of the briefcase. And that was where she had placed the larger denominations of bills when she closed her account and withdrew her money at the bank in Scranton. She pulled three thousand-dollar bills from the top of one of the bundles and closed the fake floor of the case.

She and Dr. Merchassen had decided that the illusion of false depth was created by the complex, paisley-patterned lining of the case. On top of the secret compartment she refilled the space with the folder of newspaper clippings she had been able to find about the fire and Mamie Abbott's progress. Then, the beginnings of a runner she had been crocheting on the sly for Emma, and the crochet hook. And finally Doc's Browning automatic, given to him by a distant cousin who had survived the Normandy invasion.

The barrel of the handgun carried the inscription FABRIQUE NATIONALE D'ARMES DE GUERRE HERSTAL BELGIQUE, but she didn't know what that meant. Doc Merchassen had a name for the gun she couldn't remember—maybe it was service issue, or officer's issue. No, that wasn't right. She did remember Doc telling her how to cock it by pulling the top sleeve back, and that it held thirteen shots, which seemed appropriate. To the best of her knowledge, the gun had never been fired and it frightened her. Leona imagined it packed with dirt inside, blowing up in her hand when she squeezed the trigger. And yet she kept it because it had been one of his most treasured things.

She put it in with the crochet work and shut the briefcase.

She wrapped the three big bills inside a five-dollar bill to keep in her hand, took the briefcase, and turned off the light.

Her perspective slowly changed as she went down the curved staircase. Everything seemed to float away from her—the oblong of the downstairs door, the writing table with its vase of silk chrysanthemums, Emma wearing a fresh orange-colored apron. Feeling light-headed, Leona descended the stairs carefully, holding the bannister by the hand with the money and carrying the briefcase in the other.

"I wish you could at least stay until Frank gets home. I know he'd like to say goodbye."

Leona could deal with Emma, not her husband; there was no telling what he might do. She'd planned all along to be gone before he came home from his pinochle game. Deep down, she believed he resented her being there. "Emma, if I wait, it'll be too late to get anywhere tonight and I'll never have another chance." It came out sounding too harsh, too selfish, and she tried to lighten it. "Besides, if I have to sit through watching John Cameron Swayze again, I'll just cringe."

Emma slowly looked away and went to hold the kitchen door open at the side of the house. When Leona went by, she hugged her with her free arm and kissed her cheek. "Wish me luck, Emma," she said and slipped the bills, unseen, into Emma's apron pocket.

"Where will you go?"

"Wherever she wants to go."

It wasn't an answer, but Emma didn't pursue it. "Well, let me know how you are." Her chin dimpled and creased like a peach pit and she said no more.

Then she was gone, Emma's image losing detail until it was a waving silhouette, framed in the doorway by the yellow light behind.

Slowly she drove down the street, slowly along streets she had taken night after night, streets so embedded in her memory she could walk them blind a year from now. She knew where the sidewalk bucked up from tree roots and where it was sunken, washed over with grass. Past houses that had never been and would never be hers, past families in rooms of light, glimpsed through swagged curtains. How long her heart had ached for such a place—a home and a family all her own.

Anything could go wrong. If Emma let on or started bawling or told Frank and he called the hospital; or if one of the nurses for some unknown reason decided at the wrong moment to go to the laundry room, and in the dark they collided . . . But Leona couldn't worry about that. For the last few days now, she had mentally rehearsed her going in and coming out. By merely closing her eyes, she could visualize the course she would take, the pale yellow-brown floor and the stark white walls flowing by as she passed from the dusky laundry room through the metal-plated swinging doors, up the six or eight steps of the shadowed vestibule, and to the right into the glare of the corridor where five doors away, five rooms on the left, was Mamie's room.

Now there was nothing to do but wait—wait in her old blue Buick parked in the darkest part of the lot as close to the laundry-room entrance as she could maneuver it without being conspicuously out in the open. She had backed the car up twice now to escape the moonlight, but she had gone as far as she could and the pale glow was catching in a glint on her hood ornament. She stared past it to the window with the speckled light.

Weeks ago, when she bought the blue lampshade with the tiny cutout stars to brighten Mamie's room, it hadn't occurred to her that it would make a light in Mamie's two windows unlike all the others; she'd bought the shade only because she thought the thin cones of light flying from the pinpoint cutouts might arouse a happy response in the child. Now she was waiting, her breath beginning to fog the windshield, for the speckled light to go out. That would be the first domino of the planned sequence.

Long before there was reason to plot anything, she had become familiar with certain of the hospital's night habits, and they would be used tonight as milestones: visiting hours for children ended at eight, adult patients could be visited till nine, then a brief onslaught of nursing activity followed, the taking in of night medications to patients, the plumping of pillows and turning off of lights, the good nights and sweet dreams. This ritual varied only slightly, although some nights it lasted longer than others. Somewhere around quarter to ten, the nurses would drift back to the central nurses' station (where the three long corridors converged) for a last sip of coffee, to freshen their lipstick and comb their hair, to tease each other about the night still ahead, and to pull on sweaters and wraps, anxious to be relieved by the skeleton late-night shift at eleven. Unless one of the patients pushed his buzzer in the night, the corridors would be deserted until six the next morning. That's when they would find Mamie missing.

Although he had always infuriated her with his banging and clanging as he checked and locked and rechecked the exit doors, Leona in her planning had almost overlooked the nightwatchman, who made his rounds shortly after the last shift arrived at ten-thirty. So it was in those minutes of shift change and confusion, but before the rattling passage of the watchman, that she had to make her move.

The speckled light in Mamie's room went out. Leona turned the radio on without turning it up. She checked her watch by the ghostly radio light—ten till ten, right on time. Now her breath came heavier and deeper. She shut the radio off; the pale light blinked to black. The windshield became opaque with her breath, two bluish surfaces fogging up until she couldn't see out.

But, she thought, no one can see in either. She pulled on her cream-colored tam; then, squirming and raising her body under the steering wheel, she changed from her mink coat to a tan raincoat, too thin for this early November weather but practically invisible down a long corridor of doors. From a distance, it would be almost indistinguishable from a nurse's uniform. On the seat beside her sat the shopping bag of clothes and the new white parka she had brought for Mamie to wear tonight, but it would take too long, would be too much trouble; and she stood out in the bristly cold air, easing the car door shut with only a click.

Across the asphalt in her crêpe-soled nurse's shoes, into the darkness of the laundry room, through the swinging doors into the shadowed vestibule—empty as expected. Then up the stairs to where the first-floor corridor began. She peered around the corner. Toward the end of the corridor, a nurse pushed a medicine cart and another nurse appeared from one of the distant rooms. They turned toward the station.

Moving quickly but not so quickly as to draw attention to herself, Leona went down the corridor of opened doors, staying close to the wall, down the corridor of moanings and mumbles and a radio playing softly, against the rules. She counted five doors and slipped inside. Stepping out of the slab of door light, she stood still against the inside wall to catch her breath. Blinking, she let her eyes probe the darkness.

A spill of light from the parking lot outside fell through the large window and onto one corner of the bed. In her haste, before she could see as well as she wanted to, the child's name had formed and been uttered, on a rush of breath, "Mamie?"

Slowly, as her eyesight adjusted to the dark, a flurry of disturbing impressions overtook her other concerns. The room was cold, unreasonably cold. The far wall had curtains that, when drawn, entirely covered two large windows. But tonight the curtains were partly pulled back and a draft of raw wind blew by her and out the lighted doorway. In nearly the same instant, she realized that one of the windows was open, the thin curtains on that side swelling and shifting and collapsing with the movement of the breeze. The venetian blinds had been drawn up. But oddest of all was the overbearing smell of the air itself. It was as if one of the nurses had dropped a bottle of cheap perfume and decided, rather than clean it up, to air out the room. Good Lord, she thought, what have they done? It made no sense.

Taking up less than half the bed and outlined by the sheet tucked in around it, the curled-up figure lay on its side, the top end of the sheet clutched to its chest. Its smudgy eyes seemed locked on a corner of the ceiling. For a stabbing moment, Leona gazed at the door number again to see if she might actually be in the wrong room. Then, confirming that she wasn't, she wondered if Mamie might have been moved to another room. Had they, perhaps, released her early? There was nothing to do but find out.

She took a tentative step forward. "Mamie?" she whispered across the dark depth of the room. "I've come back. Like I promised." But her voice broke.

The curtains fluttered.

Avoiding the light that fell through the doorway, she moved up past the foot of the bed. She could see that the loosened bandage covering Mamie's shoulder had shifted sideways; she could see the scabbed edges underneath, and the hard, emaciated face—the face that had been getting softer, fuller, but now seemed even more gaunt. "My God, Mamie, what're they doing to you?"

As she leaned down toward the child, a cold gust of wind lashed through the room. Half the curtains filled and collapsed so quickly that they snapped. She shuddered, all the while speaking quietly: "I'm sorry I took so long to get here, Mamie, but at least I can stop that wind." She glanced at the curtains once more and then, without taking her eyes from the doorway where a nurse might appear at any moment, she stepped back, caught the window frame, and pulled the window shut. "There," she said, hurrying back.

But through her own soft voice, she heard the slow squeak of nurses' shoes in the hall; in a panic, she glanced about for a place to hide. She thought of the curtains first, but discounted them immediately as too obvious; if she accidentally caused the curtains to move, she could bring her entire house of cards down around herself. She thought of stooping behind the wing chair, but that seemed childish and risky. Then she saw that the door to the shared bathroom near the foot of the bed had been left open; it protruded dimly into the room.

Stepping sideways, she moved behind the forty-five-degree angle of the open door—in the room's darkest corner. Clasping the edge of the door, she peeked around it, watching the front of the room. And momentarily the light coming through the hall doorway was all but blotted out by a huge Negro woman in a white uniform, buttonholes straining and gapping, the popping tight skirt riding up on her waist.

Leona found it almost impossible to breathe. It was as if she were hanging by a wire in the air, caught up on the hook of her own imagination like a fish, suffocating. She kept her mouth open and let her breath leak out silently. All around her, a dank and moldering odor drifted. It was a particular foul scent, both recognizable and familiar, but she couldn't place it.

The nurse lifted her head high and Leona heard her say, "You wearin' perfume in here? Nope? Well, I swear I smell perfume in here." Backlit, the black face caught chiaroscuro highlights. Her head seemed too small for the rest of her, and she seemed to be looking directly at Leona.

Standing near the curtain pleats and holding the bathroom door before her, Leona felt her fingertips begin to tingle with pinpricks of pain. She was afraid to move her head behind the protection of the door, afraid the movement would reveal her presence. Then, with her eyes locked on the figure at the door and all her senses heightened, she felt a vague stirring at the back of her neck, like something crawling on the outermost ends of her hair. What is that? she wondered. She wanted to slap at it, but couldn't; she wanted to shiver, but kept herself rigid. Her scalp began to prickle and itch—in a flash, she could feel every pore on her body. She took a slow breath as if pulling it through a straw. Quietly.

The nurse strayed in toward the bed, but in the hall another nurse said, "Did you tell that Wharton kid to turn off his radio?" The black nurse sniffed the air a moment longer before she shook her head, grumbling aloud to herself: "I must've brought that perfume smell in with me, from Mrs. Carruther's room." Then she backed out the doorway and was gone.

Leona stepped from behind the door, shivering and rubbing the back of her neck. She drank the air. Frowning as she turned, she squinted back at her dark hiding place and at the curtains, but they hung in perfect folds. Again the sound of nurses' shoes in the hall drew her attention. Hurrying around the bed, she went to the front of the room and eased the door shut. The light in the room shrank. She turned back to Mamie. It occurred to her to stoop over into the spill of light from the window so the little girl could see who it was, as well as hear her better. "Don't they pay any attention to you at all?"

Mamie was trembling hard, but the smudgy eyes didn't change or respond, and now that the immediate danger had passed, Leona breathed freely.

It was hopeless. Mamie didn't know who she was, had never known who she was, perhaps was even afraid of her, tonight of all nights. She had never felt less certain about what she had set out to do than she did at that moment. All those sleepless nights, fretting and hoping—all for nothing. After four days' absence, she had only wanted a glimmering of recognition, but there was nothing more than there had been, and for those endless seconds Leona wanted to change her mind, to turn and walk away and never come back.

But Mamie . . . Even if she wouldn't look at Leona or say her name, even if she didn't know who this woman was who had come to her every night, and talked and read and held her when she trembled, and kissed her goodbye in the morning while slipping a cellophane-wrapped lollipop under her pillow for good luck—even if Mamie didn't care or know or notice, one day her lips had been purple, the next day orange from the lollipop, and she was getting better. Not completely well, but better. And tonight, as Leona pulled the gray blanket from the footboard to wrap Mamie in, she told her, "If we have to start from scratch, at the very beginning all over again, one day you will know your name, Mamie, and you will tell me mine."

Mamie was still trembling; Leona had to undo the small fingers one by one in order to pull the sheet down and replace it with the blanket. "This'll keep you warm," she whispered. "We don't want you to catch pneumonia." She shoved the sheet down. Partway, then farther. Except for a top, Mamie was dressed. In clothes too big for her, but dressed. Girls' clothes, a size or two too large. Denim jeans and socks and old tennis shoes. An edge of the wadded hospital smock had slipped from under her pillow. "Oh, Mamie," Leona said, surprised, "were you going to run away? Is it that awful? Where'd you get these clothes?" She shook the blanket open and pressed it around the little girl, and as she leaned over Mamie to pick her up, she saw the curtains shift just slightly and below the bottom edge of the curtain she saw shoes. In that instant, everything—the room, Mamie, even herself—seemed surreal. Then, before that sensation had passed, the window light shining through the fabric weave delineated a moving shape, a very distinct shape of a figure standing as if it were wrapped in gauze. She tried to speak, but her voice was too dry to lift sound; finally, as she exhaled, her thin voice carried: "Who are you?" She gasped. "What do you want?" The curtains stirred and began to part. She couldn't see who it was—the emerging figure was in shadow. Her heart seemed to stop.

Pulling Mamie up into a gray bundle in her arms, she ran to the door and yanked it open. Glancing back toward the lone desk lamp at the nurses' station, she rushed along the corridor, down steps, through the doors, into the laundry room, then out into the clear, cold night, and into the car—driving away before she'd even turned on the headlights.

As she pulled the knob, the two pools of light skimmed the hedges at the back of the lot and suddenly in the road ahead, as if rising out of nowhere, came eyes—oddly tilted eyes, catching the light in gimlet slants. The Buick closed toward them, but the weird reflective eyes did not waver. It was an animal of some kind, maybe a dog. She couldn't tell what it was except that it was enormous. Her hands grew tighter on the wheel, every sinew braced. She couldn't respond fast enough to move her foot off the accelerator. Whatever it is, I'm going to hit it. . . . I'll never get out of this.

At the point of impact, she felt her reflexes snap and she turned the wheel hard, one hand flying out protectively to Mamie, and just as she swerved, it came up along her side window, a blur of teeth and slobber and a deafening growl. She saw it slide away, but before she could straighten the car, it came again, striking the side window with such force the glass cracked; the creature's black maw rimpled back on slashing teeth, so close she lunged from it, threw her arm up defensively, and jammed her foot on the gas pedal. With a loud growling noise, the creature hit the window a third time, its claws digging at the glass beside her face, but by then the Buick had shot forward. Bouncing across a low brick wall, it plunged into shrubbery, jarring Mamie up against Leona. And Mamie's arm came up across the line of Leona's sight, as if she were reaching for the animal.

"Get down! Mamie! Get down! Dear God, get down, Mamie! *Please!*" Evergreens scrubbed the length of the bucking car; swabs of black boughs lashed the windshield, and the steering wheel whipped from side to side under her weakened grip. The Buick broke through to the other side of the evergreens, struck pavement and spun past a parked car, tires squalling. As she struggled to correct the car, she saw in the rear-view mirror a figure running after them, and something else. That dog. No mistake now; she had seen it close: it was a dog, a damned crazy dog. She was so completely shaken that the muscles in her arms and legs had cramped. But she didn't stop for the intersection at the bottom of the long hill. The car squealed into the turn and fishtailed across both lanes of the highway.

They sped through Graylie and had driven several miles on the open road before Leona rubbed at the pain in her arms and rearranged Mamie on the seat beside her. Who was it? she thought. A patient? But who? Who in the hell? Now even more than when it happened, she could feel the tickling sensation at the back of her neck. Could feel it touching her hair tips. And she knew what it had been. *Breath.* Someone breathing on her hair in the room . . . watching her, waiting. She had been that close, had come that close to . . . But who? Waiting for what? And that stench she couldn't identify seemed so obvious now —it was the stink of a wet dog. She couldn't stop shaking. With her trembling right hand, she patted and smoothed the small head on her lap. And with her left hand, she gripped the steering wheel, easing the Buick through the night traffic—a speeding blue car made distinguishable by a fluttering sprig of black cedar caught on its hood ornament.

# 5

If there was any chance of catching that woman tonight, Sherman knew, it would be at the house. He crossed the last long fairway behind the hospital grounds, running as hard as he could. Ahead of him, the Chinaman sniffed the ground, then plunged through tree shadows, a mottled streak. As long as he kept going, Sherman could maintain a precarious equilibrium, concentrating on the single thought of getting to the house fast. It was when he paused to track his direction or lift the rusty tines of a wire fence to climb through that the rage surged in him again, like quick poison through all his senses. The unexpected shock of what had happened struck him in waves. The bitch, he thought again and again; the bitch, the lousy bitch.

Leaving the lawn, he jumped into the rough grass.

In the dark room, he had thought she was a nurse. Since she was dressed in pale going-home clothes, he'd thought she was coming in to say good night to his sister. As soon as she left, he'd planned to help Mamie finish dressing in the clothes he'd stolen from clotheslines; then he'd lower her out the window and escape into the night. But his plan, like all the others, had backfired. Only worse this time, much worse.

Even when the woman backed up against the curtains, practically touching him, he hadn't guessed what she was up to, afraid himself of being discovered and taken away by the police. That was why he hadn't moved, hadn't done anything to stop her. And then it was too late to do anything. It was like watching a ball of kite string unwind faster and faster in his hands until it was out of control and burning his fingers. The effect of what that woman had done went on hovering beyond his consuming rage and his ability to understand it. With Sherman, everything was quickly reduced to its simplest terms: if he caught that bitch tonight, he would kill her. You've really done it, he thought. Now you're dead.

He thrashed through the back edge of the rough and came out on an old cowpath fronting the woods. Grasping his knees, he stopped in the barren path, his breath loud and ragged, his head throbbing. Long needles of pain stitched up his arm from his bandaged, burned hand. In the east, the quarter-moon showed a rust-colored curl of light like the rim of a partly buried paint bucket. The Chinaman trotted up to him, panting, his dark eyes quizzical and his tail rolled back into a dense ball of fur. "Good boy," Sherman said between breaths. "You did your part." As if obeying just the sound of Sherman's voice, the big dog promptly sat down. But Sherman hardly paused before he was off again, turning and jogging away. The Chinaman ran along after him.

The creaking woods closed over them. Running parallel with Sherman, but straying from his side, the Chinaman loped through the underbrush. On the other side of the woods, Sherman heard the whine of a car on the highway, saw its moving headlights glittering through the trees. It was traveling in the same direction the woman had gone—into town, on the road to Scranton. Absorbed in that thought, he nearly collided with the iron palisades surrounding the cemetery; the toe of his shoe struck the stone base, a seam ripped, and the sole began to flap. Through the fence, the monuments and statues glinted feebly, catching grains of distant streetlight.

Another car passed, its engine throbbing, then fading away; in succession, headlights filtered through the obstructions and blinked along the fence. When the light was gone, Sherman stepped through the breach in the iron palings onto the soft rolling terrain of the graveyard. He moved from stone to stone, on familiar ground now. He had taken this route other times when he'd followed her home. While the road emptied of traffic, he stood beside a white obelisk, then raced down the sidewalk

toward Sand Creek Bridge and the downtown lights of Main
Street. The Chinaman ran ahead of him and plunged from sight.
When the next cars passed on the bridge, the headlights fanned
much too high to reach them as they scrambled along the slippery creek bank, going downstream.

Five minutes later, on the far corner of Battery Street and
Columbia Avenue, Sherman came to a halt, studying the white
frame house in the dim row of houses before him. He ran
forward a few steps, then slowed to walk across the intersection.
In his approach, he stayed across the street from the house,
walking very fast on lawn after dingy lawn to silence his footsteps. He could see that a light was on downstairs. At first he
thought it was the man's television set, but the light didn't
bounce or flicker; it was a faint, steady light, coming from the
hall or kitchen. When he passed the house, the living room was
quite dark, except for the beam of light from the other room.

Beside the house, the driveway was empty, the garage closed
up. The woman's blue car hadn't come back here; he was too
late. Without uttering a sound, he slumped where he stood. The
Chinaman came to him from across the street, his tongue dangling from the side of his mouth and his big grisly face masked
behind the white steam of his breath. Unless the car was hidden
in the garage, she'd done it; she'd grabbed Mamie, and nobody
knew.

But me, Sherman thought. Nobody but me.

Down the long wintry street, a car turned toward him and
he crouched back against spindly hedges and dropped to his
haunches to wait while it passed. He called the Chinaman to him
by puckering and smooching his lips, and the dog lay over on
his back to have his stomach scratched. His muzzle had been
bloodied when he attacked the car; his whiskers were now
frosted with blood. Still he lolled on his back as Sherman stroked
his furry chest. The run had not depleted Sherman's anger, but
now his body tensed with an even deeper knowledge. It's over,

he thought, nothing left to lose now, and he began to shake so hard he had to sit on the damp grass and chew on the bandage on his hand to stop. As soon as the fan of light sped past them, he stood and nodded for the Chinaman to come. He looked up and down the street.

He went to the corner and down the side street, and turned abruptly in to the alley, left unpaved and unattended between the various back-yard demarcations. Against his sweaty skin, the wind was biting cold. He chose his steps carefully through the weeds, keenly aware of the noise he made. Always before, he had entered the alley from the other end. On the back side of a shed, he paused to slow his breath and wipe his brow. When he stepped away, a high-backed cat hissed at him through the dark, leaping from the woodpile to the roof of the shed where it crouched like a gargoyle. Growling and snapping, the China-man tried to climb the wall after it and Sherman had to drag him away. But up and down the alley, then all over the neighbor-hood, a chorus of mimicking howls erupted. After a few more steps, he turned the Chinaman loose and they hurdled the low iron railing behind the Mattingly house, then crossed into the rough earth of the garden, and stood erect and silent behind the ornamental birdbath.

An upstairs window glowed with pinkish light, not in the woman's room but another bedroom. The glass in the back door shone dimly with the same shade of light he'd seen through the large front window. Somewhere in the middle of the house, then—the dining room or the hall—a light had been left on. The garage was empty. So the woman who'd taken Mamie was gone, completely gone. His last spark of hope withered, and the neces-sity of what had to be done settled over him with a weight like iron. Somebody had to know where she was, somebody close to her . . . and somebody was home.

Near the concrete urns, he stood in the darkened arch of the rose trellis, watching the upstairs light, collecting himself.

When the moon drifted free of clouds, it cast him in a pattern of drab, gnarled checkers. He breathed into his hand to trap the white fog spewing from his mouth. Freezing in his jacket, he stamped his feet slowly on the packed leaves. There was no movement or change in the upstairs room. The barking dogs dwindled to one lonely howler.

As he stood there, he knew he would go after Mamie and the woman and find them and bring Mamie back. He would go as far and as long as it took. He would need only a few things. A picture of the woman would help, and he knew where one was —on the mantel. A letter to her from somebody might give him a clue about where she was headed. And money; he'd have to try to find some money.

The house would be easy to get into. He had been in it before. Sherman checked his jacket pocket, and felt reassuringly the weight of the old leather-covered blackjack he'd found and taken one night from a desk drawer; and, in the other jacket pocket, the flashlight disguised as a pencil. In his pants pocket he felt the ridge of the folded knife with one of its two blades broken off. The Chinaman whimpered and stood, and sat down again. "You stay here," Sherman said. "Don't let anybody in. Don't let *anybody.*" The Chinaman squinted his slanted eyes and licked his muzzle.

Waiting for the light to go out, Sherman scooped two of the pain pills from his coat pocket and ate them dry from the gauze on his hand. He knew where the fuse box was, if it came to that. The medicine nibbled along his nerves and flared in his brain, numbing the throbbing ache in his hand and behind his eyes. He waited for his head to clear. Then he entered the house.


Emma opened her eyes and the room was dark. For a moment, only her eyes moved, skimming the night in the room for some half-remembered disturbance. She blinked and rubbed her eyes.

Of the little she could see, nothing appeared to be out of place, and yet she felt nervous. She couldn't recall turning off the bedside lamp, nor did she remember falling asleep, but what she did remember was far more troubling and vivid. As she slept, only brief moments ago, she'd had the distinct sensation of something very close to her, like a cat come to steal her breath away. The blind memory of it knotted in her nerves.

The old sayings and superstitions of her childhood had been stirred up. For a terrifying instant, she thought, Oh, my God, it's Leona. She's been killed and she came to me. Then she scolded herself for letting such heresy affect her reason. But nothing appeased her. She still couldn't reconcile the gnawing fear she'd experienced just as she awoke.

Shrugging higher on the pillows, she reached for the base of the lamp and slipped her fingers up on the celluloid switch. It clicked; she blinked, but the darkness remained intact. Quickly she turned the switch two more times. Again nothing happened. She stared toward the fluted lampshade with disbelief.

Watching the dark, she debated whether or not she had left an emergency candle in the bathroom the last time she'd cleaned. She decided she hadn't, which meant she'd have to go all the way downstairs to get one. She hesitated. She was afraid to go downstairs and she was ashamed to admit it. She drew her legs up in her nightgown and hugged them. As the quilts slipped, her library book fell shut, tumbling from her lap. On the nightstand, on Frank's side of the bed, the luminous dial of the alarm clock showed twenty to eleven. Frank should be home by now, she thought.

She remembered leaving the light on for him in the dining-room hallway and coming upstairs. It had been shortly after ten o'clock. In the bathroom medicine cabinet, she had found the bottle of nerve pills Leona had given her. ("They're mild," Leona had said. "You might need something for a rainy day." How obvious her scheming appeared, now that she was gone.)

Tonight, worried and jittery about how to tell Frank her bad news, Emma had taken two of the pills. Then, routinely, she'd changed into her nightgown, plumped both the pillows behind her head, and settled back with *The Fountainhead* open against her drawn-up knees. The lamp had been on.

She wondered if the bulb had burned out as she slept—if, in fact, the quiet pop and sizzle of it going out hadn't been what had awakened her. She was thinking about how long it had been since she'd changed the light bulb when she glimpsed a faint movement in the darkened doorway across the room. Her head had been turned toward the lamp and she saw the shape wrinkle and fluctuate on the outer edge of her eye. Twisting toward it, straining to see the doorway clearly, she heard the unmistakable slap of a shoe.

Her heart was pounding and the night solidified before her staring eyes—it was like peering through a tight black mesh. It's Frank, she thought, trying to relax. But she hadn't heard his car in the drive. As she struggled to grasp what was happening, she suddenly realized who it was and why the noises had been so hesitant and perplexing. Leona's come back, she thought, and her spirits lifted. Something went wrong; she'd lost her nerve, or at the last minute she'd just changed her mind and called it off. And come home. In all likelihood, she was going to her room right now, defeated and downhearted.

Emma leaned forward on the bed to listen more carefully, and the house became a vast jar of stillness. Rising from its depths came the noises, tiny wisps and spots of sound: the grind and clicking rotation of a doorknob turned, followed by the muted yawn of a door opened, and, under all the noises, the sound of that one faulty shoe. It's Leona, she concluded, nodding thoughtfully. That would explain everything.

Peeling back the covers, she stood up from the bed, shrugged into her flannel robe, and cinched the sash. She poked her toes under the side of the bed for her slippers and her foot came down hard on something ice cold and slimy and wet. She gasped and lunged from it, but it stuck to the bottom of her foot. Moaning, she caught her foot in both hands. She could feel the thing stuck to her skin. Bracing herself, she cupped her fingers and scraped it from the rigid ball of her foot. It gathered in a wad on her fingers. She could smell it in the room now, the remarkably clean odor of rotted wood and rain. The texture in her hand was webbed and veined and she held it up closer. It was wet, a crumpled leaf. *Oh, God.* She eased back against the quilts; a babble of relieved breaths interspersed her soft, embarrassed laughter. A leaf. After all, just a leaf. Lord have mercy.

It took a few seconds for her to resolve to put an end to her foolishness, once and for all. She stood up from the bed again, rearranging her robe and sash. Halfway across the room, she stepped on another leaf. Again it surprised her, the old fear trickling along her spine. She turned to look at the drawn shades on her two windows, both scarcely glowing with dull moonlight. Surely by lifting the shades she could let in enough light to see where she was going. She went immediately to the windows and pulled the shades up. Gazing out at the thin rind of the moon, she was surprised at how little light there actually was.

A trail of leaves led from the bed, through the door, and out to the staircase landing. Black, glistening leaves. Her pulse thumped in her temples. Neither Frank or Leona would have tracked filth like that into the house. She reached out blindly for something to hold, caught the bedpost, and clung to the acorn finial.

She was caught in a desperate frenzy to move, and yet she didn't know which way to turn. The telephone was downstairs. The only way out was downstairs. But whoever it was in the house stood between her and escape. If she screamed or yelled, she realized, the house would probably contain her cry; it would do nothing but alert her visitor to her fear. If she stayed quiet, maybe he would take what he wanted and go away.

Hardly breathing, holding her breath as long as she could and then inhaling a few mouthfuls of air until she could brace herself and hold it again, she stood absolutely stock-still, clutching the bedpost. She hung on the air, waiting to hear the retreat of footsteps and the quiet closing of the downstairs door, but neither happened. The wait grew interminable. At last the slow flap of the shoe recurred, but her racing heartbeat interacted with it too much for her to tell where he was. Through the bedroom door, open to the stairwell, she watched the lights of a passing car swell and disappear in the foyer below.

Her visitor was moving much faster now; she could hear his urgency so plainly that she decided he had to be upstairs, but she couldn't be certain. The darkness swarmed on her eyes: the night air had thickened to the consistency of molasses. He was stumbling through the rooms—once, she was convinced she heard him in Leona's room—attacking the house with a heedless, fumbling haste. His impatience tightened her nerves. She heard glass breaking, not once but repeatedly, and endless small shattering noises. That time the noise seemed to come from downstairs. A drawer shrieked open, then shut. Another drawer opened. Apparently he was looking for something in particular, rushing violently about in his search. Let him take what he wants, she thought; then he'll leave. She had decided he could have anything if only he would leave, when she remembered hiding Leona's three thousand dollars under the vase on the desk. She ached all over and wanted to cry.

The interior doors did not have locks; there wasn't even a chair in the room to jam under the doorknob, only the useless kidney-shaped vanity bench. She could hardly bear to stay where she was, but she was equally incapable of moving from the anchoring bedpost. She was trapped in her bedroom with the two dull traces of light glimmering through the windows to the floor at her feet. She took a step forward.

Abruptly all the noise stopped. As in a nightmare, she merely lifted her head and the noise was gone. To keep herself quiet, she clamped her hands tight over her mouth. Car lights flashed through the rooms downstairs, blooming up yellow in the staircase depression, and she saw the head and torso of a figure rising toward her in silhouette. Her pulse beat and lapsed. The car's rumbling slowed to a regulated buffeting alongside the house. It's Frank, she thought. Oh, thank God, Frank, hurry. . . .

She began to move helplessly through the room, searching about for some defense while she listened for the flapping shoe. There was utter silence. Then, outside, the garage door clattered up. If she could get to the window and raise it, she could call down to Frank and tell him to hurry. She took a full step backward toward the window, then another. The car door slammed, the motor revved. Her legs were heavy and sluggish; she could hardly move. The garage door clanked shut. Simultaneously, she heard Frank whistling and an angry snarl of drawn breath in the bedroom doorway. Her muscles crawled under her skin, her inertia spread to her will. Everything stalled.

The figure seemed hardly to move; it was like a shadow collecting density from the dark. She saw the shape contract and expand, emerging toward her. Fear rose through her throat and broke from her lips in airless whimperings. Absolutely frozen, she couldn't move or speak, couldn't think what to do. She saw that her intruder had a wrapped hand and that he was smaller than she had imagined. When he spoke, his slow, guttural voice was as cold as ice water tossed on her face. "Where's that woman?" he asked. "Where'd she take Mamie?"

Oh, not that, she thought, but the voice had spurred her to her senses. One of his hands, the unwrapped one, came up holding something that looked like a black baby rattle. It wobbled soundlessly on the top of his fist. She could hear Frank coming up the walk and an odd sound like a growl. "You shouldn't be here," she tried to say, her voice a sticky whisper. "You're in the wrong house." The moonlight bloomed brighter in the room and he was coming through it. Her breath backed up. "Why," she said, "you're just a boy," and she whirled to break past him. The blow struck her across the cheek with astonishing velocity. It felt as if she had been hit in the face with a boulder. Her jawbone and teeth exploded; a bolt of intense white light seared the backs of her eyes, burning down like embers, and incomprehensible shock waves of pain erupted in her brain. One side of her face began to puff and contort. He caught her as she fell and time stretched like elastic. She felt herself immersed with him, and his gamey animal smell was vile. His arms came up around her in a kind of embrace and clasped over her throat, front and back, and he wrenched her head backward and to the side. A sharp, distinct, very loud crack broke the air—from the base of her skull outward she grew very numb and cold, instantaneously. She fell, crumpling hard.

Her head lolled to the side. She tried to move it, but couldn't. She tried to move her fingers, couldn't. Inches from her tilted eyes, she saw one shoe with a many-knotted shoelace and one sock foot. A small pool of light snared and dazzled her face. Stooping down, her assailant smiled upon her with perfect white teeth. "You're dead," he rasped. "And that woman . . . You're all dead." He snatched and tore the words with his teeth. "I'm gonna string her up and gut her like a goddam dog." Then he told her to shut her eyes. From outside, the angry growling and barking came even louder and, through it, Frank's voice.

Emma heard her assailant move from her side, his feet twisting fast on the carpet. She strained to open her swollen eyes to slits. She saw his shape step over her, wagging his flashlight.

The end of the light chased before him like a ghost on a leash.

# 6

Stopping only once along the roadside to change clothes and dispose of Mamie's odd bits of clothing in a picnic trash barrel, they drove almost ninety miles that first night, heading south into Scranton. Disallowing some fluke, Leona believed she had eight to ten hours before Mamie's disappearance would be discovered and the search spread beyond Graylie. She claimed her reservation at the Claypool-Chase Hotel and registered as Dr. and Mrs. Arnold Merchassen, explaining that her husband would be joining her daughter and herself later. It was quarter past midnight.

The hotel lobby was like a massive rococo tunnel, and everything was accomplished quietly, quickly, impeccably. She paid for the room in advance from the spending money she kept in the coin purse in her handbag and she kept a quarter out for the bellboy. She had two of the seven suitcases brought up, but carried the black briefcase herself. Mamie gazed at everything; she seemed particularly fascinated with the elevator operator— a matronly Negro woman seated on a fold-down stool, who closed the elevator's clattering lattice gate, then shut the windowed doors and turned the crank without ever once looking up from her magazine. On a wheeze of smooth pressure they rose to the fifth floor.

As soon as the bellboy had left, Leona shut and locked the door, closed the drapes and the venetian blinds, and turned to Mamie. The gray-green eyes drilled into her from the middle of the room.

"Well, now, Mamie, what do you think of this?"

She expected no answer and she got none. She took off the mink coat, a gift from Mrs. Merchassen eight years ago, removed the hatpin with the diamond eye, and laid her feather hat on the dresser.

"Aren't you warm?" she said. "Let's take off your coat." She unbuttoned and slid the new parka off Mamie's small shoulders. "Now, isn't that better? Yes, it is. I know it is." With some surprise, she noticed that Mamie was still wearing the small identification bracelet of beads from the hospital. I missed it, Leona thought, when we changed in the dark car. It gave her a moment's start; had anyone in the lobby seen it? Would they know it came from a hospital? It was unlikely; she decided she was overreacting.

Using her fingernails, she loosened and removed the string of lettered beads from Mamie's wrist and, with it, Mamie's last link to that dreadful place—a very small thing to do and yet, to Leona, it had real significance. "Now you're free, Mamie," she said. "You'll never have to go back there again." Mamie stood staring at her naked wrist as Leona put the bracelet of beads in the zippered compartment inside her purse.

Her legs ached when she stood, still tense with what was left of her fear. "Tell you what—why don't you sit here on the edge of the bed and we'll get you ready to go to sleep? There, that's better. I know what we'll do. How would you like a soda pop?"

No reply.

Unable to shake the jitters, Leona wanted something to calm herself and also something to help them celebrate, but she didn't know what to order. She went to the telephone and asked room service for a martini and an orange soda pop. "No," she said, "not mixed together."

In the bathroom of black and white tile, she changed into her nightgown and robe. As she came back, she caught Mamie scratching at the crisp skin under the bandage on her hip, and trying to reach back to her shoulder. "Oh, Mamie," Leona said, "what're you doing? I know it must itch, but you shouldn't do that." At the sound of her voice, Mamie stopped scratching and twisted away. So this was to be the glimmering of recognition Leona had waited for. She quickly smeared cream on the red fingernail marks and pulled the hem of Mamie's jumper down.

"You'll make scars." And she showed her the jar of Pond's cold cream and where it was kept in her purse; she told Mamie how to use it when she itched, because itching meant she was getting well—took one little finger in her hand and dipped it in the cream and, guiding her, let Mamie smooth it on her own cheek.

There was a tapping at the door and a boy wearing a red pillbox hat trimmed in gold, and gloves the color of mice, delivered their drinks, and it didn't matter, as she carried the tray into the room, that Mamie had globbed cream on her face and in her hair and all down her front. It didn't matter. Leona laughed and said to her, "My goodness, Mamie, did you itch all over?"

With a towel from the bathroom, she wiped the cream away as quickly as she could and went to make sure she had remembered to lock the door. The glass of orange soda pop with its straw afloat was so large Mamie held it with both hands. In Leona's glass, the green olive with its red tip silently released a dust of fine bubbles. She took a sip, shuddered, and set it aside. Mamie simply held her drink in her lap. Condensing water puddled between her fingers. "Okay," Leona said, "I was wrong. I'll need you to stand up." She took the soda pop and set it next to her martini, then helped Mamie stand.

She unbuttoned the long-sleeved dress in the back and worked it off her arms. Then she lifted Mamie's arms and held them straight by the wrists and, catching the hem of the petticoat, pulled it up and over her head. She sat Mamie on the edge of the bed again to unbuckle her white shoes and let them drop, then her white socks. "Do you want to take your underpants off yourself? I've got brand-new pajamas for you." But of course Mamie didn't answer. Her unyielding stare was now focused on the litter of clothes at her feet. "Don't worry. I'll pick them up."

All of a sudden, now that they were completely alone, Leona wanted to pick Mamie up and dance around the room. But the unrelenting eyes held her at bay. Leona felt awkward—it was silly, but she couldn't help it. Minute by minute, she kept waiting for some inviting glance, any half-friendly response, but it was no use. She clenched her hands into fists, then forced them open.

She had to put her arm around Mamie to pull the underpants down and away from her feet. And as she held her now, great waves of feeling—and of doubt—broke through her. Maybe Mamie was too damaged. Maybe Leona didn't know what she was doing, even though she had cared for other people's children during those years in the doctor's office and had always longed for just such a moment as this. Maybe she was just trying to steal affection, as Emma had implied. This body she was holding, so frail and vulnerable, was—other than the shoulder and the hip where skin had been grafted—perfect in every respect, yet something was missing. Leona could not take Mamie's small hand without being aware of its perfection, the flawless fingers, the little fingernails. And behind those lovely eyes, a mind no one had reached. Was she still wandering lost through those smoke-filled rooms, her mother begging and praying, her brothers perhaps already smothered by fumes, dead in their sleep, and her father wetting down the quilt? Who did she think she was, to try to save such a child? Yet Leona knew that, no matter what, she had to do whatever she could to save Mamie. That single-minded premise sustained her.

She didn't know how long she had been kneeling, rocking unsteadily, her knees half asleep as she held Mamie to her, but a long shiver ran through the small body and Leona held her even tighter. "Don't worry," she said. "Nothing bad is ever going to hurt you again. Not if I can stop it." Then it occurred to her that Mamie was probably cold.

She released her and helped put on her pajamas. She pulled back the covers and laid Mamie down and sat beside her. "Go to sleep now." With her fingertips, she moved the hair from the small face. "I know you want to go home, Mamie," she said. "I don't have any home either. So we'll just have to make one for ourselves."

She stayed there for several minutes, thinking how new all this was to her and how strange it had to be for such a little girl. When Mamie burrowed her head in the pillow and closed her eyes, Leona stood up, away from the bed. Her adrenaline had begun, at last, to drain away; she was very tired. There were only a few remaining things she had to do before she could get to sleep herself. She picked up Mamie's clothes, folding and stacking them on one of the suitcases. Again she checked the fastened door, removing the key from the lock to keep under her pillow. She turned out the bedside lamp. The ceiling light was still on in the bathroom and she left it on, to burn through the night. She also left the bathroom door ajar, so that if Mamie awoke in the dark, she would know where she was, know not to be afraid. Almost as an afterthought, she pulled the cord to open the drapes. Another cord opened the blinds. The morning light would wake them and they could make an early start.

It was only then, standing alone at the dark window, having done what she had done with no possibility of turning back, that a burst of violent remorse welled up in her. She had done the unthinkable. And with one swift act she had made herself a fugitive and an outsider. Now Emma's words of foreboding returned to her: *You don't know what you're doing! What do you really know about her?*

She was staring at the night sky, the black clouds drifting along toward some unknown destination and the stars behind the clouds, cold and brilliant, staying forever in their appointed places, never touching, never once breathing, never coming alive with a word or a laugh, like so much in life. She couldn't live in that emptiness any more. There was no love in that sky —so what she had done, wherever it led her, would have to be better than that. Even with all its traps, all its failings, this had to be better.

What else could I do, Emma? she thought. Put yourself in my place.

Keeping her eyes shut, lying absolutely still, Mamie Abbott waited that night for a sound she thought would never come— the woman's breath drawn deep and slow in sleep. She waited a little while longer until there could be no doubt that the woman was sound asleep. Then, crawling silently, Mamie touched the side of the bed and slid to the floor.

From the bathroom, a thin belt of light cut across the dark reaches of the room. Standing up in the space between the beds, Mamie waited again, watching to see if the woman would wake up. The sheet rose and fell with almost invisible regularity. Not making a sound, Mamie stooped and took up the woman's pocketbook.

On tiptoe, she carried it to the far side of her bed where the light from the bathroom was brighter, and, kneeling on the carpet, she opened it a tiny fraction at a time so that it made only the faintest sound. She felt inside the compartment and retrieved the string of hospital beads spelling her name. Then she closed the zipper, dug deep in the purse for a pencil, and found one, a yellow stub with a dull point. Behind her on the other bed, the woman moaned and shifted in her sleep. Mamie did not move a hair. When she thought it was safe, she peeked above the edge of her bed and saw the shadow of the woman, asleep and motionless under the covers. She closed the pocketbook. She returned it to the floor beside the nightstand.

She needed something to write on. Holding the hospital bracelet and the stub pencil in her fist, she slowly searched the darkened room until she came to the table with the vase of flowers on it. Stuck in among the flowers was a small white envelope with its flap standing open. Slowly she pulled it out. Inside the envelope was a printed card. And the back side was blank. There Mamie wrote: STOP HER SHE GOT ME FRUM HASPIDL. Then she put the card in the envelope and slipped the bracelet in, curled around so that it would fit inside the envelope, too. She licked the flap and sealed it.

The woman had left Mamie's white parka tossed over the back of a chair. Climbing into the seat, Mamie slipped the sealed envelope down inside the coat's deep front pocket and hid the pencil beneath the cushion. Now when the moment came she would be ready. She ran back to bed, shivering with the knowledge that this would all soon be over. She was far too wound up to sleep.

They left the hotel at seven-thirty, riding down in the elevator and walking out across the expansive lobby. Carrying the briefcase, Leona held Mamie's hand and walked slowly so she could keep up. A different clerk was behind the desk now, and though there was no way he could have realized she had registered falsely, Leona avoided him. She went directly to the bellman, presented her room key, and asked for her car and for her bags to be brought down. He spoke into his archaic intercom.

She felt hemmed in by the gloom of the lobby. Picking Mamie up, she went through the revolving doors to wait for her car under the hotel canopy. The morning air was cool, mild but blustery, the sky overcast with slabs of clouds. While they waited, it began to snow.

When the attendant delivered her car, she noticed that he looked at her strangely. He opened the trunk for the bellboy who was bringing her suitcases and hurried back to the driver's door as she approached it. She thought for a moment he was waiting for his tip, but then she saw what he saw: the cracked side glass, the scratches in the blue paint below the cracked window, deep scratches down to bare metal, and, mixed in the crust of slobber, fragments of dried blood.

In the raw morning light, the dreadful episode of the night before flashed through her mind. That dog wanted to kill me, she thought. Or worse . . . it wanted Mamie. The slamming of the trunk lid jarred her back to the here and now. She was tempted to explain with a lie what had caused the damage to her car, but instead she gave the attendant and the bellboy a dollar each.

It was snowing but now the sun was shining, and the snow melted as it touched the ground. Drops beaded on the long blue snout of the Buick. As soon as they'd left the industrial outskirts of Scranton, Leona pulled the car off the road. She took a handkerchief from her purse and dampened it with melted snow from the hood, then scrubbed desperately at the dried slobber on the paint. She had to dampen the cloth several times before she had most of the mucuslike crust removed. It ruined her handkerchief and she tossed it away.

She waited for a truck to pass before she pulled back onto the highway and drove away, still headed south along the Susquehanna River, through Pittston and Cromwell, Kingston and Plymouth.

When Scranton was well behind them, Leona turned on the car radio. She found a station that played Benny Goodman records, and numbers, as they called them, from *Show Boat* and *Oklahoma!* When she knew the words, she sang, too, but when the news came on, every thirty minutes, she turned the radio off and sang alone.

Most of the sycamores and elms along the river had shed their foliage; great swarms and drifts of leaves blew around the Buick's windows as they drove through the bright open spaces. It was becoming a glorious day, but the cracked side window split the landscape in half, distorting Leona's view. As she drove, she wondered again who it had been in the hospital room hiding behind the curtains. Watching the landscape roll by her window on the passenger side, Mamie sat on two pillows, her hands in her coat pockets, her legs swaying with the motion of the car.

When they stopped at a Shell filling station some time later, to buy gas and go to the ladies' room, Leona did not see the small hand come from the pocket; nor did she see Mamie place the florist's envelope on the chair where the station attendant had been sitting, reading his newspaper. Her back was turned.

# 7

Only the sound of his footsteps and the soft padding of the Chinaman's paws broke the night silence. Sherman did not hesitate or look back, striking deftly through the dark countryside. "Goddam her," he muttered under his breath; "goddam her to hell," the words like a chant, marking his stride. The pills held his pain to a low humming at the back of his brain.

They kept to the high ground parallel to the Scranton road. When the dog wandered down too close to the ditches, Sherman called him and made him come back. Otherwise he let the Chinaman roam. Very little traffic moved on the highway this late at night; for long periods it stood completely empty. Yet he wanted to be sure that their departure wasn't noticed by anyone. He spoke to the dog sparingly and used his pencil flashlight only when he had to—when the darkness of wild bushes blocked his path or the dog slipped into a gully that opened in the ground like a trap.

Moving quickly, they crossed pastures and fences and woods. As soon as the sun came up, Sherman opened his shirt and removed the papers and pictures he'd taken from the Mattingly house. The snapshots, blown up to frame size, had faded to a bronzy orange. The two women, the one he'd just hit and the one who'd taken Mamie, were in both the photographs. He immediately folded them, scored them with his thumbnail, and tore them in two. Then he tore the two halves showing the

Mattingly woman into little chunks and threw them to the wind like confetti. In the two half-photos he kept, the woman looked younger than she did in real life. His teeth began to ache from the angry set of his jaw. From his billfold, he removed the print of Mamie's school picture that he'd torn from a newspaper, folded it with the two pictures of the woman, and returned all three, in his billfold, to his pocket.

Methodically he flipped through the sheaf of papers—most of it yesterday's mail, he guessed. All the envelopes had been opened. He separated them quickly, sorting out the circulars and bills and holding the two envelopes addressed to Leona Hillenbrandt in his teeth. The stack of useless material he tore into small pieces and let them dribble and flutter from his hands as he walked. Of the two remaining pieces, one was a letter on good-smelling paper from Cornelia Dunham, Ridgefarm Road, Brandenburg Station, Kentucky. But the other letter, from the Citizens National Bank of Scranton, held his attention and he placed the Kentucky letter inside his shirt.

Sherman tore the bank envelope apart. He paid little attention to the actual writing as he repeatedly formed the woman's name with his lips: Leona Hillenbrandt. Scranton. That had to be where she was taking Mamie. Nothing else made sense. He folded the letter with the envelope and tore them to pieces. The little wad of money he'd found wedged under the Mattingly woman's vase—the three thousand-dollar bills wrapped in a five-dollar bill—remained untouched in his jeans pocket.

It was still very early in the morning when he saw a country gas station far below and wondered if it was safe yet to hitchhike, if he was far enough away from Graylie. He was crossing an area of hills, and had wandered higher from the road than he meant to. While he looked down, two cars moved like minnows onto the asphalt drive, headed in opposite directions. He wanted to be riding in a car. He called the dog and started down the steep embankment.

He counted four cars parked on the grounds, none of them

police cars—nothing that looked suspicious. As he and the dog crossed the highway through the morning fog, he saw a clump of road signs. In black letters, one said: SCRANTON 72 MI. The idea of seventy-two miles stretched deep in his imagination and, with it, the minutes ticking away and Mamie slipping farther out of his reach. He pulled a piece of clothesline rope from his hip pocket, tied it to the Chinaman's collar, and they jogged through a display of chalk figures strung out on the ground—reindeer and donkeys pulling carts, and birdbaths—and slipped between the parked cars.

Fog hung in scraps over the road, but the traffic was fairly brisk. As they moved into the shadow of the gas station, a car came in headed north toward Graylie. The attendant ambled from the garage, pumped the gas, and went back to work, frowning at Sherman and the Chinaman as he passed. A lull settled over the station. For several minutes nothing moved on the road.

Come on, Sherman thought, his anxiety mounting. He sat down on the concrete curbing, then stood up and scuffed back and forth.

Two cars came in and stopped on either side of the gas pumps. While the attendant handled the car pointed north, Sherman tapped the passenger window of the one going south, a maroon car. The driver leaned across the seat and rolled the window down a few inches. Sherman asked for a ride to Scranton. The man seemed to consider it, lowered his head as if to decide. "I need a lift for him, too," Sherman said. "He's with me," and nodded toward the Chinaman. Without answering, the man cranked the window up and turned to stare at the road.

Before the attendant had finished with the maroon car, an old blue coupe had pulled in behind it. Sherman tapped the window glass, and again he thought he might be getting somewhere until he pointed to the big grisly dog; then the driver said, "Sorry," and went on studying the map spread on the steering wheel. The car radio was turned low, but the emphatic voice could still be heard: "*Graylie police continue to investigate last night's assault and battery of a local woman, Emma Mattingly, of 210 Columbia Avenue. Mrs. Mattingly has been listed in critical condition. . . .*"

Sherman heard only that much as he withdrew from the side of the car, concentrating on the man reading the map. Fright ran through him like quicksilver. She's still alive, he thought. If she could describe him, it would only be a matter of time before the cops figured out who he was and what he had done—not only what he'd done last night, but all the other nights and other things, the paperboy who'd taken his place, the fire. I should of finished her, he thought; I should of.

Even after the coupe had left, he went on glancing about, alert and cautious. He saw no immediate threat, except the attendant was coming toward them in his blackened coveralls, wiping his hands on a greasy rag. "You can't hang out here," the man said. "You'd better just run along." The Chinaman clambered to his feet and started to growl, his hackles rising.

"We're tryin' to catch a ride," Sherman said, pulling the dog's collar, telling the Chinaman to shut up.

"You better catch it someplace else. I want you to clear out of here." He went inside the garage.

Sherman slowly brushed the seat of his pants. Another car came in headed the wrong way, and the frowning attendant glared at them as he adjusted the pump handle. He had the hood up when a white pickup rolled in, going in the right direction. The driver's window was down, his elbow resting out in the chill November air. Sherman started talking to the man in earnest, telling him he had to get to Scranton because his sister was there and he had to take the dog, and could they ride in the back of the pickup, when the attendant came around the front of the truck. "If you don't head down that road right now and stop bothering my customers, I'm going to go inside and call the county sheriff."

Sherman opened his mouth to speak.

"No buts," the attendant said. "Either you go down that road right now or I call the cops. Take your pick."

Tugging at the dog's rope, Sherman tore from the pickup window and marched past the attendant. Angry tears stood in his eyes. He knew when the cards were stacked against him, knew when to keep his mouth shut. He jerked the dog to him, moved down the drive, crossed the highway, and slipped into the ditch so he could let the Chinaman loose. His good hand was curled tight on the blackjack in his pocket. He wanted to take it and beat that sonofabitch to death. He hadn't gone very far when he heard a horn honk and saw the white pickup truck swerve to the side of the road above the ditch. It's about god-dammed time, he thought.

He squatted down in a corner of the truck bed, pulling the dog in beside him, and the irregular houses and foothills and pockets of trees wheeled alongside the truck and sank away in an ever-deepening V.


By the time Sherman hopped down from the bed of the truck, uneasiness was nagging at him. He held the Chinaman's collar with his bandaged hand, waved thanks to the driver, and watched the pickup rattle out into the steady flow of Wednesday-afternoon traffic. They were alone in a strange place, but what he felt was more like panic than loneliness. From the truck bed, he had seen three patrolling police cars and now the air seemed charged with hostility. This is not a good place, he thought.

The highway crooked down into the basin of the city and narrowed to a street. There, as far as the eye could see, loomed the city of Scranton. At his feet, the sidewalk thrummed as if from some deep pounding. Under the vast network of poles and wires, between what seemed like stacks of buildings, rivers of cars darted and blared. The air stank of electricity and sulphur. Backfire, gunfire, blowout. The sky glimmered of itself like the green-gold wings of flies. Factory whistles blew, church bells struck, and sirens shrieked in the air with sudden death. Like evil tidings, all his worst expectations had come home to roost in his mind. If Mamie had been brought here, how would he ever find her?

He stood there transfixed for several seconds, feeling himself shrink smaller and smaller. Trembling with hate, he muttered, "We gotta get outa here. You stick with me, now. We gotta get through with this," and in a burst of furious urgency, he led the dog through the traffic to the nearest gas station.

He waited on the cement drive until the mechanic would talk to him; then Sherman asked if he'd seen a dark blue car come through here last night.

"There's lots of blue cars," the mechanic said, clicking his ballpoint with his grease-black thumb. "What kinda car was it?"

Sherman described the car with his hands. It had two doors, the trunk sloped down, it had bubble fenders in front and a snout for a hood.

The man said, "It sounds like a Chevy or Buick, '48 or '49." He turned the pages of a calendar showing naked girls posed in and around different makes of cars, and kept saying, "Does this look like it?" Sherman shook his head and shook his head, until finally he said, "That's a lot like it, only this one I'm asking about was blue." And the man said, "Now, that's a '48 Buick Roadmaster." But he hadn't seen one.

Another mechanic, in a garage, changed spark plugs while Sherman spoke to him. "Did you see a dark blue '48 Buick come through here last night about eleven o'clock?" The man studied the mean-looking dog and shook his head. Sherman had walked out into the daylight when the man said, "Who's drivin' that Buick?"

"A woman was drivin' it," Sherman said, coming back. He

took the larger photograph from his billfold and held it up, but out of reach. "Here's what she looks like," he said, "and there's this little girl with her."

The mechanic squinted his eyes and reset his cap. "Naw," he said.

Bit by bit, treading down the sides of the highway strewn with bottle caps like an idiot's spilled treasure, zigzagging back and forth through traffic from one gas station to another, he put his question together in a cohesive whole. Had any of them seen a blue '48 Buick drive through here around eleven o'clock last night? He described the car again when it was called for, showed the woman's picture, and eventually showed the picture of Mamie, although it worried him that Mamie's picture would probably appear in the newspaper soon enough and somebody might put two and two together. But nobody remembered seeing a blue Buick driven by a woman. And the afternoon passed slowly away.

Eventually he came to a gas station with an empty driveway. When the man acted friendly, Sherman said, "I was wonderin' if you could break this up for me?" He slipped one of the thousand-dollar bills from the other two and opened it with his fingers.

The man held out his hand. "Let me see that a minute."

Reluctantly, Sherman laid the bill on the calloused hand. He took a deep breath and exhaled it a little at a time.

"Where'd you get this?" the man said.

"Just found it." Under his arms, his shirt felt sticky. "You gonna break it or not?"

The man eyed him. "I don't carry that kind of money around here." He folded the bill lengthwise between his blunt fingers. "This's an awful lot of money for a kid to have in his pocket—practically brand new. S'never touched the ground." Keeping his face lowered, folding and creasing the money, the man glanced up at Sherman. "This money don't belong to you, does it? Where'd you get it?"

Sherman lunged forward and snatched the bill. "Give me back my *goddammed money!*" Hurtling at his side, the Chinaman's claws dug the glass countertop, his barking muzzle diving at the man, who had quickly stepped back. The potato-chip rack clattered to the floor. Sherman caught the rope and pulled the dog away. "There's nothing wrong with my money!" he shouted. And backed away, backed slowly away, not once taking his eyes from the man.

At five-thirty that evening, Sherman and the Chinaman stood pressed together in the doorway of a church not far from downtown Scranton. He had discovered nothing about Mamie—a whole day shot. Now he had to get some money he could spend. Soon it would be night and his head was beginning to hurt. He knew he should take another pill, shouldn't try to save them, but the pressure of the impending night weighed on his thoughts. He needed to get one of these large bills cashed before everything closed. As he struggled to piece together a scheme to break the money, a yellow taxicab rolled to the curb in front of a brick house across the street. The driver got out of the cab, cocked his cap at an angle, opened the back door, and lifted out a bag of groceries. He went to the front door of the house, rang the doorbell.

Squatting beside the Chinaman for warmth, Sherman studied the cabdriver. He was a young guy and he moved with a jaunty efficiency. A woman opened the door, they spoke, and the driver followed her into the house. Minutes later, the cabdriver reappeared, returned to the taxi, took out a big box of groceries, and went back inside the house. Sherman came to his feet. He understood what was taking place. The woman had called in an order at the grocery store and the cabbie was delivering it. His mother had done the same thing when the children had been sick with scarlet fever and she couldn't leave the house.

The cabbie came out talking to the lady, who was paying him. Sherman went down the church steps and into the street. Walking very fast, the cabdriver came through the gate and stepped out around the front of his cab.

"Hey," Sherman said, crossing the street.

The cabbie hardly glanced up. "How you doin'?" He sat down under the dome light of the cab, one leg dangling on the pavement. He spoke into a small black microphone, wrote something in a book, lit a cigarette. Sherman stood at the edge of the open car door.

The cabbie reached for the door handle. "Hey," Sherman said, "you do favors for people, ain't that right? I mean, like you took that woman her groceries. And stuff like that? Dontcha?"

The cabbie smiled. He had bad teeth. Crumbs of tobacco stuck to his lips. "Well," he said, "I don't deliver groceries for nothin'. I get paid." He gripped the padded door handle. He had a cocky, smirky grin and his face was angular and sleek and hard-boned; he looked clever like a fox, and Sherman liked him. The cabbie had his cuffs rolled up, and beneath the fine hair of his forearm a blue-and-red tattoo wiggled over his muscles.

"I've got a favor I need done," Sherman said. "I'll pay you whatever she did," and nodded toward the house.

The cabdriver glanced at him casually. "Look, kid, I don't have time to mess with you. I'm losing money." He threw his cigarette out, stepped on the butt, and pulled the door shut, but Sherman stood at the window, held the big bill up. "Look," he said through the glass. "Could you help me break this? Take it to a store or someplace and break it? I'd give you ten dollars if you would."

The sunlight was nearly gone. The car door opened, the dome light blinked on. The cabbie grinned. "What's that you've got there?" he asked.

"It's a thousand dollars," Sherman said. "A thousand-dollar bill."

"Well, where'd you get it?" He acted surprised and impressed.

"Found it."

"You did?"

"Yes, sir."

"Where'd you find it?"

"Just blowin' across the grass. It looks brand new."

"You live around here?"

Sherman looked straight at him. "Can you help me break it or not?"

"I'm thinkin' about it."

"Well, I wish you would. I need to get this broke."

"Just hold your horses," the cabbie said. "I better do some checking." He picked up the microphone and turned his head in to the cab. Sherman heard him say, "Breaker central," and then something else and, "I'm still on South Hampton. I'm gonna get a cup of coffee." The radio crackled and a woman's garbled voice fuzzed and snapped. The cabbie looked around at Sherman and winked. "Well, tell'er to keep her pants on." He laughed at his joke, signed off, and put the microphone down.

"Now," he said, turning his full attention to Sherman, "as I was saying, that's a hell of a lot of money to try to do anything with this time of day. Everything's practically closed. All the banks're closed, all the usual places. No grocery store's gonna have enough money to cash a bill that big."

As the sleek-faced cabbie talked, Sherman stuffed the bill slowly back inside his pocket. "I know it," Sherman said.

"I didn't say it was impossible," the cabbie said. "I just said it wouldn't be easy. I know a couple of places. . . . I know this one place in particular where a friend of mine's usually got a bankroll might be able to help us out. But it'd cost you—probably cost you a C-note."

"What's that?"

"A C-note's a hundred. I imagine that'd be his cut." The

cabbie sat on the edge of the car seat, in no hurry now, leaning over with his elbows on his knees and his feet planted on the pavement.

"That's pretty steep," Sherman said.

"I know it is." He was talking slow and friendly. "It sure is. But with money like that you can afford it. I'm just telling you the facts. That's one way we could go." He kept looking at Sherman from the corners of his eyes. "Then, of course, it's clear on the other side of town and I'd have to take time to arrange it and make the trip. I imagine altogether it'd run you another fifteen, twenty bucks for my time and expenses. Now that's one way we could go with this situation."

Sherman tried to calculate quickly how much it would cost all told and how much he'd have left over, but he couldn't. It was coming at him too fast, somehow; it made him extremely nervous. It seemed like a lot to pay, considering that before last night he'd never even seen a hundred dollars, much less a thousand. But even so, he thought, he and the Chinaman would still have plenty of money left afterward. "How long would it take?" he finally asked.

"Oh . . . probably half an hour, everything considered."

"How would we do it?"

"Probably the easiest way would be for me to just go and do it. You could give me the money and I'd go change it and meet you back here."

"What if you don't show up?"

The cabbie grinned; then he laughed. "Well, hell, kid, I'd show up if you paid me to do a job. What's the matter?"

"If you're gonna do it," Sherman said, "then I have to come, too."

"Okay. That can be arranged."

"And he goes, too."

The cabbie rolled his eyes toward the dog and turned back. "Look. That won't work. If somebody sees a dog in my rig, I get fired. That's the way it is. Health and safety regulations. Can't do it."

Sherman shook his head. "He goes too, or I don't go."

The cabbie put out his hand to pat Sherman's shoulder and the Chinaman barked once and began to growl. He removed his hand. "Let's see if we can't work this out. Why don't you two get in the car?"

They sped through the city, lights glowing and sinking past. Bounced across railroad tracks, and made their way through a dark area of empty-looking warehouses. At one point, they wove through traffic over a long black bridge and dropped in among rows of car lots and drive-in restaurants swarming with traffic. Sherman sat on the back seat with the Chinaman tall beside him. Once they were moving, the cabbie kept up a constant chatter. He asked Sherman what'd happened to his hand, but Sherman was busy studying their route and left his answer deliberately vague. "Hurt it," he said, "working on an old car."

"Wasn't battery acid, was it?"

"Nope."

The cabdriver had agreed to take them back to their original starting point when the transaction was over. Even so, Sherman felt swept along on an irreversible plunge through the night; he kept struggling to track their direction with landmarks he could remember. The taxi bucked and rolled with the uneven streets, stopped at red lights, then sped away. The steering wheel had a knob on it that the cabbie used to drive one-handed. The radio squawked unintelligibly, and over it the other radio played tunes. *So Halo, everybody, Halo. Halo is the shampoo that glorifies your hair. . . .*

The taxi slowed in front of a low building covered in tar-paper brick. Its name blinked in neon above a flat red door, ALIBI BAR & GRILL. Hanging in the one large window, signs glowed in the gathering dark: a fiery red dot, a delta of pale yellow, three intersecting rings, and the letters L E N M O from the middle of the Glenmore Whiskey advertisement. "Okay," the cabby said, turning back over the front seat. "I know this place don't look like much, but this guy's got the money. Runs a poker game in back sometimes. So . . . let's go. Let me see it."

Sherman just looked at him.

"Hell's fire," the cabbie said, and slapped the top of the seat. The Chinaman swung, snarling, toward the noise. "Look, I can see you're all pissed off. But you seem like a nice kid. I'm just tryin' to work things out. Hey, kid, come on. Really, now, I can't take all night."

"We have to do it together," Sherman said.

"But we are. We are doing this together. Here, I'll show you." The cabbie turned off the motor, opened the door, and got out. He closed the front door and opened the back door next to Sherman. "This is the place," the cabbie said, stooping to look in at them. "As you can see, it's a tavern. Now, you can't go in there for just one reason—you're not old enough. You know that, don't you? And they're sure as hell not gonna let a dog in there. Why don't you give me the money? I'll go in, break it, and come right back. I'm gonna leave you here in my cab. I don't never leave anybody in my cab. Nobody. You get it? This cab is my life. But because you're so het up, I'm gonna let you stay right out here, in my cab, till I get back. And—well, if that don't suit ya—if this ain't good enough for ya—well, then you can just take your mutt for a walk and we'll call it quits." Underneath his controlled voice, the cabbie sounded mad as hell.

Sherman glared at him, his face burning, his voice short and clipped: "I thought you said you'd take us back downtown."

"That's correct. Considering I was gonna make twenty, twenty-five bucks on this deal. Come on," he said, his voice hard and just as short, "let's get this over with." He snapped his fingers.

Rigid with indecision, Sherman realized he didn't trust him.

As much as he wanted to, as much as he admired the cabbie's
jaunty efficiency, when it came to handing over the money, the
suddenness of it only intensified his misgivings. And yet it had
to be done. Feeling as though he had no choice, Sherman dug
the bill from his pocket and handed it over. He immediately felt
stripped of power, immediately regretted it.

As he watched the cabbie entering the tavern, he grew more
and more suspicious that something was wrong, but he couldn't
untangle what it was. After all, he was sitting in the cab and the
driver would have to come back to it sooner or later. The beer
lights glowed on the steamy window glass above the sidewalk.
Slowly the interior of the taxi chilled. The Chinaman sat beside
Sherman, his eyes alert, scanning the night. But the driver didn't
return.

Sherman began to lose control. Scarcely five minutes had
passed before he thought he should go after the cabbie, find out
what he was doing, and get his money back one way or the
other; at the same time, he knew he shouldn't leave the cab.
What could be taking so long? He sat back in the seat, swinging
his foot, kicking the slack fabric of the seat in front of him. He
considered leaving the Chinaman in the taxi and going into the
tavern alone, but the dog would probably have a fit, tear something up inside the cab, and there'd be hell to pay. More time
went by. Sherman remained in a frenzy of indecision until his
head began to ache; then he grasped the dog's rope and got out
of the cab.

Taking the Chinaman with him, he went to the tavern door
and stepped inside. Near the door, a clump of customers strag-
gled around three pinball machines. A jukebox blared in the
corner. Deafening noise filled the air—a swirl of jukebox music,
loud talk, laughter, pinball clatter, clinking glasses. The room
was long and dim, with red light bulbs strung down the center
of the ceiling. The only real light gleamed behind the bar.
Smoke and the stench of sour beer hung in layers. Through the

reddish darkness, indistinguishable shapes moved to and fro; eyes turned toward him as he edged forward searching for the cabdriver.

A pinball player whooped as Sherman passed by. It startled him and he jerked away. He moved down the long row of stools, men swiveling around, laughing, jeering, making fun. Somebody started making barking noises; somebody else yelled "Arf, arf!" The Chinaman struggled against Sherman's grip. A waitress came toward them with her hands on her hips. She was wearing a red outfit that laced up the front. She put her hands on her knees when she stooped toward Sherman. She had to talk loud. "Honey, you can't come in here." When she bent over, somebody gave a shrill whistle. The Chinaman slung toward it.

"I'm looking for that taxicab driver that came in here," Sherman said, above the din. "He's got something belongs to me." His eyes continually roamed the room beyond her, seeking that one familiar face.

"Son, nobody's walked through that door in fifteen minutes."

"He's the last one walked through it. I watched him."

The men at the bar were still teasing the Chinaman; the dog wrenched under Sherman's grip to snap at them. One of them was trying to give the dog a drink of his beer. The waitress leaned closer. "Somebody come in to use the bathroom a little while ago, but they left. Now, come on. You can't be in here with that dog. I'll lose my license."

"But nobody came outside. He didn't come out. I was watchin'." Sherman had to strain to be heard. "He said he was gonna talk with the owner."

"Sweetie, I'm the owner and nobody's talked to me about nothin'."

"That guy that went to the bathroom, where'd he go?"

"I don't know. I wasn't payin' much attention. He could've gone out the back."

His throat went dry. "You mean there's another door?"
"Yeah."
"Can I go that way? Go look?"
"Sure," she said. "You can look all you please. Come with me." She led him back among piles of cardboard beer cases to a door that opened with a long metal bar. She pushed it down and held the door open for him. When he stepped out, drawing the Chinaman with him, the door swung shut and he noticed there was no outside latch. The sidewalk was dark and quiet and empty. Then he heard it. From the street in front, he heard a motor rev and the scratch of tires, saw leaves flutter on the sidewalk. He turned quickly, yelling *"Chinaman!"* as he ran for the front of the building.

The taxi was gone. *Gone.* His thousand dollars. *Gone.* In his head blood pummeled. That bastard. He spun toward the red tavern door, his eyes beginning to water from the dull, throbbing pain in the crown of his head. They were all in it together. Laughing now, having a good time. Every damned one of them. The guy had left by the back door and waited for Sherman to come looking for him, knowing that he would. Then he had taken off in the taxi. Sherman ran up the buckling sidewalk to its crest, but he couldn't tell which way the cab had gone. On the streets and sidewalks there was no one to be seen, no cars to speak of except some parked at the curb, no traffic—just old newspapers blowing in the street.

Sherman hated this goddammed dirty street in this goddammed place in the middle of nowhere. He hated that trestle looming in the distance and the sound of the muddy river he could smell even when he couldn't see it, and he hated the dirty little pieces of spit snow that were beginning to fall.

He drifted back to the sidewalk in front of the tavern. The old rage was flowing now, and nothing could stop him from striking back. Cold wind whetted his eyes and the colored beer signs squirmed like inventions of the uncertain night and the

radio tune kept playing in his thoughts, *So Halo, everybody, Halo*
... Hello, sucker! That would be more like it. His mind whirled
as he stomped back and forth in front of the bar, the dog turning
with him. He was casting about for something to use, anything
that would really hurt. He could see the shapeless crowd
through the large window. He walked a few paces up the sidewalk and came back. Then he went away.

He was gone maybe fifteen minutes before he reappeared on
the buckling rise of the sidewalk. He uncapped the square tin
can of lawnmower gasoline he carried, tipped it over, and let it
gurgle and pour down the sidewalk toward the tavern door.
When it stopped running, he struck a match, dropped it at the
top end of the dark streak, and watched the fire shoot and climb
toward the door. *So Halo, you bastards, halo.* An ashtray came
flying through the window of colored lights, glass shattering
outward in dark, glittering shards. Someone was screaming,
"Fire!" The hole in the glass looked like a black, ruined mouth.
Inside, the place erupted in a roar, but he was hurrying away,
ducking between parked cars, across yards, into the alley where
he returned the gas can to the garage.

He hadn't the faintest inkling where he was.


It was morning before he got his bearings. Teeth chattering,
aching from the cold, he called the dog from the wrecked car's
dark interior where they'd slept. A frozen mist hung in the air.
Crossing a withered lawn, he picked up a bundled morning
newspaper and stuck it under his arm. They shivered back along
the sidewalks to the all-night gas station where Sherman had
stolen their supper—two bags of potato chips and a root-beer
soda—the night before. The sun was just beginning to rise on
the distant mountains as they entered the men's room at the rear
and locked the door.

Drinking from the tarnished faucet, he took his morning pill and noticed that the bottle was more than half empty. He wiped his mouth on the neck of his sweatshirt and stood under the warm air duct until he could stop shaking. His bandaged hand prickled as it warmed. Quietly he told the dog to stop nosing around. Dissolving cakes of pink antiseptic in the toilets enriched the air. He unrolled the newspaper. In the bottom corner of the first page he saw the story about Mamie, but it was not the story he had expected to see.

### KIDNAPPED GIRL SEEN WITH WOMAN

*Gambria, Pa.* State police joined with county investigators here late last night to search for Mamie Abbott, the seven-year-old girl abducted from the Nathan County Memorial Hospital in upstate Graylie. The child was reported missing at 5 a.m. Wednesday by the hospital staff.

In his briefing, State Trooper James T. Whalen confirmed that a local service station owner has discovered new evidence regarding the child's whereabouts. For the safety of the child, the nature of this evidence has been withheld pending further investigation.

According to other witnesses, the girl left the service station area in the company of an unidentified woman. Officials now believe that they were last seen traveling in a 1948 or '49 black or dark blue Buick.

Sought by police in connection with the alleged kidnapping, the woman is described as approximately 35 years of age, 5'7" tall, medium weight, with auburn hair and brown eyes and wearing an expensive fur coat. Pictured above, the missing child is described as approximately 3'4" tall with blonde hair and green eyes. When last seen, she was wearing a white parka.

Persons with any information regarding the whereabouts of Mamie Abbott or the woman matching this description are asked to contact law enforcement officials immediately.

It's her, Sherman thought. I knew it. He struggled through the article again, reading the words he knew, shaping the others with his lips until he could utter them and grasp what the article said. It's her. It's that same woman. That's what she looks like. He glanced at the paper a third time, caught in a tide of urgency to leave right away. Gambria. He'd have to get a map. But he still needed some money he could use. He tore the article from the newspaper, folded it, and stuck it in his shirt.

He took one of the two remaining thousand-dollar bills from his pocket and examined it. What's wrong with this money? he thought. There must be something wrong with it, it's no good. Since the minute he'd taken the money, he'd had nothing but bad luck following him like a curse. It's no-good luck, he thought. That's what Mamie would've called it when she was little. I've gotta get rid of the damned thing. A sudden impulse struck him just to throw it away, but he knew that would be really stupid. He spoke to the dog and opened the door.

The sun was up, casting hard shadows. Traffic chrome flickered on the cold street. Sherman and the Chinaman hurried away, along sidewalks and alleys. He led the dog down a flight of stairs to a basement pool hall. The colored balls clacked across the green tables. A tough-looking guy racked the triangle of balls, laughed, and shook his head. "Kid," he said, "you must be crazy."

"Where else can I break it, then?"

"Try the pawnshop. They might carry that kind of dough."

"Where's that at?" Sherman asked.

A block and a half farther south, Sherman and the Chinaman walked through the rat's nest of musical instruments and shelves of old jewelry, moldy books, typewriters, record players—a vast panoply of junk. The cigar-smoking pawnbroker examined the bill through a black-ringed glass stuck in his eye. "I'll give you five hundred."

"But that's a thousand-dollar bill."

The pawnbroker puffed four quick smoke rings into the air. The rings shimmied one after the other, widened, and were gone. "I can let you have five hundred," he said, clearing his throat. "I don't know where this comes from. The police trace this bill back to me, who takes the heat? You? No. I lose my shirt.

So I ask you no questions and you don't tell me no lies. Five hundred. No more." He shrugged and slipped the bill back through the slot in the barred window.

"Okay," Sherman said. "If you'll break it into little bills I can spend."

Now he would get a map.

# PART TWO

# 8

Just past noon on November 17th, the icy drizzle changed to snow. It was Saturday, but the stores were nearly deserted, there was very little traffic, and the snow spilled out across the sidewalks and curbs like rippling hand-snapped sheets. Under brooding clouds, the highway through Fielding Heights, Pennsylvania, slowly lost its boundaries. The blue Buick entered the city limits at low speed.

Leona had been behind the wheel since they'd left the motel at dawn, and the monotony of travel had put Mamie back to sleep by midmorning—curled on the seat beside her under a blanket. As she drove, Leona watched the shifting alterations in the winter light and listened to the sound of the falling snow. It was like the beating of tiny wings, she thought, or an all but inaudible, wet, packing hiss. It made her so drowsy she could hardly keep her eyes open. She pulled the Buick to the curb and let it idle, relaxed against the seat and closed her eyes.

The strain of these days, the physical and nervous exhaustion, had drained her. They had been traveling for four days now, but the roads were often slick; the going was slow. At this rate, it would take longer than she'd planned to reach the place where she knew they would be safe. She hadn't been sleeping well in the motels at night, and during the day, the frightening reminder of the cracked window at her side clung to her always. With the roads becoming more and more hazardous, she knew she shouldn't go on, especially in her state of increasing fatigue, but it was almost as dangerous, she thought, to nap in the car on a city street in broad daylight. She needed to find a place where she could rest undisturbed for a little while—just long enough to regain her judgment and her strength.

But the calming hiss of the snow dispelled her logic. With her eyes closed, she heard Mamie's soft, sleeping breaths, and it was like the hypnotic music of a mermaid lulling her down into a whirlpool of sympathetic escape. For another few minutes, before she tended to Mamie and tried to go on, she dreamed of being tended to herself. It was an old memory, one that came to her rarely. She heard herself saying his name: "Alfred . . ." and her heartbeat caught in her throat; she could feel his warm embrace. Brimming with excitement, she wanted to tell him about the baby—news that would change their lives forever— but he touched her lips with his fingers and she arched beneath him, happy to be with him, happy in her body. Then, deep in the quick of her being, the yearning stirred, her old yearning for the sweetness she had only begun to enjoy. And had never forgotten. She wanted to be held that way again, to be sustained by a loving whisper. Yet she knew that if she didn't resist, she would slip even deeper toward the dark burgeoning sleep she needed so badly. Her yearning diminished to a thin ache in her thighs but the memory of innocent passion lingered like a vivid fantasy. With all the strength she could muster, she forced herself up.

She pressed the heels of her hands to her eyes, shook the cold from her hair, and straightened the blanket on Mamie. When she drove up the slippery main thoroughfare, she passed only a few cars—those that did venture by must have been handled by drivers familiar with the dimensions of the sloping street. The cars seemed to lunge forward in slow motion, tires softly walloping in the snow. At the center of each intersection, under dangling traffic lights, stood a massive corn-shock and many of the shopwindows were still decorated with cutout goblins and witches.

After only a few minutes, Leona knew she couldn't go on, not in this foul weather as tired as she was. Mamie was waking up. Still looking for a place where she could rest, Leona noticed the lights chasing through the bulbs of the Old Mill Run movie marquee and the small cluster of people buying tickets. Gene Autry and *Mighty Joe Young*, a matinée double feature.

"Why don't we go to the picture show?" Leona said, carefully making a U-turn, and going back. "Yes," she went on after a moment, "I think we should go, don't you?"

Rubbing her face, Mamie sat up, awake and rigid, staring out the window.

In the lobby they bought tickets and a red sack of popcorn for Mamie. Leona was aware that she moved rather guardedly, watching and holding on to Mamie's hand. It made her uneasy to be out with the child in public. But I can't keep her prisoner in the car, she thought, and she felt some protection in the drifting matinée crowd. A uniformed usher showed them to seats Leona chose at the side of the theater; she sent Mamie in first and took the aisle seat herself. The cartoon was ending. As soon as Mamie was comfortable, Leona settled lower in the seat until her knees touched the back of the seat ahead. If Mamie tried to leave, she would have to go past her.

There was another interlude before the first picture began; a time for the Jan Garber orchestra to perform on the screen. The music was soft and romantic, as lazy as a stream. Maybe a third of the seats were taken, but against the glow from the screen, the other moviegoers were shadowlike; faces, when they turned, were only half exposed. So for now, enclosed in semidarkness, they were safe. Leona shut her eyes.

Her sleep was half sleep, the gray figures of the mammoth

screen flickering on her eyelids and wandering thoughts. She took Mamie to the rest room between features, and afterward gave her chewing gum from her purse when she seemed restless. It was toward the end of the second movie that Leona heard a small creaking noise at the side of the screen and saw a crack of light in the exit passageway; the outside door was quickly opened and shut. She thought she heard whispering; a shadow appeared at the exit doorway and retreated. What was going on?

She straightened in her seat. After a moment, she saw emerging from the exit doorway two small children, one holding something. They stopped, whispered to each other, and then moved forward along the front-row seats, the vast screen making outlines of their heads and shoulders. They're sneaking in, Leona thought, amused and touched. They looked very small to be taking such risks and she wondered about them. Don't get caught, she wanted to tell them, or you'll be in hot water. They seemed so small and frightened. She watched them until they vanished in the dark.

At the bottom of the theater, the children stood very still, watching as the pale reflection of the movie struck the empty seats and illuminated the faces in the closer rows. "I can't see him," the little girl whispered. "There's too many faces in here." The boy turned to her, holding out a wrinkled photograph. "He's gotta be here," he said. "He's gotta be. We just have to find him." They edged forward and hesitated beside a man in an aisle seat, looking at him and then looking at the photograph. The two didn't match. Then they saw a woman and a little girl sitting together watching them, and as they went past, the woman said, "Is something wrong? What's the matter?"

But they didn't answer. Still holding the photograph before them, they went up the long aisle ramp, searching through the screen-lit faces for that one face—the only one who could make everything all right again, the way it used to be.

The letters they had waited for weren't like the other letters their mother sometimes received; they were blue envelopes of thin, crackling paper and she had to slice them open with a razor blade to read what they said. The letters didn't have any sheets of paper in them, either. The words were written on the inside of the envelope and it had to be taken apart carefully. They were like magic to Patsy and Walter.

When these letters came, their mother tore them or cut them crooked more than once hurrying to get them open, and she had to tape the bad places. She would read them through greedily, her eyes sparkling. There were parts of the letter she would read aloud to them and parts she couldn't. "Now here, for a little bit," she would explain, "he writes just to me, something for just your daddy and me to know, private things," then she would go on reading. The children stood next to her and watched and listened as she pointed to the tiny words and read. If they asked, or if she noticed they were puzzled, she stopped and told them what a canteen was and that Korea was clear on the other side of the ocean. In the end, their daddy always wrote that he loved them, and she choked sometimes and hugged them to her soft, sweet-smelling dress.

Lifting them up, she would carry them to the framed picture hanging from a red, gold-tasseled cord above the divan, and it was like a game they played over and over. She would tell Walter that the man in the picture with the Army cap on his forehead was his father, Private First Class Jerome Aldridge, and she'd ask if he remembered his daddy. "I remember him," Patsy would say. "You do, doncha, Walter?" She was a year older, ready to start school in the fall, and she liked to help him make up his mind. Walter remembered his dad coming with their mother to meet them after the picture show, the same serious-looking man who wore the uniform and brought the goldfish in the white paper box full of water, and how they had fixed it a place to live in a mason jar. The next day, the man had called them into his mother's bed to read the Sunday funny papers. But sometimes Walter, who was barely five years old, acted as if he didn't know because he liked to hear his mother answer for him, "Oh, of course you don't, but you will. You'll remember when he comes home for good. You're just like him."

"When he comes to the train station and we go to meet him," Patsy said.

"That's right," their mother would say. "There'll be hundreds of people milling about, hundreds upon hundreds, and then we'll see him in the crowd and we'll all be together."

Walter always asked, "But what if we can't find him?"

"Then we'll just have to take this picture with us, and we'll look at the soldiers and we'll look at the picture, back and forth, until they match and then we'll know we've found the right daddy."

And then Patsy would say, "But, Mommy, who do I look like, though? Am I gonna look just like you?"

"Oh, no!" their mother would exclaim. "With your red hair, you'll be lots prettier than me, like—well, like Hedy Lamarr." And sometimes she picked up a magazine from the coffee table and showed Patsy the picture of the beautiful catlike woman.

If it was Saturday, they had to hurry or they'd be late when the Turnbull girls came for them. Their mother would help them put on their coats, and then she'd stand on the porch, waving, as they left for the matinée double feature at the theater two blocks away. And she was always there waiting under the overhang of glittering lights when they came out blinking from the show, eager for them to tell her everything that had happened, starting with the cartoon and the cowboy story, the jungle show, and the newsreel with the train in it, and the hundreds upon hundreds of cheering people just like she said it would be; and she always picked the cowboy story to hear first, and she would say, "Oh, no, they didn't!" and "Oh, surely not!" and laugh as they went back home through the late afternoon. "What happened next?" And Patsy—and then Walter—would tell her. "Oh, boy, I bet you were scared then, huh? So what happened next?" And they would laugh and tell her everything. It was the best time.

For an eternity then, two or three weeks, no letters came, and when she was cross with them she told them she was at her wits' end, she had tied herself up in knots. She said they would just stop waiting for the letters and they pretended to, but another kind of letter came, and when she read it, she turned white and fell down in a chair. She held the letter up to read it again, but her hand was shaking too much and she wadded it up. In the cupboard she found a bottle with dust on it. The bottle was half full and she couldn't get it open with her shaking hands. She kept squinching her eyes to get the tears out, and they were asking, "What's the matter, Mommy? Who's it from?" Finally she grabbed up her dresstail and twisted the cap off with that. She drank from the bottle till it was empty, roaming the house from room to room, like the goldfish in the jar, with them tagging after her, asking. And she said, "I'll tell you. But please . . . give me a little time to think."

She pressed the letter flat against her knee, then folded it and put it in her purse. She sat them on the divan, arranged their clothes, their legs sticking straight out. "Now, listen carefully," she said. "Mommy has to go out now for a little while and I can't take you with me and I don't have time to find somebody to stay with you. Now, I want you to sit right here. Don't move off this couch. Will you do that for me?" They both nodded. "I'll come back or send somebody just as soon as I can. But I want you to stay sitting right here. You promise? Tell Mommy you promise."

"I promise," Walter said softly, with his chin in his shirt collar, and Patsy said she promised too.

Leaning over, with the burnt smell on her breath, she kissed them. She went into the bedroom and quickly reappeared with white crescents of powder on her face and a sweet air of perfume. Without taking her coat, she hurried out the door, clutching her purse. The mail flap clacked.

A stillness settled through the house, the light changing and shifting ever so slowly on the window blinds; the two clocks ticked—the one on the living-room shelf and the one in their mother's bedroom. Her absence was everywhere in the house, but only one thought sank in Walter's mind: something awful's happened and Mommy's not coming back. The thought kept repeating itself. And eventually he muttered his fear to Patsy, who looked just as scared as he was. "She said she'd come back," Patsy whispered. But she had never before left them like this. The afternoon droned on. The sound of the street outside came to them muffled—the throbbing passage of cars, school kids yelling on their way home. And no one came. His fear burrowed in and he wanted to go to the toilet. "You better not," Patsy said. "You promised." It was getting dark. Still he tried to wait. She's not coming home. Nighttime came into the room, and he couldn't hold on any longer. "I have to," he said, and slid off the couch, but it was too late: the hot, yellow stench fumed around him, and wet stripes darkened his pants legs. Tears flooded his eyes and his nose was running and he hid his wail in his hands.

In his misery, he didn't hear them come in, but the lights were on and Uncle Barney was there, and Aunt Maggie, and others, too, and Patsy ran to them. "Walter peed his pants." He heard his mother saying, "Let me go to him. I can make it," and she came weaving across the room, bumped the coffee table, and loomed down beside him. Her face looked mashed and red. "It's okay, it's okay, Waltie."

"I had an assident," he said, sobbing.

"Oh, that's okay. I don't care at all," she said.

"But I promised I wouldn't . . ."

"I know you didn't mean to. Mommy knows. Let's see if we can't lie down. Just the two of us."

Across the room he saw Patsy high in Uncle Barney's arms. "But I'm not tired," he wailed.

"I know," she said. "But I am. So tired, and you'll feel lots better."

She helped him clean up with soap and a washcloth. He put on his pajamas, and she was sitting by his bed asleep when Walter closed his eyes.

In the night, he awoke with the foot of his bed stacked deep with coats. The door to the living room was open a crack and a blade of light cut across the room. He could hear a buzzing spiral of voices.

"All it says is he's missing in action."

"Missing in what action?"

"I know he's gone. I can feel it."

But when Walter stepped under the arched doorway, blinking, no one was talking. They were sitting on the divan and on chairs and the arms of chairs; their heads were bowed and all the lights were on, but no one was talking. Patsy, he noticed, was asleep on Aunt Maggie's lap. "Mary, get him," someone said. "Poor little guy missed his supper. Must be starved."

"That's all right," his mother said, and picked him up. "I'll do it." And she was telling him, "We don't know for sure, but I don't believe your daddy's coming home."

Maybe the children would have remembered it as a dream, but the next morning there were cups and saucers all over the living room, on the windowsill, on the arms of chairs, on the floor, and their mother had to pick them up and Patsy and Walter helped. But there never was any funeral, just a black ribbon twined around the red cord of the photograph. And for the length of that summer their mother still waited for the mailman to come. Only now, instead of being nervous and ill-tempered when the letters didn't come, she was distracted and slow. Every day, she collected the mail from the foyer floor and shuffled through it, her face a stone of disappointment.

One hot day, the goldfish died because, she said, the water wasn't any good, but they knew she didn't like the goldfish. She had done it. She forgot to feed it and it died; the mason jar full of water, the colored rocks that grew into a weird knotty castle, the little box of food—all were gone. They would have buried the goldfish, but she threw it out with the trash and they never saw it again. Walter asked if they could get another one, but she said no, she didn't want to take care of it. Walter said he would take care of it, but she said no and that's final.

By July, she was drinking whiskey every day. She didn't worry about her looks, left her hair in bobby pins most of the time, day and night, with a cloth wrapped around her head and knotted in front. She didn't powder her face or bother to put on lipstick, and she looked as if she had washed her face too hard, it was so blank. Some days she didn't even change out of her nightgown. For a while, she hardly scolded the children at all, barely went through the motions, leaving them to their own devices. And they knew she didn't want to be bothered—she was cross most of the time—knew she didn't want them around. Every day when they were up and had dressed themselves, Patsy asked her what she wanted them to do today, and usually she said, "Don't bother me," or "Go play," or "Just get out of my way." And then she would look from Patsy to Walter. "Look after him, Patsy. He's your baby brother." She didn't like to hear the picture-show stories any more, and one Saturday she forgot to come and meet them for an extra long time. After that she just told them to come home with the Turnbull girls.

On rainy days when they couldn't go outside, she sometimes let them make her drinks. They knew how she liked them. Walter stood on the kitchen counter to get the glass and Patsy climbed on a chair to reach the ice cubes. Four ice cubes in the glass, fill it up with whiskey, then dig a red candied cherry from the slim jar and float it on top. Patsy hopped down from the chair and, using both hands, carried the full glass to the bed-room. Once, when they reached the doorway, Walter said, "Let me give it to her this time," and carefully, not spilling a drop, they switched hands on the glass. She took the glass from him but, hardly glancing at it, flung it against the wall, the glass breaking, the amber liquor splashing everywhere. "Don't ever serve me my drink in a short glass," she said, the tip of her cigarette bouncing up and down as she spoke. "I want my drinks in tall glasses. Gimme another one and do it right." Another time, when they were late coming home, she threw her drink in Patsy's face so fast she couldn't blink, and the whiskey hurt her eyes. Then, because it was their fault, she told them to mop it up.

Adrift, they did all the things she would never let them do. They climbed the high trees behind their house; they swung on grapevines; and once Walter even went to the river with the older boys. Patsy said, "You better not, Walter. She'll be mad at you. She'll be *awful* mad." But he didn't fall in the river, as his mother always said he would. No currents sucked him under.

When she thought they were really bad, she made them hold out their hands. They would beg her: "Mommy, please don't milk my mouses." But she would catch their fingers in hers, folding them down in a deep indrawing clench until the fingers nearly ruptured at the joints. And they squealed and squealed. "See," she said, "that's what bad little mice sound like." The one time Walter went to the river, she asked where he'd been and he didn't lie. He told her he didn't fall in. That night, giving him a bath, she was supposed to be washing his hair when she dipped him back to rinse it and plunged his head under the water. She held him under till he couldn't breathe. He thrashed and kicked, water flying, his body squeaking and thumping on the bottom of the tub until at last she drew him up. Patsy stood screaming in the doorway, afraid to come in and afraid to leave, shouting at her to stop. "That's what happens to bad boys who won't listen," his mother said while he coughed and spit bathwater and tried to scream. "Next time you'll drown."

Afterward she held him on her lap and pulled Patsy up in her other arm. She hugged them and asked them to forgive her. "Mommy's sorry," she said, her words slurring, "Mommy gets a little under the weather sometimes and she don't know what she's doing. But you kids have to do your part, too. You should stay away from Mommy when she's like that."

"But I told the truth," Walter said, weeping. "You said to tell the truth."

"Then let's pretend this never happened. That's what we'll do. Forget all about this like it never happened, and go back to the way we used to be. Okay? Whaddaya say?" But she couldn't go back, and it was as if they had two mothers and most of the time they couldn't tell which one she was. They tried to stay away from her, ran from her. "I'll look out for you, Walter," Patsy said. "If I yell, go hide." But now, when their mother wanted to give him a bath, he hid all by himself until she said they wouldn't use the bathtub, only a washcloth and soap, or until she just forgot and changed her mind.

Sometimes the neighbors let Patsy and Walter come to their house for supper, something the children liked to do, except that their mother might decide to come find them. She always smiled to the neighbors and made excuses, but she turned on them at home. One night, she told them to go in the shed outside and lock the door, she was so mad she didn't know what she might do otherwise. They hid under the house where she couldn't crawl. Other nights, they would go home dreading that they would find her crying or reaching from place to place to get across the room, or mad at them, ready to slap them with her wedding-ring hand that cut.

Mrs. Petrie, a big bouncy woman from down the street, appeared every so often to "wet her whistle," as she put it, with a jigger or two of whiskey. "Adele, honey," she said, "you've

got to pull yourself out of this thing. You're a living mess. Why
don't you come out with me sometime to the Capri Club, down
on Delacroix? Have yourself some fun?"

Their mother said she didn't think so.

But it didn't take many of Mrs. Petrie's visits before the
picture came down from above the divan: the black ribbon, the
gold tassels, all of it gone, like the goldfish—only "put away,"
their mother said. Where it had hung, the wallpaper was lighter
and it was worse than having the picture there, she told Mrs.
Petrie.

Even when the days began to dwindle and darken, as long
as it was warm enough to play outside, she let them stay till
night in the neighbors' yards—the Turnbulls', or the Snyders'
—and she would leave in the late afternoon for the Capri Club
in a clean dress, her hair brushed soft and pretty and her lips wet
red, almost the color of their daddy's red Ford coupe she'd
promised she wouldn't drive, but did.

About the same time, she had the telephone put in her bedroom where she spent hours, talking and laughing. On the first
day of school, she took Patsy to meet her teacher, leaving Walter
in the car while she was gone. But after that Patsy walked to
school with the neighborhood kids. One evening, Suzie Turnbull told Walter he couldn't come to their house any more
because her mommy didn't want them to associate with each
other because she didn't think highly of his mommy because she
had sex and that's bad. "*You* ask her," Patsy said as they went
to the kitchen. "No, you do it," Walter whispered and they
argued, in whispers. Most of the time it was Patsy who got them
in trouble, but it was Walter who got punished.

"Mommy, what's sex?" Walter finally asked her.

"I don't know. Why?"

"Is it like a fever?"

"It must be." And all the time she kept telling him it was a
bad dream when the noise woke him at night and he went to

crawl in with Patsy. "It's just a bad dream, Walter," she would say, coming to their door. "Just an old nightmare. Go back to sleep."

But when the night noise woke them up, it didn't end like a dream—it kept going a little louder and on and a soft, sawing, creaking noise, like a train rumbling and squeaking far away. "What is it?" Walter said, staring at his sister in the dark. Patsy stared back at him. "I think it's some monster!" And they hid under the covers—until they decided it *was* a train—the sound of a train bringing their daddy home, and they listened to the creaking lullaby rhythm, and threaded through it came their mother's whimpered complaints as if she were sad and fighting for breath, Uh-ah, again and again and quicker until it was louder than the train noise, and Patsy said "It's Mommy!" and Walter said "She's hurt!" And he had to use the toilet.

Moonbeams lit the hall in intervals. Their feet padding on the hardwood floor, they hurried to her bedroom door and took turns peeking through the keyhole where a soft light glowed on the other side. Patsy turned the knob and pushed the door open far enough for them to slide into the shadowed room; there was a smell in the room like candle wax. A man's pale back rode up in the shadows and the loud creaking noise ricocheted around the room; their mother's moaning flattened in their ears and Patsy said, "Don't hurt Mommy," but her voice faded to nothing, and then Walter tried to speak but he was too afraid—he had to go to the toilet too bad to step farther into the room. The man fell off to the side and the bed bounced. They heard him mumbling in the pillow, his voice smothered, and their mother was sitting up, holding the sheet across her. "It's okay, sweetie. We were only fooling around with each other. Just carrying on. You needn't worry. It's okay. Really."

Patsy took a step forward, but drew a quick breath and stepped back. It flickered across Walter's mind that the last time, when his dad brought the little box with the holes in the top so the fish could breathe, there had been that same noise in the morning before the funny papers and she had been hiding his dad in her room all night as a surprise. He scooted a step into the room and whispered, "Mommy, is Daddy home?"

"No, baby . . . Ah, Davy, don't be mad, don't be mad, he's just a baby—he don't know. . . . I told you, sweetie . . . I told you. Oh, hell, goddammit, Walter . . ." She put the back of her hand over her mouth because she had said a bad word, and she rubbed her eyes with the insides of her wrists the way she did when her hands were dirty and she had a bad cold. "Go back to bed now."

"I hafta go to the toilet."

Patsy said, "Walter, let's get outa here. Come on." She reached out and grasped his arm, but he pulled away from her, and their mother said, "Well, go ahead, then, Walter. You can go by yourself."

"Can't either, in the dark."

"You can turn the light on. Just close the door first and then turn it off when you leave. You can do that."

"Can't reach it."

"You can too. You reach it all the time. Do it this once for Mommy."

Louder. "Can't reach it." He looked for Patsy, who had backed all the way out to the hallway.

"All right, then." She yanked her robe into bed with her. Flopping from side to side, she covered herself. "Come on. Hurry up." She flipped the bathroom light on; the light shone fan-shaped in the bedroom and he walked through it into the bathroom. She shut the door.

On the other side of the wall, they had words, angry and hurried. The man said, "That's it, Adele, that's it." And before Walter had finished, he heard their voices trickling away in another room. He's going away, Walter thought, and flushed the toilet. The razor strap was gone from the nail. She had taken it when she reached for the light switch.

He felt a prickly quickening in his groin. Stretching above the top row of tiles, he turned the light off and went out. The pink bedside light was on and his mother sat perched on the side of the bed, legs crossed, pressing a glass of yellow ice cubes against her forehead. "I hope you're proud of yourself," she said. "Couldn't quite reach the light switch, huh? C'mere." She had on her high-heeled slippers with the puff feathers on the toes, and by swinging her leg and flexing her toes, the slipper swung and clapped against her heel. Next to her on the bed was the razor strap.

"It wasn't any nightmares," he said, his voice fluting. "You lied." He looked toward the hall again; the bedroom door was standing open and empty. "Where'd Patsy go to?"

"C'mere, Walter." Her voice was low and steady. "If I have to come get you, it'll be twice as bad. You've been asking for this for a long time."

Now the man was slouched against the door frame with a cigarette dangling from his lips, and she was off the bed, her robe falling loose and open, the dark taper of hair and the rosettes of her ponderous breasts rushing toward him. She grabbed his arm as he ran, threw him over the bed, and pushed his head down with her hand between his shoulder blades. She didn't take time to lower his pajama pants, but it didn't matter. The razor strap sizzled as it flew and struck. The sharp pain slashed into his clenched buttocks again and again.

When she let him up, he stood away from her slowly, choking to find his voice. "I don't like you no more," he told her. "You lied to me, you killed my fish. We can't ever go to the Turnbulls' again."

"I never said that," she said, returning from hanging up the razor strap, her robe shifting apart, her thighs and stomach and breasts blotchy with dark bruises.

He let loose with all his venom. "They did, though. They said we couldn't. Cause their mom don't think highly of you and she don't want them and us to *adsoserate* together with each other cause you've got *sex* and that's *why!*" He choked and pointed at the bruises. "See," he said, "you've got it."

She stopped in midstride, pulled her robe shut, her face awry. "Well, that old windbag. If that's what they talk about, it's a damned good riddance. But who taught you to talk to your mother like that? Suzie? Talking about things you don't know a damn thing about." She shoved him toward the door. "Now go back to bed, and leave me be." He started to go, but the truth of it struck him and he turned, lifting his hands up in supplication. "Now I can't never go with 'em to the picture show no more." But she pushed him—"Get going"—and he fell, scrambled up, and ran past to their room, where Patsy was hiding under the covers.

He climbed in beside her and lay there, crying, the tears running into the pillow. He cried about the letters that didn't come and the goldfish in the trash and the hundreds upon hundreds of cheering people in the newsreels he couldn't go see. And when he couldn't breathe from crying, he sat up and wiped his face and wept noisily.

Suddenly the ceiling light was on and Patsy was screaming, "Go hide! Walter, go hide!" jumping up herself and running from the bed, but the man was bending over him. "Puttin' up quite a little ruckus in here, ain't ya?" There was a strange smile on his face. "Sounds like to me you like to cry. Enjoy it. Keeping people up all night. How'd you like something to really cry about?" Quick as lightning, the man boxed his ears, first on one side, then on the other, box, box, that quick and hard, hands like iron, and it happened so fast there was no pain at first, just a drumming sound in his ears, and then the pain flowed into his head and everything blurred. His mouth sprang open, but nothing came from his lips and the room was turning dark, the light going out in dim washes, and his mother was in the room. He barely heard her say, "You've really hurt him," but the man took her by the arm and turned off the light, drawing her away, and the scream grew out of him, riding out of his body on the waves of his pain.

Walter stayed in bed most of the next morning, holding his hand on his left ear that wouldn't stop hurting. Patsy didn't go to school, but stayed with him in their room, trying to get him to play. That's when she told him, "We have to find Daddy." And they made their secret plan.

Their mother was talking on the telephone. When he went to the bathroom, he found a drying rack in front of the door to her bedroom, so he had to go in from the hall. And she told them not to come to her room any more at night unless they knocked. She didn't go to the Capri that evening, but the next day, in the afternoon, she told them to stay in the house, in their room, and behave themselves, she wouldn't be gone long.

When the front door closed and the house was quiet, Patsy wanted to leave right away, but Walter went to his mother's bedroom. He looked in all the bureau drawers, then went to the closet, which was full of a dry, woolly smell. "Come on," Patsy said. On the floor in the corner he found the picture with the dusty black ribbon and the faded red cord. Heavy as it was, he managed to get it up in his arms and was turning to bring it out when his shoe snagged on a fallen coat hanger and sent him sprawling. The picture flew out of his arms as he fell—flew out into the room and crashed. Patsy went to it and turned it over. The glass that had protected the picture was now broken in chunks and pieces.

"Uhhh," Walter moaned. "Oh, no," Patsy murmured, and they sat down, feeling across the splintered, jagged surface. All he had wanted to do was take it with him so they could pick the right face.

The picture had buckled forward on one side and he thought

he could get it out, but when he tried to, he cut three of his fingers and blood drops fell on the picture. His fingers didn't hurt, just stung, thin white cuts oozing his blood. "Now you've done it," Patsy said. Walter let out a long sigh, reached in, and pulled the picture out. The jagged edges of the glass scraped white grooves diagonally across the pictured face. He wiped the blood off the picture with his shirt, but now there was blood on its back. Patsy ran to the bathroom and got the Band-Aids. She put one on each of his three cut fingers and one on his forehead like the prizefighter in the newsreel. Walter folded the picture small and put it in his back pocket. Then they went to get their coats.

Bracing one foot against the wall, turning and pulling the big brass doorknob, they got the heavy door open and ran out into the cold afternoon, then fled down the sidewalk, the icy snow catching in their eyelashes.

At the intersection, they swung across the street in a slant and ran along the outer fringe of parked cars where the slush had been packed down by traffic. Up ahead, they could see the waterfall of the marquee lights. As he ran, Walter took the picture out, unfolded it, and then ran harder to catch up, following Patsy down the gritty brick alley beside the theater until they reached the exit door in back. "What if they won't let us in?" Walter asked her. "We forgot to get money."

"The other kids do it," Patsy told him. "Now, be quiet. Be real quiet. You go first."

"No, you go," Walter said. "I'm too scared." So while Walter studied the photograph once more, trying to memorize it, Patsy forced her fingers into the crack beside the door and got it open. Suddenly, she pushed him into the warm dark and stepped in herself, drawing the door shut behind them.

The movie cast a strange glow like moonlight on all the seats and faces. Patsy clutched at the stitch in her side while Walter held the picture, looking everywhere to see if anybody matched it, because Patsy said their father would be sitting in the audi-

ence. She had laughed at him and called him "cuckoo" when he
had told her what he believed—that this was where the train
would arrive, that the hundreds upon hundreds of cheering
people came down from the newsreel and went out with the
happy crowd. Trying to look at all the moonstruck faces, they
went up the aisle and heard the woman speak to them. But the
movie was ending; the people were standing up, putting on their
coats, and if everybody left how would he ever match the faces?
They darted across the inner lobby to the door on the other aisle,
only to find themselves in a sea of legs.

In minutes, the crowd trickled to a few stragglers. They
were too late. Walter slumped against the water fountain and
covered his eyes, sobbing with defeat.

# 9

Most of the crowd had left before Leona stood up, feeling restored. It was quarter of five. Momentarily she scanned the
gaudy trappings of the large sloping room; as the movie ended,
she had lost sight of the two children, and she wondered what
had become of them, if the ushers had caught them and run them
off. I could have paid their way, she thought, sorry that she
hadn't realized it sooner. She adjusted her coat around her, took
Mamie's hand, and headed up the ramp. As they entered the
lobby on their way out, they saw the children again—the little
girl and boy standing together near the water fountain. The boy
was crying and the girl appeared to be trying to comfort him.
Still refusing to speak, Mamie nonetheless looked at Leona and
tugged at her hand, pulling her toward the children. The little
boy was holding a large creased photograph in his hand. When
Leona asked them what was wrong, they said they were looking
for their daddy.

"Where is your daddy?"

"In the picture," the little boy said.

"You mean here in the picture show? Where is he now?"

"Right here," the girl said, and showed her the man's face in the photograph.

The lobby had emptied to three teenage girls buying licorice at the candy counter, and the few uniformed employees. Mamie pointed at the little boy's hurt fingers and the Band-Aids, then grasped Leona's coat sleeve and pointed to the bloody places on the boy's shirt. Leona thought, he must remind her of someone in her own family.

"Did he hurt himself?" she asked the little girl.

"Uh-huh," the child replied. "Taking the picture."

Talking to them—children who were lost and hurt—came to her so naturally that Leona didn't realize at first she could be risking everything. The sense of possible danger came only when she noticed they were making themselves conspicuous simply by remaining in the deserted lobby; the ushers were looking at them. And yet these children were so pitiful and helpless, how could she deny them a moment's kindness? She asked the little boy about the blue welt she could see under his hair; with a pang, she thought, He's really been hurt. His ear looks bruised. "Did you hurt your head?"

"No," he said. "Davy hit me."

"Who's Davy? Is he your daddy?"

He held his breath, then let it go all at once. "Nahh . . . he's just this guy." Looking at his feet. "He comes to our house sometimes. He comes to our house to sleep."

"But why'd he hit you?"

"Don't know." The little boy shrugged. "He said I kept him awake. That's what he said."

"Now, tell me the truth," Leona said. "Does your ear hurt?"

"No," he said, and shook his head. "It don't hurt any more."

Leona looked through the glass front of the lobby. Low in

the evening sky, the sun going down behind clouds created long, deep shadows; the angle of the light magnified the falling snow into fluttering white ribbons. It was time to take Mamie and go. She knew she couldn't get any more involved with these children; there was too much at stake. "Do you live nearby?" she asked them, and they nodded. "Then you should go on home." They looked at her doubtfully. "Really you should. Your mother and father will be worried about you. Mamie, come with me." She didn't wait for the children to reply; she had to remove her concern for them from her mind. "Go on home, now. That's the best thing to do."

She started to take Mamie's hand, but all of a sudden Mamie turned and put her arms around the little boy. "Why, Mamie," Leona said, "what're you doing?" And Mamie said, "No, they can't go. There's no more home."

It was the first time she had spoken, and her voice was small and rich. A thrill went through Leona. *That's Mamie's voice.* "Oh, Mamie," she said gently, taking her in her arms, "we can't stay here."

Once more, looking back at the children, Mamie said, "But there's no more home." She's thinking of that terrible fire, Leona thought, and she felt the depth of Mamie's loss.

She carried her down the sidewalk toward the Buick, parked five or six cars away. It was almost five o'clock, almost suppertime. In another half hour, the sky would be completely dark; in four hours, she would have to start looking for a place to spend the night. Leona dreaded getting back in the car, setting off again in the snow with night coming on. Across the street next to the corner, she saw a neon sign blink and softly begin to glow; SUGAR BOWL CAFE, it said. FAMOUS ICE CREAM.

Determined to keep the two children out of her mind, she fixed her concentration on the sign. I should at least get a cup of coffee, she thought. And Mamie needs something. "Umm," she said. "Ice cream. Doesn't that sound good? Let's get some before we go." Mamie looked up at her but otherwise didn't respond. There was no one in sight, nothing really to worry about. They crossed the street, the wet snow blowing around them.

The restaurant was in its late-afternoon lull. Two waitresses in red-and-white checked uniforms lolled against the cabinet behind the counter, chatting and painting their fingernails. Leona steered Mamie in front of her to the second table back in the long L of booths. She helped Mamie up in her seat and sat down across from her. It was chilly in the room and they would be here such a short while Leona decided they should unbutton their coats but leave them on.

"Well, Mamie," she said softly. "I know you can talk, because you just did. So you really will have to tell me what kind of ice cream you like." The gray-green eyes remained passive, looking away somewhere. "Which do you like best, chocolate or strawberry? I think I'd rather have chocolate myself."

Blowing on her spread fingers, the waitress, a very plain sixteen-year-old, came to take their order. She held the pencil with the utmost care. Leona ordered a cup of coffee, black, then a single dip of chocolate ice cream in one cone and a dip of strawberry in another. The waitress sidled away. Two women from a back booth squeaked by in galoshes and went out.

Leona had tried to position them strategically. Over the rim of Mamie's hair, she could see the front of the room, the door they had come in with its number, 211, the reverse of what it was outside, and the plate-glass window, its sill—halfway up the back side of the empty booths—lined with wilting Boston ferns. If anything suspicious happened on the sidewalk or street, she would see it in time to act. She watched passersby hurrying along outside the window. And the snow continued to fall. Somewhere a fly buzzed and it made her think of sound, snoring sleep. On the street, a car lumbered by and the errant sun's reflection on chrome blazed in her eyes. She winced, a streak of red on everything. Mamie's chin was just barely level with the tabletop. "We'll ask them to bring you a cushion," she said, squeezing her eyes shut.

In the self-created darkness, the red streaks receded and dissolved. The bell on the door jingled. When she opened her eyes, she saw the two children from the theater standing inside the door. They followed us here, she thought. They'll come over here, maybe want to sit with us. I can't have this . . . but what'll I say?

But they didn't. They looked about uncertainly for a moment and then climbed up side by side in a booth by the large window. Rising to her knees, Mamie peered at them over the top of the booth; then she waved at the little boy, who was sitting closer to her across the open corner of the L, and the little boy waved back. Who's going to look after them? Leona thought. As she fretted about them, the children looked at her and smiled. When the waitress went by, Leona said to her, "Give them whatever they want. I'll pay for it."

Only a few minutes had passed before a woman in her late twenties came through the door and walked unsteadily toward the children. "So there you are," she said, and Leona thought, That must be their mother. Blonde, blue-eyed, the woman might have been pretty if she hadn't looked messy and disarranged. The little girl was undeniably her daughter; there was no question about that now. The child was a small duplicate of her mother, except for her dark red hair. "Why don't you sit down, Adele?" the waitress said, delivering the Cokes the children had asked for. "Have a cup of coffee."

Without saying a word, the woman sat down across from the children. Her daughter said something, squirmed and shifted, her thighs squeaking on the plastic seat. "Don't lie to me," the woman said. Her voice was a surprise—hoarse, harsh. Her fingernails ticked on the table. Lifting her head, she looked for the waitress.

Three high-school boys slummed in, scuffing their heels as if they were trying to walk without lifting their feet. Suddenly they began punching each other on the shoulder, laughing, and one of them went up for an imaginary hook shot. At the counter they ordered a cherry Coke, a chocolate Coke, and a vanilla Coke. They flirted and made eyes at the waitresses. They played the jukebox. Then each of them seized a pinball machine. Everything was transformed. The air grew dense with the music and the crash-clatter-clang of the pinball machines. One of the boys started to dance with his machine, hips swaying, and now and then, he swung himself loose from it, his arms open wide in musical expression as he mouthed the words to the jukebox song: *"Baalue moon, you saw me standin' alone, you knew just what I was there for, you heard me sayin' a prayer for . . ."* Then he attacked the pinball machine again.

The waitress brought the ice-cream cones. Leona took both cones and asked for a cushion. Reluctantly the waitress brought one, lifted Mamie, and slid the cushion under her. It wasn't much of an improvement. "Your coffee'll be right up," the waitress said.

The blonde woman was sitting ramrod straight, hands folded in front of her, and the children were talking to her, but Leona couldn't hear what was being said. The street was darker now, the sunset all but gone, and in the different light Leona could see the woman's trembling fingers as they touched the tips of her hair, the vein that bounced in her tense throat. The waitress noticed that she was staring. "Don't mind her," she said, serving the coffee. "She drinks a little."

Embarrassed, Leona lowered her gaze. The jukebox had stopped playing. "Okay," she said to Mamie, "which do you think is best, the chocolate or the strawberry?" Again, Mamie leaned to the side until she could peek at the two children. "Then I'll choose. Let's see. I think I'll have the . . . the chocolate," but Mamie reached and took the chocolate cone. Leona had never before seen such determined contrariness in a child. Mamie heard everything she said, understood everything. Leona lifted the strawberry cone to her lips to conceal her smile.

Across the way, the little boy was having the same problem Mamie had had—he was swallowed up in the booth. Holding the glass of cola out like a torch, he drew one leg up under him and was bringing the other one up so he would be kneeling and tall in the seat, when the glass tipped in his hand and spilled.

There was a flash in the air; then, like the flick of a whip, the woman's hand came down and struck the little boy's face very hard. At the crack, Leona flinched, upsetting her coffee; it splashed into the saucer. No sooner did the boy cry out than he began to choke and fight back his tears.

The woman said, "I have told you and told you!" The cruelty in her voice bit into the air. "Now look at me! A goddam mess. And I spent hours."

"Mommy, we're sorry," the little girl said.

"It's a little late for your sorrys," the woman said, and her hand flew out and down. The boy was defenseless; the blow caught him broadside and he screamed and kept screaming. Mamie had come up out of her seat and was standing motionless in the aisle. "His ear!" the boy's sister pleaded. "Mommy, it's his ear! Don't hit his ear!" The woman's hand flew up again and she struck the girl square in the face, slamming her against the booth wall. In reflex, as if absorbing the blow herself, Mamie's hand crunched down on her cone, and the ice cream splattered on the floor. The woman twisted from the booth, splotchy with Coke, and tossed down a dollar. "You just wait till you get home!" She stalked out of the restaurant.

For a moment no one moved. In the booth, the children were crying. Leona looked at the waitresses and they stared back. One by one, the schoolboys slipped outside and were gone. It had happened so fast. The little girl huddled over her brother and then stumbled out into the room, the shape and definition of her mother's hand now clearly imprinted across her face. She choked to find her voice. "He's hurt! He's hurt!" She looked at Leona. "Please!" she shouted. "It's his ear! His bad ear!" The boy cowering in the booth still cried out.

Leona was too startled to act; tears stung her eyes. But Mamie had darted over to them, and suddenly she turned back. "Please," she said. "You gotta come."

"He's hurt," the little redheaded girl cried again. "He's really hurt!"

"You gotta, you gotta!" Mamie climbed into the booth, bending over the little boy, who hadn't moved. She was putting her hands around him, trying to help him get up. Leona went to them; she could hear the boy weeping and it tore her apart. She said to the waitress, "Do you have a damp cloth—anything?"

A wet dishcloth was brought to her and she said to the redheaded girl, "Now, stop crying. What're your names?" And Patsy told her.

When Leona touched the little boy, he jerked away and drew into a tighter ball. She could still hear him crying under the protection of his arms. "Mamie, here," she said. "Let me . . . let me look at him." Mamie moved out of the way.

First Leona tried to coax him out; then quickly she tried to lift him out, but it was no use. She kept asking him, "Are you okay?" He wouldn't budge. She sat down beside him and drew him into her arms. "There, now," she said, not knowing what else to say. "There, now. It's okay. It's okay. We'll make it all okay." She smoothed the unkempt hair and pressed the boy's head against her body. "Don't worry. It's okay to cry," and she could feel the small body give way against her; his arms came up around her and the anguish poured out of him in a long, trembling wail.

Leona had to look away to keep from being drawn into the child's pain. She nearly wept herself. We have to go, she thought. We have to get out of here right now.

No one else had come in. When she made a movement to

get up, the small arms held on to her even tighter. Automatically her own arms responded to his; she felt the truth of that feeling spill through her. Still holding him, she put her coat around him and slid from the booth and stood.

"This is a very fine boy here," she said, knowing the boy in her coat would hear her, too. Mamie was watching her intently, as if the words were visible as they came from her lips. "Look how fine he is." For a moment, Leona stood gazing at the little redheaded girl, the wet cheeks and eyelashes, the blood smeared on her small upper lip; then she handed her the wet dishcloth. "Here, Patsy, let's clean you up. We can't have a pretty girl like you looking like this."

"I can do it myself," Patsy said. Slowly, Mamie tilted her body and looked at the boy, who was now hardly crying at all, his face buried in Leona's coat. Leona looked compassionately at his sister. And then at Mamie. She took the dishcloth when it was handed to her, put it aside and went back to stroking the small head pressed into her shoulder.

"Patsy, I think you and Walter ought to come with us for now. You can ride in my car. We'll decide what to do. Would you like that?"

"Okay," Patsy said, excited. "Is your car very fast?"

"No," Leona said, "not very fast."

One of the waitresses said, "Hey, where're you taking them?"

Leona couldn't meet her eyes. "I'm taking them home," she said.

Ten miles out of Fielding Heights, Leona nearly lost control of the car as the enormity of what she had done struck her. From head to toe, through the very tips of her fingers, her body shook as if she had grabbed a live wire and couldn't let go. With the last of her strength, she pulled the car off the road and covered her face with her shaking hands. "I have gone crazy," she mumbled. "I have taken full leave of my senses and I didn't even know it was happening. This is a terrible thing I've done." And now there was nothing else she could do; she had to take them with her, at least for a while. She couldn't just set them out on the side of the road like unwanted puppies. And yet she wanted to stop what was happening. If only I could just turn and go back, go all the way back, she thought.

But from the corner of her eye, she saw herself reflected in the side window, and the jagged crack in the glass ran through her like a long and vicious slash. And she knew she couldn't go back, *mustn't* ever go back, because something more evil than she could imagine would be waiting for her. The thought of it made her feel weak all over.

Patsy, who had been sitting next to Mamie, stood up on the floorboard. "Why're we stopped?" she asked, not pleased. "Is the motor broke?"

"No, no," Leona said, "nothing that serious," but she couldn't hold her smile and when she turned the key in the ignition, nothing happened. She jammed the key in the slot even tighter and stamped the gas pedal. This time the motor roared. She put her foot down and the road flew away beneath them.

With the pockety-pockety of the snowy windshield wipers keeping time and the nervous light from the dashboard quivering between them, Walter and Patsy Aldridge, ages five and six, not only answered all her questions but began slowly to tell her everything. Shy as they were with strangers.

Their father's dead, Leona thought, and their mother must be out of her mind. That's all she needed to know for now, as they sped on through the patchwork towns, Eberlie and Hazelett Grove and Deer Creek Landing, on toward the immense black maw of night.

# 10

Policemen saw him that week in November as he continued through the towns along the Susquehanna River—a rough-cut, scrappy-looking boy leading a large mongrel dog. Any one of them could have picked him up on a truancy or vagrancy charge, and some of them considered it. Cruisers slowed along the curb beside him, but as long as they let him alone, the boy ignored them, kept his pace brisk, his tense face pointed straight ahead. Only if they spoke to him did he waver. Usually they asked him "Where you headed?" just to get a response. The boy would hesitate and glance at them and say, "Just passin' through." Immediately they thought, There's something wrong with him. He was smiling, or trying to smile, his mouth drawn up in an expression of snarling mischief. But it was the poisonous slither of his dead blue eyes that preyed on them. Under sleepy eyelids, his eyes darted, and the hate coming from them was unblinking and corrosive. What's he trying to hide? they wondered afterward, grasping at the commonplace. Even those who were most tempted to run him in for questioning held back, kept an eye on him, and waited for him to get out of town. He was a kid, after all, down on his luck, but they had seen all of him they wanted to see. The cruisers pulled away.

In Gambria, where the note had been found, the owner of the Shell filling station was getting ready to lock up, two nights later, when he saw a fleeting shape refract on the glass of the back door. He dropped his coffee cup, grabbed a tire iron, and gave chase. But in only a few blocks, he was out of breath and losing ground. He told his wife that he had followed what appeared to be a boy and a dog for several blocks until he decided he was probably chasing a schoolboy prankster and turned back.

The boy and dog appeared, caught a ride and left, appeared and left, but where they came from, where he ate, slept, no one knew. They were seen rising from a weed-thatched ditch alongside the road one morning, the boy picking the brown leaves of his cover from his clothes. A farmer returning to his isolated home from a church council meeting found the contents of his refrigerator upset and rummaged through and some of his son's work clothes missing, including an old pair of shoes, but nothing else had been touched. Fifty miles farther south, a country wife wiped her hands on her apron, tucked the edges of her hair into her headscarf, and opened the front door on a scraggly, misbegotten boy. "Could I get a glass of water?" he asked. "I need to take a pill for my headaches." She observed his crumpled, unwashed clothes and told him to wait there on the porch. Afterward she was certain he had been in the house. It was a feeling, a sense of things disturbed, and a lingering, almost palpable odor like the stench of a moldy dog.

To anyone who would give him a few minutes, the boy hastened to show two pictures, the first a torn snapshot of a woman. "Have you seen this woman?" he would ask. "Did she stop here, pass through here, driving an old Buick? She's got a little girl with her. Here, I'll show ya." He'd draw out the other picture ripped from a newspaper. "This one's of my sister. Her name's Mamie. Have you seen her with that woman? That woman just took her. Didn't ask anybody. She just did it. And I've got to find 'em. They're ridin' in an old Buick." He asked the same questions in much the same words again and again, until the newspaper photograph began to disintegrate at the folds.

A man wheeled his rack of tires out on the drive to open his gas station and saw the boy and dog approach from the side of the building. "Yeah," the man said in answer to Sherman's question. "It was evening, day before yesterday." In another town, in Woolworth's, the boy went from counter to counter and questioned the clerks, and one of them said, "She looks kinda familiar. Maybe I saw her, I don't know. There wasn't any girl with her, though." But when he tried to press for details, leaning close over the counters or stepping behind partitions, they saw the hard glint in his eyes and sensed more than that: a force full of rage. The dog was never far behind.

They were dirty and they stank and they moved like wraiths upon the land. Grime had collected in the creases of the boy's skin and he smelled like the dog, of soured sweat and damp wood rot and wet ferreting animals. People shrank from them because of the odor and because of the dog, but the boy seemed oblivious to it. They ate at roadside diners and dinettes, always taking the sandwiches and plate lunches outside, and when they were stranded on the road, they stole what they could to get by. They slept together in whatever place presented itself—in unlocked cars and in the unlocked bathrooms of gas stations when it was colder. In the daytime, after the boy had been up most of the night and couldn't get a ride, they slept in deserted sheds and outbuildings and in culverts along the road. Climbing out of the ditch on a lonesome stretch of highway, he stuck out his thumb and walked and waited until one of the passing cars swerved to the side of the road, only to see it tear away, throwing up gravel, when the Chinaman lumbered out of the weeds. It was hard getting rides, and getting harder all the time.

On milder days, policemen saw him hanging around gas stations, near the doorways of restaurants, in front of shops displaying the new 12-inch television sets, but never for long; a runaway, they thought without noticing how intently he listened to the news being broadcast. He begged most of his rides at gas stations when the cars and trucks were at a standstill, the drivers captive to at least some of his plea. When his luck ran out completely, he offered them five or ten dollars for a ride. Eventually someone would say, "Well, all right. Come on. Get in the back seat. But you damned well better keep a hand on that dog."

After they were on the road, if the radio wasn't already turned on, he would say, "Could we play the radio? I used to have an old radio, but it never did work right." Then, until the news came on, he studied very carefully how they drove their cars and trucks. With complete absorption, he watched the coordination of hands and feet, noticed the movement of feet on clutch, brake, and accelerator. One driver told him how to sight down the hood a distance of fifty feet and use the side of the road as a guide to steer by rather than focus on the road immediately ahead. That way a passing car at night wasn't blinding. A young driver let him shift the gears with the long floorboard stick. As he grew bolder, he told them, "If I could get somebody to turn me loose in a rig like this, I believe I could figure it out all by myself and drive it. I know I could. I've been studying how to do it. If you'd let me, I bet I could drive this car right now."

Two nights south of Gambria, in a freezing rain storm, Sherman and the Chinaman clambered down from a flap-covered truck at an all-night truck stop. Through the bright-colored calligraphy of light, truckers milled in and out of the coffee shop. Sherman stood between the main door and a pyramid of oilcans, asking for rides as the men returned to their trucks. It was after 2:00 a.m, and very cold. He wore two sets of clothes now, for the extra warmth, but also, he thought, if he got in a jam he could shuck the outer shell of clothes and look entirely different to an unsuspecting eye. When the crowd had dwindled away, he waited inside the restaurant door to get warm, and caught the end of a news broadcast: ". . . *Fielding Heights police now believe there may be a connection between the disappearance last Sunday evening of Patsy and Walter Aldridge, the six- and five-year-old children of Mrs. Adele Aldridge, and the similar disappearance of seven-year-old Mamie Louise Abbott in Graylie, a rural community north of Scranton. . . . Police have established a special telephone number . . ."*

On the inside flap of a matchbook, Sherman wrote: ADELL. He asked the waitress, who had loaned him her pencil, how to spell Aldridge.

He shook two of the pills into his mouth, swallowed them, and counted the ones remaining in his bottle. Only six left. He returned the small bottle to his pocket. The double dose of medicine jolted him with a sensation of renewal. It lifted him. His body constricted; his eyesight cleared. The world of Mill Run Drive in Fielding Heights came to him in sudden sharp clarity. He stroked the Chinaman's head with his good hand and stepped from the curb. Thunder cracked over them and two crippled shards of light danced on a rooftop lightning rod. The rain drummed harder, splattering the sidewalk. His spine shivered involuntarily as the painkillers knitted his muscles.

The house was silent and dark. He cut the telephone line with his pocketknife. He slit the screen wire down and across at the lower corner of the wood frame, reached in, and inched the window up with his fingertips until he could slide it open and crawl into the house. He stood inside the curtains and closed the window. Nothing stirred. The Chinaman watched him from the other side of the glass. Sherman motioned him down, then moved out of the curtains and away from the three tall windows overlooking the shallow porch.

The contours of furniture glowed with the penetration of streetlight. He noticed two drinking glasses and a bottle of liquor on an end table, along with a pair of high-heeled slippers. Lapping over the edge of the coffee table was a clutter of *Look* and *Photoplay* magazines. A coverlet had been left wadded on the sofa. His hair and clothes were sopping wet. He wiped his hair on the coverlet and dropped it. The beam of his pencil flashlight sliced over walls, entryways, doors, and settled on a black-and-white celluloid clock, softly grinding in the dark. Three-thirty. He shut off the light. His shadow ebbed over the furniture.

When he stepped from the living-room rug, the bare floor groaned beneath him. Listening for any other noise, he stood very still before proceeding down the hall toward the back of the house. Doors hung open in the dark. He scanned the kids' unoccupied room and eased back. In the bathroom, ghostly silk stockings hung like withered skins on a spindly rack. Behind it, a door to the other bedroom stood open a few inches. He touched the stockings and they were dry. He glimpsed his face in the medicine-cabinet mirror as he turned. Only the prominent features of his face caught the faint glimmering streetlight; the darkness covered his clothes. He backed into the hall.

Standing just outside the door to the other bedroom, he heard the short roll of bedsprings, the rustling of sheets. He waited. The door was partially open; he stepped through it carefully. A window blind had been left up; through the rainy glass, the bank of streetlight rippled as if it were alive. Tangled in the ropy covers, she was sprawled in the center of the bed, her face mashed sideways into the pillow. Her hair was pinned up in knots with crossed bobby pins. She was snoring very lightly, soft and smooth. Noiselessly he moved away from her.

He retreated to the dimly lit windows of the living room. Through a shadowed doorway, he saw a rack of dishes glowing like teeth in the semi-darkness and went toward it. The kitchen counters held the makings of a feast: pies and cakes and loaves of bread, a ham embedded with pineapple circles and cherries. He dug out one of the pineapple pieces, slipped it into his mouth, and went to find the fuse box.

He did not know until he heard the swish of her nightgown that she was very near. "Davy? Is that you?" Her voice sounded soft and dream-weary. "Davy . . . Who is it? Jerry? Oh, my

God." He lifted his head and stared at her stricken eyes, heard her sharp intake of breath. He had just stepped up from the landing to the basement. The storm had slackened; a streak of drab moonlight divided them. His excitement was like terror and her terror was very real; and so, terrified, neither of them moved, the air dangling between them. He needed a long deep breath, now that he had been discovered, but his breath stalled in his throat and he strained to stay quiet. He could not let her scream; if she tried to, he would have to stop her.

Adele Aldridge went on looking at him, stony-eyed. Then she swallowed and blinked her eyes countless quick times, a flurry of impulses shooting through her face. She looked white with fear. Even her arm, outstretched, seemed to grow whiter and more stationary with each passing moment, fossilizing in the air like Lot's wife turning to salt.

It troubled him; this was not how he had imagined it would be. But it was too late to retrace his steps.

"Nobody's gonna hurtcha," he said at last, composing his voice while he stood, no more than five feet from her, looking at the shadowed curve of her body through the skimpy film of her gown. He struggled to keep his voice calm and firm. "I didn't come to hurt you," he said, knowing if anything would keep her from screaming, short of the knife, it would have to be what he said and how he said it. "Just don't scream."

She did scream then, in a way, after all, the fear she had held in her body spewing from her lips in a long sob. She lowered her arm, closed her eyes, and licked her lips, and when she drew breath, it shuddered in.

He had started to speak to her again when she broke in: "Please . . . what do you want? How'd you get in here? Please, now—you're just a kid. What're you doing here? Take whatever you want. But please, I want you to leave—leave now."

"I don't want to hurtcha," he said, "but you gotta promise to be good, and not try anything, and listen to me—willya listen to me? And let me tell you why I'm here? Why I had to come here? I don't want your things, I'm not here to take your things . . . because, see, somebody took something that's mine, maybe the same woman that took your little kids and all I want is for you to listen to me. Wouldn't you do that and just not scream, Mrs. Aldridge?"

The mention of her children and her name sank through her face like light spreading in water, but he didn't give her much time. When she didn't answer immediately, he began to talk again, keeping his voice quiet. "I can explain. Honest, Mrs. Aldridge. Wouldn't you just listen?" He spoke on and on, his voice never pausing for long, filling the time until she gave some sign of acknowledgment. Although he knew she could not see it clearly, he took the disintegrating newspaper photograph from his pocket and shook it open. "This here's a picture of my little sister. Her name's Mamie." Then he brought out the other photograph. "And this woman took her while she was at the hospital. I know she did. She's pro'bly the one took your kids." He saw the change come to her face, the softening of fear. He folded the pictures and put them away, letting her make up her mind, waited and let the time build heavy with waiting, and she revealed herself in the most bewildering way: she began to pluck the bobby pins from her hair, raking them out with her fingers and dropping them on the metal tabletop. Finally he asked her again, softly, "Wouldn'tcha listen to me?" And she nodded, but her voice still quivered when she said, "For just a minute, if you'll leave then. Let me get a drink."

She stepped past him to the cupboard. She took out a tray which held several glasses and a bottle of whiskey. Her hands were trembling. She uncapped a bottle and poured the glass full, spilling a little down the sides. The smell of whiskey thinned in the air. She took a long drink. Then another, and filled the glass again. He didn't know what she thought of what he'd said. When she turned away, she kept her head bowed. He was drenched with sweat and rain, his clothes soaked through. "That woman," Sherman said. "I have to find her. I *have* to. She pro'bly took your little boy and girl, too."

The woman sighed, glanced at him. "Nobody knows what happened to Patsy and Walter." She crossed one arm under her breasts to prop up her drinking arm. In her trembling hand, the whiskey swished softly in the glass.

"I do," he said. "I know what happened. And sooner or later I'm gonna catch up with 'er. That's why I came here. Maybe the police told you something that might help me look for 'em. I figure she's a day ahead of me, maybe two at most. I can get your kids back." He heard a momentary shift in her breathing, but nothing registered in her face.

She shook her head and pressed the glass to her cheek. "No," she said. "I don't know. . . . I'll tell you the truth. I don't think anybody can find 'em any more. I think they're gone for good." Suddenly she was sobbing, her racked breath shuddering and harsh in the dark room. She buried her face in the crook of her arm and the sobs muffled. The woman's emotion touched him so deeply that for a moment he was seized with her loneliness as much as his own and he shared her sorrow. She lowered her arm to take a drink and the sobbing continued, raw and loud, jerking her body in long spasms. He waited for her to stop, watching the rain bead and trickle on the windows.

"Ma'am," he said finally. "Ma'am, they're not gone for good, I don't think so. She's got 'em and I'll catch 'er. Honest. She can't go forever."

"I wish I believed you," she said in her woozy, dreamy voice, tears bright on her face. "Patsy waited for the mailman to come . . . they missed their daddy so bad. And now they're gone." She was looking out the rainy window, her nose runny, not even trying to wipe her face. "The police don't tell me anything. I don't know what they're doing. To them, I'm just a nuisance."

"But they gotta tell you something."

"Not any more than what's in the newspapers. I don't know. Everything kinda went haywire. All I know is one of the waitresses said a woman took 'em—a woman like you say, with a little girl."

"I know it," he said. "She's the one that's doin' this stuff. It's crazy. I don't why she's doin' it. She don't look crazy. I showed you her picture."

"I get all kinds of crazy calls. Crank calls. Just this evenin' somebody called, some reporter, and said Walter had been seen way south of here in Deaconsville, but when I called the police, they said it wasn't confirmed." She straightened and wiped her face with her hand. "Wait here," she said. "I want to show you something." She went through the arched doorway and he heard her moving in the living room. He started to go after her, still afraid to trust her, but she returned, carrying her purse. She flipped the switch for the ceiling light. She flipped it again and looked at him. She flipped it a few more times. "Now, what's happened? Did you do something to my lights?"

"No, ma'am," he said. "It's prob'ly the storm. Line down somewhere."

She took another drink. "I hate this goddammed place more every day. Nothing works right. I don't know why I stay here. I'll rustle us up a light. You wait here. I'll be right back." She walked away unsteadily. When she came back, she had brushed her blonde hair down over one eye like Veronica Lake; she wore perfume and she carried a lighted candle. She proceeded to drag some of the contents from her purse—a compact, car keys— until her hand closed on a fat billfold.

Mrs. Aldridge showed him billfold snapshots, tearing the pictures from the straining plastic leaves and holding them up in front of him. "Here's Walter when he was three, and here's one of Patsy on her fourth birthday on a pony, and here's a fairly new picture of 'em taken last April." Another snapshot showed all four of them in front of a stage set with palm trees. "That's

Jerry, my husband. But I've got a better one of the kids," she said, slipping the pictures one behind the other like playing cards, almost shuffling them in her haste. She stood stooped at his side, leaning forward, her body warm and full in the slinky nightgown, and when she moved, the cloth seethed against her. He could feel an almost feverish heat radiating from her as he stood trapped in her adamant recital.

"Why don't you take this one of Patsy and Walter? So you'll recognize 'em. If you see 'em, you could call . . ." She laid it on the table. Slowly she straightened and looked at him. "Could I see the picture of that woman again? It was dark in here and I couldn't get a good look at her." He dug the picture out and held it up. She reached for it, but he hated to let go of it and relinquished it slowly. This time she held the photograph near the candle and studied it at length. Her hand roamed the table till it covered her drink. She took a big swig and licked her lips. "You're sure this is the woman?"

Sherman nodded. "That's her." She's drunk, he thought. That's what's wrong with this. It's been wrong all along.

She took another, slower drink. "You know quite a bit about this, doncha? For just a kid? Who are you, anyway? How'd you get in here? Did I leave the damn door open or what?" He didn't answer, watched her close. "Whew," she said. "I don't know what I was thinking of. We have to get this down to the police. I better call 'em."

"You better just give it back," he said, "and I'll go ahead." He reached for the photograph, but she swung from him, sloshing her drink. "Oh, you can't leave now," she said. "This's important."

He couldn't think of a way to explain to her in words that wouldn't betray him how much he detested and feared the police. She tucked the photograph under her arm, took the candle, and left the room, the flame lighting her face in grotesque waves. He trailed after her, saw her go to her bedroom.

Through the darkened doorway, in the pool of candlelight, he watched her dial the telephone, flick the receiver button several times, and slam the receiver down. He stopped just inside the bedroom door. "Now the damned phone's dead," she said. "This goddammed weather's knocked everything out."

"Give me back my picture," he said. "I gotta go."

"Ah, listen," she said, "you can't go now after all I've been through. I'd give anything to have my kids back. You gotta come with me. We can take my car. We'll be down at police headquarters in ten minutes. Please. You've got to. Come on." She nudged him along, ushered him back to the dark living room. "Just give me five minutes. I have to get dressed. I'll be ready in five minutes. Promise." She closed the bedroom door and left him staring at the doorknob.

His pulse moved in great jolts; shock ran through him like acid. In and around him everything was collapsing; even the grainy blue film of the air tasted sour. If only she would change her mind, return his picture, and unwind his tension in a clean, straight line. But she wouldn't; he knew she wouldn't. Not without some really bad trouble. He prowled back and forth outside her bedroom door, caught in a slipstream of desperation. Everything was speeded up and breaking down, beyond his control. He felt dizzy, and shut his eyes till he steadied. He could feel events slipping away from him just as they had that night with the cabdriver, only this time the stakes were even higher. He wouldn't go to the police with her, absolutely could not. But even if he didn't go, she would tell them all about him. He had to get his picture back. If they traced it to him, they'd find out everything and put him away forever. With dread, he unzipped his jacket, shrugged till it fell to the floor. He flicked his pocketknife open and held it prone in his hip pocket. Outside her bedroom door he tried to shake the jitters, but it only made things worse. He couldn't wait any longer. Keeping his good hand on the knife in his pocket, he turned the doorknob with his bandaged hand and slipped inside.

She had put on her high-heeled shoes, nothing else. For an instant, in the wiggly light, her image clung to his imagination —the line of her body, breasts nipping and wobbling on the air, hammocky and poised in their suspension. The high heels sculpted her legs, the double round shape of her hips rolled up by the cat-curl of her body as she drew underwear from a bureau drawer—all of her burnished with the feeble light. He could feel the moments destruct and disintegrate one by one. As she lurched up, swayed up like a cobra, his wrapped hand flicked over the candle on the nightstand and the light winked out.

"Hey, what'd you do that for?" Her voice sounded irritated, but his action had scared her. As the darkness flexed on his eyes, he could hear her breath quiver in her throat.

Until his eyes adjusted, he was only able to see her as a dark moving shape in this dark box. His muscles were vibrating and the sweat was slick on his face. The bank of dull streetlight contained his shadow for only an instant. He stepped through it and wiped his eyes on his sleeve, hurriedly calculating the distance to where she stood. "Oh, what'sa matter with you? Never seen a girl get dressed before?" Her voice had turned haughty and brash. "What are you, some kind of weirdo? Come bargin' in here?" She let her body drift into a sullen pose. "Why don't you take a good look, then? Get a real eyeful. Then get the hell outa here." She'd painted her face into a vivid mask and in the dull light he saw her now for what she was: coarse and not ashamed of anything, capable of anything. She would tell them every damned thing they wanted to know. "I mean it," she said. "Don't worry about your measly picture. It'll be right here. Now, get out of here, get out of this bedroom. You hear me? I want you OUT! GET OUT! GET OUT! RIGHT NOW!"

"*I told you not to scream!*" His voice slammed tight from his throat. "Give me back my goddammed picture!"

Very fast, as he spoke, she twisted to the bed and slipped her robe on. "Where d'you get off tellin' me what to do in my own house? I'm going to the police. And you're goin' with me."

He turned bone cold. "You can't take me to the police," he said, his voice flat and quiet. "Nobody can." He edged toward her.

"Oh, yeah? Well, we're goin'," she said. "You better believe it. They'll have to listen to us, now that we've got that picture." Just then she seemed to realize that he was moving relentlessly toward her, and in fright her glance darted past him in frantic search of escape.

"I won't go to the goddammed police," he said. "Where's my picture?" A few more steps and he could reach her before she did anything. Force it from her. But she hurled the hand mirror at him, wheeled and ran, her heels flipping behind her at odd angles. He skimmed through the dark, diving for her, and caught a fist of her hair as she yelped and sprang through the bedroom door. He yanked her back, her feet coming off the floor. With astonishing speed, his arm flung out and the knife drove deep across her throat. Her legs skipped the air, the cry severed in her voice box. Twice her arms flailed in the confusion; a fingernail opened a burning lid of flesh above his left eye. He stabbed her again and again and again, and she was reclining on the air. When at last she fell back, the force of gravity pulled him along with her and he rode through her fall. They smacked the floor hard, he straddled her, and the hot red blood poured from the opened regions of her face.

And time passed, minutes . . . and longer . . . and he stayed with her. Under the hard press of his hands he could feel her exhale the last faint breath. Just as he let go, a long rippling shudder coursed through her body, more violent and absolute than anything preceding it. When he opened his stinging eyes, the woman's blank eyes looked through and past him; nothing moved in her face, not an eyelash. She was not breathing. On

her lips a bloody bubble broke, the tip of her tongue just breaking the pale rim of her lips, and he began to tremble and gasp.

Dimly the outlines of the room returned to him, tinged with
haze. He was covered with blood. Leaning into the bed, he
picked up the chenille bedspread and wiped his face. He squatted beside her. In the abrupt stillness, as he watched the night,
he saw hundreds of glittering eyes winking at him like fish
surfacing from the black water of a magical pond, each showing
him a shattered sparkling piece of himself. He stood and pulled
the bedspread over the body and most of the broken mirror. He
wiped the blade on his pants, closed the knife, and put it away.

Holding his wrapped hand out from his side, he unbuttoned
the middle three buttons of his shirt and withdrew the collection
of papers—newspaper articles, his map, the torn photographs—
and laid them on the bureau. He removed the bloody sweatshirt,
wiped his face with it, dropped it. He pulled the T-shirt from
his pants, grabbed the bottom edge, and pulled it up, damp and
stinking, over his head. He dropped it and again took up the
sweatshirt, scrubbed it across his chest and under his arms, and
tossed it aside.

Dragging his feet with exhaustion, he went to the door and
let the Chinaman in, caught a reviving breath of cold air, and
reset the door chain. As soon as the dog smelled blood, he began
to whine and go stiff-legged. Sherman had to quickly shut the
bedroom door. Then, in the living room, the Chinaman shook
himself, slinging water high and wide, the slapdash shudder
moving down his dark coat from head to tail as he wrung
himself out. He looked woolly as he followed Sherman to the
kitchen. They ate ravenously. The dog gulped ham scraps and
chocolate cake in huge swallows, his coat heaving on his bony
frame.

Scattered on the kitchen table were the billfold photographs
Mrs. Aldridge had shown to Sherman. He picked them up, one
after another, and held them in a streak of moonlight, glancing

at the fixed smiling faces of utter strangers. I've come a long way, he thought, to get no further than this. He let the last photograph drop, the one showing the little family standing among the cardboard palm trees.

Tired and spent, his rage depleted for now, his hunger satisfied, he sat at the dinette table listening to the muffled sound of the wind and watching the last of the rain trickle on the window, and it all seemed so familiar. Slowly he lifted his head and heard far away the creaking slap of a screen door, silverware tinkling, Mamie's laughter, the sound of his family's voices as they sat around the supper table at home. He stiffened and swallowed the pain in his throat, but already the glimpse of home had vanished as if a dream had suddenly burst in his heart and dwindled to nothing. A weary sob emptied his throat for all that had been lost and set loose within him. When he spoke to the Chinaman, it was not with sorrow or remorse, but with longing. "We don't have a home," he said. "It's gone. It's gone. Burned up."

Unsteadily, he stood. Turning the dead kitchen light switch to off, he went down the basement stairs and fixed the fuses. In the living room, he told the Chinaman to get up on the couch and made him lie down. The dog lowered his head on his paws and groaned. Sherman picked the dirtied tape-flap loose and unwound the bandage on his hand.

Under the bathroom lights the sight of his ruined hand sickened him. Inflamed and swollen, the skin was cracked like old parchment. It was almost unrecognizable as a hand; it gave off a nauseating stench. As gently as he could, hardly touching it, he washed it. Braced against the cold rim of the sink, grinding his teeth, he dabbed peroxide on the infected parts and dabbed it off, yellow and singeing. Then he took a bath, letting the water saturate and warm him, the delicate odor of the soap lingering. The night's ugliness seeped from his pores. When he had dried himself, he brushed his wet hair straight back with the silver-plated brush from her boudoir set and found the torn photograph edged among the perfume bottles. He dressed his hand and wrapped it in bandages from the medicine cabinet.

He cleaned his clothes as well as he could, but the sweatshirt and the corduroy pants couldn't be saved. Stolen, they never did fit right anyway; tomorrow he would have to bury them. His other pair of pants, the jeans he wore under the corduroys, weren't stained so badly that he couldn't wear them. In her bureau, he found clean underwear and a white sweatshirt stained with yellow paint, all too big—her husband's, he guessed —but he had no choice: he had to take them. He found the woman's car keys in her purse and took them. At the first light of dawn, he and the Chinaman went outside.

Graying with light, the air was chill and wet. The freezing rain had again turned to snow. From the back of the house, he took the stone walk past the side of the garage to the alleyway. Around him, the dark windows reflected black tree shadows. He walked slowly, his hands limp at his sides. This morning he was acutely conscious of his hands.

Other than the twittering of a robin or wren, all was quiet. Among the trees a few shriveled patches of frost striped the ground; leaves scuttled. And the snow was falling. Sherman turned to listen for any odd sound. Listened. Nothing. He opened the wide garage door on its creaking pulleys and tried the key in the car trunk, where he stashed the bundle of bloody clothes and bandages. He shoved the trunk shut and tried the other keys until one of them fit the ignition. He called the Chinaman into the car.

He sat behind the steering wheel, studying the unfamiliar panel of instruments and dials. He shifted the lever into neutral. With his foot on the clutch, he turned the key in the ignition. The motor whined and throbbed. Slowly he eased the gear shift down to reverse. As he let out the clutch and touched the gas pedal, the car slipped back, caught the edge of the garage door, scraping red paint, and rolled into the dim morning. He practiced driving back and forth on side streets before he headed out of town.

On River Road Drive, the scant morning traffic came off the curved ramps and whisked by, the headlights hurtling and flickering like meteors. In no time, he passed between the statues, like bookends, on either side of Hoover Drive, the brass Indians on horseback, ancient hosts of the city of Coolidge, Pennsylvania. He could smell the age of the city. Old bricks crumbling to atoms of red dust; soot and smoke and mustiness. He crossed the metal drawbridge, and the façade of the city shimmered in the snowy morning light, while all around the red Ford coupe the occasional throb and whoosh of traffic created a beautiful pandemonium in the early dawn.

# 11

*"Maamie . . . ohhh, Maamie, time to come to supper."*

*"Comin'! . . . Now, you girls be good and when I get back we'll — Uh-oh, Elsie, your dress fell off again. Shame on you. Naughty. Naughty girl . . ."*

*"Maamie! Put those paper dolls up. Come on, now."*

*"Okay, Mama! I'm comin'!"*

*"La-di-dah,"* Toddy said. *"Look at you. Where'd you get so dressed up?"*

*"These're all my favorite clothes. Mama said I could wear 'em. Race ya."*

*"Okay. Ready, get set, go."*

*"Wheeeee!"*

*"Hey, bannisters is no fair."*

*"Look who's here,"* Sherman said. *"It's Loretta Young."*

*"Hi, Daddy."*

*"Hi, Loretta."*

*"It's the Queen of Sheba," Toddy said, "and she cheats."*

*"Pkpkppkppkppk!"*

*"Loretta, don't stick your tongue out. Not very ladylike."*

*"Tell him not to make fun of me, then. Tell him, Daddy."*

*"I think we oughta tickle her," Sherman said.*

*"Oh, no! Yiiieeee! Hahahahaha haha hahahahaha."*

*"Sherman, Toddy," her mother said. "Stop your foolishness now and come to supper. Ray, bring Mamie."*

*"Daddy, ride me piggyback. Please, please, pretty please, Daddy, let me ride."*

*"Up we go, then. Up high. Now, hold on tight."*

*"Hey, what's that? Daddy? Mama, is that my birthday cake? But how'd you make it so big? And look at that! Little birds flying round . . . Daddy . . . Daddy, look at the bluebirds with ribbons in their teeth. It's just like Cinderella. Oh, Mama! Where'd you get the little birds?"*

*"Now, who's the one I love? Whose little girl are you?"*

*"Oh, Mama!" she cried. "I'm your girl. I'm your very best girl, Mama . . . I'm your girl. . . .*

"Mamie? Mamie, wake up. You're twitching all over." The woman gently shook her shoulder. "Are you having a bad dream?"

Mamie awoke startled, her hands reaching for the bluebirds, the words of her dream still warm in her mouth. She had to withdraw suddenly inside herself to keep from crying out. She caught her breath, then let it go all at once. Closing her eyes, she tried to reclaim her dream but it was gone for now.

To Mamie, only the dream seemed real: her family gathering at the supper table, nobody sick or hurt, no scabs on her, Sherman skinned up like he always was, but not bad—everything the way it should be. That was real. It didn't seem real to be riding in this lady's car and not going home. She thought she should be going home now, even though she knew her home was no longer there. Someone had carried her away and she had seen it burning, but knowing that did not slacken her longing for it.

Every time she slept and opened her eyes, she expected to wake up in her own bed, with the sun shining through the window, kids playing in the yards below, and the Chinaman dragging his chain, barking. She wanted to feel the cool planks under her feet as she went to the bathroom half asleep and washed her face with cold water and soap and a washcloth. Sometimes, when she opened her eyes, she could almost smell the soap she had once used. Instead she awoke with empty·hands and the countryside rolling by outside and the monotonous rumbling of the car. All she wanted was to leave her eyes shut and live in the place she had just left, in her dreamland. She slept more than she should—too many hours, the woman said, for a girl her age.

In the beginning, she kept telling herself there'd been a mistake, an awful mistake, and that sooner or later the woman would realize what she'd done and take her back. Sometimes she stood in the back seat staring at the woman's head and just purely hated her for what she had done. She wanted to cry out, This is wrong, all wrong! She wanted to tell her what was wrong, but the woman was no one to talk to. She was a stranger. And besides the nurse had told her not to talk, because people would think she was crazy.

She knew what happened to crazy people. They put them with a crowd of other crazy people and never let anybody out. That's what it was like to be crazy and she didn't want to be like that. Mamie believed there had been some kind of crazy mistake, though, until the woman picked up the other little kids, and then she knew it wasn't a mistake any more. She had done it on purpose, and now they had Patsy and Walter with them all the time. At first she'd thought Walter was like Toddy. But he wasn't Toddy. It was all wrong somehow. It scared her when she thought about it, and she was afraid most of the time. She didn't want to be put away in a crowd of crazy people.

She saw the names of towns fly by her window, and they were like names in a book with the pages turned too fast. For a while, she tried to remember the names in a string, but there were too many of them and she couldn't. She tried to keep track of the days, but the days all ran together. And she never knew where they were or where they were going. It upset her beyond her ability to comprehend it.

Again and again, she thought she saw Sherman. A boy walked by a store window, turned to look down at a display of model airplanes, and she thought it was him. Her heart quickened. She trailed toward the glass. Then he glanced up and moved away, and she was left trembling with disappointment.

The last time she had seen Sherman, he was bending over her at the hospital. He still carried that strange look in his eyes and his mouth was like a cut in his face. "Come on," he said. "Let's get you dressed and get outa this dump." He was struggling with her, trying to get her to pull on some jeans he'd brought for her, and she wanted to help, wanted to go with him in the night the way she used to, but it must've been the medicine that made her so sleepy. Even so, she was surprised and glad to see him at last. "I've got the Chinaman," he told her, "and I've got a place for us to hide." Then they heard hurrying footsteps in the hall. If he hadn't told her about the Chinaman, she might not have been led astray so often, but the sight of a boy and a dog anywhere made her heart leap. She always thought it was Sherman and the Chinaman come to take her away. Her deepest feelings rushed out to meet them, only to be hit by a numbing backwash when the truth struck her. It wasn't them.

The hospital bracelet hadn't worked.

She thought if she could leave some kind of trail behind like the movie star captured by Indians who left scraps of her clothes on bushes—if she could only think of something like that while the other kids were asleep! Keeping most of her body on the seat, she leaned down to the floor of the car and opened the Little Lulu funny book to the second page. With a blue crayon she wrote across the top margin: SHE TOOK US, turned the book and wrote down the side: MAMIE. She closed the book. The next time they stopped to buy gas, she dropped the funny book and watched the wind blow it across the street. Another time, she wrote HELP SHERMAN FINE ME on the inside of a chewing-gum wrapper, and signed it, her printing jiggled by the bumping of the snowy road. She folded the wrapper in a small, tight square, and while the woman and the kids were busy buying candy, she slipped it inside the end of an opened cigarette pack lying on the counter. Then she quickly replaced the chrome lighter on top of the cigarette pack and turned away. Again and again in their passage along the road, she scribbled her little notes and dropped or hid them. And she waited for Sherman to come. She waited until she thought she could wait no longer. She would have to try to talk to somebody.

Then three nights after they had taken Walter and Patsy, very late in the night, the woman said quietly, mostly to herself, "Either my eyes are deceiving me or our lights are going out." Slumped in the corner of the back seat, Mamie heard her. The other kids had appeared to be asleep, but at the sound of her voice the two rose and stared through the windshield. "They are," Walter said finally, his voice croupy. "Didja see that flicker?" And Patsy said, "*There*. It just did it again." Mamie heard them, listened to their small voices piping back from the front seat, waiting as she had been waiting all day.

"We're having a wreck," Walter said, glancing at her, big-eyed. "You want to see it?"

"You two certainly have vivid imaginations," the woman said. "We're not having a wreck and we're not going to have one, much as I'd enjoy hearing you describe it. There must be something wrong with the battery, that's all."

They drove in silence, the road slicking away beneath them. If something's wrong with the car, Mamie thought, maybe I can get away or get somebody to help me. She stood on the floorboard next to Walter.

Snow splattered the windshield and the wipers carved it away with unremitting regularity. They passed a glowing white sign: BURDETTE, POP. 903. At a slower speed, the car stalled and sputtered and rocked forward. They entered a small downtown area, four blocks of tall ornate stores, all of them closed and dark, the shape of the Buick wriggling along the plate-glass windows like a lurking shadow. The headlight beams thinned to darkness, blazed, and went out. A half mile beyond the edge of town, a lighted sign revolved in the air. HORSESHOE COURT, it said; TOURIST COTTAGES.

The Buick coasted into the exit end of the horseshoe drive, cracked through frozen puddles, and rolled to a stop. The woman turned everything off in the car, the wipers, the heater, the radio, before she turned the key in the ignition once again and the motor gave a guttering moan. "Well," Patsy said, "what're we gonna do now? Camp out?"

The woman said, "That was close." She undid her scarf from her neck and tied it around her head. "At least we can get a room." She told them to stay in the car and leave all the knobs alone, and they watched her disappear toward the blinking vacancy sign. Not yet, Mamie thought.


After Leona had brought in the few things they would need from the car—one of the suitcases, her shopping bag, and the briefcase—she locked the cottage door. Like most of the other places she had rented, Cottage 12 was outdated and meagerly furnished, but with the storm blowing up outside, it seemed warm, almost cozy. Once they were all safe inside, she went to the window, spread the venetian blinds with both hands, and peered across the bleak peninsula of horseshoe drive. Taking a last look out had become part of her nightly ritual; somehow it answered a deep abiding need to believe that all was well. There was nothing to see—her stalled car, the falling snow. She let the slats go shut momentarily and stepped back. Silent, except for the soft bleating of its exhaust, a car moved round the horseshoe drive, passed her window, and proceeded on its way. This time when she parted the blinds, she let her eyes stray beyond the vacancy sign to the long curve of road leading to the Monongahela River and eventually to Hastings, West Virginia, the road that would take them away.

Their already slow progress had now come to a standstill. After she'd taken Walter and Patsy, Leona thought it best to remain hidden; she had avoided the main highways as much as possible, choosing instead the country roads that skirted the patrolled thoroughfares. And of course the side roads were often poorly maintained and much more hazardous; seldom did her speedometer climb above forty. Tomorrow, at last, they would cross into West Virginia and the going should be easier, but tonight, before they left Pennsylvania for good, she would try once more to write that miserable woman a letter. And yet no sooner had the thought crossed her mind than she wished it hadn't. *Dear Mrs. Aldridge* . . . Who was she trying to fool? Just trying to come up with exactly the right thing to say in that kind of letter was enough to drive her to distraction. *Dear Mrs. Aldridge, this is to say your children are safe.* . . . *Dear Mrs. Aldridge* . . . She should forget this unreasonable urge to explain and confess and tell her side of the story, she told herself. She should be changing the children's clothes, getting them ready for bed.

*Dear Mrs. Aldridge* . . . She went among the children in this shoddy rented room. *Please forgive me.* . . . They were looking at her, waiting for their pajamas. She knelt and opened her suitcase, then handed out their nightclothes and said, "Now, Walter, remember, before you wash up, I want to look at your ear." And sad-eyed, shy Walter shrugged and said, "Okay."

*Forgive me for the terrible news I have to send you. . . .* "You and Patsy can change first—in the bathroom, please." *I've taken your little boy and girl.* Leaning sideways into the edge of the double bed, her feet sliding slowly out from under her, Mamie stared at the pajamas clutched in her fist with an expression of curious disgust. "Mamie," Leona said, "I'll help you in a minute." She set out her own nightclothes and snapped the suitcase shut. *I'll be keeping them with me for a while. . . .*

Mamie hadn't spoken to her since the night they fled the restaurant.

Walter stuck his head around the open bathroom door. "Hey," he said, "you want to look at it?"

"Yes," Leona said, "I'm coming." She looked steadily at Mamie, who stood alone, always alone, and she wondered what it would take to really break through to her. She watched her until the walls—the cheap pictures of herons, the mirror, the mock-candle wall lights—all of it began to reel away from her and she pushed herself up to her feet. *I know this will come as a shock to you. . . . Maybe you will appreciate them more when they are returned to you. . . .*

In the bathroom, she turned Walter so the side of his head was to the light, and examined his ear. Patsy stood close by, protectively, to watch. The swelling at the hinge of his jaw and the welt above his ear had receded. "Does it hurt?" she asked him softly, and she realized, not for the first time, that he had trouble hearing. She couldn't get used to it in such a small child. "Walter," she said a little louder, looking at him. "Does your ear hurt? If it does, I'll put bandages back on it." He shrugged and rolled his head. "Nahh," he said. "Is it okay?"

She smiled. "Yes, it looks okay." *You see, I have a little girl who desperately needs other children. . . .* "Are you two ready for bed?"

Patsy nodded enthusiastically and Walter looked doubtful. Leona had seen these children in one form or another all her life. There had been children like these two when she attended grade school. It was a quality in their faces that always struck her, something beaten down and yet indomitable, as if their character had been forged at the first spank of life. Now they were with her, getting ready for bed. At times it seemed unreal.

"That's strange," she said. "You don't look ready. Patsy, wash your face and brush your teeth. And maybe you could help Walter wash his face, too." She stepped to the doorway. "Mamie, come here. And—well, look at me. I'm not ready either. Mamie . . ."

Mamie came into the bathroom as Leona was handing the two children a towel. Walter insisted on drying his own face, and Leona told them to go ahead; they could get into bed. She changed Mamie's clothes, checked the bandages on her hip and shoulder, and told her that tomorrow they would leave the bandages off altogether. Shut away from the other children, she lifted Mamie onto the countertop of the sink. When the child still wouldn't acknowledge her, Leona cupped her chin and turned the small face till it was level with her own. "Aren't you ever going to talk to me again? I mean really talk to me? I know this is all strange to you, Mamie, but they've had their bad times, too, you know. Probably not as bad as yours, but bad times just the same. I want to tell you something, Mamie—we had to bring them with us." Mamie was beginning to tremble, and her trembling grew more pronounced the longer Leona talked. And yet at that moment Leona needed to explain to someone what she had done. "Yes, that's right, we did—I'm sure of it. And now we have to take care of them." There was more she'd meant to say, but Mamie's thin hand came up and touched Leona's cheek in no touch at all, like the touch of someone blind. She thought she felt the slight dig of fingernails and it chilled her for a moment. Mamie jumped down, away from her, and ran out of the room.

*You see, Mrs. Aldridge, I didn't know what to do. . . .*

That night, as she tucked them in, Leona sat on the side of the bed. "You must be tired of this," she said. "I'm tired, too. But I know a place where all this trouble will end. A place where it's safe and they'll never find us—at least, not this winter. Do you understand?"

Mamie just stared at her, but the other two shook their heads.

"All right," she said. "Try to imagine an island. A beautiful little island in the middle of a river. It's still a long way from here. We'll have to take a boat. You can't reach it by road—no road even goes near the closest riverbank. And on this island there's a house made of stone, a nice, clean little house with pine trees all around it." She watched their faces, looking from one to the other.

"It's really a wonderful place. I used to go there in the summertime with some friends of mine. It's like a little fort off all by itself, but we could stoke up the furnace and have all the heat we want. And I could cook for you. I could make all the things you like. And when it rains on the roof you could sleep forever. Does that sound all right to you?"

Imagining it herself, Leona could see the island now, breaking through layers of fog, could practically smell the surround of pine trees. Then she had to laugh because Walter and Patsy were muttering, and had been for some time, that it was all right with them. "Okay, then," Leona said. "That's where we'll go."

Patsy twisted her head on the pillow and looked at her. "At your place—does it have any kitty cats?"

"Yes," she said, "I think I do recall some kitty cats. They lived off all by themselves. They're kind of wild and hard to find. You'd have to be awfully careful. Because they could scratch you, and they can disappear just like *that!*" She snapped her fingers.

"That's the kind I like," Patsy said.

She kissed them good night, shut off the light, and went to the bed she'd made for herself in a lounge chair by the window. She was nearly asleep when she heard footsteps and realized that Walter, head bowed, was beside her. But he wouldn't look up, waited instead for her to lean down for his whisper. "Muz . . ." he said. It was the name he and Patsy had given her, although they used it very sparingly. He rose on tiptoe, closer to her ear. "I think I want to go home now."

She never knew what to say. "Oh, Walter, I do too," she whispered to him earnestly. "I'm so lonesome for home it's a disgrace. I miss so many things. That's why I told you about the place I have all picked out for us. And you'll like it, too, Walter —really you will."

"Okay," he whispered, leaning up to her again. "But I really want to go home right now."

She lifted him to her lap. "You miss your mother, don't you? Yes, I know you do. Even if she hurts you sometimes, you still miss her." It was much the same answer she had given him other nights. "I think you're better off with us for a little while, Walter. Things'll be better, you'll see."

He studied her for several seconds and tonight he said, "Muz, don't sleep in a chair. Come stay in our bed."

"No," she told him. "You stay with me." Then she saw that Patsy had come toward them in the dark and Leona motioned for her to join them.


In a few minutes, Mamie knew, the woman would bring the children back to the bed. Find me, Sherman, she thought, find me, please find me, before I'm all gone. She could feel an immense loneliness filling her up. Please, somebody, hurry. I don't want to go to no ireland with river water all around it. She peered into the dark until tears filled her eyes. Then she hid her face in the pillow. Without uttering a sound, her lips shaped the only prayer she had ever really learned: "Now I lay me down to sleep, I pray the Lord my soul to keep . . ." Again and again, into the smothering dark.

The next morning, while Leona talked to the garage mechanic about the car, Mamie wrote her last note, in a *Field and Stream* magazine: SHES TAKEN US TO IRLAN. Seated on a plastic-covered bench in the waiting room, she glanced past the heads of the other two children, who were standing at the glass, and saw the woman giving the man some money. She returned her crayon to her coat pocket and put the magazine among the others.

Just then the door to the glassed-in room opened and the woman and the garageman came in. "You're lucky it's the battery," the man said. Leona said she'd like to hold on to the trunk key unless he needed it. He shrugged, went into his dark cubbyhole, and brought out a receipt. Still writing it, he asked for her name. "Merchassen," said the woman whose name was Leona, "Helen Merchassen," and she spelled it for him. She acted cheerful, but a little nervous and talkative. "This won't take long, maybe half an hour, if you want to wait," the garageman said. "No," Leona told him. "Maybe we'll do some shopping. We'll be back by then."

Outside, Leona looked around carefully, up and down the row of stores, before they started along the sidewalk. She asked them whether, if she gave them some money, they could take care of it or should she tie it in a hanky. "I want mine tied," Patsy said, and Walter nodded and said, "I always lose my money."

She took three quarters and three little handkerchiefs of different colors from her purse, knotted one quarter in a corner of each one, and passed them out. The sky was gray and murky as they crossed through dirtied snow and entered the bright interior of the dime store. "All right," she said, looking straight at them. "You can spend your quarter on anything you want that costs a quarter. Just like before. You pick it out."

Walter whispered to Patsy, "We get to pick it out."

"Walter, do you understand that you have to be good?"
He nodded.

"I want you to have a good time, but if you're bad I can't
give you any more quarters. Mamie, pay attention. Now, go
ahead. I'll be right around here if you want me." She stayed at
the front of the store to watch them as they went their separate
ways. Walter soon found the wall of aquariums and stood gazing
up at the bright darting fish. Patsy's hand squeaked down the
long glass cases of candy.

Clutching her lavender handkerchief in her fist, Mamie
walked slowly beside the display of dolls, her eyes switching to
Leona and back. The children were still within six feet of each
other. How carefully Mamie moved now, slowly, quietly,
hardly lifting her feet. Never far away, Leona tucked her purse
under her arm and strolled down the aisle one counter over.
Mamie leaned back and watched her pause at the sewing counter
and turn farther into the store. Leona was now two aisles away,
looking down, looking at something. Mamie could see the
shoulders of her fur coat through the neatly arranged shelves.

Again Mamie checked the others. Walter stood with his
hands clasped behind him, gazing up at the tanks; Patsy had
stopped in front of a glass case of jelly beans. Mamie looked
beyond them to the chute beside the cash register where two
middle-aged clerks were chatting across the counter. If she went
that way, the other kids would try to follow her and she'd have
to get past the clerks. She glanced back. The patch of Leona's
fur coat was still visible through the shelves. Mamie peered
down the long funnel of goods broken by intersecting aisles and
saw another woman, two sections away, stooping to investigate
the stacks of merchandise under the display.

Now was her chance. She spun on her toe and dashed
straight for the woman shopper, scampering past a bank of
artificial flowers, some ironing boards, and a high teetering stack
of detergent. She broke through the intersecting aisle, her heart

pounding, and plunged forward. The stooping woman wore a turban. Hearing Mamie's approach, she lifted her head and turned. Without hesitation, Mamie ran through the next aisle, and she had already started to spill her words before she reached the woman. "Help me!" she gasped. "Help me get away." She pointed frantically behind her, down the empty aisle. "She took us. She did, and—and—I want to go home. I have to go home now. Please, help me, please! I—" She stumbled to a stop near the woman, huffing for breath, too choked with emotion to express the depth of her anguish. She began to sob. Tears smudged her eyes and she felt dizzy with urgency.

The woman in the turban said, "Whoa, there. Now, slow down and tell me again." Mamie wiped the tears from her eyes, and breathlessly tried to explain. "I don't want to, but she came to the hospital and got me and—but I didn't want to—I don't want to go in the car." Something brushed her shoulder; she jerked away from it and saw Walter. Behind him was Patsy, and looming behind both of them stood Leona. Mamie groaned and sidestepped into a wall of hanging mop handles. Leona slipped between the two kids and said to the turbaned woman, "Don't mind Mamie. There's no telling what she might've said, if she said anything. She has such a vivid imagination. Don't you, Mamie?"

But it was Leona's face that was ashen and frightened, not Mamie's. She stepped quickly to Mamie and reached for her, but Mamie swung out hard and pivoted before she was drawn up at the waist. Through the fur coat, she could feel Leona's body shaking. Mamie twisted in the clasping arms.

The other woman, still stooping, was trying to talk to Patsy. Mamie heard her say, "What's your name?" and Patsy glanced aside to murmur her reply. "You look awfully familiar," the woman said. Leona let Mamie down, keeping a grip on her forearm, and rushed toward Patsy as the woman said, "Why, you're the little girl I saw in the newspaper, aren't you?" Suddenly, Leona caught Patsy's hand and they were moving. "Aren't you?" the woman said, now staring at Leona. *That's the little girl!*"

And they were practically running. Leona told Walter to hurry, *hurry;* the dime-store lights slid by them, bright boxes clattered to the floor, and all the pretty colors blurred away.

Outside, Mamie tried to plant her shoes and brace herself, but they were moving so fast that she was momentarily dragged through the air. "Hurry!" Leona said. "Hurry, Walter. Try to keep up. Take Patsy's hand. That's it." She dipped down and grabbed Mamie in the crook of her arm, and they were crossing the street, running for the garage and the old car.

They fled down the winter sidewalk, past stores decorated for Thanksgiving, past a huge wedding cake in a baker's window. Leona's hair was coming undone, her feet skittered on the ice, and now it was snowing quite hard. "Let's go!" she said, with the wind blowing the snow straight at them. "Come on, let's go!" shooing them before her like chickens, picking them up when they lagged behind, and carrying them until she could let them down again. "Run!" She could hear the fright in her voice. They had only a few minutes to get away. That woman knows who we are. She'll get the police.

At the end of the storefronts, Leona saw the Buick parked outside the garage, ready for her. Still pushing the children along, she hurried to get her key from the mechanic, who was now working on a red car in the driveway. The mechanic said, "It'll start for ya—I just now drove it out." Then he told her he'd left the key in the ignition, and Leona turned to go. But Patsy stopped, and then Walter stopped with her. They stood gazing at the little red Ford. "That's Mommy's car," Walter said. "That looks like my mommy's car." Trembling and out of breath, Leona said there must be hundreds of cars like that one, and caught Patsy's hand. "Come on, now, Walter. Never mind. We have to go. Oh, my God, *hurry.*"

# 12

"How's it comin'?" Sherman said, leading the Chinaman toward the red coupe.

From the shadows under the hood, the mechanic squinted at him through the snow. "Just about finished," he said. "All you needed was a fan belt."

With a shrewd and nimble watchfulness, Sherman again scanned the layout of intersections and stores. No police in sight. And no sign of Mamie. He had been driving all night. "I thought I heard it squeakin'," he said.

"I see you got your groceries," the man remarked, collecting his tools and drop cloth and slamming the hood.

"Yeah," Sherman said. "How much do I owe ya?"

"I better check." The mechanic went into the garage.

Still glancing from side to side, Sherman put the sack of groceries in the back seat and took out a Hershey bar. The Chinaman jumped into the car and immediately sat down, his tail twitching. Sherman snapped off some pieces of the chocolate and flipped them to the dog; then he ate a few pieces himself. "Is this your favorite?" he said, teasing the dog as he chewed. "Or what? What's your favorite?" But the dog wouldn't bark or break his concentration from the candy, a rich, brown drool leaking from his muzzle. Sherman fed the dog the rest of the bar. What's taking so long? he wondered. Thirty miles back, a man in a restaurant said he'd seen the woman in the Buick headed this way, but now all trace of her had vanished. Again, Sherman scanned the streets. Through the snow, he saw the mechanic come out.

Sherman counted six dollars from the wad of bills in his pocket and took the receipt. He was about to show the mechanic the picture of the woman when the man said, "You sure you're old enough to drive this baby?"

"Yeah," Sherman told him, his voice suddenly cold and flat. "I'm old enough." He returned the picture to his pocket.

"Okay," the mechanic said, backing away. "You are if you say you are. That's my motto."

Through the snowstorm, the red coupe headed out of town. With his head pounding, Sherman sat erect but low in the driver's seat, peering above the rim of the steering wheel. On the seat beside him lay the bottle containing his last pill, saved since yesterday noon. The sleepless hours of driving were beginning to take their toll. His eyelids drooped and blinked. The road was already slippery with new snow—he'd have to be careful not to end up in a ditch. He took his foot off the accelerator and pumped the brake pedal. In swerving dips the Ford slowed to a crawl. The dull ache throbbed in his temples and his eyes watered until he could hardly see. He squeezed his eyes shut momentarily, blinked, and saw a rusty neon sign appearing in the falling snow. HORSESHOE COURT. TOURIST COTTAGES.

As he drove past the horseshoe-shaped drive, he drowsily glanced in at the little string of cottages and went on down the road. He drove another thirty or forty yards before it struck him. What had he just seen? He let a car pass, shifted the Ford to reverse, and crept back. There it was, parked at one of the cottages: the blue Buick.

Still, it startled him.

"*That's it!*" he yelled. "*That's it! That's it!*"

Its grille dappled with snow, the Buick faced the road; it had been parked back toward the cottage. Suddenly everything around him grew sharper. Again he shifted gears. Inching forward, he glanced at the road, then back, the parked Buick rotating slowly on the axis of his sight. He saw the woman and three kids coming out of the cottage and rushing for the car. Then, clearly, he saw that one of the kids was Mamie.

"*Mamie!*" he shouted, "*Mamie! Mamie! Mamie!*" pulling himself up on the wheel, bouncing in the seat. He couldn't stifle his outcry, his voice contained in the closed car. He was filled with joy. He smacked the steering wheel, turned quickly into the front entrance of the drive, and stopped the car just beyond the motel office.

From that distance, he watched the woman as he made his plan. He wanted to surprise her. He wanted her to beg. Uncapping the bottle, he swallowed his pill. "Boy," he said to the Chinaman, "do you see what I see?"

That awful woman, Leona thought; she's called the police by now. Her nerves were so on edge she didn't know what she should be preparing for. She could feel the gravity of the danger bearing down on her. She needed some kind of defense, something to restore her equilibrium. She leaned into the trunk, pushed aside the other suitcases, and opened the lizard-skin briefcase. It was as if everything she had done had led her inexorably to this moment. Grasping the Browning automatic in its mass of crochet cotton, she transferred it, cotton and all, to her purse.

"Is that a gun?"

Ambushed by the child's voice, Leona flinched and glanced back. Not three feet away, Patsy stood watching. And stepping away behind Patsy was Mamie.

"Can I see it? Can I see in your purse?" Patsy said, her voice almost a whisper.

"No," Leona said, and they stared at each other. "Patsy, I'm not playing now. I told you to get in the car."

"Okay," the little girl said, "but you don't have to be mad at me," and turned away.

Leona slipped her hand into her purse, gripped the cold pistol, and flipped the safety off.

The snow continued to fall, heavier and heavier. With the doors on the passenger side open, she lifted the children, one by one, into the car: Patsy and Walter in back; Mamie taking her turn to ride in front. Leona locked the doors on the inside, slammed them shut. Head down, clutching her collar tight, she ran to the other side of the car. Over the snow-swept roof of the Buick she noticed that the red car the children had pointed out at the garage was now parked near the motel office. The driver's door had been left standing open. . . .

She heard an odd sound on the wind. The falling snow obscured her vision, but she was certain she saw something move; yet when she blinked, it was gone. It's just the snow, she thought. She slipped behind the wheel. Placing her purse on her lap, she pulled the door shut. Crusty ice had darkened the windows in scallops and eddies, a packed, uneven dimness. Dear God, she thought, please start this car. She turned the ignition key and the motor revved beneath them. The wipers cleared most of the windshield, leaving frozen patches. But she couldn't take time to clean it. The car broke forward, cracking on ice.

At fifteen feet, he heard her start the car. Now at ten feet, through the ice-crusted side window, he could see the mottled shape of her head as the car pulled forward. Stop her, he thought, and he plunged through the deep snow. The Chinaman, breaking through drifts, raced beside him. Sherman pulled the blackjack from his pocket, ran out on the slippery ice, and flung himself at the moving car, his arm whipping around. The blackjack exploded on the side glass with a deafening crash.

At the moment of impact, Leona's head whirled away from the inward spew of glass and she pitched across the seat to hide herself and protect Mamie. *My God, what was that?* In that moment she was seized by fear so profound she felt that her heart had wrenched sideways. It took her completely by surprise; she thought someone had shot a bullet. Her bedraggled hair and her coat caught much of the flying glass, but grains and slivers of it were stuck to her cheek and in her left eyebrow. She was afraid to open her eyes.

When the Buick swerved from his blow, the rear fender caught Sherman broadside and knocked him off balance. He spun to his knees and came up, still clutching the blackjack. Again he went toward the car and the woman inside it, but then he saw a blinking red light stain the snow around him and glanced back. Everything in him froze. In front of the unlit motel office at the other end of the drive, a shiny black car slowed beside the red Ford.

Police.

Moving as little as possible, he drew to a standstill. The snow fell in a thick biting slant. It was his only cover. He could hear the Buick rolling slowly away. He wanted desperately to go after it, but he couldn't. He had to hide. Across the windy divide, a state trooper got out of the black cruiser and strode toward the little red car. As soon as the trooper turned his back, Sherman darted and swiveled down between two cars that had been parked in the drive overnight. He pulled the Chinaman to him and held the black mouth muffled with his good hand, ready to silence him if he started to bark.

She still felt as if an enormous muscle had been pulled to the point of breaking deep in her breast. Cowering in the front seat, Leona gasped for breath and touched the sharp bits of glass on her face. She wiped and picked enough of them away so that she could open her eyes. Miraculously the already cracked side window in the driver's door had held, but she wondered if it was safe to sit up. Yet she had no choice: she couldn't let the car idle along any farther.

Taking a deep breath, she pushed herself up from Mamie and sat behind the wheel. Her foot trembled on the brake. She looked back at Patsy and Walter. Their faces were terror-stricken, shocked beyond tears. "Are you hurt?" she asked them, her own voice hoarse with fright. "Is anybody hurt?" She reached inside her purse and fitted her hand on the Browning.

"I think I feel pale," Patsy said, whitefaced, and Walter began to sob, his fingers digging into the top of the seat. But before she could turn to him or make any effort to comfort him, a ray of reddish light fluttered into the car's interior. It flashed through Leona like a current. Police, she thought. That woman did tell.

*Did they fire at us?* She couldn't see through the shattered side window, and snow had covered the window in back. But through the patchy windshield she saw a black police car skid across the exit end of the drive and block it. Her heartbeat jumped in her throat. Horrified, she let go of the Browning. I can't do that, she thought. We've got to get out of here. We'll have to go out the other end.

To Sherman, watching, none of it seemed real. The red coupe was cut off by the police. Two black cruisers sat angled in front of it now, their pale insignias glinting through the snow. Four troopers had congregated at the rear of the car; they were prying the trunk open with crowbars. He could hear them. Then, in the arc of their headlights, he saw them lift out his bloodied clothes. I knew it all along, he thought; it's me they're after. Not her. But the confirmation of it ran in his veins like ice. He was trapped. He straightened up between the parked cars.

Tugging at the dog, he darted like a frightened animal, rely-ing on gut instinct, terrified beyond thought. Crashing through the snow to Cottage 10, he caught the doorknob but the door wouldn't open. At the next cottage, he hit the door with his shoulder; the latch jangled but the door held tight.

He heard a crunching sound behind him like footsteps. His heart jammed as he lunged around. Nothing. Nobody with a gun. Yet something was wrong. The Chinaman was wandering away though the snow.

Keeping his voice low, hardly above a whisper, he tried to call the dog back, "C'mere." He smooched the air with his lips two or three times. The dog stopped and raised his head. "Come on, Chinaman, c'mere." Urging the dog back, Sherman patted his knee and inched from the shadowed doorway, but it was no use. The Chinaman was still slipping through the snow, his dark, ragged coat working on his long muscles. "Go ahead, then, you bastard," he muttered. But he could see that the dog was moving at an odd gait, almost stalking, head pitched low. Then he saw why.

The Buick was turning back.

That's when the Chinaman started to bark.

"*Chinaman!*" Mamie screamed, "*Chinaman! Chinaman! Chinaman! It's him! It's him!*" She twisted and climbed on the seat, straining to look out. "It's him! It's him! Chinaman! It's him!" Her eyes frantic and searching, she pulled the lock knob up with both hands.

The passenger door flew open and Mamie plunged out. She fell in the snow and scrambled up, saw the Chinaman's head rise through the snow, and ran from the car toward him. "*Chinaman!*" She threw her arms around his ugly face, all her pent-up feelings overflowing, tears running from her eyes. He barked once, gruff and mean, then nuzzled and licked her face. "Oh, Chinaman," she gasped against the swipe of his tongue. "Oh, Chinaman, let's go! Where's Sherman at?" she whispered. "Take me, take me."

The dog back-stepped from her and barked. "Take me home," she said. He started to go, swung his head back, then barked again and pumped away through the snow. She chased after him. "I'm comin', Chinaman. I'm comin'. Wait for me!"

Immobilized at first by shock and fear, Leona shoved her purse under the seat, grabbed the key, and ran from the car, oblivious to everything but retrieving the child. "Mamie, don't! Don't go there!"

She swooped and caught her runaway and it was like holding a wild screeching cat. All teeth and fingernails, Mamie shrieked and struck out blindly. Leona tried to hold her in a tight clasp.

As they started back to the car, she glimpsed an odd movement in the snow. She looked again and saw a dark snow-speckled mass rushing toward her. A wail broke from her lips. *It's that dog!* Swinging Mamie against her hip, she ran for the car. And the Chinaman hit her like a blast. His teeth snagged her hair and the back collar of her coat. The force of his hurtling body carried them around and lifted her off her feet; Leona could feel the dog hanging on to her coat, riding with her through the air. They were thrown down in a hard slamming spin. She tried to break her fall with her arm and still hold Mamie; heard her coat tear away as she sprawled across the icy ruts in the drive.

The Chinaman rolled to his feet at once, rending the torn piece of coat like slaughtered meat. "Oh, Mamie, get up! Try to get in the car!" The dog dropped the piece of fur. Tightening her arm around Mamie, she heaved up. "Get to the car!" she gasped. She knew he was coming, saw the hackles on his back, saw his hindquarters gathering.

Panicked, she stepped to the side and ran, but he was at her, tearing at her, dragging to get her down. She felt the coat ripping on her back as she fell. Mamie squealed when Leona again tried to protect her. "Lemme go!" she yelled. "Lemme go!"

Leona slapped the dog hard across its muzzle, threw her arm up and absorbed the flailing wrench of his jaws. Part of her sleeve was gone. She was struggling with all her might, but he was too fast and too strong, eclipsing her with his hideous weight. The flesh of her ear stung and bled. I'm all in, she thought, I can't stop it, and felt the teeth jab at her body.

In the glittering air, one of the policemen yelled "Hey!" and quickly there came a low, shrill whistle. The dog twisted up, ears cocked. Again the whistle sounded. Through her torn sleeve, Leona saw the dog tramp away, his paws beating the snow in soft explosions. Still calling out to the dog, Mamie chased after him until Leona caught her again. And even then Mamie went on struggling, her eyes searching the cottages as the dog vanished from sight. "Let him go," Leona said, still dazed. "Mamie, for God's sake." Then she noticed what Mamie must have seen—a snowy, white-on-white shape like a snow-man withdrawing itself into the space between two cottages. And Mamie screamed out across the empty expanse: *"No-o-o!"*

From the crest of the drive, two policemen were hustling toward them saying something, but Leona couldn't hear it. They've got us, she thought. She tried to move quickly, but her legs wobbled like stilts. She called out, "Officer . . . My little girl, she's my little girl," and clambered to the car.

The policemen drew closer. "Lady, don't you hear good?" one of them shouted. "Get going! Get outa here! *Get out!* We've got a murderer loose in here!"

She put Mamie in the back seat, then got in and drove past the police cars angled in front of the red coupe. She couldn't stop shaking. Without pausing at the stop sign, she skidded the car onto the highway and sped away from the swarming red lights. Slowly, Mamie turned from looking out the back window. When Leona glanced in the rear-view mirror, Mamie's tear-stained eyes met hers with a gaze of fierce triumph.

.  .  .

It was like the taste of blood in his mouth.

In the falling snow, he watched the roof of the Buick speed along the motel's front embankment, gain ground, and sink down the road. Again she had got away from him, just as she had that night in the hospital, but this time he had drawn blood. The next time she wouldn't get off so easy. The Chinaman nudged his wrapped hand. "Good boy," Sherman said.

Another cruiser skidded toward the Ford, red lights flaring. Car doors slammed. Metal cracked and ratcheted as they loaded shotguns.

*You bastards.*

And yet the fear and the rage revived him. Had anybody seen him? he wondered. Do the police know me, know who I am? *Risk it,* he told himself. Gotta risk it. Shivering with fear, he took a step forward. He was flirting with danger and he knew it, could feel it surge through him. "Chinaman," he said, "come on." Braced inside himself, he walked out into the open drive. Scooping up a snowball, he looked around. Policemen were spread out everywhere. "You can't stop me," he muttered. "Nobody can. Just try it."

Quickly he hurled the snowball. The Chinaman bounded after it and Sherman ran along behind him toward the highway. A clipped cop voice yelled for him to stop. Bastards, he thought, gathering up more snow; I dare ya.

"Aw, hell, leave him alone," one of the troopers said. "It's just some kid playing with that damned dog." And the men lowered their guns and turned away.

# 13

Her hand still trembling, Leona gripped the rear-view mirror and adjusted it downward until the small staring face slid into the reflecting oblong. She placed her hand back on the steering wheel, but time and again her eyes flicked up to Mamie in the mirror. She knows all about this, Leona thought. Whoever it is chasing after us, doing these things—Mamie knows them. She knows that dog; she was calling its name. So many things were beginning to make sense. Someone had been with the dog. That shape like a snowman. And Mamie had tried to follow the dog to that shape. But who was it?

The wind caused the shattered window to flex and flutter at her side and fear pulsed through her. That's when it had started: with that window, the night she took Mamie. She could still see the shoes stepping from the curtains in Mamie's hospital room, could feel herself lift Mamie and rush outside, and the dog—she cringed, remembering—the dog attacking her car. It was all the same, the same dog, the same . . . The policeman had said murderer. The realization chilled her. Mamie had run toward a murderer.

Little details kept nagging at Leona, little things she had once overlooked or dismissed, like the tramped-down place in Emma's garden littered with bits of string and cigarette butts. Emma knew. She had been so unyielding, trying to tell her something wasn't right. What a fool I've been, Leona thought, I should have guessed Emma knew more about this than she said.

Oh, Emma, what was it you said? What have I done? A murderer. *A murderer*, Emma. Oh, my God.

Since leaving Graylie, she hadn't tried to call her sister for the most obvious reason: the police would probably expect her to. But now she had to, just as soon as she could get to a telephone. Assuming that everything was all right, she would ask Emma to tell her again what dreadful thing had happened in Mamie Abbott's family.

Her left ear was still bleeding a little from the scrape of the dog's teeth. Already it was swollen and stiff. She could feel it throb. And in the back of her mind was the knowledge that she would have to ditch her car, the 1948 Buick Roadmaster, the only car she had ever owned. She had never believed the authorities would endanger the children by attempting to capture them in a moving car. But the police, she realized, were a secondary threat; today had proved just how wrongheaded and sentimental she had been about the car. Now there was no choice; she had to get rid of it and cover her tracks.

She had driven perhaps twenty miles before they came to a gas station. Knowing that the shattered window would eventually cave in and leave them exposed to the weather, she asked the attendant if he could tape something over it, to keep it from flying into the car when the glass crumbled apart. "Lady," he said. "What the hell happened to you?" She asked if she could use the telephone.

But no one answered at Emma's house. In the rest room, she washed her face and her bloodied ear and tried to tidy herself. Undoing her clothes, she quickly examined herself. Though the dog had attacked her mercilessly, his teeth for the most part had only jabbed into the thickness of her coat. Across her abdomen and thighs her skin was scratched and bruised, but not torn and punctured as she had first feared. Still, it felt as if every bone in her body had been hurt. She straightened out her clothes and pulled on a sweater and her summer raincoat. What remained of the ruined fur coat she dropped in an outside barrel where trash was burning. Never again would she leave an obvious trail. Then she quickly returned the Browning automatic to the briefcase and took it with her to the front seat of the car, to have it close at hand if she needed it. The attendant had knocked out the shattered glass and replaced it with a piece of taped-in cardboard.

She drove another thirty miles and stopped and called again. She stood shivering in the roadside booth, listening to the telephone ring on the distant line. No answer. At the drive-in restaurant where she next called, she ordered hamburgers to take out. Still no answer. She tried to figure out where Emma might be but, of course, she could be almost anywhere. It was Thursday. Maybe she was out shopping or visiting with neighbors.

They entered West Virginia at about three o'clock in the afternoon and just before they crossed the Monongahela River, Leona tried to call again. The telephone rang and rang. Answer it, Leona pleaded, rapping her fingers on the metal shelf of the booth. Come on, Emma, answer. But no one did. They went on south and west through Barrackville and Pine Grove Hollow, driving and telephoning. As the afternoon moved toward nightfall, the pain caused by the dog's attack grew stronger.

A single band of blue winter light streaked the darkening sky. Surely she's home by now, Leona thought; it's nearly dark. In Fairmont, West Virginia, she saw a lighted telephone booth at the edge of the public-library lawn and pulled to the curb. The two Aldridge children had gone to sleep, but Mamie still watched her.

She gave the operator Emma's number. Feeling apprehensive, she listened to the distant telephone ring and ring; then it was picked up.

She gripped the telephone tight against her ear, but still it was difficult to hear. "Frank . . . Hello, Frank?"

"Leona . . . is that you?"

A little breathless, she said, "Yes, Frank, I—"

"Where are you?"

"I'm on the road, Frank. And the weather's so bad—"

"Leona . . . I've been wondering if you'd call."

"Frank, could I talk to Emma? Is she there? I've been trying to call. I need to talk to Emma—"

"Damn you, Leona, you know what you did? It's all because of you . . ." The telephone banged. It sounded as if it had been dropped or thrown down. After a moment it was taken up again.

"Aunt Leona, this is Charlie—you know, Emma's boy? Dad's all worked up, but he wants you—me to tell you Mom's in the hospital. It's pretty bad, we don't know . . . It's really bad, Aunt Leona. Can you hear me? The night you left, somebody broke in here and beat Mom up—beat her nearly to death. She's in a coma. . . . Aunt Leona, are you there? Dad's all upset, so don't blame yourself. They've moved her to Scranton—to a hospital in Scranton. . . . Aunt Leona? Are you there?"

Leona tried to answer but her voice was strangled in her throat. Tears welled in her eyes. She was standing outside the booth, holding her face in her hands. She stumbled out across the library lawn, gasping for air, beginning to weep. When the waves of nausea and tears subsided, she nearly reached the car but then had to rush from it, moaning and retching. Bending down beside some hedges bordering the lawn, she couldn't hold it inside her and stood there heaving, so weak she could hardly stay on her feet. At last, wiping her face, she made her way back to the car.

Head spinning, she told the children, "I don't feel well," and for once they kept their distance, perhaps sensing the depth of her pain. Again and again, tears filled her eyes. Leaning her sore ear against her hand, Leona drove into the night, the lights of cars approaching and focusing, horns blaring and yawning away, lights, endless lights taking shape like the evil, slanted eyes of that dog.

Emma, she thought, I never meant to hurt you, God knows. I'm so tired . . . worn to a frazzle . . . can't sleep, can't get hold of myself. I can't come to you and I want to, I want to. Oh, Emma, if that madman comes at me again, Emma, if he comes after any of these children or sends that dog, I'll kill him—I swear to God I will—for both of us. . . . Somehow I'll kill that vicious bastard if it's the last thing I ever do.

The children slept around her in the darkened car as free from worry, it seemed, as cattle roaming in moonlight. In her grief she felt utterly alone and apart from them. If only I'd never left, she thought. Emma would still be all right. I could have stayed with her and talked to her, and everything would be the way it was. Suddenly she remembered Emma dancing across the windy garden just before she left. And she saw the pennies, those sweet, silly pennies, in Emma's shoes. Oh, Emma, Emma. She had to pull off the road; she was crying hysterically, unable to control herself. She folded her arms on the steering wheel and hid her face and the grief poured from her. Finally, Walter woke up, leaned over the top of the front seat, and said, "Why're you cryin'? Did that dog hurt you?"

"Yes," she said before she realized how it would sound. "Oh, Walter, no, it's not that. I just don't want anybody to get hurt any more."

She did not know how long she drove. The bleary lights trickled away and the highway narrowed to an asphalt road among hills. This isn't right, she thought; this isn't the highway. Somewhere she had missed a turn or turned once too often. She slowed and went on, looking for a wide place where she could turn the car around.

The road was packed with snow. She wasn't aware that they were riding on ice until she felt the back end of the car slip to the side. Quickly she turned the wheel against the slide and for a moment the car seemed to correct itself. Then the rear end spun out completely and the Buick was gliding sideways down the road in a smooth, effortless slant.

She turned the wheel to no avail. She pumped the brakes but

couldn't stop the skid. Stunned, she realized they were sliding crosswise down a long, gradual slope. In front of her, the headlights ghosted through a snowy wire fence to nothing. And the children were sitting up, sleepy and puzzled. "What happened?" they asked. "Where are we?"

Very little time had passed. She could tell by the drift of the car that they were headed for the snowbank edging the road. When they hit it, the impact would at least slow them or maybe even stop them. "Get up here," she said, throwing them a glance, both her hands clenched on the wheel. "Walter, you and Mamie get up here beside Patsy." If she tried to get them out through the driver's door, they would fall in the path of the car. "Come on," she commanded. "Quick, get up here!"

They were climbing over the seat when the Buick jolted into the snowbank. With its back end dragging through the snow, the car crested forward, temporarily slowed. All at once, she had a terrible premonition of what was to come. She strained past the three of them and pushed the passenger door open. "Get out!" she cried. "I can't get it to stop. Go! Get out! Get out!" Patsy jumped out and fell. "Go, Mamie. Quick, get out!" Mamie jumped. Walter scooted to the edge of the seat, but hesitated; Leona had to push him out.

With a faint tamping of snow, the car straightened along the raised spine of the road and gained speed. She reached for the doorway herself but everything dipped—the headlights, the nose of the car, the track of her eyes—and she knew she was moving much too fast.

Brush and gravel scraped the undercarriage with a scattering noise and then nothing, no sound. The road lay in a steep trough, one side shelved with stone slabs, the other side woods. She could see ice, full plates of ice, where the wind had blown the road smooth and luminous. And in between the plates of ice, drifts of purest silver.

The front end of the Buick was already sliding when it hit

the first expanse of ice and sped forward. The foreground of shelved sandstone went by in a blur. She tried to stop the car; she pressed down on the brake with all her strength. "Please," she moaned, "please, God, get me out of this."

The Buick crashed like a bullet against a wall of snow six feet high. Glass shattered. The steering wheel wrenched from her hands so quickly that both her wrists snapped and throbbed. She grabbed the wheel and jammed down on the brakes, again using the full power of her body. But the car erupted onto the ice once more. Ice as far as she could see. And it was like moving out across the mute drum of the universe.

Then she realized that the land was falling away. The empty roar of the engine came to her and she knew the car was aloft, flying through the air.

Suddenly before her staring eyes, the concrete sidewalls of a bridge jutted through the night. In a thunderous crash landing, the Buick straddled one of the walls and flew forth as if on a rail. She was pitched forward. Her body crumpled, her head smacked the windshield glass, and she was slammed back. Like a spent meteor, the car spewed a few feet down the concrete length, the gutting of the undercarriage awesome. In the midst of the jarring clatter, the door flew open and Leona was thrown out into the snow, unconscious.

Then, silence.

Snow fell off the trees. Water in the creek below trickled on its way. The wind whined on the road and under the bridge it snored like sleep itself. Perched delicately atop the low girder, the old blue car groaned and tottered and fell, crashing into the snow. The quiet of the woods resumed.

Still brushing the snow from their clothes, the children scurried to the bridge and down the bank. One by one they went to her, the three of them gathering to look down on the woman who had watched over them as they slept and saved them from the wreck. She was sprawled face up on the snowbank among some brush, her arms flung wide as if to greet the heavens. There was blood on her face. They stood as if spellbound. Then, bending down, Mamie reached out and touched the blood on Leona's forehead. After a moment she drew away. Slowly she turned and beckoned the others to follow. And they left her lying there.

Leaning into the wind, the three children set off down the moon-swept road that vanished in the waiting trees.

# PART THREE

## 14

Night branches swooped down at them; shadows darted across the phantom road in a crazy web, surrounding them, flickering over them. And the moon chased through the sky, appearing and disappearing in clouds. Once, Patsy cried out, "I can't see. I can't see nothing!" She groped for the other two children and fell silent, overcome with the immensity of their solitude.

One by one, they sobbed for breath, shuddering from the cold and to keep from breaking down completely. Each child's face was stricken, on the verge of crying out. They ran a few steps, then walked, huddled, then split apart, their shoes creaking through the snow.

Slowly, Patsy and Walter began to whisper to each other; then more excitedly they debated what to do, their voices growing loud and edgy. "Let's go back and wait till somebody comes," Walter pleaded. "Who else'll take care of us?" Hurrying along beside them, Mamie kept quiet, paying no attention to their argument. Walter craned his head back, then drew it down inside his coat collar like a turtle. "Please," he said. "Come on. We gotta go back there."

"No," Patsy said, her voice sharp, surprisingly vehement. "Let's get outa here! There's monsters out here! Can't you hear 'em?"

"I do," Walter said. "I hear 'em. That's why we gotta go back."

"I won't go back. I have to go home. *There was blood on her!* I saw it. Didn't you see it? *Blood?* I did."

"But we'll get lost," Walter said. "We're all gonna get *real lost.* And *freeze to death.*"

From the woods by the road came a wild thrashing of sticks and twigs, bushes stamped on, stones clattering. Terrified, the children wheeled toward the violent noise. "See?" Patsy exclaimed, "There *is* something out there! *See?* I toldja." But the wind howled in their ears, drowning any recurrence of the sound. Together they moved backward, staring toward the dark place where the noise had been. No one spoke. They exchanged frightened looks, and Mamie turned, hurrying farther and farther away down the white winter road, and the other two children fell in behind her. "What *was* that?" Patsy asked quietly.

"Don't know," Walter said, his voice strange. They crossed a bridge of snow-covered planks that bounced lightly under their feet. The wind blew from the trees; it was as if the storm had never stopped. "It's that monster," Patsy decided. "It's watching us. It's gonna get us. It's *gonna get us!*" Uncontrollably she began to chant it, each word gasped and quivering, *"It's gonna get us! It's gonna get us!"*

Suddenly behind them, on the far side of the bridge they had crossed, the snowy bushes combusted in a furious spasm. Like a wild engine of snow and wind, something swung out onto the road and raced at them. "Run!" Walter shouted. *"Run! Run!"* They scattered down the empty length of road but the whirlwind quickly engulfed them. Shrieking, they pitched into the snow-ditch weeds; then as the churned-up snow sifted down around them, the terrible presence materialized under the moonlight: a deer, ice-frocked and majestic, stood at the edge of the road. For a split second, the children thought they shouldn't be afraid, but the deer was so big and domineering—the air around them shook with the snorted blasts from his black nostrils.

Regal and towering, the buck loomed over them. The massive expanse of his chest twitched with packed energy. The sight of it drew away what little courage the children had left and held their eyes suspended in terrified wonder. Lifted very high and erect, the murderous points of its antlers gleamed yellow-tipped. In a rush of nervous muscle, its hooves stabbed the snow and the buck took an abrupt step forward, snorting white streams. Frightened beyond limits they could endure, the children whimpered and squirmed back from the animal. For something so large, the deer's carriage was tipsy and delicate. The ponderous crown of killing bone tipped and nodded lightly, then grew still. His black liquid eyes studied the night above them. With a long slow droop of his mighty head, the buck peered at them and they saw the pure cruelty of his eyes. They moaned for breath. Immediately, without any noticeable gathering of power, the buck vaulted over them and thudded away into the night.

The glittering silence returned to the road.

Badly shaken, the children climbed from the ditch. As they dusted the snow from their clothes, Mamie finally spoke. She was every bit as frightened as they were, but what she told them that night changed the way they thought of her for a very long time. It was the night she told them about Sherman.

The cold wind wailed in the trees like a continuous lament of voices. When it blew very hard, it nearly lifted the children, as if to push them on their way. In the dull moonlight, Mamie's eyes looked smoke-colored. She was shivering, too, walking fast beside the others, but the small features of her face were determined and hard-set. She said they couldn't get away by themselves, but that someone was coming after them, to take them away. She would tell them a secret, she said, if they would cross their hearts. They drew X's on their coats. The cold, cutting wind blew; they turned their backs to it; their teeth chattered, yet they went on. Mamie told them what had happened that afternoon in the motel drive, that she had seen the Chinaman with her brother Sherman. She asked them if they had seen the dog, and they said they had. "The one that hurt her," Walter said, and Mamie nodded. "That was the Chinaman," she said, "and I used to give him sugar." She cringed against the cold, her voice shaky. Hurriedly she told them about her house burning up, fire everywhere, and she got out of it and Sherman got out, but nobody else did, not her mommy or her daddy or Toddy —all killed in it. And how Sherman had come to get her in the hospital, but that woman, Leona, took her away instead.

Their eyes were apprehensive, yet they were mesmerized by her sudden revelations. Then she told them her awful truth, the fearful thing she had kept swallowed up inside her these many weeks. "If you tell—if you say anything, people will think you're crazy. That's what the nurse told me. *So don't ever tell.* They'll put you in a room with other crazy people in it, without any doors or windows, and you can't never get out. You can't come home or go anyplace, cause they won't letcha. Because people will think you're crazy. If you tell . . ." She saw the terribleness of it strike them and sink through them, and afterward they looked about, almost incoherent with their imaginings.

"Will we go to jail?" Walter asked finally, his face contorted with dread.

"It's like jail," Mamie said, "only you can't never get out." Afraid of what she said, they scooted away from her and shuddered, drawing their coats tighter about them. They went over a hill that seemed large to them and down the other side of it. Then, deep in trees, they saw the lighted windows.

"Remember," Mamie said, "not to tell. If you do, they'll call the police and take us away."

At the two mailboxes they turned down the snow-flattened

lane. As they passed the barn, Patsy lagged behind. "I'm not goin' over there," she said, staring at the tall dark eaves of the house some distance away. "What if there's witches in there? What if it's like that story? I don't want to be changed into something." They looked at each other, then across the lot strewn with chicken pens and stacks of firewood. It was snowing again, the air suddenly dense and white.

"There's no place else," Walter said. "Look all around. There's no place else but this one."

"Patsy, we can't wait to go home out here," Mamie said. "There's not been any cars go by. Not even one."

"Yeah," Walter said, "and we're freezin'."

They passed the scatter of sheds and outbuildings and pens and came to the gate in the picket fence that surrounded the house. Their mittens and gloves closed on the wooden latch and turned it, and they crossed the flawless snow to the screen door. "What was that?" Patsy said, and ran back to the other side of the gate. Walter shrugged. "I didn't hear nuthin'," he said.

The screen door led to a dark, screened-in porch cluttered with tools and washtubs, old harnesses and horse collars, a pump built into a box. When they knocked on the door, it clapped in the frame. "They can't hear us," Mamie said. Cupping their hands to the sides of their eyes, Mamie and Walter peeked through the screen and saw two other doors, one on either side of the enclosed entryway. "I'm not goin' in there," Patsy said, standing outside the gate. "You can't make me."

"Me neither," Walter said. "It's scary in there."

"Somebody has to," Mamie said. "Remember, don't tell."

They dug the ends of their gloved fingers into the crack of the door until they could squeeze it open, and Mamie stepped up across the stone threshold, crept to the door inside the porch, struck it with her fist, and dashed back. They closed the screen door and stood there, shivering, peering in.

Slowly the door opened and they stepped back even farther.

A hand holding a lighted lamp emerged slowly through the opened doorway. "Hey," Mamie said, her voice shaking. "We're out here."

The upheld lamp came toward them. Light spilled down a woman's sleeve and burnished half her long face; the other half melted in darkness. She was a tall woman and she was wearing a sweater over her apron and blue work shirt. A knotted scarf hid her hair. "Who is it?" she said. "Who's out there? . . . Kids? Little kids? What on earth . . ."

"Wreck," Patsy cried, running in. "Wreck, we've had a wreck!"

Holding the small of her back, the woman leaned down, shining the lamplight over them, turning her head from one to the other as they all talked. Then, as Patsy ran out of breath, Walter pointed out across the white fields. "She's hurt," he said. "She's bleeding. *She's died!*"

"Come in here," the woman said. "I can't understand a word you're saying. Don't let my heat out, now. Come on in here and tell me what happened from the beginning."

Near the warm cookstove in the kitchen, she gathered them to her, loosening their coats and rubbing their cold hands, and when she understood what had happened, she said, "Now, listen. Where was it? How far?" And they told her about the bridge, the low bridge.

She went immediately to the telephone and dialed it. She said, "Mark, this is Vivian, up here. Come quick! There's been a wreck down by Forky Creek bridge. Somebody's hurt." She slipped into her coat, sat in a chair to pull on rubber boots. As soon as she was ready to go, she ushered the children into the living room where the drum of another wood stove glowed with heat. "Mom," she said to the woman sitting near the stove. "Mama, you look after these children, now. While I'm gone." And they were left alone in that tall room quaking with light, alone except for an old woman whose eyes glowed from the deepest crevices of her face. Coming inside from the violence of all that had happened, their bodies still vibrant with fright, they stood gazing across the stove at the creaking chair that had slowly, very slowly, stopped rocking.

They brought Leona back to the farmhouse in Mark Hardesty's old Willys car, and he carried her in his arms to Vivian's bed in the living room. To the children, Mark was a provocative and beguiling sight, tall, dark-haired, a man of action. Murmuring among themselves, they crept forward to see him better in the lamplight. "I like him," Walter whispered. "He's kinda like my daddy." But Mamie whispered, "Sh-h-h. Don't say that any more. They'll know something's wrong." Her small white fingers were like knobs pressing through his coat sleeve. Straightaway, Vivian tried to call a doctor but after a moment she hung up the receiver. "I cain't get through," she said. "We'll have to do the best we can."

"Maybe if I left right now," Mark Hardesty said. "Maybe I could still get to town."

Vivian shook her head. "In this storm, you'd never make it. And even if you did, you'd never get back. Don't you leave me stuck out here. We're just lucky we got back here with 'er." Then, while Vivian swiftly attended to Leona's most critical needs, wrapping her in quilts and heaping wood on the fire, Hardesty brought in suitcases from the car. Vivian asked the children which of the suitcases their clothes were in and Mamie pointed to two of them. "All right. Now, tell me, what would her name be?" Patsy and Walter turned to peer at Mamie. "It's Leona," Mamie said without looking up. Vivian slid the two suitcases away from the others, pulled more blankets from the wardrobe, gave them to Hardesty, and told him to put the kids to bed upstairs. Hearing their footsteps on the staircase, she turned immediately to her mother, who had been watching throughout the commotion. "Mama, you're gonna have to put yourself to bed tonight. I got work to do."

The old woman's cane tapped the floor. Slowly she stood; then her face twitched as if she had walked through spiderwebs, and her quivering voice began, "Vivy, listen to me. There's somebody in yore bed. Hit's some gypsy woman with a whole passel of kids. Ye oughter watch out. They're gonna steal ye blind. . . ." Vivian went with her as far as the kitchen door and turned back.

The snowstorm lashed the old farmhouse in great, droning gusts; against the winter blasts, the kerosene lamps in the room guttered and throbbed with smoky light. Much later, after Vivian had cut away Leona's bloodied clothes and bathed and covered her in one of her own gowns, after Hardesty had closed the vicious head wound with mercerized thread, they stood by her, waiting for some remnant of color to return to her stone-white face. They couldn't have marveled at her more if she had plummeted from the sky. "My God, look at her," Vivian said, her voice constrained with worry. "I wonder who she is."

"Come on, now, Vee. She looks healthy. She'll come through this all right."

"She'd be pretty if she didn't look so nearly done in. Surely, somewhere, her people must be waitin' for her."

"We could find out who she is if you want to," Hardesty said. "We could go through her purse."

"No, sir," Vivian told him. "I'd hate to do that—unless we have to. I wouldn't want somebody rummagin' through my things. I guess it don't matter who she is right now—we cain't get word out anyhow."

When it appeared that Leona would, indeed, survive the night, Vivian sent Hardesty home, with the understanding that he would be on hand the next day while she did her chores. She didn't tell him what she had seen.

Leona's clothes had been well tailored, so unlike Vivian's clothes she had hated to cut them, and there were welts and scratches on her abdomen and thighs that did not correspond to any of the tears in her clothing. So what had really happened? And why had her car crashed in this isolated place? She wore no wedding ring, yet she had three children. Who are you? Vivian thought. What sent you out on that mean stretch of road on a night like this? With three kids in the car? And why get them out of the car and not yourself? But finally . . . Lord, she looked so hurt and helpless. Vivian took her limp hand momentarily and patted it. "Well, Leona," she said, "you don't make any sense to me. You look like you've been through livin' hell."

The next morning, while Hardesty and her mother watched over Leona and entertained the children, Vivian went out to do her chores, glad to be outside even in a blowing storm. Hardesty had offered to do her work for her but she refused him, taking some pride in the little farm work she left for herself. She treated the children in the only way she knew how, with a warm place to sleep and good food from the stove and cheer in her heart. Even her mother, who was eighty-three and feeble, cantankerous, growing dimmer and weaker every day, rejoiced in the three little imps, as she called them.

For three days and four nights, Leona lay on Vivian's bed in the living room, wounds wrapped in bandages, as still and exotic as a mummy. Every now and then, she would rouse up and say something, but her ramblings made no sense. The enigma she created just by being there remained intact; the entire household revolved around her, and it was with a kind of freighted expectancy that Vivian waited for the woman to regain consciousness. I'll know what this is all about when she opens her eyes, Vivian thought, as if the unknown were suddenly going to solidify into a definite shape.

"Try to lay still and rest. You've had a bad spill."

The voice came to Leona in ripples, like the surface of a pond broken in disappearing waves, and the air itself condensed to the consistency of water, smooth and slick and easy to drink. She was aware of footsteps shifting quietly around her. From farther away, she heard a soft whirl of giggles. She opened her eyes and the place was full of light. Shapes were standing nearby, just barely out of focus. This is a dream, she thought, but realized it wasn't; she seemed to be stranded in some bright void. Closest was a man, a stranger.

She started to edge up on her elbows to see and talk, but a hand settled on her breastbone. The man said, "Don't try to get up. You'll fall down." Then he spoke again: "Look at me," he said. Leona strained to see him clearly, but against the glare her eyes began to water. "Look at me," he repeated. "Do you see me?" She opened her lips and nothing came out. "Don't try to answer," he said. "If you hear me, just follow my finger with your eyes." He moved his finger from left to right and up and down. The space where he had been grew clouded.

The soft weight on her chest was too heavy to lift. She sagged where she lay, her mouth cottony inside, forming and forcing from her lips all she had to know. "The"—drawing in breath, licking her lips—"the children . . ." A cool cloth pressed against her forehead and a voice trickled away inside her brain. "They're safe. You're all safe now. Don't worry."

The next time she awoke, the room was dark, murky-colored. Light pulsed on the walls and she heard a dry, snapping noise. Leona rolled her head and saw shooting flames inside a wood stove. With her fingers she touched her face, lips, eyebrow, and found the thick patch of bandages on her forehead. Her fingers collapsed there for a moment, searching, before her hand fell away. Under the covers she slipped her other hand out in a wide arc from her body, out across the cool expanse of the bed sheet, and it felt good and fresh against her parched fingers. Quickly she moved her toes. Nothing's broken, she thought.

On the other side of the firelight, a chair stirred with a cracking sound like the fire. A spindly shadow jutted and receded, sliding up and down the wall. The cadenced motion of the rocker, the creak and snap of the runners on the floor, fell into rhythm with her own heartbeat and in time it seemed as though her heart were out there softly fighting in the dark. *D-rump, ramp. D-rump, ramp.*

A figure stood from the chair and came through the amber half-light, a tall, long-boned woman of coarse features. "So," the gaunt woman said, seating herself in the cane-bottomed rocker by the bed. "You've finally come to."

"Yes," Leona said, "I think so," her voice as slow as her breath. "Where . . ."

"Sh-h-h," the woman said, leaning down. Age had softened the rough features of her face with a finely etched crosshatching, but the woman's eyes were intelligent and unblemished, an almost glacial blue. "Mind you, everybody's asleep. I even caught a little catnap myself." She smiled. Her hair was streaked with gray, her cheeks windburned and ruddy. "It's three o'clock in the morning. Now, don't fret yourself. Everything's under control." As she spoke, she tipped a pitcher and poured water into a glass. "Here," she said, "take a little of this. It'll help bring you around." Sliding her arm under Leona's pillow, the woman lifted her until she could drink a few sips of the water. Then she eased her back down, extracted her arm, and took the glass. "I've made some chicken soup. Would you take some if I brought it out?"

Leona closed her eyes and slowly shook her head on the pillow. "Are the children all right?"

"They're fine," the woman said, "all tucked in upstairs, fast asleep." She smiled and rocked back and forth. "I've told you that so many times it's gettin' to be monotonous."

Leona closed her eyes and slowly drew them open again. "What happened?" she asked.

"Don't you know? It's nigh onto impossible to get an ounce

of sense out of them kids. They said you made them get out of the car?"

"That's right," Leona said. "I couldn't stop it. I thought I was done for."

"You wasn't by yourself in that," the woman said and sat back. *D-rump, ramp,* her friendly firelit face swimming in and out of Leona's loose focus.

"Did you come get me?"

"Um-hum. Me along with Mark Hardesty. He lives just down under the hill. We didn't know what to treat you for first, the knock on the head or frostbite."

"I'm glad you did anything at all," Leona said. Then it came to her. Terrifying images tore through her thoughts—windows crashing, yellow ripping teeth, the hideous sensation of flying uncontrollably through black space. She pitched upright on the bed and a sharp ringing pain erupted in her head. Struggling, she said, "I have to get up. Please. We shouldn't be here."

"Easy does it," the woman said, holding her. "Take it real easy. We've been expecting you to fly off the handle. You took a pretty hard lick."

"No," Leona said anxiously. "You don't understand. We're in danger. There's a man, a madman . . ."

"Yes," the kind woman said, soothing her, "but the danger's all over now. You mustn't work yourself up. There's no reason to," she said, easing her down, patting the pillow. "There's nowhere to go, nothing to see. This blizzard's fixed us proper. Nobody could get to you even if they wanted to. We've got two feet of snow on the ground already, and more on its way. Our electricity's down, the phone's dead. Our pipes've been froze up since yesterday. I have to pump well water. Nothing's been through here, not even the mailman."

The exertion of trying to get up left Leona exhausted. She caught her breath and held it, then let it go. "What day is this?"

"Well, let's see. Unless I lost count, this is Monday. You've been here now three days."

Three days, Leona thought, three lost days with that lunatic still out there, still coming after us. But her resistance was gone. Increasingly, the motion of the woman in the rocker was making her dizzy. Questions went on drifting drunkenly in her mind, but even as she tried to voice them, her eyelids drooped closed. "Who are you?" Leona asked, dragging her words.

"My name's Vivian Turner," she heard the woman say. "But I go by Vee. And we live about eight miles this side of Rocky Comfort, West Virginia." *D-rump, ramp.* "Right smack-dab in the middle of nowhere."

The aroma of breakfast, of side bacon and eggs, fried potatoes, fresh buttermilk biscuits, and the lovely tart scent of perked coffee—all overlaid with the faint hint of wood smoke in the room next to where she lay. The old kitchen held the ingrained aromas of smoked meat, of all the bounty of the land—potatoes and turnips and onions, the lingering residue of good home-cooked meals prepared and eaten there. It saturated everything, the wainscoting, the moldings, the fabric on the chairs. *It's like home.* Somehow on the battered waves of her unconsciousness, Leona had been brought here. She had come home.

The house sagged in the middle like a rickety ship. The walls were out of plumb. Pictures of stern ancestors in ornate chalk frames dangled away from the wall as if hovering there. The floor had buckled and banked. With a groan, massive oak wardrobes and dressers skittered forward now and then. Doors clicked open unexpectedly as much as the width of a body before they stopped. The house was settling, corner by creaking corner, into the ground.

That morning the door opened and the wonderful flavor of country breakfast flooded the room. Without wasting time, Vivian Turner went to the two radios stacked on top of each other and flipped a dial. The morning light revealed a mottle of brown spots edging her gray temples. She shoved her sweater sleeves up, put her hands on her hips to listen, and glanced at Leona. "Oh," she said, "I'm glad you're awake. Now I won't worry about botherin' you. Don't want to miss my weatherman." She turned the dial up a bit more. The battery radio hummed; static crackled; the polished voice became more and more distinct.

"... *Road crews continued to work round the clock last night and early this morning in an effort to clear the streets of our nation's capital as the worst blizzard in two decades battered the Eastern Seaboard. Record amounts of snow have fallen from North Carolina to New Jersey, only to be complicated by high winds. Cities and towns in hardest-hit Virginia, West Virginia, and Maryland are reported to be without power. In some areas telephone service has been disrupted. Forecasters now predict another three to five inches of snow today in most areas before the storm moves out to sea.*"

"That's us," Vivian said. "Snow ever' which way and no end in sight."

Static hissed and snapped in the radio. "*Now from our local desk: Police report no progress in the suspected kidnapping of two Pennsylvania children—*" Vivian turned the dial and the staticky voice faded to nothing.

Aghast, Leona sat staring at the wooden cabinet of the radio. The announcer's voice went on reverberating in her mind like a recurring spasm. The contraction around her eyes and nostrils was slight, the whitening of her lips faint, but as she struggled for self-control she could almost feel her cheeks grow scarlet, as if she had been slapped very hard. Fearing the worst, she still had to face Vivian and see what effect the news had had.

Burning with guilt, Leona looked straight at Vivian, and the kind woman stared back, hard, for a moment. Does she know? Does she think it's me? Did the kids tell her?

Vivian frowned. "We saved what we could from your car." She nodded toward the row of luggage near the foot of the bed. "I'm afraid we didn't get everything. Hardesty even walked back down there the next morning, but he didn't come up with much. He did get your keys. Thought you might want 'em. I hope you don't care, but I had them kids pick out their suitcases so they'd have something to wear."

Fear again, raking Leona's nerves. Did they go through everything? "No," Leona said, unable to look at her. "It's all right. Is my car—it's completely ruined, isn't it?"

"It's upside down on the creek bank. From the looks of things, you musta been flyin'."

Leona nodded distractedly. "Yes. It got completely away from me." She looked at the battered suitcases. Her fingers were shaking when she touched her forehead. "I'd like to get up and see the children. Why haven't they been in to see me?"

"Well, for one thing, they're still asleep. And furthermore I told 'em, I said, 'You kids just stay outa here and leave Leona alone. She needs to lay up and heal herself.' But I'll leave the door open, if you want me to, so you can see that they're all right." Then she was gone.

A wave of nausea rose in Leona's throat, followed by a flush of weakness. What does she know? They must have gone through my things. She knows my name. When she heard Vivian go upstairs to wake the children, she forced herself up in spite of the pain, slipped to the end of the bed and checked the briefcase. The bottles of medicine were smashed—they'd have to be thrown out, along with the newspaper clippings about Mamie—but the Browning and the money appeared to be undisturbed. At least, it appeared that they hadn't gone through it. She let her body sink backward on the bed, and slipped the briefcase down between the night table and the dust ruffle, to keep it safe from other hands. Turning her head on the pillow, she looked out the snowy window.

She didn't know what she expected to see outside, but her sense of foreboding was bottomless, and one thing was certain —out there somewhere, perhaps not very far away, the police were looking for them right now. And someone else was, too. Someone else.

Throughout that first slow day of wakefulness, Leona listened to the children in the kitchen, catching glimpses of them and picking out their voices. "That's mine," Walter said. "No, she gave it to me. She said I could have it." Patsy's chatter. "Give it to me, then," Vee said. "If you're gonna fight over an old dress sash, I'll just put it up." Then Walter said, sulking, "But I need it for my sword." Twice Leona heard another child's voice and thought it must be Mamie, but she couldn't be certain. The children called the tall, gaunt woman Aunt Vee. She took care of things: settled their disputes, soothed their ruffled feathers, fed them, tucked them in at night. She was coarse-acting and coarse-talking and usually she wore men's clothes—work shirts and bib overalls and frayed sweaters. She was strict but kind with them. There was another voice, too, scratchy and tremulous but quieter, harder to hear.

It was toward evening before Leona really allowed herself a respite from her tension and fear. She opened her eyes to a pure, harmonious peace. The house seemed empty and vast, an infinite well of tiny noises: the fire still burned in the stove near her bed, a clock ticked quietly. She could no longer hear the children, but through the window she could see them dashing about in the snow. Her head was clear; she realized she felt very little pain in her body. What a luxury it was to allow herself to bask in this lull of deep comfort and tranquillity.

The storm had abated; against the darkening sky, the snow-fields glowed like a luminous, depthless pearl. For the first time, Leona began to assimilate exactly where she was, situating the house in relation to the sheds and outbuildings and the more distant, snow-shrouded barn. Into the view framed by the window came Vivian, carrying a large basket. Dressed in her thick winter clothes, she paused, spoke over her shoulder, and a man came into the frame behind her. They took different paths: Vivian went into a shed with the children trailing after her, and the man stooped at the woodpile just beyond the weathered picket fence. That must be Hardesty, Leona thought.

Even wrapped up for the raw cold, he presented an image of vitality and good health. That was her initial impression of him—how vigorous he looked. He seemed unaffected by the weather, moving about through the snow with easy unconcern.

Immediately, he launched into his task, setting the logs on the low stump, then straightening and lifting the axe and driving it down into the wood. Although it was muffled by the window glass, she could hear the dull crack of the axe as it met its mark, the splintering of the wood. His actions seemed to be a natural extension of the cold weather, the glowing dusk. Again and again, he brought the axe down, the air ringing with the recurrent crack. How perfect, she thought.

There was a hard, rough elegance about him. He hung his coat and hat on the fence palings, then wiped his forehead with his shirt sleeve, unaware of her, unaware of himself. She guessed him to be about her age, but from some angles he looked older and, she thought, dignified in his own way. His lack of self-consciousness appealed to her. He shifted his shoulders lightly and glanced into the woods, watchful; then his vitality rose and he went back to work. She could see his shoulders shift, pressing into his shirt when he swung the axe. An ordinary action for him, but she found it almost hypnotic. Occasional breezes stirred up whirling ghosts of frost, and when they settled he was there; she was transfixed by him, drawn to him. The heave of his shoulders became a continuous natural rhythm in the air.

Eventually, Vivian and the children reappeared, coming toward the house. He gathered an armload of kindling and joined them. Leona heard the kitchen door close behind them—he was speaking to Vivian. The timbre of his voice sounded out of place in the house.

All at once, his voice grew closer. He's coming in here, Leona thought. She quickly pushed herself up and a sharp pain beat inside her head. She tried to straighten the bodice of her gown, but before she had time to do much of anything, he came through the doorway and handed her a cup of steaming coffee. "You should have something," he said. "A little coffee won't hurt you."

She was so unaccustomed to having anything brought to her by a man that it rendered her speechless for a moment. How kind, she thought. "How nice of you," she said. She tried to look at him, but the room was as gloomy as the evening outside, and the pain in her head made it difficult. Perhaps mistaking her hesitation for reluctance, he had withdrawn to the doorway, holding his hat in his hand.

She started to ease around to sit up. "Stay where you are," he said. "I'm just glad to see you're feeling better. We've been through quite a lot together, you and me." A grin widened his cheeks.

"You must be Mark Hardesty. Vivian's neighbor."

"That's right," he said. "And you're Leona. We know that much."

"I've wanted to say thank you," she said. "You came to get me, didn't you? With Vivian?"

"Yes, ma'am," he said, shifting to formality. "But don't feel obligated. I was glad to do it." He rubbed his chin with the back of his hand as if he hadn't shaved. He's almost shy, she thought, but she was flattered by his concern and his old-fashioned manners. Then he did look at her clear and straight with his dark eyes, and there was a trace of something in them as if he were about to speak. But the moment was left incomplete. With an excuse he turned to go. And yet the opening gesture he had made with the coffee lingered in her thoughts long after Vivian had brought in her supper tray.

Outside, the pale blue peripheries of earth and sky blurred
and the wind-forsaken house seemed to drift above the slow
turning of the planet as if all time had been erased, all past
mistakes and sins and fears removed. Through that strange evening light, a procession entered the living room, the children
still in their play clothes, chicken feathers dangling from head-
bands, a shoe-tongue pirate's eye patch worn flipped up on
Walter's forehead. Mamie led them, carrying the lighted lamp
with little scooting steps, the chimney clattering in its holder.
Patsy looked at Leona. "We're a parade," she said.

"Yes," Leona answered. "I can see you are."

Behind them came a small old woman, not much more than
four feet tall, and she walked with a gold-handled cane. Her
head was so tiny it looked shrunken; the bones of her face
seemed to show through her skin.

The children called her Funny Grandma because she made
them feel *funny*, they said. That was all the explanation they
gave. In the days that followed, Leona told them, "I'm not so
sure that's a nice name to give somebody. Why do you call her
that? Because she makes you laugh?"

"Sometimes she does," Walter said.

"Sometimes she scares us," Patsy put in, and made herself
shudder.

"How does she scare you?"

"Well . . . she does weird stuff."

Funny Grandma smelled faintly of mothballs and lavender
perfume, but it was her eyes and mouth that told her age. En-
larged behind cheap octagonal glasses—which she wore now
and then—her eyes were sunk in her head. Her mouth was
empty; where teeth had been, her lips drew together into a tight
little knot like the end of a drawstring tobacco sack. After she
was seated in a rocking chair, her hands unfolded from her lap,
and they were large thorny hands on frail stems, shaped, Leona
thought, by years of manual labor.

The night closed down around the old house like an enormous black tent. The children listened to the radio and played the simple card games Aunt Vee had taught them: War and Crazy Eights. When the dishes were done, Aunt Vee joined them, sitting beside her mother to talk and rest, her hands inflamed and still smelling of Oxydol soap powder. It was a quiet time, a soft murmur of voices, the trickling ebb of radio programs.

A more eloquent language was spoken then, the women's voices becoming intimate, remembering their lives and the lives of those around them in a thread of memory that was never broken, but was picked up again and again each evening. "Now, Bessie Silk married Clarence Hargis," the old woman said. "Yes," said Aunt Vee, "and that was the sorriest day of her life. Never again owned a moment's peace. When her second boy was killed— Oh, what was his name?"

"Jacob . . . twarn't it?" Their talk seemed imbued with the mystery, the awesome wonder and capriciousness of life.

*"From Hollywood, International Sterling presents the 'Adventures of Ozzie and Harriet,' starring America's favorite young couple, Ozzie Nelson and Harriet Hilliard."*

It touched Leona to see how delicate and patient the children were with the old woman. They dealt hands of cards for her, which she held obediently in her gnarled clasp or fumbled in her skirts. "Funny Grandma," Walter scolded playfully, "you dropped your cards *again*. I'll get 'em for you." Then, while the two older women listened to Ozzie and Harriet, chatting intermittently, Patsy stood next to the rocker and drew ticktacktoe games on a small school slate. She and the old woman took turns with the bit of chalk, drawing the X's and O's. "Draw an X," Patsy reminded her. And the palsied hand descended to the board. The radio program changed.

"Now, Bessie's brother Urban used to live over by Sandison, Ohio," Vivian said. "He sold hardware around through these parts. Drove a red truck." Seldom did she look directly at Leona;

she nodded or frowned or stared at the fire. Only when Leona's head was turned did she feel the brush of those shrewd blue eyes. Several times that evening, when she glanced up, she saw Vivian's head turn slowly away. She knows something, Leona thought, and the tension drew tighter and tighter in her stomach.

*"Mortimer, how can you be so stupid?"*

*"Uh . . . just lucky, I guess."*

The children, even Mamie, laughed. Walter looked at the radio and spoke directly to it. "Oh, Mortimer," he said, letting his hands rise buoyantly at his sides, "you really are stupid."

When the clock struck eight, the children were led away to bed in the attic. As she rocked, Funny Grandma's long, knobby fingers moved awkwardly through the Bible in her lap. Minutes later, Vivian returned and the old woman cowered in her chair. "I'm ashamed of you, Mama. It's your own flesh and blood. It's me, Vivian."

Only one eye looked up. "Go play."

"Mama . . ."

"Go play, smart aleck."

"Mama, it's time to go to bed."

"No." She started to rock again, her slippered feet tapping the floor. The Bible sank into her skirt and snapped shut. "Now see what ye did? How'll I ever find my place?"

"Let's go to bed, Mama. Come on, up we go. It's late."

Still shaking her head, Funny Grandma took the cane, grasped the handle until it fit her hand, and, leaning on it, stood. Vivian was gone with her for quite a long time before she came back and sat down with a cup of coffee. "Would you like some?" she asked. Leona smiled and said no. Except for the ticking clock and the occasional hiss and crackle in the wood stove, nothing disturbed the night silence.

Vivian leaned her elbows on her spread knees. "You mustn't mind my old mama," she said at last. "In her heyday she was nothin' to be monkeyed with. But now, half the time, she don't know who she is. She thinks she sees things, reads signs in all kindsa things. Sometimes she thinks these kids are hers. She's been saying she'll come visit 'em from the dead. It's one of her favorite things to promise people, but they don't know that."

"I don't think they mind," Leona said.

The wind shook the windowpanes. Hardly lifting her head, Vivian glanced at the night outside, then at Leona, and turned back to her coffee. "I don't mean to insult you, but I have to ask you something." She rolled the sides of the cup in the palms of her hands. "There's something wrong, ain't there?"

Before Leona could formulate an evasive answer, Vivian's head came up and she was staring straight at her. "Them kids," she said. "They're not yours, are they?"

Leona's heart was beating very fast. She was pinned by those intelligent blue eyes. What or how much the woman knew was impossible to guess. If she lied, Vivian might easily trip her up. Frantically she searched the tangle of her thoughts for a plausible answer that wouldn't incriminate her. Time stretched between them until Leona knew she couldn't delay her response any longer. Tears stood in her eyes. "No," she said softly, "no, they're not."

Vivian was still staring at her. Then she said, "I didn't think so," and, as if embarrassed by their frank exchange, she dropped her gaze again. "Too many things just didn't add up. Whose are they, then? Kin of yours?"

"Yes," Leona said, her mouth as dry as a stick.

"How'd you happen to end up with 'em?"

"I was taking them home," Leona said, not knowing what else to say. "For Thanksgiving." In a way, it was true.

Vivian rocked, biting her lower lip thoughtfully. "Well, that makes sense," she said. "Have you had some trouble with 'em?"

Leona closed her eyes and let out a deep soundless breath. Now, what's she leading up to?

"Oh, you needn't tell me. It's just . . . I keep missing things. I put a spoon down and reach for it and it's gone. Biscuits disappear, my old pack of cigarettes. It's all little stuff. I keep a couple of silver dollars in a dish in the cupboard. They went. I said to my mama, 'Looks like somebody's fixin' to take a trip, collectin' all my stuff.' And *she* said, 'Or else they's plannin' on company,' " Vivian laughed.

Leona said nothing, staring at the night that made faint mirrors of the windows. From a hook inside the wardrobe, Vivian removed a gown and robe and, picking up her coffee cup, went to the kitchen. Soon she was back, in her nightclothes, lowering the window shades, fluffing a pillow on the couch, unfurling a quilt. "Oh, Vee," Leona said, "you don't have to stay with me tonight. I'm feeling better. Really, you should go to bed."

Cupping her hand to a lamp chimney, Vivian blew out the light. "When bad weather sets in, I always move out here by my stove. It's too cold in yonder." Through the dark reddish light of the stove, she motioned toward the draped doorway beside the wardrobe. "Besides I've got this 'ere couch broke in just the way I like it. Don't you worry 'bout me."

Leona started to protest again, but Vivian wouldn't hear of it and then, as the night settled into the room, somewhat shyly they said good night.

It was snowing harder; hour after slow hour it fell, obliterating any trace of them, isolating them from that other, brutal world. No one will find us here, Leona thought, and it was true. Nothing had moved on the county road beyond the barn; no one had stopped by except Hardesty; the telephone could not ring. And even if the Turner women had been suspicious and wanted to report the children's whereabouts to the authorities, Vee couldn't have done it.

It suddenly dawned on Leona that after she had received the terrible news about Emma, all her other concerns had been answered—but with a spiteful vengeance. She had needed to get rid of the car and it was gone. Desperately needing rest, she had it now—in the extreme. She had yearned for a little safe time with these children and that, too, had come to them. Their lives —the terror and desperation, the fear of capture, the hiding and the night driving, the endless flight from that maniac—all of it had been reduced to this house of crumbling firelight, programs on the radio, the children playing in these lofty rooms, yelps of surprise, laughter, time spent in bare simplicity. How long can this possibly last?

At eleven o'clock, Leona made another attempt to fall asleep, pulling the quilt up under her chin, only to lie there staring through the amber dark, expecting at any moment and against all logic to see a madman emerge from the kitchen doorway and the glowing eyes of that monstrous dog.

# 15

*"This is the 'Arthur Godfrey Show,' and Arthur's not here. Please stay tuned."* Music started to play. The kitchen and living room were suffused with light; the children had finished their breakfast. Aunt Vee carried a tray to Leona. "Now, I like Arthur Godfrey," she said, "but it irks me that he can't get to work on time. You'd think he could. Did you hear it when he talked about F.D.R.'s funeral parade? I'll tell you, it broke my heart when he started to cry."

Leona said she hadn't heard it, and Funny Grandma said, "Did ye say F.D.R.'s dead?" And Aunt Vee had to explain all over again that it had happened some years ago, that Funny Grandma had just forgotten about it.

To the children, the farmhouse was like nothing they had ever seen before, a source of almost endless curiosity and adventure. They would never in their lives adequately describe what it was like to awaken in a cold attic and go down those rickety stairs to the warmth of that kitchen. It was their room, where they stayed, where things were brought to them from the hidden regions of the house for them to play with, and it was primarily from the kitchen that Mamie took things.

She didn't know why she did it—she liked Aunt Vee. It was something she felt compelled to do, as if by returning to the way she had been with Sherman, she could hold tighter to that part of herself she remembered most deeply. This morning, through the glass sides of a jar of odds and ends, she had seen a small picture in a gold frame, a tiny picture of a man and a woman. And she wanted it.

Patsy and Walter were playing Chinese checkers on the kitchen floor and the three women were still talking about F.D.R. "He's flown off to Heaven," Funny Grandma said, "and nary a soul told me." With her back to them, Mamie opened the cupboard door a crack, looked back toward the living room—the radio had come on. "*Howarya? Howarya? Howarya?*" the gravelly radio voice exclaimed, and a ukulele was strumming. Using the tips of her fingers, Mamie turned the jar lid. "Hey," Walter said to Patsy, "that's cheatin'." Then from the living room, the radio announcer said, "*And now the news from our international desk, this Wednesday morning, November eighteenth...*"

Mamie withdrew her hand from the cupboard and slowly turned on her toes. She heard nothing else. November eighteenth. It's my birthday, she thought. And nobody knows. She remembered the last time she had a birthday and how she had waited. "You cheat," Walter said, abruptly standing up from the star-shaped game. "Aunt Vee," he moaned, trotting into the living room. "Patsy's cheatin' me. She won't play right."

Mamie bent to Patsy, clasping her knees, and said, "Patsy, guess what?"

She shrugged.

"Patsy, it's my birthday. *Today is.* I'm eight years old," and when Patsy looked at her blankly, with none of her excitement, Mamie whispered, "When Aunt Vee comes, tell her. And then act like you don't know. I want it to be a surprise."


"How'er you feelin'?" Vee asked Leona. "Do you feel like sittin' up?" It was just after twelve, the time of day when everything hummed with light.

"Yes," Leona said, "I think so. I'm really sore, but my head seems clearer." And she started to edge up.

"No, no, not now," Vee said, walking toward her. "Something's come up."

"What is it," Leona asked, a little alarmed, pushing herself up higher against her pillows.

"Sh-h-h," Vee said with her finger to her lips. "Stay where you are." She pulled the rocker over and sat down quickly on the edge of the seat. "I don't want them to hear us." She shot a glance toward the kitchen. "That little girl of yours—the blonde one—she's been puttin' out the word that today's her birthday. She's the wise old age of eight."

"Mamie?"

"Uh-hum. That one."

Careful not to reveal too much, Leona thought for a moment before she answered. "I hadn't thought of it. But I guess it might be. I guess it is. It slipped my mind."

"Well, sir," Vee said excitedly, but Walter ran to the doorway.

"Can I have another toast?"

"You shore can," Vee said. "In a minute. I'll be in there directly and I'll fix you one."

"Patsy wants one, too."

"That'll be all right, you can tell'er I said so." She turned to Leona. "So we have to do somethin', don't we? It'd be a crime to let it pass." She smiled. " 'Specially since she's goin' to so much trouble."

"Yes, of course," Leona said. "But, Vee . . . I don't have anything to give her. Not something a little girl would want for a birthday present. If you're thinking of having a party, she'll be really disappointed if she doesn't get presents."

"You leave that to me," Vee said. "When you're stuck in a place like this, you just have to make do. We're gonna have to be a little resourceful, that's all. Now"—she looked again toward the kitchen—"after a while, I'll get them all outa the house. We'll . . . we'll build a snowman. Mark's already said he'd help. So when we're outside, could you mix up the cake batter? Then, while Mark entertains 'em, I'll come back in and bake it. I'll put ever'thing you need on the bottom shelf of the cupboard. Now, tell me. Are you sure you're up to this?"

"Yes," Leona said. "If I can get to the kitchen, I'm up to it."

"Good," Vee said. "She don't think so, but she's gonna be surprised."

Not much time had passed when Vee backed through the doorway again, talking to the children, and finally turned toward the bed. She was hiding a cigar box under her apron, a box that turned out to be crammed full of small toys and trinkets—a yo-yo, a ball, a few jacks, old jewelry, a doll's head, a shiny new tin kazoo, and more. "I've saved this stuff a long time," Vee said. "My cousin Emery used to bring his kids to visit, so I started collectin' things for them to play with. Then he moved the whole tribe to Arkansas. So . . . d'you think she'd like this?"

"I don't know," Leona said. "I think she would. There's so much there it'd take her a while just to go through it."

"Then it's settled. I'll find you some wrappin' paper. You can give it to 'er."

"But, Vee, I can't do that. These are your things—if you want her to have them, you should give them to her. I'll think of something else."

"Oh, you won't neither, no such a thing. No, sir. It should come from you." Vee closed the cigar box, set it on Leona's lap, and, with a wink, went back to the kitchen.

Running her fingers through the box of trinkets, stirring them, Leona turned up a rhinestone brooch, then an arrowhead. She had no idea if Mamie would like these things. If the situation was different, she would have liked to give her something new and wonderful—a bicycle, maybe, or a puppy. But there was nothing she could do. More than anything, she couldn't belittle Vee's kindness. Maybe she would wrap one of the dresses she'd bought for Mamie in the beginning. That would really be her present to her.

Leona listened to them go out. When she sat up straight in the bed, her head throbbed so painfully she nearly fainted. She waited for the pain to subside before she stood up. She felt wretched. "I'm not as far along as I thought," she muttered. Pressing a hand to her throbbing head, she went to the kitchen, pulled a chair to the cupboard, and, holding the bowl on her knees, began to mix the ingredients for the cake. I really shouldn't be up, she thought.

The house was silent. Funny Grandma had gone to her room for her afternoon nap. The minutes stretched slowly away like minutes in a dream. Now and then, Leona stopped what she was doing and held her head in her hands. The throbbing didn't slacken for a moment. And yet she wanted to do her part for Mamie's birthday; it was important. Through the side window she could see the three children working with Vee to build the snowman, occasionally heard them call out in their delight. After she had stirred in all the ingredients, she thought there was too much batter and wondered if she had done something wrong; what kind of cake did Vee have in mind? She hadn't the strength to question it further.

After a time, she grew aware that the voices outside had stopped and she lifted her head. The neighbor, Hardesty, was talking to Vee, the children leaping around them in a kind of spontaneous dance. Watching them was like watching a movie with no sound. Hardesty turned and swung Mamie up on his shoulders, took Patsy's hand, and they set off through the trees with Walter leading. How right they looked together like that, Leona thought. How happy.

Vee was coming to her across the kitchen. She took the bowl from Leona's lap. "I knew it," she said. "I don't know why I even said anything. You're not fit to be up yet, and this's all my fault. Come on, get ahold of me. You gotta get back to bed."

When Vee helped her stand, Leona thought the top of her head would fly off. She caught and steadied herself. "But, Vee," she protested, "I'm going to be all right. It's her birthday. I can't miss it."

"Don't worry about that," Vee said, supporting her. "Nobody's gonna leave you out."

"Where's he taking them?"

"Oh," Vee said, "he's been tellin' 'em stories about his blind fish. It's all a pack of lies but they enjoy it. He's goin' to show 'em his fish."

"Are they really blind?"

"Of course not. Who ever heard of such a thing?"


She heard a soft scuttle of activity around her and opened her eyes. Directly in front of her, on the piano stool, sat a four-layered birthday cake covered with white icing, and punched into the top of it were eight small pink candles. "She's awake," Walter said, hovering just beyond the cake. "Patsy, go tell Aunt Vee she's woke up." Patsy broke from him at a run. Standing next to Walter was Mamie, and behind the two of them, in her rocking chair, sat Funny Grandma. Still deeper in the room, near the wood stove, Mark Hardesty stood like a dark column. Night was settling in; a single lamp had been lit on the piano across the room. Leona still couldn't see him clearly, but she was aware of him. And she felt better. When she shrugged up on the bed, rearranging her pillows, there was only a faint throb at her temples. Turning on her side, she felt something brush against her thigh under the covers, and as she shrank from it, she realized what it was—the box of trinkets for Mamie. Vee must have put it there, she thought, while I was asleep.

Vee came to the foot of the bed, folding her arms. "You look better than the last time I looked in," she announced, and Leona said, "Yes. I must have slept a long time. What time is it?" But already the children were beginning to clamor.

"Is it time to light the candles?" Walter asked.

"They're not new candles," Patsy said, elbowing him. "They've been used."

Vee was feeling in her sweater pockets for matches. "We made up for these old candles by making an extra big cake." She looked at Mark. "Couldn't you set that cake afire and let that pretty girl get on with her birthday? She's about to bust at the seams."

Leona watched Mamie, who was beaming. Hardesty came toward them, striking a match with his thumbnail. Leaning over the children, cupping the fire in the palm of his hand, he lit the eight candles one at a time. The wick blazed up and the flame stabilized before he went on to the next one; little by little, the small flames exposed his face.

What struck Leona about him now was the absence of anything boyish in his face. Most of the men she knew, even Dr. Merchassen at the age of seventy-nine, carried some remnant of their boyhood in their faces all their lives. Not Mark Hardesty; his was entirely a man's face. He was a lean, rugged-looking man; his eyes were warm and dark and crinkled at the corners. She noticed that his hands were weathered, accustomed to work. "I understand," she said as he lit the last two candles, "that you have blind fish."

"That's right," he replied. But the children disrupted anything else he might have said. "Yeah," Walter told her. "We fed 'em corn. *Field* corn." And Patsy said, "Uh-huh, we went inside their cave."

When Leona lowered her eyes, she saw that the three of them were looking straight at her. "I'll bet they liked that," she said, and then turned again to Mark. "You must consider yourself very lucky? To have such fish."

"They're something everybody should see," Hardesty said to her, unable to keep from grinning. He winked at her and shook out the match, stepping back. She could no longer see his face.

With the eight birthday candles flickering, they all turned to Mamie. "You have to make a wish," Patsy said, and Walter added, "But close your eyes first."

"I know how to do it," Mamie said.

"Hurry up," Walter persisted, "they're gonna go out," and Leona said, "Walter, let Mamie do it. We should sing," and she started, "Happy birthday to you," and Vee sang along. Walter and Patsy muttered the words, rapt, watching closely as Mamie bent over the eight yellow flames and blew them all out in one breath.

"What did you wish for?" Patsy asked.

"Don't tell 'er," Walter said. "It's s'posed to be a secret."

Vee diverted them. "Why don't we cut that cake and eat it? We'll all have some. Patsy, if you'd help me get the plates, and, Walter, you can hand out the forks."

The candles were smoking, each sending up a tendril of white vapor. To keep the blackened ends from falling in the icing, Leona reached to take them out, but Mamie stepped forward possessively, blocking her hand.

Mark Hardesty noticed Mamie's spite and the hurt expression that sank quickly on Leona's face. But Mamie didn't object when Vee removed the candles and cut the cake.

Served on saucers, the pieces lapped over the sides. When Mamie was through with her cake, Leona said to her, "Mamie, there's a present here for you . . . from your Aunt Vee and me." And she lifted the wrapped box from the covers. Funny Grandma said, "I seen the light come from the East in a hail of glory."

Vee had wrapped the box in cooking foil. Mamie took it from Leona, sat with it on the floor. "It's heavy," she said quietly. Eyes bright with anticipation, Patsy and Walter gravitated to her, going to their knees, setting down their cake plates.

"Wonder what it is," Walter said.

Mamie tore the wrapping away. "It's everything," said. "There's everything in it. Just look."

Vee caught Leona's eye and nodded; then she said, "Mamie, you should share with them," and obediently Mamie pulled out the yo-yo for Walter and the kazoo for Patsy, but they were more interested in everything still in the box. As the children went on exclaiming over their treasures, Vee collected the plates. She started to take Mark's, but he said he had to be going, and they turned toward the kitchen when suddenly, without warning, a scream ripped through the room like a knife to the heart. Leona leaped up from the bed; Vee and Mark wheeled in the doorway; Funny Grandma pitched forward. And then Mamie screamed again. The box of trinkets spilled from her skirt. She raced around the room. "Look!" she cried. "Look! Oh, look! Look!" Tears were running down her face. "*Look*, it's Toddy's ring! *It's Toddy's ring!*"

She ran from one of them to the next, holding up the metal ring in the shape of a skull with glass eyes. "It's Toddy's ring!" Pausing hardly a moment, she cried, "It's Toddy's ring that he gave me. It's Toddy's Phantom ring." She showed it to Vee and Hardesty and Funny Grandma. She was crying, brushing the tears from her face. She showed it to Patsy and Walter, whirled and stopped short directly in front of Leona. Mamie wept uncontrollably then, covering her face with her hands, and when she drew her hands away, her face was shiny with tears. She swallowed. "Oh, thank you," she said to Leona. "Where'd you ever find it?"

Mamie didn't wait for an answer, and it was just as well. Leona couldn't speak.

"It's my Toddy's ring," Mamie said, examining it once again. ". . . That *he* threw away." She wiped away her tears and turned to the other children, sliding the ring down onto her finger. "See," she said, "it's adjustable."

Leona couldn't stop looking at her. Suddenly there was something warm and different in Mamie's eyes.


In bed that night, Patsy said, "I think she likes him. Did you see how she looks at him? Maybe we can just stay here."

"I like *Harkestry*," Walter said. "He looks just like my daddy."

Lying in the dark, Patsy said, "He don't *either*. Stop saying that. He looks like somebody else."

"Who, then?" Walter asked.

*Toddy's really a good boy, Mr. Abbott. He works so hard. . . . None of us knew he was so deeply troubled. . . .* Mamie remembered that time. And she remembered asking Sherman, "Is Toddy comin' with us?" And Sherman said, "He's all right." But Toddy wasn't all right. He wasn't all right any more. Tonight she couldn't stop thinking about Toddy, just like he'd said he couldn't stop thinking about Sherman. Without making a sound, she lay there in bed, crying, holding his Phantom's ring in both her hands. It was a year ago tonight that he had come to her room and given her the cuff-link box with this ring in it. No one else had remembered. It seemed like forever ago.

Finally she had to bury her face in the pillow to keep from making any noise. She knew she had to be quiet tonight. It would be a long wait before she could sneak downstairs and put back Aunt Vee's things: the buttons, the bobby pins, the silver dollars.

She was eight years old. She had her ring back. And Leona had given it to her.

# 16

Dawn.

A hinge squeaked.

Leona started and opened her eyes. Daybreak was just beginning to illuminate the drawn window shades. What was that? she thought. Her mind amplified a host of tiny sounds, but for several seconds she recognized nothing out of the ordinary. Then she heard two distinct footsteps. It's somebody, she thought; it must be one of the children. And yet the noise was too measured and surefooted to be the sleepy wanderings of a child. Someone was in the house. An inkling of who it might be sent a chill through her. "Oh, no . . . no," she murmured, trying to dismiss it. But who else would come sneaking in so early? On the sofa across the room, Vivian was sound asleep. Leona had slept with her arm back over her head, hiding her face. Now, under the canopy of her sleeve, she could see only part of the room.

A dark figure came to the edge of her perspective and stood near the row of windows, as much as ten or twelve feet away, but the reddish glow from the stove didn't reach him and the thin morning light left him unexposed. *This must be what he did to Emma.* Standing at the other end of the dingy brown shades, he was hardly more than a shape—as if a shadow had drawn itself together there. *It's him!* she thought. *He's found us.* He just stood there, very still. Her heart was pounding so hard she wondered if it showed through the covers, but at the thought of Emma, her fright was tempered with an even colder resolve. Her eyes scanned the room for something to use against him, but she could see nothing that would stop him. Then she remembered placing the briefcase next to the bed and thought, If only I could get the gun.

The pale morning light filtered through the shades in dim, diagonal streaks. It was like looking through ribbons of gauze. Otherwise the room was dark. She wondered if he could see her any better than she could see him, and decided she had to take the chance.

Slowly, under the quilts, she slipped her concealed hand to the edge of the cool bed sheet and began to lower her fingers. She thought: When he comes . . . if he sees what I'm doing, he'll come very fast. He moved. He lit a cigarette. She saw the cupped flame bloom in his hands. She concentrated all her will into the quiet descent of her hand, and eventually her fingertips touched the top of the case. Muffling the spring-loaded latches under the ball of her hand, she undid them, first one, then the other. Wedged between the bed runner and the night table, the briefcase stood open a crack.

He was putting out his cigarette.

Shifting slightly, still hiding her face, she fumbled for the Browning, finally snatched the upright barrel end of it and carefully retracted her arm. She could follow the path of her hand under the covers: the surface of the quilt swelled and flattened like the track of a mole in soft earth. She slid the Browning into the warm air pocket near her body where she could manipulate it undetected. Then, like a slippery shadow, the figure at the window took a step and turned, and she closed her eyes, playing possum. If he came toward her, if she heard him or even sensed him coming at her, she would kill him. Shoot straight through the quilts.

Trying to keep her eyelids relaxed and her breathing steady, she found the small metal safety catch and released it. At the same time, she heard him shift, then nothing else. She tensed beneath the covers and felt a change in the air as the warmth from the stove was momentarily blocked from her. Her forefinger closed down like a knot on the trigger. To locate him exactly, she opened and closed her eyes very fast and saw the blur of his hand so close to her face that she couldn't move, couldn't even scream—her throat had slammed shut. Then, recovering, she threw herself up from the pillow, tearing the covers off, and glimpsed only his sleeve vanishing through the doorway.

The gun shuddered in her rigid grip. From the kitchen, she heard the door open and close, the double squeak of that dry hinge. Eyes wild, studying the uncertain dark, Leona finally sank back, sitting upright on the bed. She had been poised for abrupt, explosive violence. Now she was unable to grasp what had happened. On the corner of her pillow slip was a matchbox still warm from the hand that had held it. To put the gun down, she had to force her fingers to relax. She lifted the small oblong box, turned it, and slid it open. She was still so panicked it took a moment to comprehend what it contained: a small blossom carved from wood, about the size of a half-dollar. What . . . *Oh, my God!*

Still trembling, she raised the nearest window shade and saw Hardesty headed home through the trees, his white breath trailing over his shoulder like a ghostly scarf.

*My God! My God!* It was Hardesty! *I almost shot him! I could've killed him. I came so close!* Tears stung her eyes.

Overwhelmed with relief, long after he had passed from sight she went on staring at the place among the trees where he had gone. Again and again, she examined the carved blossom in her open palm. It looked so strange and small, so innocent. Even with the proof of it in her hand, what had taken place didn't seem quite real or possible. It was completely unexpected, seemed so unlikely.

I've got to stop this, she thought. I can't live like this! I must just stop it! I've got to, before I do something horrible! She wiped her eyes with her forefingers. I'm not like this, she thought, still shocked at herself. Nobody's going to hurt us here.

She could hardly bear to look at the gun. Quickly she returned it to the briefcase, snapped the latches, and slid the case down under the foot of the bed. Away, out of reach. The decisiveness of her act gave her an immediate, almost tangible sense of liberation.

Bed-weary and stiff-jointed, she stood upright under her own power for the second time in as many days. Her legs still trembled with fright. Holding on to the bedpost, then to the window frame, she quietly raised the other blinds, and the winter light opened the room in merging sections. Soon the new light would awaken Vee and the day would begin. On tiptoe, Leona made her way to the long mirror in the wardrobe.

The image of herself in the mirror was disconcerting. She looked pale, exhausted, not at all as well as she felt. The muslin bandage binding her head seemed uncannily out of place; it was unnerving to look so weak and undone. Yet, except for a faint shading under one eye, her face bore hardly a trace of the disaster she had endured.

Why did he do it? she wondered. In the tilt of the mirror she could see the matchbox and the carved flower still on the pillow where she'd left them. What if he comes back? Immediately she wanted to make herself look presentable. She found the strip of adhesive tape that held the bandage and undid the layers of wrappings. Behind her, Vivian sat up and wiped her face. "You shouldn't do that. These things take time."

"Yes," Leona said, oddly elated. "I know." She laughed softly to herself as she collected the band of muslin. "But have you looked at me lately? I can't lie about looking like this and do nothing. It's time I started taking care of myself."

Hearing the self-mockery in Leona's voice, Vivian smiled. "Well, it's your head. Fool with it if you want to." She shivered and yawned again. "Next you'll be wantin' to wash up," she said, opening the stove to add firewood. "I know I would. Feel lots better."

Leona turned and said yes, she would, if it wasn't too much trouble. "More than anything, I'd like to wash my hair." She removed the final compress of bandages. High on her forehead, near the hairline, was a cut about two inches long. Five tight black stitches held it shut and it looked bruised and gruesome, but most of the swelling was gone. The wound felt tight and tender beneath her cautious fingers. If she moved her hair just so, it would cover it.

Vee hurried in and out, tying on her apron, listening to her weatherman, then switching stations when Arthur Godfrey came on, and the morning was under way. For a moment, Leona allowed herself to be frivolous: she was thinking quite deliberately about Hardesty—that she would need some color in her cheeks. Leaving a towel and washcloth, soap and shampoo on the nightstand, Vivian filled a basin with water and put it on the stove near Leona's bed. "Here's that bath we talked about," she said, and grinned. "Let it warm before you try to use it." Returning to the kitchen, she brought in a smaller pail of water. "Rinse water for your hair." She pulled the blinds and wiped her hands on her hip pockets. "There," she said. "Nobody'll bother you. Mama's in her room and I promised them kids they could go with me to feed the chickens. I'll keep 'em with me for a while. So take your time."

And then he'll be here, Leona thought.

Nearly a half hour passed before she heard them go out. Still unsteady on her feet, Leona lifted the edge of the window shade and watched the warmly dressed children scatter ahead of Aunt Vee. Turning back, she put the rough cloth in the basin of water and held it, wet and steaming, against her face. A blissful warmth spread through her. The pink bar of soap was so old its edges had turned white; with it she washed her face and throat and the back of her sore neck. She imagined a box of tissue-wrapped bars given to Vivian long ago as a gift; for her uninvited guest, she had broken the set. It was touching and sweet, but sad too.

She heard shouts outside and went back to the window, peeking out on a furious snowball fight. Mamie and Patsy and Aunt Vee, stooped down behind a woodpile, were hurling snowballs at Walter and Mark Hardesty, who were crouched behind an old broken wagon. So he had come back. Now she tried to look at him carefully, but the sun had come out and the morning was so bright, reflecting from the snow, that she had to squint to see through it. Hardesty was quickly packing together an arsenal of snowballs while talking to Walter. Vee ran out, heaving snowballs, and suddenly one from Hardesty disintegrated at the side of her head. Her old cap sailed off; the wind caught it and blew it into the fray. She slunk back, laughing, shaking her fist.

More snowballs flew back and forth. Then Mamie darted for the cap. The snow was deep and she plunged through it. Watch out, Leona thought; watch out, hurry. Under a barrage of snowballs, Mamie grabbed the cap just as Hardesty ran from his shelter and caught her, swinging her up in his arms, both of them laughing. There was such a directness about him, Leona thought; nothing confused or false.

She let go of the shade and took a deep breath. Mamie's long silence was finally over. Thank God. That smile, she thought; how she smiled at me. Who would've guessed such a cheap little ring could do so much? "Walter, duck! They're gonna get you," she heard Hardesty shout. And then laughter. What am I doing just standing here? She shrugged off the cotton gown Vivian had provided her with, caught it, and cinched it with a loose knot at her waist. She washed her shoulders and arms and wiped her breasts clean, her nipples growing hard against the rough chafing.

From time to time as she bathed, she caught glimpses of herself in the long mirror, and finally she stepped to the glass, loosened the gown on her waist, and let it slide down her legs in a soft bunch. The scratches and bruises on her abdomen and thighs were receding in yellow and gray smudges. It was not often that she looked at herself completely naked, never before in a room so unfamiliar. Outlined against the cozy backdrop, she appraised herself and decided she was still fairly willowy and well-shaped. You look naughty, she thought, and you're enjoying it. At least, she hadn't completely wasted away. She heard them laughing outside again.

Leaning over the basin, she wet her hair with handfuls of water and washed it with the shampoo; then, stooping over the bucket, she lifted the dipper and rinsed the suds from her hair. A trickle of soap burned her eyes. Dripping water, she reached for the towel and heard the children coming in with Hardesty. She grabbed the towel and wiped her eyes, then dried her body and wrapped her hair in the towel. Sunlight transformed the window shades into rich, bronze panels. Opening the suitcase on the floor, she took clothes from it and quickly dressed. When she stood up straight, all at once she felt clean and attractive and new.

She wanted to see Hardesty up close, yet wanted her curiosity to go unnoticed. With her hair still wrapped in the towel, she went to the door, opened it quietly, and paused there, looking for an excuse to enter the kitchen. She glanced at him surreptitiously, but he was turned from her, talking with the children, and she saw only his shoulder and the back of his head, his dark wavy hair—darker than hers—just touching the edge of his collar.

Walter looked toward her, and she gestured for him to come. "Your shoe's untied," she said to him. "Let me help you." And she stooped and drew the lace tight. Lapping the ends, she lifted her head to look at Hardesty. He turned, and their eyes met and disengaged like dragonflies darting across water. His eyes were even darker in clear daylight. Near her ear, Walter said, "You've tied it enough," and moved his foot, and she hid her smile, seeing the clumsy knot she'd made in his shoelace. She stood and withdrew from the doorway, feeling real excitement, and her first resistance to it. This can't be, she thought.

Morning and evening, he came to the Turner farmhouse. Often from her window she saw him cross under the spindly walnut trees beyond the fenced yard and heard him enter through the kitchen door, a room away. When she missed seeing him pass, she heard the children welcoming him and his gruff, cheerful salutations. Time after time, he wore the same slouch hat of an indeterminate brown felt, a khaki-colored mackinaw, and green rubber mudboots that came nearly to his knees. His shirts were always clean and pressed, his hair neatly combed, and every morning he was freshly shaven, carrying a hint of some lime tonic. Invariably he looked comfortable and very much at ease. After she was moving around the house more routinely, she glimpsed him seated at the old kitchen table, stirring his coffee and teasing the children with another elaborate story, watched him one afternoon trying to show the three of them how to shoot marbles across the white tablecloth.

Once, some years ago, she had nearly been married—nearly, she had thought, to the point of buying a wedding dress and talking to a minister. It was long after the time she had loved Alfred; she had been with the Merchassens five years when she met him, and in many respects she had truly entered her womanhood with him—at least, she thought of it in those terms. His name was Jack Wilkinson and he had come to the doctor's office selling pharmaceuticals. He usually arrived in the evening, and she began to go out with him to the picture show or to dinner. He had money to spend and, as he said, time on his hands.

From the beginning, she thought he was married—so much so that one night she had gone through his wallet while he slept, looking for some telltale scrap of evidence, but found nothing. He had never really acted married, was never in a hurry to leave, never had to be somewhere at a particular time. After the movie, they would drive to another town, where he invariably wanted to stop for a drink, and what she had admired about him most was that he would listen to anyone. Drunks who could hardly stay on their stools found a listener in him. When she asked him why he did it, he said, "They all have their stories. I always learn something." But it was more than that; he liked those down-and-out people, cared about them in some unspoken way. She wondered sometimes if perhaps he had come from people like them and it was his way of touching home base. She never knew.

But she had loved him for that; now, from this time and distance, she thought perhaps she loved him for that only. And then they would find a room, or if he already had one, go to it. She must have known that he was lying and yet she couldn't deny herself to him. And, of course, it ended as she thought it might. He stopped coming around. He disappeared. And she waited a long time with the need to confront him, knowing quite well that if he should reappear, she might not be able to, might once again ride with him through the night in his open car to look for a room. But she never had the chance to find out.

Nothing had prepared her for the subtle effect Mark Hardesty began to have on her; so thoroughly had she, years ago, renounced her dreams of finding happiness with a man that his charm and attention caught her completely by surprise. To her, his presence was like a warm and flickering fire in the midst of a very long, very dark night. Every glance, every word, every half-hidden smile resounded with layers of importance, as if the moments themselves contained the sparks of something larger. And yet as inviting as it all was, she was afraid of rushing toward it.

All day she waited for evening to come when she would see

him again. He always spoke to her then, asking how she was, telling her about the quirks in the weather, usually with the children clustered about, Vivian coming in red-cheeked from the cold and Funny Grandma babbling some nonsense. But it wasn't what he said or the pleasing sound of his voice that she dwelled on most. He was watching her. Even when they were in different rooms, Leona knew he was as aware of her as she was of him. And the way he looked at her with that slight tilt of his head and the dark softening in his eyes was like enchantment. At night, after he was gone and the children had been put to bed, while Vee pottered about, adding wood to the stove, preparing for the winter night, Leona blew out the bedside lamp and felt the night shrink around her, more eager than ever for morning. Wishing my life away, she thought, and smiled ruefully at the truth of the old cliché.

One evening, as he was preparing to leave, she went to the living room to get his coat, lifting it from the back of a chair. Slowly she looked back toward the kitchen where he was and heard him talking with Vee. On impulse, she drew the coat— full of the smell of him—up around her shoulders. She was consumed by it. The scent of leather and tobacco and that hint of lime tonic flooded her senses. She imagined him touching her, and a hot, wicked sensation ran through her. Then, in the other room, he laughed. She thought she'd been seen, glanced behind her. The doorway stood empty.

When he wasn't there, she plotted to put him out of her thoughts. But if there was still light outside, she would see the distant column of smoke from his chimney and imagine him there, tending to his stock, chopping wood.

Though it was still a few days away, Vee began telling the children what they'd be having for Thanksgiving dinner; some of the neighbors would be coming, she said, and they'd bring other good things to eat. At first, Leona felt like an outsider who would be intruding on a neighborly event, but since she lacked the means or a graceful way to excuse herself and the children, she volunteered to help in the preparations. Happy to be useful, she tied up her hair in a scarf and, with mops and rags and buckets of soapy water, she joined Vee in the housecleaning. Repeatedly while she cleaned or served the children their lunch or helped Vee wash the dishes, her gaze would stray to the windows and out across the fence and through those spindly black trees, following the path he had taken earlier to the lane that dropped from sight. There the chimney smoke would seem closer—like a presence emerging from nothing.

The feelings between them accumulated like the slow inevitable gathering of snow on the ground. From Vee she learned only a few things about him. He had grown up here, gone to school here, and enlisted in the Army at seventeen. He had lived overseas for some time and had returned a few years ago, to farm. Vee didn't know why. Leona guessed him to be older than she was, maybe close to forty. She waited for a chance to talk to him while the children were occupied elsewhere, but when it came, the things she wanted to know seemed too personal, so she asked him instead if he could drive her to the nearest town when the roads became passable.

He grinned. "Where is it you want to go?"

"I'm afraid we won't be going anywhere unless I get a car. I'm still not quite sure where we are . . . exactly. But I can arrange to buy a car, if you could take us just that far."

He nodded. Again, like two dragonflies, that swift telltale glance passed between them, as brief as a spark. Then he squinted through the window at the morning sky. "We'll see how it goes. When the roads are bad, I leave my old Willys out in Vee's barn. It wouldn't start the last time I tried it." He chuckled. "I'm thinking about walking over to Mose Yerby's place later on. He's got an old two-way radio he keeps in his tack room. If you want me to, I could let somebody know that you're all right."

She thought at once of asking him to find out about Emma, but the likelihood of his getting information without causing new risks was remote.

"No," she said. "There's no one."

Vivian set the hoop on the post to close the fence gate and saw Hardesty coming toward her through the dusk. "Let me give you a hand with that," he said.

"I'll get it," she told him. "You can carry my light." She handed him the lantern, then stooped and lifted her bucket of milk. They started toward the house.

"The big storm's about over," he said. "It's getting warmer."

"Yeah," she said. "I'll be glad when spring comes. Where've you been—cuttin' across my pasture from that direction?"

"Over to see Mose. Did you hear that somebody's breaking into places all over Guthrie? Broke into that drugstore, the one you always go to. Damn near demolished it, Mose said. People wake up and find their clothes gone, iceboxes ransacked. The town's in an uproar, to hear him tell it."

Vivian squinted at him and shifted the milk pail to her other hand. She shook her head. "Well, weather like we had some people just go a little berserk sometimes. But what goes on in Guthrie ain't no business of mine."

"You never know," Hardesty said, and nudged her. "Good-looking woman like you. Might be one of your old boyfriends looking for you." Then the playfulness left his face. "We don't need to tell her about this. With those kids she's got enough to think about."

Vivian regarded him carefully. What he said had very little to do with what he wanted to know. "She's gonna be all right," Vivian told him. "She's gone through something. I don't know what. Maybe a man." Setting her milk bucket down, she hugged herself, staring at the lighted windows of the house. "We might not never know. I won't ask her. I'd rather just leave well enough alone." She glanced at him and he was looking at his rubber boots, listening. "She sure is involved with them kids. Her face just lights up. I like her for that especially."

He smiled at her and the humor returned to his eyes. "Vee," he said, "anybody that nice-lookin' can't be good all the time."

"You better just mind your manners," she said, and mocked him with a smile like his own as they parted.

"I'm going out and see if my car'll start," Hardesty called back.

That evening as he headed home, Hardesty paused at the edge of the fence to watch the living-room windows, searching for Leona in the place where she had lain unconscious those first few days. In the beginning, he had thought: She's like those cats that live under Vee's house, skittish and flighty and afraid of her own shadow. But every day—it was like setting a pan of milk among the stones—he had gone out of his way to make some pleasant remark or to talk to her in some small way, because he knew that as surely as a cat would eventually poke its nose toward the milk, so would Leona find her way out of her fears.

Suddenly, through the window, he saw the children racing about and she was among them, laughing, playing some game. She seemed, at that moment, to speak to him in ways neither of them would ever express. She was what a home would be like. She looked happy and full of life as she hugged the children and mussed their hair. Briefly she turned to the window, exhilarated, as if to beckon him in. But he knew she couldn't see him; it was fully dark now. All at once, she hid her eyes with her hands and began to count, her lips moving, shaping the numbers, allowing herself to be like them: innocent, daring, vital. He wanted her then with that part of himself he had hidden away and sworn never to open again.

On the day before Thanksgiving, in the morning, he said, "It's time we took those stitches out." She had forced herself to ignore them for so long she had nearly forgotten them.

He went out of the room and came back, carrying a clean cloth, a bottle of alcohol, and small scissors.

"Should I be sitting up or lying down?"

A smile played over his lips. "You can stay where you are. It won't take long." She settled back in the rocking chair and he leaned over her, drawing her hair gently away from the wound.

It was as close as they had ever been. She could feel his warmth, breathe that scent of lime. "Is this going to hurt?" she asked. "I've never had stitches before."

"That's not my plan," he said. His voice strummed at the deepest recesses of her tension. "Hold still."

She saw his curving eyelash very close, felt his breath blow softly across her face, and an almost irrepressible urge came over her to raise her lips to him. She felt his fingers and the cold tips of the scissors nibbling at the tender crusty skin of the cut. "This will sting," he said. He dampened a corner of the cloth with alcohol and held it pressed against his handiwork. Then, putting the cloth aside, he said, "Let's have a look at you." Very solemn, she thought. His hard hands touched the sides of her face with such delicacy it sent a thrill flying through her. "You're going to have a scar," he said quietly, almost apologetically, "but the way you fix your hair"—she was looking at him, and for a moment he seemed to lose track of his thoughts—"nobody'll ever notice. It could have been a lot worse."

Leona said, "If that's the worst that happens—" But she stopped herself and smiled. "Really, I don't mind," she told him. "I'm just glad to be here." She touched the thin, feverish ridge of the wound. "Thank you."

"Don't thank me," he said. "Thank your Maker." He gathered his materials and started to go.

"Stay here for a little while," she said, "and keep me company."

He smiled as he turned. "I'll put this up." When he came back, he brought two cups of coffee and handed one to her. It was like a warm glow in her hands.

"What do you do when you're not here?" she asked him.

He pulled a rocker toward her and sat down. "I farm."

"Yes," she said, sipping the coffee, watching him over the cup rim. "And you have some fish?"

The corners of his eyes crinkled. "That's true."

She started to laugh. "Tell me about these fish. You know how children get things mixed up."

"Sure," he said, enjoying her response. "What would you like to know? They've been blind since the time of the red man. I don't know how they ended up here. They look a lot like a salmon. I'll show you sometime."

"When?" Leona felt happy, radiant. This was what she wanted for now, easy talk, a careless laugh. She liked having him here; she felt safe with him in the house. The resistance she'd felt in the beginning was gone. She had almost forgotten what it was like—to flirt with a man, to enjoy this slow movement toward some degree of intimacy. "Vivian said you live alone."

"Yes," he said, "it was my granddad's place before he died. I used to come here when I was a kid. I remember Vee when she was about thirty. A true hellcat."

"I don't believe it." With her next question, Leona felt her throat constrict a little. "You're not married, then?"

He looked at her, then lowered his eyes. "No," he said. "Not any more. I was, once."

She waited for him to go on, but he sat across from her staring at the fire in the grate. She didn't want to pry and yet suddenly she wanted to know everything about him. Very slowly, she tilted her head toward him. "Tell me what happened."

Before the sound of her voice had ended, he answered her automatically. "She died." Then he looked at her and she could see the pain edging into his eyes. It looked wrong in his rugged, clean-cut face. Inadvertently she had led him into painful territory. "Look," he said, "I don't like to talk about it much. It's not very interesting."

"But it still hurts you," she said softly. "Doesn't it?"

The muscles in his face had hardened; he looked almost angry. "She seemed so scared in the end. That's what I regret. . . . Frightened and alone and I couldn't help her, couldn't do anything to ease her way." His speech was halting now. "I felt completely helpless, outside of everything. One day something happens you never dreamed possible. It's as if your life crosses some invisible line and then for a long time afterward you can't believe it. But it happened. And it lasts a long, long time." He raised his head. "I'm sorry," he said finally. "I've never tried to put it into words before. I can't expect you to understand."

"But I do," she said. "I do know, exactly. You loved her." She wanted to touch him.

"Oh, yes," he said. "Yes, I certainly did that." He cleared his throat. As he stood, he reached for her coffee cup and she also stood, across from him. When his fingers came forward to take the saucer, they both nearly let go of it at once. The cup clattered on its dish as if the closeness of their emotions had set off a physical reaction. Then she released the cup and in silence they looked at each other. Never had his eyes been so dark, so tender, and the moment left Leona so profoundly exposed that she had to sit down to keep from falling.

She heard Mark Hardesty turn and go out through the kitchen. Yet when the door closed, she felt his presence still there: even the charmed silence of the morning was like a part of him left behind. Leona had no thought beyond evening when she would listen again for the sound of his footsteps in the snow. At the window, she watched him retreat to the path among the trees and her concentration was so strong that nothing interrupted it. She didn't hear the curtains shift at the far end of the windows.

Unnoticed, Mamie ventured a few steps forward and stopped. Little by little, over these last snowy days, Leona had changed. Mamie could feel it now quite clearly. Leona didn't see her, didn't turn or look around, hadn't heard her small secret steps—she stood at the window, looking out, her arms crossed. It was as if a familiar and accustomed warmth had suddenly been withdrawn from Mamie. Despite the lingering resentment she still felt toward Leona, who had taken her from Sherman, she knew she was losing her, and for a moment Mamie forgot her resentment and let the bleak disappointment surface in her heart.

# 17

In the dark morning hours of Thanksgiving Day, men armed with shotguns and high-powered rifles spread out through the woodland bluffs of Prescott and Otello counties. Keeping some distance apart, they angled around rotten limbs, ducked under icy branches, looking for tracks. No one spoke. The fields and thickets glowed chalk-white with snow; the air was chilled and astringent. In a cove of frosted pines, a doe lifted her head from the low delicate shoots, her eyes at once still and as shiny as jelly. Her nostrils flared, her large ears tensed. Suddenly her white flag sprang up and she leapt in a long arc, then flickered through saplings, the darkness behind her vivid with gunfire. Afterward the hunters searched for blood in the place where she had been and, finding none, moved on.

By midmorning, they were returning to the little towns, the carcasses of slain deer tied to their cars. In Guthrie, the hunters gathered at Willingham's Garage to have their game tagged and recorded. A boastful recounting of the morning's events started up; whiskey was sent for. As others continued to arrive, the hunters lit a fire in an empty oil drum and clustered around it, drinking and passing the whiskey around, telling their tales. To the edge of this gathering of men came a ragged boy leading a large mongrel dog.

A few of the hunters saw Sherman clearly that morning, but to most of them he was just another blurry passerby. He had come from the back of the garage; for several seconds, he stood at the front edge of the curb. His face was dirty and he was unkempt; his hair fell in slabs. He wore a shabby jacket, two sets of clothes and a pair of oversized galoshes. A sweatshirt rode up on his narrow waist, exposing another shirt that had been left partially unbuttoned.

There was something wrong with him. Patch Willingham, who was at the pumps waiting on customers, thought, He's sick. Or he's been sick. In the way the boy just stood there, he seemed bewildered, as if he weren't quite awake. Or else, Patch thought, maybe he's just not quite right. Certainly there was something different about him, something wrong with his face—like someone whose eyes are a little crossed. But that wasn't it. And beside him stood that mean, starved-looking dog.

Taking a nervous breath, Sherman tugged at the Chinaman's rope and stepped away from the curb. To Sherman, these were rough, dangerous men—men who drank whiskey, chewed tobacco, and passed their guns back and forth. He was afraid of them. The smell of wild blood hung over them like a stench, and the loud laughter, the milling drunkenness, made the situation seem all the more explosive. When one of the men stumbled toward him, Sherman got out of the way, moving very fast.

All trace of Mamie and the woman had vanished as if the snowstorm had swallowed them. In town after dreary town, he had shown his pictures and asked his questions until finally, it seemed, her trail had completely dried up. He knew she had come in this direction and he knew she couldn't have gotten far in the storm, but he had gone through four or five towns before the snow made it impossible for even him to go on. And nobody had seen her. Then to get some more pills, he had broken into a drugstore, and afterward he'd stayed hidden, waiting for the weather to break. Every day, standing in some doorway, he tried to listen to the radio playing inside. At night, he sat inside cars in used-car lots and listened to their radios, if he could get them to work, but he had lost the trail. For a week now, nothing new about the woman had come over the airwaves. This morning, as he led the Chinaman through the deer hunters, he was at loose ends, not knowing what to do next. "Yes, sir. Feels like it's gonna clear off," one of them said as Sherman passed. Voices came to him in scraps. "S'pose to get up to almost fifty," said another. Then, when he had all but given up hope, Sherman heard what he had been waiting to hear these many days. "You shoulda seen it," said an unshaven man. "Buick, looked like. Turned over in a creek out by old Bess Turner's place. You know where I mean—out there on Forky Creek Road. Tore all to hell."

Sherman felt light-headed. A tremendous weight was lifted inside him, only to be replaced by a feeling of dread. A wreck? Mamie, in a wreck? "What color was that car?" he asked the man.

"Aw . . . black, maybe. I don't know. It was dark."

"How far out was it?"

"Lessee. Ten miles or so, ain't it, Tom? Yeah, that's about right if you go over through Rocky Comfort. But you're not thinkin' of goin' out there, are ye? Son, you oughtn't to go out there. Ye cain't get through. The road's a mess."

. . .

At the farmhouse, after the morning light reached a certain gray consistency, the sun broke through the layers of fog, and the dreary, overcast day was brilliantly transformed. Beyond the barn, the county road was becoming a bed of swimming vapor.

At ten-thirty, Hardesty still hadn't arrived. Leona glanced at the clock. She had taken Vivian's good silver to the living room to polish it. There, her hands busy with the flannel cloth, she watched for him with growing impatience. It was just after eleven when she heard him walk into the kitchen.

"I have to go on home," he said. "I really came by to tell you, Leona,"—and she thought, It's the first time he's said my name —"I can take you to town whenever you're ready. My car starts now. I remember you said you didn't know exactly where we are. If you'd tell me where you're going, I'd bring you a map."

"You mean the kids haven't told you?"

"Well, they told me about an island, but that could be anywhere. Now, don't be cross with them. I had to squeeze it out of them."

"Yes," she said. "I bet it was pure torture," and she laughed.

She thought she could tell him anything and he would believe her, but it was more important that she not lie to him. Her reluctance, all the secrets she had struggled to protect, paled beside her feelings for him. Without hesitation, she told him she had planned to go home, to Brandenburg Station, Kentucky, and he smiled and said goodbye. I'll make you something, she thought. Something marvelous. It'll be my surprise.

Shortly before noon, the electricity flickered and returned to the farmhouse. "Well, well, well," Vee said. "Now, at least, we can have a decent bath before our company comes." And Walter said, "I don't want a decent bath. I want my bath in a pan. Like we always do."

Vee laughed and hugged him. "Honey," she said, "I've

twisted your mind with my old ways. Don't you know we've got a bathtub?"

Another hour passed, the minutes slipping away. It's ending, Leona thought. She had gone to the root cellar for apples, gathering them in the hamper she made of her apron skirt and carrying them out that way. With her free hand she lifted stray hair from her face. Out on the road, a snow-covered car lumbered by, the first she had seen pass. She turned toward the front of the house and stood looking at the snow shriveling to ice, the weathered fence, the loose fabric of twigs above her head. Waterdrops from the trees splattered around her with a sudden ripe velocity. At the edges of her borrowed boots, mud oozed through the snow. This is the real world, she thought; this is what I wanted, all along. And now, too soon, the snowplows would come and the Buick would be discovered, and then the police . . . We should go, she thought, while this feeling lasts. But the prospect of leaving held no attraction for her now. Knowing their time was short only increased the strength of her feelings. She had loved these days at the farmhouse more than she could have ever imagined possible.

Everything was clear in her mind; her life was no longer just a meaningless confusion of terror and flight; it was so much larger than thoughts of escape. And it was almost enough—to feel so good and alive, gathering the apples to take inside, peeling and coring them and arranging the hard white crescents inside a piecrust. To make something with her hands for Mark. She crossed the screened porch, opened the door, and stepped into the kitchen.

Tomorrow, she thought. I'll talk to Mark and we'll go tomorrow.

From time to time all that bright afternoon, as they prepared the Thanksgiving dinner, Leona caught herself staring fixedly at an empty vase or the tin match holder beside the door or the box of Cream of Wheat in the cupboard—studying them as if she could memorize them and in that way take something of this place with her when she was gone.

Evidence of the wreck remained scattered down the roadbed like fragments of an explosion. A chrome headlight ring dangled in black twigs; long streaks of blue paint glittered beneath vertical icicles on the cliff wall. Removing his one glove, Sherman touched bits of water-green glass in the running ditch, then stood and ran down the steep curve.

The sun was beginning to set in the west; the air had slowly chilled. Sharp, piercing rays shot through the weave of branches —the tall silver poplars, the black elms. His stolen galoshes sucked noisily on his shoes. A full moon had risen, muddy-colored on a distant blue ridge. Shadowlike ahead of him, the Chinaman trotted up the ramp of a long bridge. The wind blew the damp evening fog in spirals. When Sherman glimpsed the car overturned on the embankment below, he grasped the bridge railing, a shout of recognition pouring from his throat.

Scrambling, he hurtled down the snowbank. The Buick had been there at the edge of the creek for some time; its doors were sprung open and mired in the frozen ground. Snow had blown around and through it in drifted water shapes. Twisting, the Chinaman wriggled through the car's inverted interior. It's her car, Sherman thought. Apprehension filled him. *Nobody knows about this!* Neither the woman nor the children had been found or he would have heard some news of it on the radio. Going to his knees, he began to dig at the snow inside the crushed roof, dragging out handfuls of wet comic books. He scanned the immediate basin of snow for any unnatural lump or protrusion that might be a body, then stared at the creek—green water rippling through brackish ice grottos. Did the crash throw them out? Did they drown?

At once he ran wildly down the creek bank, ice-coated

witchgrass breaking around him like glass, but he saw nothing, no trace of them in the water. He turned and hurried back, his heart still hammering in his throat. "Damn her," he muttered. *"Goddamn* her!" He crawled into the shadowed compartment and poked his head up toward the broken steering wheel, explored the baggy hanging seats, looking for blood or some clue to their disappearance. There was nothing. Even the windshield had been busted out completely. He reached higher, desperate for some sign of what had happened. Then he realized he was looking for the wrong things. *The car keys are gone!* He clambered out, suddenly warmer in his jacket. They got out of it, didn't they? Or else why'd she take the key? They're around here someplace. And his eyes swerved up the bank toward the winding road.

By five o'clock, the kitchen glowed with the red sundown and the neighbors were coming into the kitchen: the Holts arrived first, carrying jars of homemade relish; then the Jessups left two pumpkin pies on the dry sink. They were soon followed by a barrel of a man called Grudge Drummond and his beautiful wife, whose curly hair and wide lusty hips shook when she laughed at some remark. A few minutes later, a woman named Hoot Lawrence appeared and her husband, Filmore, then the Hostettler twins, Imogene and Flo, the room made lively with their harmonious racket. Leona was introduced amid the raucous good cheer and the crisscross of voices, but she began to lose track of them as still others arrived. "Go on in," Aunt Vee said. "You menfolk go in there by the fire and let us set this table."

In the living room, the men spoke to Funny Grandma and pulled up rocking chairs. "How's this weather been treatin' you, Miz Turner?" Her face wobbled as she collected her voice. "Toler'ble fine," she said. From dark velvet-lined cases, a guitar, a fiddle, and a mandolin were produced, and a gangling boy named Billy jostled through the kitchen with a bass fiddle. The wood of the instruments gleamed softly with age: long necks had knobs and strings; frets were inlaid with mother-of-pearl. Walter, in particular, stood fascinated as the men, with tortoise-shell picks, began to tune their pieces. "What key're you in? G?"

Hoot Lawrence said, "If you're gonna pick around on them things, at least play something we know. Play that blackbird song." And so the music started, and in spontaneous celebration the women's feet began to tap and shift comically and somebody was singing, "*So make my bed and light the light. I'll be home late tonight, blackbird, bye bye . . .*" It was infectious and irresistible: even Leona could feel her body sway lightly to the beat of the music. Skeeter Johnson, a small tidy man with his work shirt buttoned tight on his reedy throat, walked in from the porch and blew a few notes on his French harp.

The room frolicked with laughter and the women's quick shuffling steps. The plates and bowls in the old cupboard rattled and the beautiful hanging lights swayed and pitched. Leona glanced at the clock.

Mamie whirled; she danced; she strutted. Caught up on the tide of festivity, she laughed through her hands at the strangers who reached for her, twisted and dashed away. "Whose little girl're you?" one of them asked her. "I'm nobody's girl," she told him, and shot off in another direction. Wearing her frilly white party dress, she hid behind curtains, darted beneath the table, and ran out again. "Bless your heart, chile," a neighbor woman said, "slow down 'fore you strain yourself." Her cheeks were bur-nished red, her face damp with sweat. Catching her breath at the edge of the cupboard, Mamie watched Hardesty come in and saw Leona turn, watched their hands almost touch, the smiles that slipped across their faces as they talked. He leaned to whisper in her ear, then bent down to listen to her and they drew close.

Folding card tables were brought in from another room and butted end to end against the kitchen table, then covered with overlapping white tablecloths, some patterned, some not, while women tied on aprons, stirred the pots, added a pinch of salt here, pepper there, and repeated local gossip. Still another woman appeared at the door, carrying a tray of homemade candy. "Oh, May, I've dreamed about your bonbons," Aunt Vee said.

"I hope you still do after you've tasted these."

In Mamie's dreams it was always a day just like this. There was music and laughter and her mother setting the table. Home from work, her father might be standing in the doorway, his voice deep and resonant like Hardesty's, half-listening to the radio, smoking his cigarette, and there was that delicious sweet mixture of good smells saturating the air just like now. Outside, the sun would be going down, a bird flying home to roost, and this music was like radio music: the old kitchen blurred with Mamie's memory. Looking at Leona, she remembered, before things were bad, seeing that same look in her mommy's eyes, something she couldn't say or shape with her hands.

Every so often, Leona would stop what she was doing and glance about until she saw Hardesty, and then their eyes were so secret, so unaware of anyone else. The other women were busy taking up dinner; none of them seemed to notice. But Mamie did. It was happening with tiny suggestions in the way they moved, in their friendly, sweet eyes and smiles. Only once before had she seen faces so open with feeling it almost hurt to watch, and it caused an emptiness in Mamie like hunger—she wanted to be somebody's girl, their little girl. She wanted to be included in the beautiful unseen thing that was happening. She could almost feel that deep sense of belonging rush around her and raise her up. Because now they were just like her mommy and daddy. And for that short interval of time while the table was being set everything seemed so real. So possible.

Aunt Vee went to the doorway and called the others. Laying aside their instruments, the men stood to make a passage for the matron of the house, the gold-handled cane tapping the floor, the little steps shuffling. Funny Grandma entered the kitchen first. Passed from hand to hand, the serving dishes were placed down the middle of the long irregular table: the platters of fried chicken, the sage dressing, a sliced ham falling apart like pages in an open book, bowls of mashed potatoes capped with oozing puddles of butter, candied sweet potatoes, green beans piled high and fresh-canned corn, the boats of gravy and chicken dumplings so rich and yellow they stuck to the spoon. Relishes, jellies, and jams, fresh-churned butter, hot breads: all down the table the dishes released steaming threads of the delightful aroma. The women and children took their places first, then the men. Aunt Vee said, "Filmore, would you say our blessing?" And a reverent silence settled over the table of friends.

"Let's bow our heads. Our Heavenly Father, on this fine Thanksgiving Day . . ."

It was all turning dim and fading away. Mamie could no longer hold on to it—her father's voice was gone from the room. Nothing looked familiar. All the faces were strangers. Hide, she thought. Go hide. Go hide before anyone sees you. But she couldn't leave the table—dinner was just now beginning. She couldn't leave in the middle of a prayer. Hide, she thought. Hide right here behind your face.

Leona raised her eyes just enough to see the others. How grateful she felt to be here among these good country people. How lucky, how fortunate. The silver she had polished sparkled. The old china shone. The water glasses seemed so bright. She and the children sat near the end of the table, Patsy and

Walter next to her, heads bowed, hands folded. How small they seemed now among the others. How innocent and lovely. Mark had taken his place across the table from her, and next to him sat Mamie, who had lifted her face, her eyes quivering with tears.

"We're thankful for the fellowship of such good company . . ."

The tears broke down Mamie's cheeks, but she sat very still. At last, she slipped sideways from her chair, hurried down the length of chairbacks, and ran upstairs. Heads swiveled at the noise. The blessing was quickly concluded. "Amen," the neighbors murmured, clearing their throats, and the friendly weave of conversation resumed while hands passed the serving dishes and plates.

"Mark," Leona said quietly, "would you help these two if they need anything?" He nodded. She pushed her chair back and stood. "I'll look after her," she said to Aunt Vee. "Don't wait for us."

Before she reached the top of the stairs, she could hear Mamie moving about, whimpering. The sunlight had nearly withdrawn from the long room; an eerie shine illuminated the two opposing end windows. In that delicate but steely light, Mamie was little more than an outline. She saw Leona coming. "Don't come up here," she warned. "You better not."

Leona stepped into the warp of cold evening light. Flushed and wild-looking, Mamie glared at her. She had taken off the party dress and thrown it down. In her slip and her Buster Brown shoes, she stood utterly defiant. Her eyes still shimmered with tears. How hard it must be for you, Leona thought, how terribly hard. And on this day meant to be spent at home. "Mamie . . ."

"Go 'way!" Mamie shouted.

"Mamie, what is it? Please. We have to stop this." Leona reached for her, but Mamie twisted away.

"Who says I do?"

"Surely nothing can be this bad." For a moment, Leona remembered a wretched little girl abandoned in the hospital, alone and frightened, and she thought, Lord, I'd do it again. I know what it's like to feel so alone. "Please," she said, "tell me what it is you want."

Again Mamie cried, "Go 'way!" and stamped her foot. "This is my room. Go to your room." Her voice was filled with rage, her words punctuated with hard sobs. "Get out! I hate you! *I hate you!* Doncha see straight?"

"I know it hurts," Leona told her, "to miss them so much." If she let herself, she would enter Mamie's mood. She thought of Emma, lying alone in some bleak white room. The anguish tore inside her as it tore at Mamie—the torment and desolation. She swallowed and found her voice. "Those women downstairs, Mamie, they've worked very hard to make this a nice Thanksgiving for you. Don't be unhappy. Come with me. I'll show you. You looked so pretty in your new dress."

"Liar!" Mamie cried. "You *liar!*"

"Oh, Mamie . . ." Her voice flagged.

With a restless clenching of her small fists, Mamie's body shuddered in hard spasms; spittle formed at the corners of her mouth. "You lied to me!" Her face contorted, her voice heaved out. "You lied! You just lied! You don't like us any more. You don't like *me!* I watched! *You like him! You don't like me!*" It was terrible to see, pitiful and unapproachable.

You're jealous! Leona thought. She felt flooded with light, with understanding. In that instant, every other consideration swept from her mind. While she had been regaining herself, Mamie had been left behind.

"Mamie, I didn't ever mean to neglect you," she said. It was as if she had gone through all the torment for this one joyous moment. *My God, Mamie, you're jealous! Don't you know what that means?* Mamie took a step forward, still demanding that

Leona go. Now that her feelings had been exposed, it was as if she had to vent all her anger; passionate intensity was crammed into every word, every step.

Leona said, "Don't you see, Mamie,"—leaning down for her —"you're jealous of him." Mamie flew at her, screaming, "I hate you! I hate you!" flailing with her knobby fists and those boxy schoolgirl shoes. "You lied to me! You lied to me!"

Leona lifted her up, but Mamie struck out, fists flying, teeth sinking and tearing at Leona's hair. They wrestled up close until Mamie's face dissolved to tears. "You promised," she said, sobbing. "You promised you'd like me. I don't want you to like him."

"Oh, Mamie, I do like him," Leona said earnestly, "that's true, but not the way I care about you."

"No!" Mamie gasped, squirming again, dragging for breath. "You don't like us like before."

"Of course I like you. Surely you know I do. God knows I'd do anything for you, Mamie. I've lied for you. I've cheated. All for you."

The door down on the stairs opened and Vee called out, "Leona. Is everything okay? Are you two comin' down?"

"Not right now," Leona answered. "Vee, we're all right. It's all right."

The strangled tears spilled from Mamie, falling onto both of them. "I don't want you to like anybody else. I want it back . . . like it was." She was making herself sick with it; Leona could taste her sour little breath.

"Please," she said. "Mamie, you have to stop."

All at once, Mamie slumped against her. And with a sudden compulsive flutter as if something had struck her in the spine, her small arms flew up and around Leona. Heaving for breath, Mamie clung to her then in a way neither of them had expected —so hard and tight Leona could feel the tiny bones of her wrists on the back of her neck. "I want to be somebody's girl."

Chasms of feeling opened in Leona. "Well, you're *my* girl. I know you miss them," she told her, "miss being home so much." And then she heard herself saying, "But I love you, Mamie, don't think I don't. You're my girl," all the time fighting against the tears accumulating in her own eyes. "Nothing that happens, nothing you do will ever make me not love you. I don't know why these things happen, Mamie. I don't know. I wish we could go back and change things, but we can't. We can't ever go back there. You know that, don't you? You know it now." She lost track of time, holding Mamie to her, talking quietly. The sunset had dwindled to moonlight.

A long time later, Leona went downstairs. She stepped into the dark kitchen as if entering life on a different plane. She felt changed, effervescent, disoriented. The supper was over, the dishes washed and put away, the long impromptu table disassembled and gone. The door to the living room had been blocked open with a crochet-covered brick. Like figures around a campfire, the string band played informally: music drifted in the air like her reawakened dreams, whirling around in a happy, glittering brew. She turned, looking through the window, and saw dark movements out by the fence: men smoking, she realized, taking the night air. Aunt Vee came to the doorway, stepped through it, and became shadow. "I saved you a plate," she said. "Let me get the light."

"Oh, please," Leona said. "Please don't. You've done so much already. I'd rather not have a light right now. I don't think I want anything at all."

"Shoot, it's Thanksgiving. You should have your supper. We kept it warm." Vee removed a brimming plate from the oven and put it at the old oak table. As she took out dinnerware from a drawer and arranged it by Leona's plate, Hardesty crossed the porch outside and opened the door. "Come on, now," Vee said. "It's still warm. I'll have to go sit in for my mama in a minute. She's playin' the piano but she wears out pretty fast." Then to Hardesty, she said, "Where've you been? Out stargazin'?" And they laughed.

Leona did as she was told. She went to the table and sat down; Vivian paused a moment longer. "You've got the strangest look. Is Mamie all right?"

"Oh, yes," Leona said, unable to hide the flood of emotion. "Yes, she's fine. She's asleep. I wanted her to come back down, but she wouldn't." She felt disconnected from her own voice. The words seemed to originate elsewhere in the room. "I hope we didn't disturb your dinner."

"Don't worry about us," Vivian said. "Nothing puts a damper on these folks. If Mamie changes her mind, there's another plate in the stove." She went back into the living room. Leona nibbled at the chicken, the dressing, the fresh-cooked cranberries. I don't want this, she thought as she tried to eat.

"We missed you," Hardesty said, and when Leona heard his voice, she knew that Mamie was right. Her feelings for him were larger than she could grasp. She started to gather the silver and get up, but he came toward her. "I've got something for you," he said. From his shirt pocket he took a folded paper and opened it. "I meant to give it to you earlier," he said, "but I just got around to it." It was a map, a page from an atlas. He showed her what he had done, reading the names of roads and telling her where to turn, his fingernail following the line he had drawn across the state of Kentucky until it ended at Brandenburg Station. He folded the map. "Take it," he said. "Put it somewhere safe."

"I'll put it with the carving you gave me," she told him, and smiled. Leona edged around the neighbors in rocking chairs, slipped the map into her purse, and returned to the kitchen. She touched her brow; her fingers were damp. When Hardesty took her hands, she was so pleased he could have done anything with her. After a moment she said, "Do you know how to dance?"

"Yes, ma'am," he replied. "Or at least I used to."

"Would you dance with me, then . . . just here in the kitchen?"

There was a moment's breathlessness between them like the inhalation of fresh, vibrant air. He tilted his head and smiled, and the space dividing them closed. His courtliness touched her. She lowered her cheek to his shoulder, and slowly they began to move to the easy drifting rhythm and the voice singing in the other room. She closed her eyes and gave herself over to it. *"A picture from the past comes slowly stealin' . . . Then suddenly I get that old-time feelin'. I can't help it if I'm still in love with you. . . ."*

As long as she let her thoughts dissolve, she could follow him effortlessly, but when she grew too aware of their closeness and the faint sinking sensation it caused in her, she faltered. She asked him where he had learned to dance. High school, he said, a long time ago, but she was listening to his voice, not the words. I'm making a fool of myself, she thought. The music was drawing to an end; Leona started to break from him. "Come with me," he said into her hair. "I'll show you my cabin." She looked at him carefully. "I shouldn't," she said. "The children . . ."

"You know Vee'll look after them," he said. "You couldn't leave them in better hands. It's not far. Come with me just this once before you leave." The band was playing again. One of the women started to sing in a high, quavery church voice, *"Many a night while you lay sleepin', dreamin' of your amber skies . . . was a poor boy broken-hearted, listenin' to the winds that sigh."*

"I know you feel it, too," Hardesty said, standing behind her. "Sometimes at night I miss you so bad. Look at me and tell me you don't want to come." She was gripped by anxiety, torn with her refusal.

*"Many a day with you I rambled, happiest hours with you I've spent . . . Thought I had your heart forever, now I find it's only lent."*

It reminded Leona so much of the country dances of her youth, the muggy summer nights, the katydids, paper lanterns strung among trees, excursion-boat dances. Emma was already married and pregnant, riding along beside her in what Frank called his "enclosed car"—and then afterward, gone from Emma, in Alfred's arms. The longing stirred like a narcotic memory. She had a sense of losing herself, of drowning in this world of charm and music and desire. "Let me put Patsy and Walter to bed," she told him. It was nearly nine-thirty.

She waited for the song to end to summon the children. The woman she remembered only as Grudge's wife was still singing, her immense happy hips swaying ever so lightly from the wiggle of her foot. *"My little darlin', oh how I love you, how I love you none can tell . . . In your heart you love another, little darlin', pal of mine."*

Two other women lifted their heads and joined in the chorus, the music romping along toward a final crescendo. But the song didn't end with a flourish as Leona expected. Grudge's wife sat down, and one by one the players stopped until only the piano strummed away and Funny Grandma was playing a kind of daft solo, bits of a sonata, then raking the keys in a long, tinkling run. Vee stood up from the bench and faced the small audience. " 'Scuse us, everybody," she said, "while my mama shows off." The musicians looked at each other and laughed.

In the attic, Leona stayed with the children until they were sound asleep; then, bending over Mamie, she pulled the covers up around her, whispered good night, and kissed her warm cheek. Then she drew away. The music still rippled from the living room, and, beneath it, the slow churn of voices. In the dark kitchen, she slipped into the coat Hardesty held for her. "My purse," she said.

"You don't need it," he said, "and nobody'll bother it. Why give them something else to talk about?"

She smiled and glanced toward the light in the doorway. "I should at least say something to Vee."

"She'll know," he said, and after a moment Leona nodded and went out ahead of him. A mist was falling as they went through the gate. The night sky was mottled with wispy clouds, and ahead of them the barn and outbuildings stood black against the sleight-of-hand moonlight. They turned, following the path around the fence. Music leaked from the side of the house like an impudent melody sprung to life in a packed-away music box. In the rays of window light, the threads of falling mist satinized the ensemble inside. Leona glimpsed their shapes arranged around the country band, saw the high-spired neck of the bass fiddle, and immediately felt younger—as if she had slipped backward through time.

The path meandered at the edge of an orchard, then joined the lane marked off by taller trees. Icy twigs snapped underfoot. The air tasted as clean as rain, a fresh and tinny fragrance. They reached the high mound in the road and she saw Hardesty's ice-shrouded cabin in a grove of trees below.

Again the soft whisking noise of the knife being sharpened subsided in the toolshed. Twice earlier that night, Sherman had thought he heard stray footsteps, not the sounds of the men outside by their trucks but footsteps walking in the snow, and each time he had gone to the window to look and listen.

Now he heard the same noise, like steps, and held the knife still. Quiet as a shadow, he rose to the small, flyspecked window and gazed toward the pickup trucks and a horse-drawn wagon tethered to the fence. But no one was there. In the high-gabled farmhouse, shafts of light poured from the downstairs windows. Dim music swam to him through the night. When the clouds parted, an enormous moon loomed over the black chimneys, exposing a jagged half of his boy's face. It was like granite, lips drawn almost white with purpose. His stark blue eyes moved so quickly they seemed to twitch in him. Unable to do anything but wait, Sherman stepped out of the moonlight. With his bandaged hand, he stroked the Chinaman's broad forehead. "They're here," he said. "I know they are." The Chinaman began to whine softly but Sherman scolded him. "Don't do that," he whispered. "It won't be much longer." He spit on the stone, and in the toolshed, out by the barn, the soft abrasive grating resumed, the steel knife blade winking blue and silver in the dark.

When they reached his cabin and went in, she was still full of her remembered self, still full of a delighted irrational excitement. It was intoxicating—like stepping to the edge of a very high diving board, apprehensive and exhilarated. Through the small-paned window she saw the way they had come, the snowy hills and the long night laid out before them, and then she looked around the room itself, this cabin in the woods with the firelight brandishing softly around her while their voices, his and hers, drifted back and forth.

"So this is where you live?" she said; her eyes, a little embarrassed now, restless, searched the rustic walls, the spaces set apart by furniture and screens. The main room was very much like him—ordered and confident, arranged for work. Next to the stone fireplace, a large window overlooked a ravine and there he had a worktable.

He was watching her. She looked at the clutter of his work —he was in the midst of carving several ducks from wood. She lifted an elaborate mallard, fully painted in shades of green and gold and red. "You're very good at this, aren't you?"

"I just do it for my own fun," he said. "Winter's a slow time around here."

Unable to concentrate, her eyes came to rest on the patch of black hair in the collar of his shirt. If she could open that shirt and put her hand there, touch him there and feel . . . and press her head to him . . . then he would cover her like the night. "You know," she said, "don't you, I really shouldn't have come here." She glanced at him. "I should go back. I didn't tell them where I was going. Why don't you come back with me?"

"Why don't you stay?" he said. "Linger a while." It sounded so unlikely, so odd and quaint, like a voice from a more chivalrous age.

"What did you say?" The light from the fireplace quivered like wingbeats across her pale face. She gathered herself to go, but suddenly turned back, awkward for a moment in his arms, leaning into him while he sought and found her mouth. With a little trembling spasm, her lips parted. She wanted the kiss to last a long time. Without any trace of clumsiness, his hands touched her hair and lifted it tenderly from her face, touched the delicate curve of her cheek, her throat. Through her drowning senses, she said, "You look so pleased with yourself. You've been expecting this."

"You knew what was happening," he said. He straightened up and looked at her. "You can't get away with this, you know."

She was trapped in that disarming gaze. It was only then that she let herself admit that she loved him. The idea asserted itself and she accepted it. Until then, she hadn't. She would miss his little actions and expressions, his laugh, his voice that touched her so, his clarity. The moments loomed between them, charged with everything that would remain unsaid. She knew it had already been decided; she had the sensation of rushing toward an unavoidable fate. Searchingly, she touched his face. All the feelings she'd kept in silence these days gave way to the folds of peace that surrounded them. She remembered thinking, If I'm really going to do this, I'll do it to last me the rest of my life. She kissed him again and trembled, anticipating what would happen now, what had to happen, what she would do. He began to loosen her clothes. "No," she murmured, "not like this," and let out a convulsive breath. "I'll do it."

Nothing else was said. She turned from him blindly, and moved down the hall to the room where he slept. Still feeling where his fingers had touched her through her clothes, she lifted the glass chimney from the lamp and lit it with a match from the holder. The flame nibbled blue on the wick. He had not yet come into the room, but she could sense him in the doorway, watching her, silent. Her body rocked forward a little on the throb of her heartbeat; she began to undo her clothes. Look at me, he had said that first morning when she opened her eyes. Look at me, she thought. With a twinge of self-consciousness, she undressed, then watched him enter the room and undo his trousers. She turned from him to pull the covers back on the bed, her breasts yielding to his hands. Her pulse deepened and flashed.

She trembled as she turned back to him, letting her arms close around him and lifting herself up to his mouth. And the rhythm that had lain dormant in her for so long was alive in her lips. "I've wanted you," she said, and she was still trembling when he lifted her and laid her back on the bed.

Suddenly, passionately, without any thought or even the will to think, she gave herself to him. It hurt a little at first and she thought she was tearing inside like new leaves, but he was bending over her, between her legs. "Mark," she murmured. "Mark . . ."

Then they were apart and his dark eyes, full of admiration, devoured her. She moaned watching him and drew his head down to her, to feel him there again. "Don't stop," she murmured, "don't stop," still smoldering inside.

He touched her lips to silence her. "The night's still ahead of us," he said.

She looked at him, and smiled. "Do you suppose they'll know what we've done?"

He looked amused. "You worry too much."

"No," she said, "it's not that. It's just . . . this night will have to last me a very long time."

"Nothing lasts as long as we want it to," he said.

"Maybe it will for me. I want to be everything with you." She could see the kindling in his eyes; he was about to speak again. "Please," she said, suffused with tenderness. "Don't talk . . . don't talk."

Her lips roamed his body, never stopping; his long muscles shivered under the slow brush of her mouth. She lavished herself with him, nuzzled and caressed him with her flesh, touching him everywhere, her breasts trailing over him, feeling his chest with them, his mouth, his eyes. She kissed the soft plush skin of his belly. As if from far away, she heard him groan. "Ah," she laughed and, rising on her arms, leaned over to kiss him fully. "Let me look at you," he said. She sat astride him, bedazzled. His hands covered and caressed her nipples, sending liquid contractions all through her. She wanted to let her flesh absorb his in an act like fire. She thought his eyes had narrowed. "What is it?" she murmured. "Tell me."

"Leona . . ." His voice throbbed inside her. She closed her eyes. "I swear to God, Leona. You take my breath away." They were like words from another time, cloaked in his man's voice.

Folding to him and arching back just a little, she received him in a gentle smothered meeting, and her body began to move in a rhythm of its own, to and fro, as fluent and unrestrained as light switching through prisms. She abandoned herself to her own pleasure. The lamplight shattered to filaments; she could hardly see the shadowed blur of his face. All her movements began to gain speed; an indescribable, sweet pressure ripened inside her. "Mark. Touch me." And when she couldn't contain it any longer, she threw herself upright on him, arched and tensed, her thighs shuddering with exertion, and a scream rose deep in her throat. "My God! . . . God! . . . God!" Her hair hung in her face. Strumming inside, she toppled to him. Rapture flooded through her—wave upon wave, as if a long sweet ribbon were being drawn from her.

# 18

On the edge of sleep, Funny Grandma heard Vivian out by the gate saying goodbye to their company. "Now, don't stay away so long next time," she called to them.

"Goodbye, Vee. Thanks for everything."

Her old fingers pecked the nightstand and closed on her eyeglasses. Funny Grandma set the springlike wires over her ears. Now she could see. Leaning to her window, she peered through the long depression of tree shadows and fence, woodpiles and sheds. Headlight beams flashed across her face, dazzled her glasses, and made her squint. "They're out there waitin'," she muttered, her mouth working on the words. "Just waitin'. If you listen, you'll hear 'em."

"Good night," Vivian called. "Don't forget, now. Come see us. Goodbye. Bye." Doors slammed, metal doors out in the night; motors started up. The gate closed. Vivian's footsteps crossed to the porch, the screen door clapped.

Funny Grandma nestled her head in the crook of her arm to watch the night. Moments later, she was talking though there was no one there to hear her. "Vivy," she was saying, "why won't ye listen to me? I am an old, old woman, not very long for this world. I have seed many things and did many things I shouldn't, but Vivy, if I never knowed anything else, if I never draw another breath, I will prove to ye once and for all what ye won't hear of. That no account, lowlife trash ye feed on the porch is stealin' us blind." Her head curled and rolled to the pillow, her eyelids sagged shut, her breathing grew deeper and slower. "I don't know why yer daddy puts up with it. Why don't he just drive 'em off?" She dreamed she could see them crouched behind bushes, eyes flashing in the moonlight.

Vivian was coming in to say good night. "Mama, shame on you. You've still got your clothes on."

Funny Grandma rose toward the face whose features were like her own but younger for all eternity. "Vivy, ye have to listen to me. Will ye listen?" And it began again. "They's out there stealin' our corn we slaved for."

"I know, Mama," Vee said. "I know. But it's all right. . . . I know. Let's see if we can't put this nightgown on."


Through the walls of the toolshed came the sound of a truck motor, and the growl went on building in the Chinaman. "That's the last one," Sherman told him and held the black mouth tighter. Thin razors of light flickered through gaps in the crude plank wall, expanded and rotated in the air above his head. In the barnyard, the truck turned; the Chinaman's growl deepened.

The last of the pickups rumbled past the shed. Minutes passed. The Chinaman struggled to get up, but Sherman held him, speaking directly into his ear. "Now, be still," he whispered. "Lay still. I mean it." Out on the main road, the noise of the truck engine gradually sank to a distant buzz. Then silence.

Sherman pulled the loose galoshes from his shoes. Tapping the pill bottle to his mouth, he gulped three of the pills, then stared at the bottle while he capped it. These new pills ain't as good as the others, he thought. Not near as good. He unfastened the toolshed door, patted his leg, and the Chinaman followed him out. Under the dim full moon, the mist stung his face like needles. When he walked across the untrodden snow, it cracked under his feet, and the noise made him even more jittery than he had been.

Only that snowman in the yard told him children were here, that they were really here.

At the woodpile, he studied the quiet house. He scanned the shadowed porch where the others had come out, saying good-bye; then he looked back to the side of the house where the tall windows flickered with stovelight. Keeping the Chinaman close, he followed the path around the picket fence until he could look directly through the four windows and into the dim interior.

Then the medicine took hold, so hard he swayed with it. The surrounding night distorted and slipped into place, then grew so sharp it was almost painful. And Sherman felt it come over him like ice water, his muscles pulled tight, his breath drawn in short, deep gasps. There was nothing but the house now and the people in it, Mamie in it. Nothing else reached him, there was no other world. If that woman tried to stop him, that woman he had hated so long . . . If anybody tried to stop him, he would do whatever had to be done. He would kill them all. The knife blade glistened at the end of his fist. Nothing would keep him from Mamie this time. He looked again at the firelit windows where nothing moved, then back at the gate in the picket fence and slowly turned and beckoned the dog.

Untying her sash, Vee slipped the bright collar over her head and dropped the apron on the back of a kitchen chair. With the neighbors gone, the house seemed hollow and lonely. She hadn't missed Leona until she stood up from the piano an hour ago to offer her neighbors dessert and a late-night cup of coffee. Hardesty was gone, too; she knew immediately what had happened. She smiled. Well, I hope they have a good time, she thought. It'd do her good. Now, except for the unwashed coffee cups and dessert dishes left on the table, everything was in its place, the kids' playthings still upstairs where she had stashed them, the room pretty much in order. It was almost too tidy for her taste; she had grown used to having the kids and their things underfoot. Through the doorway to the living room, the light from the stove throbbed.

After the festivities, she felt her solitude acutely. She opened one of the tall windows a crack to air out the room. The pall of tobacco smoke began to seep away. The night sky looked so close now. With a barn ladder, she could crawl right up into that moon and go to sleep with no regrets. She stood looking through the window at all that was hers and thought, Shame on you, Vee Turner, what've you got to feel so low about? There's corn aplenty in that crib, chickens brooding on eggs this very minute, and three little babes fast asleep in your attic. Then she knew what she wanted to do. I'll go upstairs and keep 'em company till Leona gets back. I don't need to stand here feelin' so blue. She shut the window, turned back the covers on Leona's bed, and went toward the stairs.

Hearing footsteps, Mamie sat up in bed. "You're not her," she said.

"No, I'm not," Aunt Vee told her quietly. "But I'm the next best thing. Slide on over there a little bit. I'm goin' to keep you company."

"Stay," Sherman whispered, bending down, his voice a dry husk. "Stay. Wait here." Obediently the Chinaman sat down, his matted tail sweeping the snow. Sherman straightened up to study the night.

The gate opened, silent as ball bearings, and stuck in an icy drift. He stepped into the yard. Clouds drifted across the moon. The mist was changing to rain.

Leaning toward the window, Funny Grandma watched him come through the misty haze. Then she heard him entering the house—a muffled sound that struck at some deep chord in her heart.

A plate was set aclatter. All at once, it was stilled. Sitting upright in bed, her heart pounding, Funny Grandma strained to hear him through the drafty walls of the house. "I'll show ye," she muttered. "I'll show ye, damn ye! Won't let an old woman catch 'er breath." She shifted to the side of her bed and squinted through sleep-tilted glasses at the door. "Vivy!" she called, and choked; her heart twisted painfully. No voice answered her, no one came to the door. *Somethin's afoot in the house.*

Out of the dark, Sherman emerged in the doorway. The wood stove left burning in the living room gave off little light. Across the room a bed was turned down and even that was hard to see. He wondered what it meant—that bed. He wished he hadn't lost his pencil flashlight. He lit a match. Yellow light leapt from his fingers and he held it higher. He saw nothing to indicate that children had been here. The match burned out; he dropped it and struck another, then another, wandering past the stove. Is this the wrong place? His eyes roamed back to the turned-down covers. He struck a match and stepped toward the bed. Suddenly he bit his lips and flung the smoking black stick from his scorched fingers. "Ah, shit," he mumbled, sucking at his fingers. The bed had been turned down, but why? Who for? He had seen all the others leave. *Where is everybody?* At the foot of the bed, wedged among suitcases, was a purse.

He looked back toward the dark doorway and heard nothing. He grabbed the purse, opened it. Feeling inside, he pulled out some papers and set them out on the bed. Then he dug down inside the purse until he found a billfold. Quickly he flipped through the plastic sleeves, past meaningless snapshots, looking for something with a name—and saw the driver's license. He struck a match, his next to last, and read the signature. Leona Hillenbrandt. Seeing her name sent sparks through his blood. He shook out the match. I knew it! he thought, thrusting the billfold back into the purse. I knew it.

Then he saw the map.

. . .

In her house slippers, Funny Grandma crossed the painted floor to her wardrobe. *They come in here, Vivy, at night, in here. To steal our corn . . . in my own house.* She could feel her heartbeat in her runaway hands, but she caught the wooden knob, opened the mirrored door, and pulled out, through hanging clothes, her dead husband's 10-gauge shotgun, the big gun, the one he'd once used to kill a bear. From the hat shelf on the other side, Funny Grandma took down a box of shells. The exertion only increased the wildness in her hands. The box shook like a live hornets' nest. *Don't respeck nothin', nobody!* She tore the box open and dumped the cartridges on her bed, where they fell together in a loose clutter of thuds.

Her arms ached and her joints were beginning to stiffen. Her heart would not slow down. She managed to break open the breech of the shotgun. Humped over the bed in a bank of hazy moonlight, she caught up one of the red waxed shells and jammed it into the first of the two empty chambers. "Ha!" she exclaimed, under her breath. She reached for another shell, but her hands were shaking too much. She dropped it. The weighted casing struck the floor with a loud clack, then rolled in noisy rim runs. "Damn ye," she mumbled, startled, and held her breath. Then she snatched up another cartridge. The shell stuttered against the chamber opening and slipped in. She cranked the double barrels upright. The breech plunked to. She let loose a sigh and drew the hammers back to cock the gun. Holding it cradled against her chest, she went to the door and crossed the porch, her right-hand forefinger on the trigger.

The kitchen door was standing open. She squeezed her eyes and stared at it. The door was ajar, nothing else. Dim moonlight fell through it in a long broken crack, exposing part of a chair and the edge of the kitchen table. *The wind's ablowin',* she thought; *fixin' to rain.* She opened the door wider and peered over her shoulder. Setting her feet, she swung around and the shape of darkness on the wall changed into harness. "Shadder," she said, and let go all her breath, "you ain't nothin' but night standin' still." But afterward, to keep her courage up against the terrible thing that was afoot, she began to talk to herself. "I ain't afeared," she murmured. "I ain't afeared." Drifting forward, tottering from side to side, she crossed the worn threshold. Not a plank announced her passage.

*Brandenburg Station.*

He held the map down in the stovelight to see it clearer. With his finger, he followed the pencil line across the map of Kentucky till it ended. A town on the river, circled. In the flickering dimness, his eyes smarted. Even down close to the stove, he had trouble reading the tiny map words. Again and again, he shaped the name with his mouth to remember it. He had started to take the papers—had unbuttoned his shirt to stuff them in—when he thought, No. Put them back. Just in case. Then she won't never know the difference. Quickly he returned the papers to the purse and slid it back in its place. From some other room, he heard a noise, and somebody talking very low. Then silence. Bent in concentration, he listened and heard it again, a soft garbled voice like somebody talking in their sleep. He drew rigid, turned and glimpsed a shadow drifting toward the doorway: a woman, it looked like. Wavering ahead of her, the long double barrels of a gun protruded into the firelit room.

Twisting, darting for a place to hide, he bumped a rocker and shadows leapt around him, like crazy laughter.

"I have seed all kindsa things good and bad come my way. I have seed women built up wi' child and tore down and put asunder. I have seed men strung up and shot down. . . ." Outside, the black night shook with loud thunder. Her arms began to cramp.

The big gun was too heavy. She had to stop and rearrange it in her hands.

Next to the turned-down bed, Sherman stood inside the filmy curtains watching her come.

"I know of things ye'll never know. . . ." In the glimmering light, the doorway rose up around her. She stood straight as a stake. In that terrible instant, Sherman saw her as he had never seen anything in his life. She was small, smaller than him, and old, her skin as patterned as a snake's hide. Blurred behind glasses, her deep-socketed eyes watched the room with hawklike scrutiny. Her lips were puckered together, absolutely expressionless and unchanging. She was making a little noise, humming or moaning. His fist grew slippery on the knife. In her hands, she carried a shotgun that looked longer than she was.

Everything was swaying and uncertain: the stovelight ebbed and receded, her flannel nightdress shifted, her face quivered uncontrollably. She heard a sound, but even in that suspended silence it was so low she couldn't make out what it was. "Whar are ye?" she demanded.

Only his eyes moved.

"Who the hell are ye?" she snapped even louder. "Botherin' me and mine." Suddenly there was a noise—a grating noise tearing across her nerves—and she turned swiftly toward it. Standing boldly at the window was a monstrous shadow thing. She staggered forward and stared at it. Hit's some man, she thought, peerin' at me. In my bedclothes. A big man, black, mulled by the rain on the windowpane. Her spine stiffened with fright. The glass fogged and cleared under its breath, but it made no sound just then. Trembling all over, she drew her mouth even tighter. "Who are ye?" she demanded sharply. "Show yerself!"

It just stood there, breathing on the window glass.

Never taking her eyes from it, Funny Grandma edged back into the room. The dark sank around her. "Git outa here, Goddamn ye!" It tore at the screen, that sharp grating sound.

Poised like a cat, Sherman watched her. It's the Chinaman, he thought. But as long as she commanded the doorway, he was trapped. She's liable to shoot. He wiped his hand on his pants and gripped the knife harder. Thunder rumbled in the high beyond and the Chinaman was whining outside, crying to get in.

Lightning. The flash struck the windows and she saw—not a man. The thing had fur and glowing eyes. "Ye ain't nobody!" Funny Grandma exclaimed, bringing the gun around and up toward it. "Hit's some dog!"

She's gonna shoot him! Sherman felt a sickening jolt. *She's really gonna shoot him!* He tore through the curtains. "Hey! Hey, that's my dog!"

The dark figure hurtled at her, flying fast, crosswise, at an angle to her. Weighted by the gun, she reeled on her feet, trying to track him, raw instinct tearing through her tired muscles. She saw, in his fist, a blade slung back in an arc, closing with blinking speed. His bandaged hand reached, swung at the long barrels to knock them aside, and her spidery finger closed down.

The room exploded with blazing incandescence.

The recoil knocked Funny Grandma backward, completely off her feet, and the deafening blast took out the first of the four tall windows. The shot pattern honeycombed the wall, reducing to slivers the entire window glass and splintering the woodwork and wallpaper in a wide, dense configuration. Stray pellets pinged and whined on the stovepipe; curtains shredded; a light dust of plaster, gunpowder, and soot floated through the air. Someone was screaming upstairs. Footsteps scurried. Dazed, his head still ringing from the concussion, Sherman rose to his knees and saw no one. She had missed him, though the gun seemed to go off right in his face. He pushed up on legs gone to rubber, staggered to the destroyed window, and vanished through it.

. . .

The noise broke through the layers of Leona's unconsciousness like a stone falling through deep water. Her eyelids wrinkled and fluttered. That wasn't thunder, she thought. Still woozy and half asleep, she rose on an elbow, listening intently, then drew herself up away from Hardesty. "Did you hear that? Mark?"

He shifted toward her and rubbed his face. "It's just the weather," he said sleepily. "It's not anything." His fingers stroked her waist and stopped. He sat up slowly and squinted toward the dark window. "You know, it did sound odd . . . like a shot."

"It sounded close," she said. "I think it came from Vee's." Covering herself with the sheet, she slipped to the edge of the bed and quickly began to dress. "I want to go back. Will you take me?" He struck a match and lamplight spread around them. A sensual stupor clung to Leona; all her flesh, every tiny vein was exhausted. Her movements seemed exaggerated and clumsy. Her fingers were awkward. Her shoes wouldn't go on. She tried to rearrange her hair and decided to leave it down. But though her thoughts were muddled, the fear went on mounting.

*A shot.*

The cabin door opened and Hardesty sent her ahead. "I have to get something," he told her. "I'll catch up. I'll be right behind you." Unable to hold herself back any longer, Leona started to run. The path through the snow unreeled before her. Rocks loomed up in the night and slipped away, twigs snapped against her, icy branches cracked and sprang back, a rusty fence appeared beside her momentarily, yet she seemed to make no progress. An excruciating twist tightened in her stomach. I shouldn't have left them. My God, my God. Rain trickled on her face, ran into her eyes. She failed to see the ropy tree roots lying in the path—her feet caught in them and she pitched headlong into the icy brush.

Hardesty drew her up, the rain splattering over them. "Take it easy," he said. "You won't get there any faster acting like this." He tried to take her hand. Under his arm he carried a black rifle; seeing it sent terror all through her. Her worst imaginings converged in that weapon. "My God, what's happened? What if they're hurt? Oh, Mark . . ." She ran from him, abandoning the path, tearing through the shortcut of the orchard. And the old house broke above the rim of night, growing closer as she rushed toward it, the living-room windows ablaze with light. Vee hurrying about. Something terribly wrong.

By the time she turned in at the gate, a heavy dread had closed around her; it was like pushing herself through lead. She could hardly open the screen door. The kitchen door stood ajar, and she entered the house in slow motion. "Vee!" she cried, but the name came out in a whimper. She could hear a shuffling noise from the lighted living room, then muted voices, then weeping. She stepped toward the rectangle of light as if walking a tightrope. "My God, Vee!" she gasped, overcome with her imaginings.

"We're in here," Patsy said, peeking around the woodwork. Then the other two children appeared behind Patsy, and beyond them, near the stove, Vee was tending to Funny Grandma. As Leona knelt to the children, she saw the empty window frame and the shredded wall. "Vee, my God—is everybody all right?" Vee glanced toward her and nodded. "I think so." In her wet coat, Leona drew the children to her. "Kids," she said, steadying her voice, "tell me. What happened?"

"We helped Funny Grandma get up," Patsy said. Her face was like a harlequin's—white, cheeks red and splotchy. She started to cry.

"Patsy, don't cry. Oh, don't cry. Just tell me what happened."

"Funny Grandma's gun blew up," Mamie said, gulping air through her open mouth.

"Yeah," Walter said. "She killed somebody." His eyelashes were wet, clinging together.

Vee stood away from the old woman in the rocking chair and crossed her arms. "Mama," she said, "nobody thinks you're makin' it up."

Funny Grandma pointed at the windows and smacked her empty lips.

"I know," Aunt Vee said. "But they're gone now. They're all gone. And you need t'settle down. Look what you done to the kids—look how scared they are. You shouldn't scare these little kids." The children were breaking away from Leona, gazing at the shattered wall, skirting it as if it were a danger zone. Vee turned to Leona. "I'm not gettin' anywhere with her. There's no humorin' her. She's too worked up. I still don't know what really happened."

Hardesty, carrying the rifle, came through the kitchen toward them. "I thought I heard something out by the barn," he said. "But in the rain—"

Before he could go on, Vee interrupted him. "Put that gun away," she said, "and stop this talk." She looked toward the children. "Some folks around here's still pretty scared." Then she took a step toward him and leaned forward. "She thinks she saw somethin' and she shot it. I reckon it was bound to happen sometime or other. She sees things, believe me."

"That's right," Funny Grandma said. "Come in on me with a knife. Just come at me. Come like a damn streak."

"You're all okay, then?" Mark said, looking at Vee. She nodded and let out a breath. "All right," he said. "I'll check around outside a little closer." And he was gone.

Mamie turned back to the rocking chair and tilted her head. "Funny Grandma, did you hurt yourself?"

Funny Grandma peered down at her. "Why, ye look just like my baby girl. Ye look like my li'l Phoebe."

"We was asleep," Patsy said, and rubbed her face.

"Yeah," Walter said. "It shook the floor."

The palsied voice chased after theirs, demanding its own

attention. "He come through that winder. Hit's one of them Frakes boys."

Vee said, "Mama. The Frakes boys went to school with you. They been buried in Hope Cemetery for twenty years. Who knows what you saw."

"Then I cain't reckon who it was," Funny Grandma said peevishly, her chin thrust out. "I seed 'im. Yonder there. Plain as day."

"You shouldn't be down here in your bare feet," Leona told the children. "Let's go upstairs and go back to bed."

"I can't sleep any more," Patsy said. "It's too loud."

"It's way past your bedtime," Aunt Vee said. "Don't want you catchin' pneumonia. The excitement's all over. Come along —I'll go up with ya." Then to Leona, "Let me take 'em up. Maybe I can get my wits about me. I tell ya it shook the whole house. Just about scared me to death in my dreams." She gathered the children and smiled at Leona as they started up the stairs. "I like your hair down like that. Makes you look younger."

Leona glanced at her and laughed softly to herself, and it broke the tension. Too much had happened. Everything was unclear to her, but her fear, her worst fear, had proved unfounded. The children were safe. Deeply relieved, she sat down on the third step, listening to the others climb the stairs behind her. Through the dark windows, she could glimpse Hardesty outside, walking in the rain. Presently he crossed the porch and entered the kitchen. She went to meet him and his hand came up and touched her cheek, and she caught his fingers in her hands. "There's nobody out there," he said, "nobody shot or I'd have found traces. There's some tracks, but in this rain it could be anything. If somebody was here, they're gone." He leaned down close to her. "Really, Leona, it's all right." He went toward the old woman and Leona turned to go after him. What a night, she thought. What a night.

The wind was blowing the rain through the empty window frame. The rocker stopped. "I never seed nothin' like it. Old woman cain't sleep in her own bed any more. I shain't put up with it, I tell you, Vivy." Funny Grandma craned her head forward till it was only inches from Mark. "Hit stood rightcher at my winder and growled." She pointed. "Yonder. Lookin' in on my sleep. Not afeared of nothin'. Mean! Crazy, mean dog!"

*Dog!* Leona was stabbed by terror. All the fear she had been struggling against broke loose inside her. It *was* him! Her stomach twisted so hard she winced. *It was him, after all. It was him!* Abruptly she stood. "Mark, he's out there! Nothing'll stop him."

Doubtful, he looked at her, then squinted out at the night. "Did you see something?"

"No!" Leona cried. "No! But he's here. He's still out there. Mark, he'll come back. *He'll come back!*" Hardesty reached for her, but she pulled away from him. "Listen, Mark, please—he's out there. He won't stop. We're all in danger. I've got to do something!" In desperation, she leaned down to Funny Grandma and grasped her thin, papery arms. "Tell me . . . Funny Grandma! What did he look like?"

The old head sagged against the wooden headrest of the rocker. "Goodbye," she said in that coarse, faltering voice. "Bye, bye. Glad ye come by."

"Yes," Leona persisted. "But, Funny Grandma, don't you remember? The man. The man with the dog. What did he look like? *Try to remember!*"

Funny Grandma shut her eyes, but her mouth kept opening and closing. She was starting to rock, humming, grumbling to herself, her slippers tapping the floor. It was no use.

Leona turned to Hardesty. "Oh, Mark, I'm so scared." And then she realized what had to be done. "We have to go," she told him. "We have to leave right now. Me and the children." He started to protest, but she couldn't let him interfere. Turning, she noticed her purse, and went quickly and inspected it, but everything was in order, the map still there, just as she had left it.

Hardesty was watching her. "What is it?" he said. "What's going on? Leona, tell me."

"I can't," she said. Nor could she look at him squarely. "We can't stay here. We're not safe any more. Nobody will be safe here. We've got to go."


Leona knelt among the children, buttoning their coats, smoothing their hair back under their stocking caps. Hardesty passed through the room carrying suitcases to the car. When the children were ready to leave, Aunt Vee beckoned them. "I believe your Funny Grandma's got a sack of Christmas presents for you kids to take with you. Just some things she put together. Why don't we go in and see her a minute?" As she directed the children toward the doorway, she turned to Leona. "Tell me the truth," she said. "Is this because of what you mentioned before? Remember, you said something about a man followin' you?"

"Yes!" Leona said, amazed that Vee had remembered. She glanced at the children and held her finger to her lips. "Yes, Vee. It just never ends."

"I thought so," Vee said, and turned to go with the children.

Alone in the room, Leona pulled out the briefcase from under the foot of the bed. The thumb latches were open. Suddenly she was afraid to touch it, but she forced herself to lift the lid. In a glance, she saw that the gun was gone. *No . . . God!* He'd found something he wanted all right. *Gone!* So that's what the bastard went into, she thought. Instead of my purse. He must have . . . He took the gun. Now what can I use, she thought with horror. What can I use to stop him with?

From the direction of the kitchen she heard Vee saying,

"Mamie, I told you. Quit fussin' around with that Christmas sack. Leave it be."

Leona shut the briefcase, gripped its handle, and hurried to them.

Then they were saying goodbye, walking toward the gate, the children going ahead of them through the long white corridor of headlights. Leona peered about, still afraid, still expecting some specter to rise up in the dark. I've got to go out there, she thought.

"I'm sorry you have to leave, Leona," Vee said, and she brought her arms up around her and held her firmly. "Me, too," Leona muttered, "me, too," and when they drew apart, she saw the abiding kindness in Vee's warm blue eyes, the caring and the strength, and felt it flowing out to her. I'm saying goodbye to Vee, Leona thought sadly. I'll never see her again. What a good friend. And the love and pain came flooding through. "Oh, Vee," she said, reaching, clasping her rough hand as warmly as she knew how to.

But the gaunt woman silenced her. "Now, you just take care," she said. "Godspeed."

And Leona was in the Willys with Hardesty and the children, the headlights skimming down along the fence, catching a glimpse of Vee still standing there in the doorway, hand raised. Leona strained back to see her once more, but the tears in her eyes distorted the night around her.


"Take my car," Hardesty said.

"No, Mark! Your car? I can't do that."

"You have to," he said. "It'll take you where you want to go. I'll walk back and stay with Vee till morning. Drive into Kentucky, buy a car there, if that's what you want to do, and leave mine. Just drop me a postcard where it is. I'll pick it up." But his eyes said something else entirely.

The rain had tapered off. They stood in the soft, gray world of the country road, hardly a mile from Vivian Turner's farmhouse, to say goodbye. Hardesty gently took her shoulders. When finally he spoke again, it was to ask her to stay. "Don't do this," he said. "I can't imagine living here without you. What'll I have left when you're gone? A memory? That's no good, Leona. How can we make a mistake this wrong? Don't go. I swear to you, I'll take care of you." The quiet vehemence of his plea touched her as nothing ever had. All that she wanted was to surrender, to stay here with him and to let him have his way.

"I can't. I can't," she said. "How could I know this would happen? I should never have involved you in this. I thought— I felt safe here with you, and it was . . ." Tears sprang to her eyes and she quickly wiped them away, trying to maintain some scrap of composure. "Oh, don't be in love with me, Mark. I'll break your heart."

"Then you'll have to break it. What are you afraid of?"

"Of staying," she said. "Of leaving." The children were drawing faces in the steam of the car windows. Leona saw them and smiled grimly. The wind hurled down the road, clattering through the high dripping branches of the trees, and Hardesty drew her close into his coat.

"Then don't tell me," he said. "Don't tell me some story. I don't care what it is. I'll just leave this, leave everything behind and come find you one of these days."

"Maybe you won't want to," she said. "You don't know me. I know you think you do, but, Mark—"

"You're like something wonderful that fell from the sky one night."

The moment arrived when there was nothing left to say. They stood there then a while longer, not talking, not even touching. It hurt, inexpressibly. It would be like a blindness, not to see each other. At last, he said her name. He said he loved her.

But nothing could hold down the fear. She tried to tell him she would never forget him, all her life. It was tearing her inside. She looked up and down the desolate road. Scarcely breathing, she clung to him, and then she kissed him with passion—to last her for the rest of her life.

# 19

Roosters crowed in the black and white distance. Time crept by. Dawn hung like a pall of smoke in the air, the rain had turned to frost, and the country road meandered through the rough terrain like a snail's shiny track. Among the trees, the morning light fell through the high branches in thin ecclesiastic beams, sliding over the boy. But in the ravines and creek beds the night's darkness still prevailed, silent, undisturbed, the color of indigo.

The left side of Sherman's face still burned from the shotgun blast; he pressed his cold sleeve against it. Of all the damn luck. He shuddered and hugged his outer arms for warmth. "Chinaman," he said, "c'mon."

Walking on stones, he crossed the creek and went on. Beneath his footsteps, the thawed ground oozed through ice as thin and crackling as paper. He wondered what time it was. Sherman kept walking, muttering, cursing to himself. He patted his leg for the Chinaman to come, but there was no movement beside him. He stopped and glanced back. "Chinaman," he said louder. "Come on, boy. Let's go." But nothing moved in the shadowed ravine. No dark shape ran across the stippled woods to meet him. And then there came a sound he had never heard before—a howl that was nothing like a howl—a terrible cry of pain.

On the far side of the creek, some distance behind him, the

Chinaman staggered up through the weeds and fell. And the cry rose again, an anguished throb in the air.

Feeling weak in his knees, Sherman ran back across the stones. "Boy," he said, "what'sa matter?" He reached for him but the dog drew his head back and growled. "It's me! Chinaman, it's me! What's wrong? It's too dark down here. I can't see you, where's it hurt?" But the black muzzle wrenched upward in yet another wail.

At first, Sherman couldn't grasp what had happened or what the trouble was. In the dark seeping light of the ravine, nothing showed. It seemed inconceivable to him that the Chinaman was really hurt. Slowly, speaking quietly, he was able to pat the dog and finally his arm went around the Chinaman and his hand fell across a wet, warm patch of fur. "Boy," he said softly. "She hit you, didn't she? It musta been that woman, that crazy old woman. You got shot." He smelled the blood on his hand. The realization sank into him, deeper and deeper. Trembling, he looked frantically around. "We can't just stay here," he said.

High above, through the wilderness of branches, the cold sky was gradually filling with light. Little by little, the shadows were abandoning the creek bank. Sherman withdrew his arm from the dog and stood. "Chinaman, get up. We have to wash you off. I'll take care of you. C'mon, now, get up." He backed away, still coaxing, and on the second try the Chinaman rocked upright on his paws. Pulling his shirttail from his pants, Sherman tore loose a wide strip of the cloth.

"Chinaman," Sherman said, "you'll be okay." Again he dipped the torn piece of shirt in the cold running creek, and a stain of blood darkened the water. He shook out the rag, folded it, and started to hold it against the Chinaman's black chest, but the dog wouldn't stay still. He squirmed and whimpered, trying to wipe at the hurt places with his big tufted paw. "Hold still," Sherman said. "Come on, boy. Lemme look at you."

But everywhere Sherman looked now—across the dog's face and shoulders, and down along his forelegs and chest—the Chinaman was bleeding. Only his back and hindquarters had been spared, and they glinted with long, thin slivers of glass. At least some of the blast from that old woman's gun had caught the Chinaman as he stood at the windowsill. It looks bad, Sherman thought, wringing out the rag once more. It's real bad.

All over the Chinaman's stubby nose and around his slanted eyes, the hair was cut in a web of bloody markings, and from the cuts bits of glass protruded, sparkling like ice. Grasping the worn collar with his bandaged hand, Sherman wiped the dog's face with the cold rag and shook it out over the water, and the glass slivers fell with hardly a sound. He worked carefully, edging the glass out with the pointed end of the cloth, then shaking the cloth out and dipping it into the creek and beginning where he'd left off until his hand stung with the cold water. But he couldn't get all the glass, the cuts were too many.

There were other places, too, where the skin was hardly punctured and the blood just trickled out, and near them, Sherman could feel the lead pellets, hard foreign matter, lying under the skin. One place was particularly bad, a deep, torn wound on the Chinaman's chest below the collarbone. There the skin was ripped open in a loose bleeding flap, but when Sherman tried to examine it, the dog snarled and bared his teeth. And Sherman backed off.

In the far distance, the sun had risen a little higher; somewhere, dimly, one lonely rooster still crowed. Maybe you'll feel better now, Sherman thought. Things always seemed different in the daylight. "Get a drink," Sherman told him, and the Chinaman clambered up on his paws and padded to the edge of the creek, lowered his head, and drank. But he was still bleeding and he seemed more and more unsteady on his legs. Sherman stayed close to him, talking to him. "Damn that crazy old woman. See what happened? See what you caused? Now you're hurt real bad."

An uprooted tree had fallen across the creek, and Sherman climbed it to its highest point and looked around. He didn't know where he was. A sharp wind blew down the creek, sending eddies of water before it. "By nighttime, it'll be freezin'," he said. Behind him, on the ground, the Chinaman moaned and swiped at his face with his paws, and Sherman scrambled down to him. "Don't do that," he scolded, "Chinaman, don't do that. I know it hurts. I'll get you something." He took up the rag and went back to work on the dog's face, thinking, I don't know what to do. The Chinaman sat very rigid under his hand, panting, whining, his weird trusting eyes gazing at Sherman through the web of cuts. "I wish you could talk."

With his good hand, Sherman scooped the slate-tasting water to his mouth and drank. Time was getting away. "We gotta find a town and get you some help." He splashed a last cold handful of water on his face and wiped his eyes with his jacket sleeve.

Not far away, car tires slip-slapped back and forth on a bridge. That would be a road. "Come on, boy. We gotta get over there. You hafta try. You're too big to carry. C'mon. C'mon." And together they followed the creek bank until it leveled beside a tended field and the Chinaman didn't have to climb the embankment.

At the end of the field was the road, and farther away a white steeple broke the rim of wintry branches. Crossing that bare strip of land seemed interminable; over and over Sherman stopped and talked to the Chinaman, went to his knees and patted him. Out on the road the few passing cars flew by like rockets. Somewhere, Sherman thought, on some road, that woman's getting away. He could follow her in his mind—the road signs, the little towns flying away behind her speeding car.

They came to the town and Sherman read the sign, DOOLIT-
TLE FALLS POP. 530, and turned in at the first gas station. Among
stacks of tires piled outside, he stooped and coaxed the Chinaman to lie down. "Stay here," he said. "Stay right here. I'll be
back in a minute." Then he went into the garage and said to the
man, "My dog's been hurt. I don't know what to give him. Is
there somebody in town where I could take him? Some doctor?"

"No, sir."

"Then've you got anything to help him out?"

The man asked what was wrong with him.

"He got in some glass and cut himself up," Sherman said.
"He's bleedin' pretty bad."

"No, sir, there's nothing here," the man said, and went back
to his work. Sherman stepped into the display room, and as he
passed a dusty glass counter of cigars and candy bars, he noticed
some tins of aspirin. Returning to the doorway, he said, "D'you
think some aspirin would help him?" And the mechanic came
forward wiping his hands. "Might," he said.

"Lemme try some," Sherman said and laid his dime on the
counter.

Hobbled and weaving, the Chinaman had wandered to the
edge of the drive by the time Sherman went outside. He had to
lead the dog back among the piles of tires. "Here," he said, "just
wait a little bit longer. This'll help you." But he couldn't get the
aspirin tin open. At last he set it on edge and hit it with a rock
until the small metal box sprang apart. Some of the pills crumbled under the impact, but from the smashed remains Sherman
picked out an undamaged pill. He held it on the ends of his
fingers and said, "Here, Chinaman, take this."

The dog sniffed at the aspirin and turned his head.

"Come on, Chinaman, take it. This won't hurtcha. You'll
feel better."

Again that terrible cry rose from the dog, building louder
and louder, tearing through Sherman's nerves like a drill, but

there was nothing he could do to stop it—the sound went on
and on, and he just had to wait until it ended. He kept patting
him, catching glass slivers in his bandaged hand and flinging
them off. Finally he clasped the Chinaman's nose and forced his
mouth apart and set the aspirin back on his tongue. And some
time after that, the Chinaman leaned into him and settled down
against his leg.

It's okay, he thought; we have to rest anyway. Slowly his
pants leg, where the Chinaman's head lay against it, grew
bloody, but he didn't move his leg. From behind the tires, Sherman listened to cars pulling into the drive for gas, heard laughter, heard the mechanic remark about the hellish weather, the
deer count, and the minutes ticked by irreversibly. It had taken
them all night to get just this far. Sitting there leaning back
against the tires, Sherman closed his eyes for just a minute. With
his arm around the Chinaman, feeling the dog's heartbeat under
his hand, he dozed.

He awoke with the dog breathing on his face. He didn't
know how much time had passed. The Chinaman whimpered
and nuzzled his cheek like his old self, but the wet blood hung
matted on his chest in a frightening bib. Just seeing it made
Sherman feel queasy and anxious. "Oh, Chinaman," he said,
"it's gettin' worse." He wiped the sleep from his face and pushed
himself up. "We gotta hurry and find another place."

In spite of the blood, the Chinaman at first seemed better.
They took their time, walking slow, and the dog kept up with
Sherman. Little bursts of shoppers, their arms full of boxes and
paper sacks, split around them, but Sherman ignored them. At
the sight of blood, women sometimes moved to the side, clutching their collars, gathering their children and drawing them off
the curb to let the dog pass. A man in a blue apron came to a
doorway. "Son, you ought to take him back through the alley.
You're tracking blood all over the sidewalk." Another man
leaned out of the cab of his pickup and yelled, "Hey, what's

wrong with your dog?" At the corner, they turned away from the stores and the noise. Taking the alleyways, they crossed through the end of town, without further notice, undisturbed. Sherman's head was pounding. He pulled out his pill bottle and tapped out two pills, swallowed one, and bit the other one in two, then swallowed half and forced the other half into the Chinaman's mouth. "This'll make you feel good," he said. The wind blew through the trees, bending branches back, dislodging a few of the last yellow leaves. The air was suddenly warmer; thaw softened the weeds.

At a crossroads, they passed a sign—HAVERSTOWN 3 MI.—and they eventually got there, a town at the foot of a mountain. Leaving the dog outside for just minutes at a time, Sherman hurried into garages and filling stations and barbershops, anyplace where men were gathered, and he spoke to them plainly and in earnest, convinced that somebody would know how to help the Chinaman. "My dog's been hurt," he told them. "I think somebody musta shot him. He's bleedin' real bad. There's glass all over him like he went through a window. Come here. I'll show ya." And a few of the men followed him out.

At one place, a heavyset man chewed on an inch of cigar, as he looked down at the boy and the dog with skepticism. "Ain't nothin' you can do for him," he said. "He's tore up inside. See that little pink ring there on his nose? He's breathin' through blood. He might go on like that for a day or so, but he's done for."

"*You don't know!*" Sherman shouted, jamming his fist in his pocket to keep from striking out at the fat man. "He's been tryin' to lick hisself. *That's what caused it.* There's gotta be somethin' to help him."

The man shrugged. "If it was me, I know what I'd do. I'd put him outa his misery."

Sherman's dread tightened like a coil. For a second, he stood staring at the man in utter refusal, then looked down. "No," he said, his mouth as dry as wool. "You gotta be crazy. I couldn't do that. He just needs patchin' up."

"Suit yourself," the man said.

It was noon; then it was two o'clock. Sherman lost track of time. They were on a road. He didn't remember coming to the road or how they happened to get there. The Chinaman was walking beside him, his claws ticking on the pavement. Now the blood was thick on his forelegs; once in a while, it blew in a dark trickle from his nostrils and made a harsh rasping noise in his throat. Sherman felt fear all over him. He couldn't think what to do. "I wish this was over with," he muttered. "I wish this'd never happened."

Nothing was straight in his mind. He shook his head trying to clear it. They're all against me, he thought. He saw how the men drew away from him, turned away from the Chinaman when he asked them what he should do. They knew what to do but they wouldn't tell him. The world was smarter than he was. All Sherman knew right now was how to get to that woman. "I know her," he muttered to himself. He hadn't tracked her this far without getting to know her—she had her weakness just as much as he did. And this time he knew where she was heading.

It was his last chance. He knew that. He couldn't go on and on, not with the Chinaman as hurt as he was. And he had to be careful. If he scared her off again, he'd never find them. Time was running out. His headaches kept getting worse; the pills didn't help much any more. Sometimes he saw things. He had to stop her and end it. *Had to!* Had to get Mamie and get away and then . . . Suddenly from behind him came that sound again, that sound unlike any other, the Chinaman's anguished howl. It cut through Sherman, and he whirled around. A few yards behind him, the Chinaman had fallen at the edge of the pavement. He was trying to pull himself up. Down the road, a truck appeared out of a curve and closed very fast toward them. Sherman plunged for the dog but couldn't reach him, threw his hands up in the air just as the truck swerved to miss them and slammed past. The turbulent air blasted around Sherman, nearly hurled him off balance.

Again the Chinaman's howl reached him, a curdling wail. Sherman ran, dropped to his knees, trying to gather the dog in his arms. In the concrete under his knees, he felt the road strumming, and abruptly lifted his head. A car flew forward, sizzling on the pavement, bearing down on them. Sherman shot up, stepped deeper into the road, waving wildly, but the car veered, horn blaring—snaked by them. "You bastard!" Sherman yelled and swung his fist after the speeding car. He pivoted, and ran back to the Chinaman. "Get up!" he cried. "Chinaman, get up!" He grabbed the dog's collar and tugged at him and the terrible wail struck him like a strap. Another car was coming. Then another. "Please," Sherman gasped, "you gotta get up!" Tears stood in his eyes, blurred his sight. *Chinaman! You gotta! You gotta!*" And then, hardly aware that he was doing it, with his arms wrapped under the Chinaman's forelegs, Sherman had lifted him, lifted his dog that was bigger than he was, and dragged him off the road, and for those few moments the dog felt insanely light. With loud, hollow noises, the cars blew past them, tires throwing grit and dirt into Sherman's hair and jacket.

The pure wintry silence returned.

At the side of the highway, the Chinaman slowly, feebly, hauled himself up. Sherman heaved for breath. Nothing seemed real. The highway was empty. In the distance, not the suggestion of a car appeared.

Sherman knew what he had to do. It seemed as if he had known all along. And yet everything in him went on resisting it. He drew the dog into his arms, stroking the thick coat. No thought, no words came to comfort him. Waiting for a ride, they stayed there, close together as they had been for so long, while the afternoon light fled into the trees.

In the gray dusk, a coal truck slowed on the outskirts of Gentryville, Kentucky. The high door on the driver's side opened and the driver stood down, turning toward the back of the truck where Sherman had dropped to the ground, talking softly to the dog. The driver helped him lift the Chinaman down. Slowly, laboriously, the dog rose to his feet. The driver pointed to a mailbox and a lane. "If you take this lane up to that white house, somebody there might help you. Ask for old Tom Phelps."

Sherman watched the truck pull away.

They followed the lane marked off by evergreen trees and entered a cluster of white buildings edging a beautiful wide lawn of frosted grass. In the main house, lights glowed through the windows. Sherman went to the door and knocked.

Wiping her hands on a dishcloth, Mrs. Phelps turned from the casserole on the drainboard and went to answer the front door. As she approached the door, a formless shape shielded its eyes and peered into the foyer. Mrs. Phelps saw the outer edge of an upheld hand pressed to the glass. She flipped on the porch light. It was not until the boy stepped into the hall that Mrs. Phelps could have sworn with any certainty that the figure on the porch was indeed a boy. There was blood on him. Huddled in his shabby jacket, without looking up, he said, "It's my dog. He's hurt real bad." His voice sounded weak with exhaustion. "That truck driver said maybe you could help. I'm s'posed to ask for Tom." The boy lifted his head and glanced at her, and the look in his eyes caused her to step back quickly. But just as quickly his expression dissolved and his pupils seemed to soften and catch reflection like the eyes of a changeling. There were tears in his eyes.

His head was spinning. He tried to focus, watching her lips as she spoke. "The doctor's not here," the lips said. "I'm his daughter-in-law. I keep house for him." She was still talking. "Ben Sizemore's mare is in foal," but Sherman turned blindly and stepped out onto the porch.

With his back to her, he gulped down two more of his pills. And the woman, grasping the door to shut it, saw the dog sitting at the edge of the light, head bowed nearly to the ground, its chest covered with blood. It took her breath. "Oh, dear God." Suddenly she felt herself drawn into the boy's desperate predicament and she hastily added, "You could wait. Tom'll be back any minute."

Sherman's head had started to clear. He looked at her, then glanced through the evergreens at the highway and the fringe of lights from the town. "Okay," he said.

She pointed to a shed and told him to take the dog to it. "There's a light switch just inside the door and some old gunnysacks you can use to make him a bed. You wait there," she said. "I'll send Tom out just as soon as he gets home."

Speaking to the Chinaman, Sherman twice looked back at the woman in the doorway with the light streaming around her. Mrs. Phelps closed and locked the door and went back to the kitchen. She wished she could do more to help him. There were sandwiches in the refrigerator, which she had made that afternoon, and apples in a bowl. With paper napkins she lined the bottom of a small basket and set three of the sandwiches in it and an apple. And that poor dog. She drew warm water into a pan and pulled out some housecleaning rags to take to him. Through the kitchen window, she noticed that the light was on now in the shed. She had the basket on her arm and had lifted the pan of water before she set it all down and went to the telephone.

She dialed Ben Sizemore's number and said, "Marcella, this is Ruth Phelps. Could you get Tom to the telephone?" She did not see the boy come to the square of light on the lawn, then edge up close to her kitchen window. Presently, she said,

"There's a boy here with a dog. It gave me something of a fright. I don't know, I think the dog must've been shot. He looks awful bad. . . .

"All right," she said finally. "All right. Come just as soon as you can."

Even in his panic, Sherman avoided the square of light.

*I knew it!* he thought.

*She called the police!*

It was dark. Night.

Though he fought to hold on, he could feel himself coming apart.

His head was throbbing like a faulty circuit. He had no idea where he was; he had lost all sense of time and direction. Now they were walking alongside plate-glass windows. The cold wind made his eyes sting. Moving on the glass, their shadowed reflections looked like apparitions. A car passed, its taillights bleeding on the black night. It streaked across his eyes. On a rooftop scaffold at the corner, a sketch of a dog was tirelessly running in blue neon, its legs switching back and forth. It looked beautiful, effortless. Above it, in white neon, the word GREYHOUND blinked off and on.

From the side of the bus station came an enormous chrome bus. With a ratcheting of gears, the bus swayed by him, spewing fumes and blowing exhaust, the cameo lights along its sides shining bright colors like a beautiful ship setting off for the stars. A bus, Sherman thought. Light wires fluttered over it as it sank from sight. *A bus!* I'd like to be on that bus. Shaking with cold and hunger, leading the Chinaman, he walked past gas pumps crowned with mock torches. The artificial light glowed everywhere around them.

"What the hell happened to your dog?" the attendant asked.

Sherman stared at him, turned and started to go, unable to

remember why he was there. Suddenly he said, "How far is it to Kentucky anyway?"

"You're in Kentucky," the man said. "Where is it you're tryin' to go?"

Sherman stared at him again, then looked over his shoulder at the empty driveway. "I'd know where it is on one of your maps," he said.

With a shrewd glance at him, the man produced a map and unfolded it; Sherman studied it and showed him the dot and the name, Brandenburg Station, and the man said, "Well, sir, that's clear over by Louisville."

"So how far's that?"

"I don't rightly know," the man said. "From here, I reckon it must be three, four hundred miles."

"So how long'd it take somebody to drive there?"

The man squinted. "Lessee. Roads like they are, oughta be able to make it in three days. Two maybe, if they've got the roads cleared."

"Three days?"

"Yes, sir. I imagine that's 'bout right."

Outside, Sherman slipped into the rest room in back, coaxed the Chinaman in, and locked the door. Three days, he thought. Three days and this is one day and it's almost over. Quickly he took off his jacket. She was getting away from him. And now that housewife had called the police and they would be looking for him. He pulled out all the papers in his shirt—the crumbling newspaper pieces, the last thousand-dollar bill he'd saved for his getaway with Mamie, the torn photographs of the woman, which he stared at closely now to refresh his memory. Everything had gone bad. He looked down at the Chinaman and saw him slumped in his own blood. He had to accept then that the dog couldn't make it, couldn't go with him, and a terrible, heartbreaking loneliness swept through him. I'll be all alone without you, he thought. All alone. Only Mamie was left. He had to go find her right away. Just as soon as he got rid of that woman, he'd take Mamie—he had the money. . . . They would find some place to live, a new place. She was all he had.

He picked up his jacket. Around the sleeve hole, the lining had ripped loose and he shoved his mess of papers down inside the jacket—they slid down to the waistband just where he wanted them. Now if the police felt in his shirt they wouldn't find anything. He helped the Chinaman stand and they went outside. A police car turned the corner in a cloud of exhaust and black gutter leaves. Sherman rocked back, everything too bright to see.

After that he remembered that they went through the chrome metal doors of the bus station. Sherman stood at a blackboard of chalked-in schedules, scanning for the name of the town he wanted. But he couldn't read it; the letters wouldn't hold still.

The bus station was a big, empty room with benches for sleepers and talkers. He didn't wait for the watchman, who was headed for him, to tell him to take the dog outside. The nebula of high ceiling lights whirled around him. I gotta do something, he thought. There was a red candy machine; he took nickels from his pocket and quickly pulled the plunger. Three Hershey bars appeared in his hand. He put them in his pocket, then led the dog out of the station.

The Chinaman staggered at his side. Sherman looked down at him. They were in among some railroad tracks. Farther and farther they wandered from the downtown lights, the muffled noise of traffic, and entered into a dark region of boxcars and weeds. Now he looked back to where the street crossed the tracks—the small lighted crossing bloomed in his eyes like a distant mirage. He unwrapped the first Hershey bar and broke it into chunks, his hands shaking so hard he almost dropped it. He fed the dog a piece. "You like this kind, doncha?" Sherman said, watching him carefully, spending these last few moments entirely with him. "Does it hurt you to eat, boy? It's your favorite." The Chinaman settled back and lay down. Sherman gave him another chunk, then the last one, and turned away while the Chinaman chewed on the chocolate. The boy drew the knife from his pocket, opened it, saw it glassily in his fist, and laid it on the iron hitch of a boxcar. Then he pulled off his jacket.

Suddenly he paced down the dark glimmering track, gasping for breath, turned and came back. He unwrapped another candy bar, broke it in pieces, and gave it to the dog. Wave after wave of sweat broke across Sherman's brow, and he could do nothing but wipe it away on his shirt sleeve. The wind was blowing, colder and colder. He let out a long shuddering sigh. He knew, the way an animal knows, what had to be done and how to do it, but his grief held him back. With his bandaged hand, he stroked the Chinaman's broad sleek head. "You're okay," he murmured. "Chinaman, you'll be okay." The night rose up around him in a brilliant black haze and slowly began to whirl. "We're just alike, you and me."

Fits of trembling ran through him as he unwrapped the last candy bar and laid it intact on the ground. He inched to the side. No longer trying to chew, the dog gulped the chocolate in hard swallows, the mottled sheen of his coat heaving on his frame. Sherman wiped his hand on his pants and clasped the knife. His dread grew monstrous; he expelled the air trapped in his lungs. Now. Abruptly he bent over the Chinaman. His bandaged hand stroked down under the dog's head and gripped the fur already stiff with blood. Although he acted with speed, the knife seemed to fly downward with excruciating slowness. Sensing danger, the Chinaman twisted too late and looked up. The blade sank and tore across the furry throat.

A hideous, strangling growl wrenched the air and the Chinaman pitched sideways in a paroxysm of astonished strength. Blood blew in a spray from the wound. Sherman stumbled forward, aghast. Terror struck him in hard convulsions. The dog thrashed about and came up, the wound reducing the flow of his movement to a spastic tossing, an odd broken cry tearing apart in his throat. *"Stop it!"* Sherman screamed. *"Don't cry!"* In a frenzy to end it, before he could think to stop himself, he swung again, savagely. *"Don't cry!"* The knife whipped down, missing, inflicting surface wounds as the Chinaman snapped at him, teeth flashing, then howled and squirmed. "Don't cry," Sherman gasped, "don't cry, don't cry," driving the knife down again and again until he couldn't lift his arm any more. The Chinaman rocked back and pulled himself up dazedly, fell and came up again, stumbling sideways, and with a burst of his old speed, tore into the brush.

Sherman's pain was as large as the air. Filled with horror at what he had done, he began to weep as never before, his voice breaking with grief. "I'm s-sorry," he stammered. "I'm s-sorry, I'm sorry, boy, I'm sorry." He ran blindly into the brush to find the Chinaman. Through his mind, as he ran, went that broken, unhinged cry. He reached the Chinaman and knelt for him, his hands sliding up the rigid lattice of the dog's ribs, lifting him gently, slowly, into his arms, speaking to him, begging. "I take it back," he said, "Chinaman, I take it back, I take it back," the tears blinding him.

It seemed a long time before he had secured the dog firmly against him, drawing him up on his body in a series of shrugging, sliding movements, still asking him, still pleading, "Come on, Chinaman, come on, I'm sorry," and finding it almost impossible to move himself as the paws dragged and scraped around his shoes. Once, he picked the dog up and carried him and then fell back to his knees. No matter what he did, the black eyes, still open and alive-looking, were fixed on him.

His hands and shirt turned dark with blood. He went on struggling with the dog, as if he could somehow make it be all right if he only tried hard enough, but the body was falling through his arms; the big head nodded loose against him, and he felt a spasm fly through the crooked hindlegs like a wild shudder of breath. And at once Sherman let go and shrank back, staring transfixed, unable to utter a sound. His hand reached out and stroked the Chinaman's head, and from the dog's stubby face the eyes now stared with a dull, milk-black luster.

He was dead.

Sherman reached out and took the big tufted paw and held it tenderly, stroking it, to rub all the pain away. He couldn't find his breath. Then a cry broke from his mouth so loud and high-pitched it carried out over the freight yard, and from the neighborhoods of that little town a cry rose with his, a reverberation of grief from every back-yard dog that heard him. And the wind blew, ruffling the Chinaman's fur, gently lifting the sleek, black ruff around his face, as if somehow that small part of him were still alive.

# PART FOUR

# 20

With a soft whir of tires, the new black Pontiac slipped smoothly through the night. Glancing at the river beyond the trees, Leona could see the first rays of morning pierce the dark and then the light washed across fields and trees and dim houses, drawing them up in sudden levitation, like faded water-color landscapes in pop-up Christmas cards. Moments later, as if sensing the new light, the children began to wake up around her. "We're almost there," she told them. "It's not much further."

In the cold, luminous dawn, the Pontiac sped through the outskirts of Brandenburg Station, slowed to the speed limit, and turned down the steep main street. The town was still asleep. All night the temperature had hovered near zero and now, driving down the empty street, Leona saw the effect of the unusually cold weather spread before her in a wide perspective. Beyond the small gazebo of the waterfront park, under sketchy layers of fog, the Ohio River had frozen over in great tilting slabs of ice.

At the bottom of the hill, near the edge of the little park, she brought the car to a standstill. Hazard Road, which would take them through winding curves to a point near the island, was barricaded. Signs read: ABSOLUTELY NO ONE PERMITTED ON

RIVER. ICE UNSTABLE EXTREMELY DANGEROUS. NO DRIVING ON ICE. VIOLATORS WILL BE PROSECUTED. Leona hesitated scarcely a moment. Would the police expect to find her here? She couldn't risk being seen. She turned the steering wheel, jockeyed around the barricades, and headed out Hazard Road. She had seen those signs before. Inevitably, every few years the river froze over, and just as inevitably, parties of daredevils walked or skated or—if the temperature was really severe and the ice deep—drove across the river to the Indiana shore. After a bitter cold spell, the ice posed little danger; it was an adventure, something to recall for their grandchildren. The warning signs were routine. To Leona, the thought of crossing the ice on foot, even with children, presented no real danger.

She was home. Everything looked familiar. Even the withered brown stalks of weeds, protruding through snow, took on a special nostalgia. She drove effortlessly. The air continued to brighten above the shifting fog. Hazard Road was an old highway laid between the water's edge and the adjacent sandstone bluffs. Where the cliffs gapped, the crumbling pavement was ribbed with thin horizontal bands of snow. Leona slowed the car. In a long hooking curve, they passed a smattering of fishermen's shacks; then the road dipped and swerved through a bog and trickled away through a stand of tall loblolly poplars. Offshore, rising through the frozen crust of the river, was the island. Île des Chats. Cat Island.

The Pontiac crossed frozen puddles and came to a stop among the trees. Leona turned the ignition off and settled back, rubbing her tired eyes, filled with relief and a sense of final victory. "Look, everybody," she said. "There's what I promised you." She opened the door and let it swing away from her, enjoying the fresh, cold air that struck her face.

The children were clamoring to get out. She reminded them to put on their caps and gloves, then let them step into the pure cold morning.

"Where is this place?" Patsy said.

"It's the Ohio River, just as I told you."

"But how'll we get out there? There's no boat."

"We can just walk across," Leona told them.

"That's river water out there."

"Yes," she said, and laughed. "And when it melts, it'll be wet."

"What if we fall in?" Walter asked her.

"Oh, you won't fall in. I won't let you."

"My mommy said I would. She said I'd fall in."

"Walter, trust me, this is different."

From the trunk, Leona collected the few things they would need immediately, the can of gasoline and the smallest bag of groceries. "Can we take the Christmas presents?" Mamie said. "I want to carry 'em." Leona saw no harm in it and said, "Of course you can. Now, who wants to carry my briefcase?" Both Patsy and Walter jumped forward. "All right," Leona said, "you'll have to take turns." The other, heavier suitcases and the large box of groceries would have to wait until she had time to move them piece by piece. Leading the children through the trees, she came to the bank at the river's edge. In the narrow channel, wind kept the ice clear of snow; where a corner of ice jutted up, it was sometimes possible to see the depth of the frozen mosaic. The ice was universally solid and deep. Nothing moved.

"I'm afraid," Patsy said. "I don't want to walk on froze-up water."

"Then you all can wait here. I'll come back and carry you."

But Leona had gone only a few steps on the ice when she heard Mamie yell, "Hey, wait for us," and watched them scramble down the bank and trail toward her.

"Be careful," she warned them. "Walk very slow and easy." And she waited till they drew near.

The waterway spanned through the rooty tufts of the small

outer islands; each landmass jutted a yard above the ice, crowned thick with weeds and saplings. Around these outcroppings of earth and rock, the ice was thin and green, bubbling with air pockets. Leona pointed out the thin places and warned them of the danger. They passed down the crooked aisle of solid ice and saw the stone house, much as Leona had described it, through the morning fog.

The little wooden pier, where Doc Merchassen had tied his motorboat each summer, still stood, its pilings mired in pale green socks of ice. Uncertain of its stability, Leona bypassed the weathered wood and lifted the children to land where the shallow cove met the slope of the yard. Without blemish or track, a crisp mantle of snow covered the entire irregular terrain. There was no path to take. They went directly toward the house, past a dilapidated rose trellis. Icicles hung from the high gables and eaves of the two-story cottage, some so long they nearly touched the ground.

Leaving everything they had carried on the cistern cover, Leona removed the padlock on the cellar and lifted the slanted door. It made an eerie noise and she saw the apprehension on the children's faces. "I'll tell you what," she said. "We'll need to make a fire until I can get the furnace going. Why don't you try to find some dry wood?"

Looking at the other two children, Walter said, "Firewood like at Aunt Vee's?"

"That's right. Just stack it up out here. And I'll go in and try to get the front door open."

In the cellar she found a soggy box of candles and, setting them in mason jars, managed to light four of them. With the gasoline she started the old generator.

"What's that thing?" Mamie asked, standing at the bottom of the cellar steps.

"It's a generator. I hope it'll make electricity so we can have lights." As soon as it was running smoothly, Leona plugged in the water pump and the hot-water heater. When she glanced back again, Mamie was gone, the spill of gray morning light now unbroken on the cellar steps. She loosened the bottled-gas spigot and lit the pilot light in the small furnace. Taking one of the lighted candles, she went up the dark basement stairs toward the living quarters, not knowing what she might find there, although from the outside of the house nothing appeared to have been tampered with.

As far as she could tell, the rooms above ground were just as she had left them months ago. She stood in the vaulted living room. Except for the light from the candle she held in her hand, she stood in total darkness and it accentuated the little sounds she made, the sound of her breathing against the bone-chilling cold. She lit the kerosene lamp, and in the small walnut table in the hall found the front-door key where she had hidden it so many months ago. The door opened on a sheet of plywood. Using an old wooden mallet from the kitchen, she knocked the wood panel away, and the morning light spread through the door.

She went outside and called the children. Then she gathered her supplies together—the red can of gasoline and the bag of groceries—cautioned the children not to play down there, and shut the slanted cellar door. Carrying the briefcase and the sack of Christmas presents, the children followed her to the pantry where she began putting her things away. "Just leave those there," she told them.

The minutes passed quickly. Together they built a fire in the fireplace. She gave the children tasks to do—let them remove the dust covers from the furniture and take the sheets outside—while, with the mallet and the claw end of a hammer, she pulled the plywood panels from three of the windows, one in the living room and two in the kitchen. An hour had gone by. Quickly she got a pot of soup cooking on the stove for their supper. Letting the water run to clear the pipes, she peeled potatoes and carrots and let the kids cut them up, placating them in the meantime with graham crackers and peanut butter. The next time she looked up, she was surprised to see that it had started to snow again, flakes falling through the sunlight. It's too cold to snow, she thought; it's just a snow shower.

The day revolved around her and she worked joyfully, moved happily. What a luxury it was just to bang around as much as she wanted to. Here at last was the safe, hidden world where she could protect the children from the threat of violence. Filled with energy, she whirled through the house with a broom, dragging down cobwebs; then with a basin of pine-scented soapsuds, she began to wipe down the wooden furniture. There was so much to do—beds to be made, linens to wash, meals to prepare—and she addressed it willingly, vigorously, refreshed in mind and spirit. She would be tired from work. She *wanted* to be tired.

If no one came poking around, she was convinced they could live here safely into the new year, maybe longer. Plenty of time to decide what to do. Now and then, from one of the windows or turning in a doorway, she caught glimpses of Mamie. How remarkable it all seemed now, that she had actually made it here with these children—with Mamie. Leona watched her with the others, watched her dash about, huddle with them, whisper, every bit a little girl.

The children were in and out of the house. Once, when they had come in to ask for a drink of water, Mamie turned, holding her glass in both hands, and asked, "Is this where you live?"

"Yes, Mamie," Leona answered, stooping to her. "But it's where you live, too. You and me and Patsy and Walter. We'll all live here together. Do you like it?"

Mamie held the glass very still and looked at the floor as if to decide. At last, without raising her head, she slowly nodded. "It's a fairy-tale place," she murmured, and stepped back toward the other children.

With its nooks and crannies and Victorian woodwork, the summer house must look like a fantasy to a child, Leona realized; like an elf's cottage in a storybook.

By three o'clock that afternoon, the sun had slipped behind the towering river cliffs, casting the island in shadow as deep and blue as dusk. As she worked, Leona made a mental list of the things she would need eventually. Somehow she would have to secure another tank of bottled gas. And the makings for a cake —a tall chocolate layer cake, she thought. Except for the pie she'd made for Mark Hardesty, it had been years since she'd had a good reason to bake anything. The few times she'd made even a batch of muffins for Helen Merchassen, they had eaten only two or three and the rest had gone to waste. Then, in Graylie, Emma had done almost all the cooking. Emma! When Leona went to get supplies, she would try to call the hospital again. She had called two days ago and Emma was stable, still in the coma. She thought of Frank; she could hear his accusations ringing in her mind, but there was nothing she could say to him that would ease his suffering. To keep her grief at a distance, she forced her thoughts elsewhere—to her last few moments with Mark Hardesty. Don't go, he had said; please don't do this. She remembered the warmth of his arms around her and the way he had cupped her face in his hands; could almost feel the slow and unmistakable movements with which her body had responded to his. She let the fantasy linger as she drew clean water. How often she thought of him now, missed him, wanted to see his warm dark eyes crinkle with laughter, wanted that and so much more. I must write to him at once, Leona thought.

The children came upon her standing very still, her pale face turned toward the front window. "What'sa matter?" Walter said, and she turned, startled, and smiled. "Oh, I was just remembering your Aunt Vee. What a good time we had."

With a few wooden poker chips and a saucer, she showed them how to play tiddlywinks. And when they had tired of that, she gave them a damp deck of playing cards and said she would play the first one who won three games of Crazy Eights.

"We played Crazy Eights at Funny Grandma's house," Mamie said, and Leona smiled. "Yes," she replied. "I know you did. I remember."

But before the card game was finished, Walter came to her. "Can we make a snowman?"

"You can try if you want to, but the snow's too hard and dry. It won't stick together." Still relieved to be out of the car, they wanted to romp and play outside and Leona immediately chided herself for dampening their enthusiasm. "Why don't you see if you can't make that snowman?"

"You want a big one?" Walter said.

"Yes," she said. "A very great big one."

"O-*kay.*" And they put on their warm clothes and ran out.

The stairway to the balcony and second-floor bedrooms ran against the lower wall with a small landing halfway up. The balcony itself was bare except for the small Queen Anne table Helen Merchassen had insisted on bringing here, and two delicate, spindle-back chairs, so old the glue was loose in their joints. Leona ran up and down those stairs all afternoon. With the mallet, she knocked the plywood covers from two of the bedroom windows, but was unable to budge the third. Once, sitting on the side of her bed, she took from her purse the wooden flower Mark had carved for her and set it up against the vanity mirror. And it all came flooding back again—his laugh, his voice that strummed within her, the slow tilting nod when he first said hello to her, morning and evening, so careful and effortless at the same time. But now her memories stung her so deeply, she could hardly bear to look at the small carving.

She went back to work. Mark would like it here, she thought. Although it was cold, she left the windows open for a while to air out the rooms. The beautiful blue afternoon light ebbed toward darkness. She was making the beds with fresh linen when Patsy called to her from downstairs. "Hey?"

"What?"

"Where *are* you?"

Leona gathered up an armful of musty bedclothes and stepped out to the balcony. "I'm up here," she said, looking down on the living room. "Why?"

"I don't think Walter feels very good," Patsy said, gazing upward. "I think he's sick."

Carrying the wadded pile of sheets, Leona came downstairs. "He seemed all right a while ago." She dropped the load in an armchair.

"Well, he's not okay now."

"Where is he? Still outside?"

"Uh-huh."

Walter was flushed. He had vomited on his gloves and coat and was sobbing because of the mess. Leona brought him in by the fire. "What's the matter, Walter?" she said. "Don't you feel good?" The two girls stood behind the sofa, ceremoniously looking on.

"I don't feel *real* good," he said. "I'm fr-freezing."

"Here, then, let's have a look at you." She pulled off his gloves and drew his coat off his shoulders; she would clean them later. Then she held her hand to his forehead. "Why don't you climb up here on the couch and we'll cover you up, see if we can't get you warm?"

He lay with his head on the fringed sofa pillows and she tucked the afghan around him. "You girls go on and play," she said. "I'll look after Walter." In the bathroom medicine cabinet she found a thermometer, wiped it with rubbing alcohol, and took his temperature. A hundred and three.

The girls had not strayed. Patsy sat in a chair by the fire and Mamie lingered at the opposite edge of the fireplace. "If you're going to stay indoors," Leona told them, "you should take off your coats. You don't want to turn up with whatever it is he's got."

A fever that high bothered Leona, even if it wasn't so uncommon in a small child. She said to him, "Walter, where do you feel bad?" and he said, "My ear really hurts."

She lifted him and turned his head. "Here, let me see it," but she hardly had to look at it. On the pillow where his head had been, there was a trace of pus. His ear. His damaged ear. "I'll need to clean it," she told him. "I'll be very gentle," and with a damp cloth she washed the inside of his ear. It was infected, perhaps had been infecting for some time. And she had nothing to give him except the aspirin she kept in her purse. She gave him a tablet. Sitting beside him, she bathed his feverish face again and again.

The sun was going down. When he had gone to sleep, she motioned the girls to the kitchen and ladled the soup into bowls. She opened a tin of crackers and they ate their soup, dipping the crackers into the broth until it cooled. They were subdued now, no one saying much of anything, and Leona had little desire for the soup. "Come on, now, Patsy, eat your supper. We have to keep our strength up."

The next time she looked in on Walter, he had kicked the cover off. He was sweating and he still complained that his ear hurt. Again she gently bathed his face. The aspirin had done him no good. If only she still had the medicine in her briefcase, if only . . . But she didn't. When he woke, she would take his temperature again, but she needed something to give him. She knew that an ear infection could become serious, that without medicine and proper treatment it would only get worse. After all, they were all run down from their days and nights on the road.

At six-fifteen, she took his temperature again and it was unchanged. Still a hundred and three. Now she began to worry. She woke him and gave him another aspirin. "Walter, do you feel dizzy?"

"Nahh," he said, "it just hurts."

"Your ear hurts?"

And he nodded, rolling his head. "Way inside," he told her.

If she let it go, it might . . . What if it turned into something dreadful like meningitis? She just couldn't take that chance. If he was really run down, as he well might be . . . She sat staring at the dark window in the living room. Night. In fifteen minutes, she took his temperature a third time. Still a hundred and three. The aspirin wasn't working. He was really sick; he needed something. His breath wheezed from his open mouth.

Throughout this part of the country, one drugstore in every town stayed open till eight. It was a law. And unless things had changed, there was only one drugstore in Brandenburg Station —Wetzel's. It was dark; at least that would be to her advantage. She knew the risk she would be taking, perhaps being seen and identified. Even more, she hated to leave the children alone in this isolated place. But she had to do something to help Walter, and to carry him back across the ice would only expose him to the weather again. Impossible for a child in his condition. In the end, it was simple: she had a sick child who needed medication.

Dressed to go out, with the briefcase in her hand, she drew the girls aside. "Walter's sick. He has an ear infection," she said. "He needs medicine and I'll have to try to get it. Understand? Mamie, do you understand me?" Mamie nodded. "I won't be gone any longer than I have to. I'm sorry to leave you here, but I need you to stay with Walter. If he wakes up, give him some water and tell him I'll be right back. Don't worry. I'll hurry. Okay?"

"I'm kinda scared," Patsy said.

"I know," Leona said. "But just lock the door after I leave. Nobody'll come. You'll be all right. And I'll come right back, I promise."

Quickly she made her way across the bumpy ice and started the car. Again, fleetingly, she worried about the Browning, but she had resigned herself to its absence. She had to drive in reverse for nearly a quarter of a mile before the road widened beside the fishing huts and she could turn the car around. She had thought she might be able to drive to town with her running lights off, but the moon had slipped behind clouds. It was impossible, though when she saw the streetlights of Brandenburg Station strung out down the steep hill, she lowered her speed and put out the car lights, and darkness fell against the windshield like a curtain. Even after the road had straightened, she drove slowly, picking her way across the thin drifts of snow. The Pontiac slipped past the barricades and idled to the curb beside the Paragon Theater. From there she could see up the long hill street; across it and two doors up was Wetzel's Drugstore, ablaze with light.

As she tried to decide how to proceed, she thought she saw something move on the other side of the road. She looked over and saw a boy standing motionless at the edge of the waterfront park, his breath clouding the air. He must have been there all along, she thought; I just didn't see him. Even at that distance, she thought she could tell that he was shivering; with the wind, it would feel like ten below zero out there. He stood hunched inside his jacket—just a kid, a young kid. Poor devil, she thought, and her heart went out to him. She turned on her headlights, pulled across the intersection, and parked. Then she took a few bills from the briefcase and slipped it under the front seat where it would be safe. She locked the car. A few minutes later Leona was entering the drugstore.

Pretending to look at a circular rack of greeting cards, she waited for two women to conclude their business at the pharmacist's counter. Somewhere above her head a fluorescent light buzzed. She stood very still near the center of the store, able to scan it thoroughly every few seconds. No one else had come in. One of the two customers went out carrying a paper bag; as the woman passed, Leona reached low on the rack to hide her face. The bell jingled on the door. When she looked toward the door the next time, she noticed that the boy she'd seen standing outside had come up to the display window. She could see that he was shabbily and poorly dressed, especially for this weather. He wore a scuffed old jacket that was too big for him. But there was nothing she could do for him, not now. She had her own troubles to deal with.

Come on, she thought. What's taking so long? Come on, come on! In her mind, she could picture the children alone out on the island. Completely alone. When she heard the second customer walking toward her, she quickly turned her back and bent down to one of the low shelves. The clicking high heels passed her. The doorbell jingled.

As she approached the high pharmacist's counter, Charlie Wetzel glanced up at her, then quickly lowered his head and went on working. Leona cleared her throat. "Don't you remember me?" she said.

"Of course I remember you," he said, sorting pills, his eyes still averted. "Leona, what the hell you doin' here?"

"I need a favor."

"You probably need more than one."

The doorbell chimed.

"Could you possibly help me?"

"Go back to my office," the druggist said. "I'll get back there as soon as I can. Go. Go right now."

Leona turned down the hallway next to the counter and opened the door marked "Private." She waited there, restlessly paging through magazines that had been left lying on the coffee table of his cluttered living room. If he calls the police, she thought, I'm finished. When the door opened, she stood straight up.

Charlie Wetzel removed his rimless glasses and closed his eyes, pinching the bridge of his nose. Leona explained the circumstances: she needed penicillin. Slowly his hand came down his face and pinched his lower lip. "Leona," he said, and looked away, "if I hear what you're saying—" He stopped in midsentence, ran his hand through his thin hair, and scratched the back of his head. "You've put me in a helluva spot. You know I'm supposed to turn you in if you show up here," he said. "I believe you know that."

Leona noticed that her fingernails were rattling on the back of a chair and took her hand away. "I've got a really sick little boy on my hands, Charlie. It's getting worse and worse and all I have is aspirin. I remembered Doc Merchassen said you sometimes helped people without prescriptions. I have some money," and she held out the folded bills from her pocket. "Charlie, I really need some penicillin."

"Put that away," he said. "Don't insult me flashing money around. Don't you know what you're asking for is against the law?"

"Yes, I know," she said, and closed her eyes on a moment of vertigo, "but—"

"Whatever happened before was between Doc and me."

"I'm not trying to trade on his good name."

"I don't know what you'd call it, then, because you damn well are."

He took his glasses off and wiped them on the bottom of his white coat, then put them back on. His face was without expression. "And I'll never— Don't ever ask me again," he said. He peered over the tops of his glasses at her. "Well, wait here. I may have to wait on customers. Don't come out. Stay here."

It was ten minutes before he returned. He handed her a white paper envelope containing a tube of ointment and the penicillin tablets in a plain unmarked bottle—he told her the dosage and the frequency. Then he gave her another envelope.

"What's in this?" she asked.

"Just a sedative. You look like you could use a good night's sleep."

She offered to pay him, but again he refused. "Let's just chalk this one up to the Doc. If you get caught with this stuff, I'll swear to God I've never seen it before."

"One last thing, Charlie," she said. "I want that sled you've got in your window."

"Leona, that's not for sale. That's my display, goddammit."

"But you can buy another one. And I can't. I know a little boy who needs a sled. What's a good sled worth to you anyway?"

He squinted at her. "I'll set it out by the sidewalk." He accepted a twenty-dollar bill for the sled. "Where you parked?"

"Down alongside Sibley's seed store."

He glanced toward the private door. "You have to get out of here. Go out the back way. I'll get that sled down to the corner. Leona, if I was you, I wouldn't stay around here. There's a reward out for you and people poor enough to take it."

As she left the alleyway and turned toward her car, an unaccountable fear struck her. She stopped, and the crisp crack of her shoes fell silent. I've been seen, she thought, they're watching me. She looked toward the end of the sidewalk and on across the wide intersection where rows of marquee light bulbs blinked. The druggist leaned the sled against the corner and retreated. No one else appeared on the sidewalk; no one entered or left the theater. Snow was falling again, quicker and quicker, seeming to feed on its own momentum. The intersection was empty; the traffic light clicked from red to yellow to green. Nothing. And yet she couldn't shake the pervasive sense that something wasn't right, that something was very, very wrong —here and now.

Holding the bright new sled under her arm, she unlocked the back door on the passenger side and shoved the sled into the car. She shut the door and again glanced around through the snow. No one, except that boy at the edge of the park huddled down in his jacket—so shrunken within it she couldn't tell if he was even looking her way. Just herself and that solitary boy on this lonely street. She wondered if maybe she should wave at him, and decided not to. But she ought to do something. Such a cruel night to be standing alone, apparently with no one to turn to. The driving snow fell in a hard slant. Maybe she would offer to buy him a cup of coffee. She remembered she had a box of cocoa among the remaining groceries in the trunk.

She started the car and changed gears, drove to the end of the block, and turned and came back. The foremost trace of her headlight beam slid over the boy and flew beyond the snowy barricades of the closed road. Not taking any chances, she waited until the traffic light changed. No other car passed through her field of vision. Warmed by the air blowing from the car heater, she crossed the intersection toward the yellow reflectors of the barricade. She passed the boy. Whether he leaned toward the car or it was just a fleeting image created by the warp of her windows, she couldn't tell, but she felt a pang of remorse as she passed him.

In her rear-view mirror, she could see that he hadn't moved. She had nearly reached the barricade before she stopped the car, slipped the gear to reverse, and eased back toward him. He slid into the frame of her side window. Leaning across the seat, she rolled the passenger window partway down and looked at him. "Waiting for somebody?" she asked him.

He shuddered. "Kinda," he said. The snow blew between them. She could see that he was twelve, maybe thirteen, and his clothes were ragged and soiled. Snow had collected thickly on his cap, his eyebrows and shoulders; he was shaking with cold.

"You live around here?"

When he spoke, he was shivering so hard she couldn't understand him. In the dim light from the street, she could see that his nose was running and his teeth were chattering. "You shouldn't be out in this," she said. "How long've you been out here?"

"While," he said finally with some difficulty, the wind draining his voice away. With his hands shoved into his jacket pockets, he seemed to be trying to move in one place to keep warm.

He was a little taller than the roof of the car and he leaned toward the window to try to answer her, then straightened up again.

"Why don't you get in here for a minute, anyhow? At least get in long enough to warm up a little."

He said, "Okay," and quickly reached for the door handle.

Leona set the emergency brake and shifted the car to neutral, knowing that when she removed her foot from the brake, the brake light would go out. Nothing would look suspicious. She turned the headlights off and flipped the heater knob as high as it would go. "Roll the window up," she told the boy, and he complied.

He tried to hold himself still and could not, so that his chattering breaths came in sudden noisy bursts. He was all huddled up, trembling in his jacket. Across the expanse of upholstery, she could feel him shake in the seat. She asked him what his name was and thought he said "Bud."

"What?" she said. "Bud? Is that it?"

He nodded a couple of times very fast. "Yeah," he whispered. The streetlight was skimpy inside the car, yet she tried to examine him closely. He had a scrapper's face, but he had come out on the wrong end of a few fights. It was a stirring and painful sight: the face of a boy who had seen some very bad times. He began to grow less agitated.

"How'd you end up here?"

He ran his hand under his nose. "I just did—" he took a deep breath—"that's all." He looked at her suddenly, almost angrily, and with a swipe of the same hand he scrubbed the tears from his eyes.

"Do you have a place for the night?" she asked him quietly.

But he wouldn't answer, wouldn't look at her now, as if, even at his young age, the tears had exposed some vulnerable part of him and he felt cheaper and weaker for it.

"What're you going to do?"

He shrugged. Finally, he said, "I'll just—I don't know. I'll wait till I catch a ride."

A car came down the hill, casting misty yellow beams through the Pontiac. For a fraction of a second, Leona's heart leapt. *The police? No.* She took a breath. "You can't go back out there. You're just a kid. Nobody'll pass through here tonight, not in this kind of weather. You'd better come with me." Then she told him about the big pot of soup she had on the stove, and the hot cocoa she could make, and she released the emergency brake, shifting gears, the yellow reflectors gleaming like scattered eyes as they swung past the barricades toward the Isle of Cats.

Dimly, against the sound of the wiper blades, the boy heard her say, "You'll get to meet my children," and Sherman turned his face away toward the window glass and smiled.

# 21

*Sherman!*

The cry swelled in her throat and hung suspended on her tongue; Mamie clapped her hands over her mouth. *It was Sherman! Her brother Sherman!* Behind Leona's back, he signaled for her to be quiet and Mamie turned away and dropped her gaze. In the happy confusion of their arrival, Leona was introducing them. Sherman tried to grin. He stood just inside the front door, hands in his pockets, arms like lead. He wanted to rush to Mamie, lift her up, hug her. But he couldn't yet—not while the woman was in the room.

"And this is Mamie," Leona said, her hand hovering, then patting the top of Mamie's head. It cut inside him, seeing them so close when he couldn't be close at all, couldn't move.

Patsy ambled toward him. "Who're you?" she asked.

"What're you doin' here?" But Leona caught her by the shoulders and turned her back. "Come on, now, Patsy, be a good girl. Let him catch his breath."

He was exhausted, but his scheme had worked and he felt some elation in that. Seeing Mamie revived him. Slowly he turned his head, tracking the woman. Just wait, he thought—you don't stand a chance now. Mamie watched him eagerly, her small face tilted toward him, her gray-green eyes bright with excitement. She began to smile, then bit her lips. *We're in this together, Mamie, you and me.* Leaning over the couch, the woman lifted Walter in her arms and started toward the stairs. "I'll be right back," she said. "One of you girls bring me a glass of water."

"I will," Patsy said. Sherman stood stiffly, furtively watching the woman. He wasn't going to make another mistake now, not when he was this close, not when he had her at his mercy.

From the landing, Leona said, "Then, Mamie, you can help bring in our things from outside." She went on up and Patsy followed her, the glass of water tipping in her hands. How long's it been since we were together? Sherman thought. How long? He couldn't count the weeks in his mind.

Left downstairs together, Mamie and Sherman looked at the lighted doorway upstairs through which the woman carrying Walter, and then Patsy, had vanished. Their hands reached out, and when Mamie leapt he caught her in his arms and whirled her round and round, all restraint gone. Mamie wanted to shriek with joy, just to be held by him, and Sherman almost cried out his happiness, burying his mouth against her small shoulder to silence himself. They clung together, tears of triumph standing in their eyes, while his battered shoes skipped and turned soundlessly on the old patterned rug.

Swallowing her voice, Mamie breathed in his ear, *"Sherman,"* and then a little louder, in a whisper, "Sherman . . . Oh, Sherman, how'd you ever do it?" He sought to caution her with a look, but he had waited so long and they were both far too excited. His face twisted in a big grin. "Oh, boy," he said, softly. "Am I glad to see you." Then he drew her into the kitchen, where the shadows fell on their faces. "I waited for her to bring me to you," he said, and he laughed very softly. "I knew what to do so she'd stop for me. I had to, because I didn't know where you were."

In her excitement, Mamie kept saying his name until he finally put his hand over her mouth and she covered his hand with hers, the way they had that one night, so many weeks ago, when he lay on the wicker lounge and she had gone to tell him to run away. "Everything's all right," he whispered into her ear. "Everything'll be all right now." Then he added, "Don't let on like you know me. Don't let her know," and he nodded toward the lighted room. And all the time he kept putting his finger to his lips so Mamie had to say it quietly. "Sherman, look what I got." And she showed him her skull ring. "It's Toddy's ring." He hardly glanced at it. "Let's go home, Sherman." There was such happy expectation in her eyes. "Let's go back home right now."

*Back home?* He could've laughed. And yet, for the moment, Sherman allowed himself to bask in her certainty. At last, he said, "Mamie, we can't go right now. I almost froze to death out there. I'm too tired. She'd just chase us down." He was tired all over, tired to death. He hadn't slept in nearly two days. "Wait till everybody goes to sleep," Sherman told her. "I'll come getcha."

"But we shouldn't stay here," Mamie whispered. "She'll figure out who you are. She'll never let us get away."

"Ha, that's what she thinks," he muttered. Behind him, the wind blew branches against the porch and he spun toward the sound, his knees gripped in panic.

"Sherman," Mamie whispered. "Where's the Chinaman?"

He looked at her and then looked away.

"I saw him that one day. At that driveway," Mamie said.

"Didn't you bring him?" Sherman's face looked so odd and tense that she didn't know what to think. "Where is he, Sherman? I'd sure like to see him."

Her small voice beat against him but he didn't answer. She could see something in his face, something like a secret or a lie. Impulsively she grasped his arm. "Sherman, what's the matter? Where's the Chinaman? Is somethin' wrong?"

They were standing near the pantry, on the far side of the table and chairs. Coming nearer, Sherman looked at her closely, and then he was telling her: "He got shot in that house where you went—you know, that crazy old lady. She shot him. I was gonna get that old lady, but the Chinaman he stood up on the windowsill and she shot him. I was gonna kill 'er. I shoulda. I shoulda gone back and done it."

It was like a little stab of pain in her heart. "But, Sherman," she murmured, "that was Funny Grandma," and she thought, *He was gonna kill Funny Grandma!* It was frightening and it didn't make sense. "Why?" she said softly. "Sherman, she took care of me."

But he didn't seem to hear her. "I tried everything," he said. Then he told her about going to the doctor's house, and how the woman called the police, and the three Hershey bars. And as he spoke, Mamie let go of his arm. It had struck her—what he couldn't quite bring himself to say. *"You killed the Chinaman?"*

"It's her fault," Sherman said, and pointed toward the lighted room, the muscles in his face drawing very tight. "If it wasn't for her, none of this woulda happened. She did it." He scrubbed his sleeve across his face. When he looked at Mamie again, there were tears in his eyes. "Mamie, I'm sorry," he said. "I'll make up for it. We can get another dog—a new dog. It'll be just like it used to be, just you and me. And him. I got some money. We'll get you some new clothes and everything, soon's we get outa here. I got lotsa money."

A pulse throbbed in her throat. "But you were gonna kill Funny Grandma," she murmured. ". . . And you killed the Chinaman." Suddenly she took a step back and turned and ran into the other room before he could reach out to stop her. Around him the air seemed to rise and shift sideways in a slow inexorable drift.

"I'll get that," Leona said to the boy as she came down the porch steps. "You'd better go in by the fire. You're still shivering." Sherman followed her instructions submissively, hardly aware of moving. When they passed each other, he realized she wasn't actually as large as his mind had made her. Standing still, he would come within an inch or two of her shoulders. For the first time, he really looked at her, not in the dim lights of the car's dashboard or in the snow as they crossed the ice, but close and in light, an arm's distance away. She was a nice-looking woman, with friendly eyes and reddish hair drawn up in a bun. He hated her. It stirred deep inside him then, that first anticipatory gathering of strength and savagery.

As Leona lifted the large box of groceries from the sled and carried it into the kitchen, she said to Patsy, "I know you're worried about Walter, but now that we have some medicine, he'll be all right. I promise you." Turning the burner on under the pot of soup, she wiped her hands on her apron and went back to the living room. Almost eight-thirty. Time to get them ready for bed. Patsy was sitting on the arm of a chair and Mamie was standing near her, rubbing the ring on her finger, but when Leona came through, Mamie stepped forward. With his hands in his jacket pockets, the boy stood by the fireplace. "I promised you something warm to eat, didn't I?" Leona said to him. She wasn't surprised when he failed to answer. "I've put the soup on the stove."

The woman went past him, talking to the two girls, laughing

at something Patsy had said. Leona's hair was coming loose. "My hair's wet," she said, "I'm sure yours is, too." With her fingertips, she flicked the beads of melted snow from her hair as she went to the linen closet under the stairs and pulled down a clean towel for herself and one for him. "Here," she said.

The boy said, "That looks good," and took the towel. As she patted her hair and dried her face, she felt something brush against her thigh. Mamie was standing immediately in front of her, looking at the boy. Long ago, when a stranger had come to the house, Leona remembered that she, too, had played peeka-boo in her mother's skirts, and it made her happy that Mamie was doing it now. Patsy was talking to the boy. "Are you gonna stay with us?" she asked.

With Mamie still standing against her skirt, Leona reached down and tousled Patsy's red hair. "I think we could let him stay until tomorrow, don't you?" Patsy looked at him and shrugged. "I guess so," she said. Leona smiled at the boy. His eyes were staring directly into hers, and for a moment she tensed with uncertainty. It gave her a queer, unwholesome feeling when he looked at her so closely. He went back to drying his face and hair with the towel, and she noticed that his left hand was wrapped in dirty, yellowish bandages. Taking a step toward her, the boy returned the damp soiled towel. *It's his eyes. What's wrong with his eyes?* Then she thought she recognized what it was. Good Lord, he must be scared to death. I haven't done much to make him feel at home. "You're hurt," she said. "You must be in pain. What happened to your hand?"

He glanced at her as if startled, jerked away, and slipped his bandaged hand behind him. "Hurt it," he said. "Workin' on an old car. Battery acid." The air circled again, whirled maliciously before his eyes, faster, dizzying.

"That sounds serious. Has a doctor looked at it?"

Sherman had to concentrate on what she was saying. He shook his head. "It's doin' okay."

When she spoke, her mouth came partly open and he could glimpse her white teeth. "Would you like me to look at it? Maybe I could—"

"No," he said, a little too sharply.

"All right," she said. "But you should have it looked after." She started to go to the kitchen and had taken a few steps before she turned back. "At least let me hang up your jacket." She reached to take it. As unerring as a magnet, Mamie again stepped in front of her, between them. Leona stumbled into her, looked down, and then swept Mamie up in her arms, laughing softly just to her. "What're you doing, Mamie? You're always getting in the way." But Mamie wouldn't look at her and shriveled in her arms. Now I've embarrassed her, Leona thought, and set her down. Mamie rocked back on her heels, watching, listening. She's absolutely fascinated with our company, Leona thought.

"I better just keep my jacket," the boy said.

"All right," Leona said, "but at least take it off. It's wet. You might catch a cold."

Sherman did as he was told, drawing his arms out of the sleeves. On the black screen of the window, he watched the ghostly white oblong of the woman recede and diminish as she went toward the kitchen. Look at her, he thought; she don't know nuthin'. He studied the room arranged behind him, the room that would be familiar in every detail before the night was through. Snow blew against the window, snow falling everywhere, covering the ground as if there were no other world. He pulled the bottle of pills from his pocket, shook out a handful, and swallowed them all.

"That's too many to take," Mamie whispered.

"It don't matter," Sherman told her, while Patsy sat on the chair arm, watching him, swinging her legs. "They don't work very good anyway. Sometimes when I get my real bad headaches, I have to take them like this."

But he waited, and tonight the pills failed him completely.

There was no rippling relief, no jolt, just that glassiness at the edges of his sight. Sherman turned his head, struggling to hold his eyes open. The air had never been so swift, spinning around him in a blur. He reached for a place to sit on the couch and leaned back. With his hand under his jacket, he pulled the knife from his pocket and shoved it down between the thick cushions. Then he put the jacket to one side. His hand came up from his knee and floated to the side, and there, for just a moment, on the tips of his fingers he felt the coarse phantom hair of the China-man, waiting, standing guard. Only then could he let his mind close like an eye, let it think nothing and be very still. Sleep sank through him like a breath.

"He's asleep," Patsy said, peeking into the kitchen as Leona set out a napkin and silverware. "Come look."

And so he was. Leona saw his face slack with sleep, his eyelids peacefully shut, his mouth slightly open against the cushion. What a strange, lonely boy. She beckoned to the girls. "Sh-h-h," she said, "let him sleep. He's had a hard time. And besides it's time you two were in bed." She withdrew pajamas from a suitcase and told them to change upstairs. As she undid the high buttons at the back of Mamie's dress, she thought Mamie's skin seemed unnaturally warm, almost feverish. "Do you feel all right, Mamie? You're so warm and restless."

"No, I'm not," Mamie said, and twisted away from her. She stepped back, drifting slowly toward the couch. "Can I stay down here?"

How unpredictable Mamie's moods were. "No, no," Leona said. "It's bedtime. Now, leave him alone and let him sleep. We have a lot to do tomorrow. Maybe we'll get a Christmas tree."

"A Christmas tree?" Patsy said.

"Yes," Leona said, "maybe, if the weather's nice." She took their small hands and walked with them to the stairs; she told them which room was theirs and let them go up unattended, giving Mamie her independence. "I'll come say good night in a little while." From the bottom of the stairs, Leona watched them cross the balcony. Patsy scampered to their bedroom, but Mamie kept hanging back, her fingers trailing on the bannister, moving slower and slower until she stopped and looked down. "Mamie, go on," Leona said. "Go on to bed, now. It's late."

"Will you be comin' up pretty soon?"

"Soon," Leona said, and laughed. "Very soon. Go on, Mamie."

For a moment Mamie continued to look at her; then she went on, very slowly, dragging her heels. Once more, she looked down. "When're you comin' up?"

"Mamie, for heaven's sake, what's the matter with you? Please. Now, go—" but before she could finish, Mamie went into the bedroom. When the door swung shut, Leona crossed the living room, shaking her head. She's so stubborn, she thought; determined to have her way.

In the kitchen, Leona emptied the boy's soup into the kettle, washed and rinsed the crockery bowl, and set it out on a dishtowel to dry. It was as if all the world had condensed to this small lamplit place in a vast wilderness of sky and trees and snow. The warmth of the air around her, the hint of wood smoke from the fireplace mingling with the river mustiness of the house, the lingering residue of the pine soap she had used all converged in a feeling of lightheartedness, a sense of peace and well-being. In less than an hour, she would give Walter his second dose of medicine and go to bed herself, under the roof made heavy and silent with snow. She lifted a drinking glass from the shelf to take along upstairs, added a few twigs to the fire, and turned off the lights. As she passed through the living room, she hesitated by the sleeping boy. When she had questioned him about his hand, she had seen panic in his eyes and it raised a curious sympathy in her. So afraid, she thought. So distrustful.

Now he slept, his fears and enemies temporarily laid to rest. A string bean, her mother would have called him. Yes, Leona thought, stringy and tough. Tomorrow, when they had plenty of hot water, she would insist he take a bath before he left. She untied his battered shoes and carefully removed them. She pulled a coverlet up around him. And as she stepped away from him, she noticed his ragged jacket. It was so torn and filthy. She thought, maybe I could at least sew it up before he goes. Picking up the water glass for Walter, Leona took the jacket from the end of the couch and turned toward the stairway.

Suddenly, Sherman opened his eyes. He watched her go up the stairs and shrink to nothing in the night.


Spidering her hands up along her spine, Leona unhooked the clasps of her clothes and changed to her robe. In the small adjoining bathroom, she turned the plump porcelain knobs, started her bathwater, and went back to the bedroom. Tonight, sitting before the vanity mirrors, brushing her hair, she again confronted the small wooden carving she'd left there earlier. With the wind whining outside and the glow of the bedside lamps creating a beautiful mistiness across the pillows, she was reminded of the night she'd spent in Mark's cabin. Linger a while, he had said, and the way he said it sounded so quaint and old-fashioned. . . .

I must stop this, she thought. It's doing me no good. And yet the memory clung so vividly.

She went to the side of the bathtub, wiped the steam from her face on the inside of her robe, and adjusted the taps. Gradually her memory dispelled even the vaguest sense of the present. The robe dropped from her shoulders. She could remember standing before the mirror in Vee's living room, examining herself, while Mark was outside throwing snowballs. They had been so close then. She could almost hear him outside, laughing with the children. She tested the water, turned the taps off, and stepped over the rim into the hot water. The heat of the bath soaked through her skin, and she closed her eyes, feeling his hands gently shape and touch her, his length moving over her. A fragment of a song she'd heard on the car radio came to her, and softly she sang the little she remembered: *"I'll be seeing you . . . In all the old, familiar places."* The bathwater lapped inside the tub like the melody in the back of her mind, like the sound their bodies had made together that one time only. When her fingertips were beginning to wrinkle, she reached down the length of the tub, her mind adrift in that other, romantic world, for the bar of soap.

Minutes later, she stood up in the bath and the water dripped around her. Opening her towel, she stepped from the tub, and while her skin was still damp, she rubbed lotion on herself, then put on her nightgown and robe and went into the bedroom. She checked her watch: twenty minutes more and she could give Walter his medicine. Then she would kiss the girls good night and go to bed. She'd left the boy's ragged jacket lying across the foot of the bed. Should I wait until morning? she thought. No, there'll be too much to do tomorrow. Better take care of it now.

In the handkerchief drawer of the bureau, she found a spool of dark thread and Helen Merchassen's old pincushion still holding a few bright needles. Leona chose one and threaded it, knotting the doubled strand with an adept twist of her fingers. Turning, she picked up the jacket and held it open at arm's length to examine it. The lining was torn around the sleeve and down the back, coming loose at nearly every seam. It was simply worn out. If I had time, she thought, I'd put in a new lining. But, of course, there wasn't time for that. The stitching on the collar had come undone, dangling against the yoke. That'll be easy to fix. Shaking the jacket out a bit, deciding where to start, she sat down on the vanity bench and spread the jacket over her knees. Just then, she heard a soft flutter behind her and she looked over her shoulder. On the floor, from the foot of the bed to where she sat, was a trail of what appeared to be torn scraps of paper. Now what've I done? she thought. Again she held the jacket up, and felt in the pockets, but they were empty. She squeezed the body of the coat, felt nothing but the soft wadding of the shabby material. She looked down at the path of scattered papers. They must have come from the boy's jacket.

With the jacket over her arm, she stooped and picked up the nearest scrap. It was a folded strip of torn newspaper with the headline MOTHER OF MISSING CHILDREN FOUND SLAIN, and printed below the bold letters was a family photograph of a woman and . . . Patsy and Walter. *Their mother?* Spellbound, Leona stared at the woman's pretty face, then forced her eyes downward and read the first few lines of type: "Police are continuing their investigation into the brutal slaying of Mrs. Adele Aldridge . . ."

*Dear God, their mother was murdered!* But why would the boy have this in his jacket? It made no sense to her, no sense at all. Quickly she picked up the next scrap—another newspaper photograph. It had been folded in lopsided quarters and was falling apart. She had to arrange the four pieces on the floor to make out who or what it was. *Mamie!* She pressed her hands to her lips. *What is this?* It seemed impossible—an old crumbling picture of Mamie. There were words, fragments of words, around the picture, but they had deteriorated so badly she couldn't decipher what they said. Mamie looked younger in the picture; it must have been taken in school, Leona thought. But what did it mean?

She shifted on her knees and picked up yet another scrap. The paper had been folded very tight; she had to pick it apart —it was an envelope from Cornelia Dunham, Ridgefarm Road, Brandenburg Station, Kentucky, addressed to *her*.

Seeing her own name hit her like a stone.

Inside the envelope, bearing its same tight folds, was a thousand-dollar bill. *Why would he have . . .*

And then she began to know. A violent dizziness swarmed through her. Her legs were growing numb. I've got to stand up, she thought.

Reaching for the few remaining pieces of paper, she pushed herself to her feet. Against her fingertips, the underside of the bottom piece felt odd, rather slick. As she straightened up, Leona turned it over and found herself looking into her own face. It was a torn photograph *of herself.* My God, she thought. All the other scraps of paper fell from her hands. *What've I done?* The blood rushed from her face. She felt fear so intense she couldn't move, couldn't breathe or utter a sound. *Oh, my God. What've I done?*

*It's him! It's him!*

*I brought him here!*

Her entire life reduced itself to this moment. *He's in the house!* Her legs wouldn't hold her. Blindly, she reached out for the vanity bench, but the photograph seemed stuck to her fingers; she couldn't let go of it, couldn't get rid of it. Her legs were dissolving. Her head swam. Suddenly she thrust out her hand, flicked the photograph to the floor, and slumped back, clasping the dirty jacket to her breasts. Then she realized what she was doing and flung the ragged thing from her, and when finally she drew breath, the air made an ugly, rasping noise in her throat.

*It can't be,* she thought. *It just can't be! He's just a boy. There's some mistake.* And yet what mistake could there be? There on the floor was the photograph of herself.

The jacket had landed in a clump on the floor; the papers were strewn about where they had spilled from her, and she stepped among them, afraid to touch them, as she crossed the room to sit on the side of the bed. Her eyes fell on the folded envelope from Cornelia Dunham. He could only have got that envelope from Emma—she remembered reading Cornelia's letter the day before she left Graylie. *My God!* She nearly cried out, and knew that she mustn't; her hands flew to cover her mouth. Again, unable to resist, she picked up the torn snapshot and stared at her own face. She could remember in detail the day the picture was taken. She and Emma had been laughing, arms thrown round each other, showing off for the sake of the camera. Now only Emma's arm and hand remained, dangling around Leona's shoulders. The rest had been torn away.

She sat on the side of the bed, paralyzed. As if to mock her, everywhere she turned now she saw herself. In the three vanity mirrors, her face looked back at her. On the cold window, her pale reflection swam and shimmied. In her mind, she saw herself utterly isolated in this house, this secret hiding place. *It's him!* The seconds passed in slow, unyielding procession. But who is he?

*Mamie! He wants Mamie!* The chill spread through her. *I must go to them! I must get Mamie and . . . I must protect . . .* She told herself also that she mustn't give in to her terrible fear, but it had her in its grip. *He's in the house!* She had to get Mamie and the children and go. Go just as fast as they could. Leave everything . . . Throwing on some clothes, she tried to clench herself back into control, because now her fear had grown too deep within her to allow her to do anything else. *The children!*

*I have to go out that door.*

Her body was sapped of strength. Trying to move was like struggling through quicksand. And yet, carefully, soundlessly, she crossed the narrow room. Leaning forward, she reached for the doorknob, stopped, withdrew her hand and listened. There was no sound on the other side of the door. Again she lowered her hand to the cold knob and now heard a sound so slight it was hardly audible. Just outside, on the balcony, a board creaked.

And slowly the light in the two bedside lamps dwindled, bloomed softly, and shrank to utter darkness. Beneath the house, the faint humming of the generator had stopped. *He got the lights!*

Her fingers on her cheeks were like sticks of ice. With the lights out, the bedroom lost all definition—like a world seen fading through dark water. She was weak to the bone. Now's my chance, Leona thought. *I've got to go now.* He's in the cellar. Still, she turned the knob a hairbreadth at a time before she drew it open and peered out. The dark balcony was, to her eyes, deserted. The house was totally silent now, dead quiet. Staying close to the wall, feeling the grain of the wallpaper slide beneath her fingertips, Leona made her way to the next bedroom. The door was ajar, the room dark, not a speck of light anywhere. She slipped her hand out across the sheet. The bed was warm but empty. "Wal-ter?" Her voice cracked. She swallowed, and licked her lips. "Walter?" she whispered. "Don't be afraid. Where are you?"

No answer.

"Where are you, Walter? Are you in here?"

She pulled a book of matches from her pocket, tore out a match, and struck it.

Walter was gone.

She knew she must force herself to be calm. He must be in with the girls. The outline of a glass lamp shone faintly in the dark. She struck a second match. Very little coal oil remained in the glass well. Cupping the flame in her hands, she lit the wick and adjusted the flame down, small and low. Again she listened, again no sound.

Carrying the lamp before her, she checked the balcony a second time and almost ran to the girls' bedroom. Drab winter light filtered through the one window. The room met her gaze in shifting notches—the tall mirrored dresser, the footpost, the bed. But no one was there. One side of the bed hadn't even been mussed. "Kids?" she said, her voice choking. "Mamie?" She slipped back through the door. Holding the lamp up away from her eyes, she stared down the length of the balcony. No one. *What's he done to them?* Now, from somewhere else, she could just barely hear another noise, a small shuffle like footsteps.

She stopped abruptly where she was. The fear had burrowed into her now; she started at every infinitesimal sound. She stood perfectly still—tense, listening—afraid that even a breath might drown out some telling noise.

"Kids?"

The silence returned and hung poised in the air. She stepped to the railing of the balcony and looked down. The fire in the fireplace was still burning, casting a dull orange glow into half the room. Moonlight poured through the one uncovered window in a long creamy stripe. The couch was rumpled, vacant.

*He's taken them! He's got Mamie! He's got them all!*

In panic, she whirled, dashing toward the top of the stairs and glimpsed sudden movement in a doorway, very close, a quickening blur at the boundary of her light. The darkness swam around her like a tremulous pool; the lamplight washed over his battered shoes and pants and up, slowly, to his malignant blue eyes. "Who—" she gasped, then swallowed. "Who are you?" She hadn't heard him come up the stairs.

The air seemed to stir like a magnetic field and the boy flew through it. A scream broke from her lips, and at once, before she could properly turn or defend herself, he was at her. She swung the kerosene lamp and struck at him. The blade whispered by her eyes, the fist, whitened by the force of his grip, brushing her cheek. The glass chimney exploded in the dark. A face darted over her, a flash of teeth. His strength was like iron. Leona began to shriek, all the sound her breath would carry, just as his bandaged hand closed on her throat, pinning her to the railing. And the knife flew at her again, the blade coming at unbelievable speed. Trying to wheel and duck, Leona wrenched her head to one side and buried her teeth in his bandages. The stench of corruption and decay assailed her. His body stiffened, thrashed about in agony; the knife dropped away, his mouth opened wide, and the noise he made was so loud and piercing it hurt her ears—a howl and a scream, one contained within the other. Still crying out, the boy yanked his hand from the unwinding bandages and shoved her away. He shouted at her then, yelled something, but she couldn't hear him. She was falling, falling backward.

She struck the wall, the railing, the stairs, and lay in an excruciating tangle on the landing. Speeding points of light converged in her eyes; a horrible ringing ache sank into her brain. Everywhere her body felt jagged with pain. Slowly she opened her eyes and saw nothing but a firelit haze. Dimly, the familiar outlines of the room revealed themselves. She clutched the railing and pulled herself up, wildly searching the gray void at the top of the stairs and then out along the balcony. But the boy had vanished. He's still up there, she thought. He'll come down.

The night silence had returned to the house. "Children!" she tried to shout, but the word broke painfully in her throat. Except for the light in the fireplace, the room was dark. I'll find them. I have to. I'll get a light. She turned, stumbled to the table near the front door which held another kerosene lamp and tried to strike a match.

Her hands were shaking too violently; she couldn't keep the matches burning. One after another, they flared and went out and she threw the smoking ends onto the table. Sulphur corroded the air. Suddenly all the hysteria broke inside her and she felt a resurgence of strength. And then a wave of deadly rage swept through her. She struck a match and held it without faltering. She was calm. Her head was perfectly clear. A light, she thought, would favor him, not her. She shook out the match.

*I know this house.*

. . .

Slumped against the bedroom wall, Sherman drew a long, staggered breath. He pressed his thumb against the veins in his wrist to ease the throbbing in his torn hand. On the bed, across the room, white pillows gleamed with dull moonlight.

Quickly, with his knife, he cut the pillowcase lengthwise in three horizontal strips, then ripped them loose at the ends. She won't go nowhere without Mamie, he thought. And Mamie won't go with her. Not now that I'm here. He took the first strip of cloth and wound it tight around his hand. Blood soaked through it in an instant. He wound the next strip even tighter, to stop the pain and the bleeding. With his teeth, he tore the end of the third, wound part of it, and tied it with his good hand. He was trembling. He gripped his hand a few times until he could hold it in a fist, then took up his knife and went out the bedroom door.

The house was as still and hollow-sounding as a cave. The front door had been left standing open. Gusts of wind blew through it, snow flying halfway across the room. Where is she? The open door bothered him, the possibility that she'd gone. But she wouldn't go, he told himself, not without the kids. She's still down there. He drew back from the railing and started down the stairs.

The room seemed to rise to meet him. His eyes hurt, his heart was pounding, yet desperately he studied the depths of the room. Things were somehow getting out of control. He was being drawn deeper and deeper toward some place where he had never meant to go. Why had she left the door open? It made no sense. Uncertainty moved inside him like nausea.

Soundlessly he stalked down the stairs and the living room unreeled around him. He took another step. Shadows lay cluttered in his path like bottomless holes. He stood very still, listening, but heard nothing, not even a breath. Her disappearance only doubled his rage.

*Where'd she go?*

Coldly, like a machine, Sherman analyzed the room. To his left stood a tall wooden secretary filled with books; beyond that was the entrance to the kitchen. Directly ahead of him, twenty feet or so, loomed the open front door, a rectangle of hard blue light, snow blowing through it. Next to the door was the one uncovered window, shot through with faint moonlight. To his right, beyond the chairs and couch, was the stone fireplace. On either side of it were bookcases and windows and cabinets. He glanced back over his shoulder. Behind him, under the staircase, was the linen closet.

He turned on his toes. He wiped his sleeve across his forehead, and then, in a streak, darted to the closet, threw the door open, and raised his knife. Shelves of towels and sheets met him. He stared, took a deep breath, and pivoted. A long, weaving cry of wind blew snow toward him, and running through it a voice —a very cold, very angry voice. Sherman couldn't make out what it said. His skin was tingling and clammy.

It was as if the wind had created the voice. It hung on the air like a lingering shred of sound. He ran a few steps into the room. *It was her! That woman! Her voice!* His mind repeated the sound; he heard it again, like an echo against the back of his brain. He still couldn't make out the words, but the unexpected ominous tone of her voice chilled him. Suddenly he spun, gazing, searching the balcony, all the time knowing it was impossible for her to be there. But she was somewhere. Close. The balcony was dark, empty. Only dead silence drifted back to him. She's watching me, he thought. He could feel her eyes hovering on him, wanted to slash at them. He shrank back into the stairwell, then stepped even deeper in until the protecting shadows surrounded him.

And then the same voice came again, very cold, very hard, ringing against the walls.

*"What did you do to my sister!"*

Sherman swallowed.

He couldn't move. A feeling like ice, like a fine cold spray of ice, spread outward from his chest. The woman was alive with hatred; he could feel it radiating from her voice. Sweat ran into his eyes and he squeezed them shut, dragging his sleeve across his face. He stared through the bannister supports, but he knew before he looked there was no one out there. The living room was empty. Snow blew across it—over chairs, couch, the rug. Where was she? Where was the voice coming from?

Suddenly the voice said, *"You bastard."* Still hard, iron hard. Then: *"You murderer!"*

The darkness coiled and closed on him like a fist. He straightened, stood bolt upright, twisting his head toward all the blackest shadow places. The voice had been quieter this time, chilling, spoken under her breath. She's right here someplace. Watchin' me. But why? This is crazy! She had to be right there in front of him, watching everything he did without being seen. It wasn't possible. He could feel his control crumbling away.

Suddenly he ran from the stairwell, tore wildly across the room, past the dark shapes of furniture to the blue rectangle of night. He flew out onto the moonlit porch, and the night wind hit him like a barrage of ice, ruffling his shirt, freezing his sweat. The snow-covered planks had been touched by nothing but his own shoes. I knew it, he thought; she didn't come out here. He hurled back through the doorway, his shadow leaping and disappearing in the room. "Say somethin' now!" he yelled.

He ran through the kitchen doorway, throwing doors open, slamming them shut, pitching out anything he could grab— dishes crashing, exploding on the floor and walls, utensils flying. "Talk to me now!" he yelled. "Say somethin' now!" It seemed to him that somehow she was always behind him, invisible, hovering very close in the dark, whispering, whispering. Still tearing about, he ran past the sink. On the counter, in a neat even row, was a row of kitchen knives—six or eight of them, all laid out. They drew him to a halt. It was very strange, knives laid out like that. She did this, he thought, to rattle me. With a vicious lunge, Sherman swept them off into the air, heard them clatter away. Treading on broken china, gasping for breath, he rushed back to the doorway, his eyes searching the gloom. And the wind blew. And that voice rose through it, not loud, but there, fierce and alive, hard as metal.

*"You can't hurt us. I won't let you."*

"THEN STOP ME!" he yelled. "STOP ME, GODDAM YOU!" His voice pierced the room, the gusty snow flying around him.

As if the night itself had shifted, something stirred in the fabric of air immediately in front of him. His concentration gathered, grew sharp. Very slowly he lifted his head and turned; his eyes peered through the quivering flashes of firelight. Something was wrong about that door. Two or three steps away, swung back from the opening to the porch, the front door stood, its glass windowpane facing him, thin curtains backing it. Reflected on the glass he could see his own faint image, and there was something else there, too—her ghostly shape, taller than he was, looming over him. *Behind me!* The realization struck him. *She's crept up behind me!* He plunged, twisted sideways, slashed out with his knife.

On air. Empty air.

He came up, thrust himself around. Her image was gone from the glass. Only the thin curtains hung behind the windowpane, gossamer, white as fog. "That goddam door," he muttered. Every damned thing had turned against him. All his frustration, all his hatred, attached itself to that door. Heaving his body into it, he caught its edge and hurled it shut against the snow.

*And there she was!*

All at once . . . there, behind the door.

He saw her hands drawn up, glimpsed the flash of a knife plummeting toward him. He pitched back, weaved sideways to avoid it. But there was no time. With a hard, grinding rip, the kitchen knife sank into him, just below his collarbone. Leona could feel the blow vibrate upward through the wooden handle and out through her arms.

The boy screamed.

She clung to the knife as if it were something solid that had roots in the ground, and when he drew away, the bloody end of the knife slipped out of him. For a startled split second their eyes caught. Horror-struck, breathing very fast, Leona thought, as she had before, He's just a boy, and felt sickened. *No. Think of Emma.* Unable to strike at him again, she tore away and hid from the sight of what she had done.

Again Sherman cried out. The pain struck him, staggered him in waves. He fell back, covering the wound with his hands, the pain erupting sharper and sharper in his body. Blood spilled through his fingers. *"Mamie!"* he screamed, *"Mamie! Mamie!"*

In the kitchen doorway, still clutching himself, he nearly collapsed. Burying his mouth in the crook of his arm, he could feel his strength seeping away, but his rage flared as never before. *She tried to kill me!* His hatred restored him. In the pantry he saw something gleam. Driven by his fury, he reached for it. A can of gasoline.

Leona was drowning in panic and remorse. I did it, she thought. He's hurt really bad. She found it hard to think. Should I . . . What should I do? Go to him? But just the thought of it intensified the horror within her. She realized she was still clutching the bloody knife and threw it aside. "Think," she muttered aloud. "Get the kids." She had reached the stairs when she remembered she had already looked up there. They must be . . . where? They must be in the cellar. She turned back. But he was in the kitchen. It meant she would have to go by him, look at him, and she didn't want to. *I have to.* Forcing herself to move, she was passing the bookcase when the boy came through the doorway.

He was pulling tight sips of breath from the air. Blood

stained one side of his shirt. He stared at Leona, his eyes filled with passionate rage. "You . . . you," he mumbled. In that dark end of the room, it took a moment for Leona to realize what he was carrying in his hands. And then it was all too clear.

Holding the bottom of the gas can in his stiff left hand, Sherman tipped it and swung it in an arc before him. The gasoline sloshed and flew in a wide crescent near her. Leona swallowed her breath. "What're you doing?" Again he swung the can and splashes of gasoline flew toward her. She stepped back to dodge it. *"My God, stop it!"* she shouted. *"You'll set the house on fire! There's children in here! Mamie's here!"*

The swinging motion did not stop. The gasoline gurgled and slopped and flew toward her again. She whirled away from it. "Please!" she cried.

"Shut up," he said. He lifted his head. "MAMIE!" he yelled, advancing into the room. "MAMIE, COME HERE!"

Then he slung the gasoline again.


On the balcony, Mamie watched Sherman raise his head and call for her, but she was trembling uncontrollably, afraid to move, afraid to go to him. Without knowing it, she was moaning to herself.

*The air was full of gas.*

In her arms, she carried the sack of Funny Grandma's Christmas presents and she flung it down. One after another, she threw the presents out into the dark until she found the one she wanted, the one she had put there herself, and then her hands were flying, tearing the wrapping away.


The moment the gas can was empty, Sherman cast it aside and turned swiftly toward the fireplace where the thatch of twigs lay burning. "Please!" Leona cried. "You can't! You'll set us on fire!" Desperately she ran at him, grabbed the back of his shirt collar, and spun him back.

Off balance, Sherman swung at her with his good fist.


A shot cracked the air.

The bullet spanked a fireplace stone, spewing grit, and sang off into the night. The concussion spread through the depths of the house. It froze the moment. Everything stopped. Before either Sherman or Leona could recover, a small shrill voice yelled, *"No-o-o, Sherman,"* and footsteps raced along the length of the balcony. Mamie darted down the stairs, reached the landing, and turned, looking down at them. The air stank with fumes.

*"Sherman!"* Mamie screamed. *"No, Sherman, don't do it again. Don't burn us up!"* In her hands, she clutched the Browning automatic.

The muzzle of the gun drifted and steadied on Sherman.

Sherman stared in disbelief. "Mamie, whataya doin' with that?"

Stunned, Leona looked up at her. "Mamie, it was you. You took the gun." She gasped for air. "You know him. Mamie, who is he?"

"He's my brother," Mamie said, not once removing her gaze from him, her voice so small it hardly carried.

"Point it at her," Sherman demanded. "She did it." He stepped toward her. *"Kill her, Mamie! She did it.* She caused everything!"

"No, Sherman," Mamie said. "You did it." Holding the gun very still, she came down the remaining stairs. "You killed 'em all. You did it, Sherman." And her wrath shattered the night. "You killed Mommy! Daddy! You killed Toddy! *The Chinaman . . ."* She stepped toward him, bringing the gun closer. *"You burned us up!"*

Sherman shrank back.

Suddenly he looked strange. Terror swarmed into his face.

Something had come up behind him. There was something climbing on his back.

*The fire.*

He tried to reach for it. He screamed. It was feeding on him, spreading all over him, bursting through his gas-stained clothes, curling on his fingers—flickering white leaves of fire.

It made a hissing noise at first. Before he could stop it, before anyone could do anything, a towering white scallop of fire engulfed him completely. It caught Leona and Mamie like a camera flash, trapping them in light. Spontaneously the fire on the floor shot from him in runners, eating through the room, flying in zigzags from one splash of gasoline to another. They were all snared in it, screaming, casting about for something to help him, but there was nothing they could do. And then Sherman screamed again, an agonized cry so full of pain it shook the air.

"The kids!" Leona cried, above the circling white roar. "They'll burn up! Mamie! *Where are they?*"

"I don't know!" she shouted as Leona reached for her. "*He took them!*"

"*Where? Mamie, where? What'd he do to them?*"

Sherman emerged from the fireball engulfing him, the stench of his burning flesh hideous, beyond imagining. In a fluttering white nimbus of light, he stretched out his hand in a hopeless gesture. "May-mie," he said from the depths of his withering. "May-mie."

In flames, he reached for her.

"*Sherman!*" Mamie screamed, and tore herself from Leona. "*Sherman!*" She stumbled toward him, lifting her hands.

"*Mamie, get back!*"

Leona swept Mamie up and pitched back through the rim of fire so fast she hardly felt it lick at her legs. She could hear them then—the children, banging in the cellar. She grabbed her coat from the rack, threw it around Mamie, and ran through the kitchen.

With Mamie screaming and fighting in her arms, Leona ran down the rickety wooden steps to the cellar. The red light of the fire showed through the guttering floorboards above them, casting thin smoky shafts of light into the moldy room. She could hear Patsy and Walter kicking, could hear muffled crying out in the potato bin.

Clutching Mamie to her, Leona slid the latch open. The children's hands had been tied, handkerchiefs knotted across their mouths, and they were huddled together in the cramped box. With one arm still around Mamie, Leona hurriedly untied them and helped them out.

"Quick!" she shouted. "Let's go! We can still get out. Let's go! Let's go! Run!"

"Sherman!" Mamie was screaming. She never for a moment stopped screaming his name. They started up the cellar stairs. From the kitchen there came a quiver of radiant light.

He was there!

All at once, in flames, Sherman's fire-ravaged arms opened, reaching out. The children screamed and clung to Leona, drawing back. Scraps of burning matter fell from him, tumbling at them down the stairs, and the door frame blazed up, a bright flickering all around him.

"This way!" Leona cried. "This way. Go out the back!" And she pushed open the creaking, slanted doors onto a sky full of stars. Mamie broke away from her and ran back toward the stairs and her brother. "Sherman, I'm sorry," she wailed. And then she screamed, *"I love you, Sherman!"*

"Mamie!" Leona gasped, running after her. "Oh, Mamie, please, you can't . . ." She snatched her up, and Mamie clawed at her so violently that Leona had to pin her arms against her body. Then she grabbed Walter in her other arm. "Hold on! Hold on tight!"

At the top of the stairs, Sherman was slowly bending to his knees.

The light from the fire stormed over the waterway like a malediction. It was as if the dark texture of the air itself were ablaze. Behind them, with a loud, staccato crack, the cottage roof caved in and a platinum brightness exploded around them, scorching their backs like a rocket's tail. The ice, catching the vast reflection, magnified the white convulsion a thousand times over. And then, moments later, a pulsing red corona of light rose from the gutted stone shell. Nothing escaped its eerie glow.

They fled from it, their shadows jutting in long, violent streaks across the frozen plain. On the riverbank, the effect of the red light was no less vivid. Shadows stretched behind the flame-stained trees and the new black Pontiac was alive with the reflected burning. And, finally, they were in the car.

Then they were flying backward toward the place where the car could turn around. "Please!" Mamie cried. "Let me go. He's my brother!" It would never be the same, and it would never be over. It was happening all over again. Once again she was being taken away.

Mamie flew wildly inside the car, sliding up and over the front seat, her pale hands beating at the glass, reaching for the flashing red flickers that sliced through the car and beckoned to her. She called his name, hurling herself from window to window like a bird inextricably trapped in a forgotten room.

The red light seemed to stalk after them as they pulled away, seemed to wink and reach for her through the trees. The Pontiac quickly gained speed, weaving through the bogs and curves near the cliffs, leaving him—leaving her Sherman—in his fiery red glow.

She could no longer scream. Her mouth still carried the shape of her immense desolation, but the sound in her throat had constricted to a small, repeated shriek. And even that was getting weaker.

Leona looked at her. Oh, Mamie, she thought. I'm losing Mamie, and she started to sob. I'm losing her. And Mamie's sob answered her own. The sound of their pain rebounded in the other two children, who had begun, once again, to cry. *Losing her. I must do something.*

Leona wanted to stop the car and comfort her, but she knew the fire would be visible for miles. They'll be coming, she thought, and yielded to her first concern—to get them to a place of safety.

They drove through the night up the high hill street of Brandenburg Station, past houses she remembered from that other, happy time. She took remote river roads. It was midnight before she noticed the blinking motel sign on the horizon and pulled the car in across gravel.

Leona signed someone else's name and carried the children into the room like all the other rooms, so many lives ago. In her pocket, she felt the paper envelope of sedatives and Walter's medicine and she drew water in a glass. She looked at Mamie, who was standing by herself, alone, alone in the world. And Mamie looked at her. The set of the little girl's shoulders, the terrified loneliness in her eyes were heartbreaking. They had lived through a burning hell and now stood on the far side of it, smoke-drenched, weak with exhaustion. Mamie was sobbing, gulping dry, shallow breaths.

Patsy and Walter had stopped crying, but they were still upset, still terrified. Leona broke one of the sedatives in two, giving them each a half, and then she gave Walter his medicine. Without losing sight of Mamie, she told them just to sleep in their underwear for the night and she helped them undo their clothes.

Then she put them to bed with a warm hug and a kiss, telling them not to worry. "Good night," she said softly, going from one to the other. "Sleep tight." Drawing the covers up around them, she straightened and turned. Mamie was gone; the door stood ajar.

With the last of her strength, Leona ran outside and saw Mamie stumbling slowly away through the night. She was weeping uncontrollably, her small shoulders heaving. It tore at Leona. Not knowing what to do or say, she followed after her, pulled along by Mamie's grief. The pain, the desolation were unbearable and she began to weep with Mamie and for her, for her suffering and for the terrible boy Mamie had loved so dearly.

"I'm sorry," Leona said. "Oh, Mamie, I'm sorry. I'm sorry," unable to stanch her tears.

Still grieving, Mamie turned, and from the depths of her despair, she gave voice to what would haunt her forever. "He wasn't"—she choked and her voice rose, fluttering out on a wail —"he wasn't my Sherman any more."

Kneeling in the snow, Leona took her in her arms and held her. "I know," she said. "Mamie, I know, I know . . ."

When at last they had stopped crying, Leona carried Mamie inside. With a wet washcloth, she bathed the child's face as she had long ago through sleepless nights at the hospital. Then she took her in her arms again and, holding her close, turned off the light and carried Mamie to her bed.

Lying in the dark, she smoothed the hair from Mamie's cheek. Outside on the empty road the wind scurried away, and little by little the motel room sank to deep silence. Time drifted from them in a slow, quiet stream. Mamie turned her head. "Sherman," she murmured, "Sherman, Sherman." In her longing, she saw him standing with the Chinaman at the foot of the bed, waiting to take her away. Then they were gone in the night.

So who's here? Mamie thought. She could see Leona's shadowy outline on the bed right next to her. Slowly she reached out and touched Leona's face and felt Leona's hand on hers. The dark stood still between them. "Yes, Mamie," Leona said, "I'm here," and she held her hand through the night, through their sleep.

Watched by the day flooding in. Day, with its trackless blue splendor.

A NOTE ON THE TYPE

This book was set in a digitized version of Janson. The hot-metal version of Janson was a recutting made direct from type cast from matrices long thought to have been made by the Dutchman Anton Janson, who was a practicing type founder in Leipzig during the years 1668–1687. However, it has been conclusively demonstrated that these types are actually the work of Nicholas Kis (1650–1702), a Hungarian, who most probably learned his trade from the master Dutch type founder Dirk Voskens. The type is an excellent example of the influential and sturdy Dutch types that prevailed in England up to the time William Caslon (1692–1766) developed his own incomparable designs from them.

Composed, printed, and bound by
The Haddon Craftsmen, Scranton, Pennsylvania
Designed by Virginia Tan